BROTHERS IN SERVICE
THROUGH THICK & THIN

LINDY BELL

Day Agency Publishing
Salt Lake City, UT
84065

Editor: Sean Linton
Cover Designer: Unique Covers
Interior Print Design & eBook Design: Dayna Linton • Day Agency • www.dayagency.com

Library of Congress Control Number: Pending

ISBN: 978-1-7365604-4-0 (Paperback)
ISBN: 978-1-7365604-5-7 (Digital Book)

First Edition: 2023

10 9 8 7 6 5 4 3 2 1

Printed in the USA

For My Nephew - Zac Bell

*Fire Service Lieutenant, Paramedic, Firefighter.
I am so proud of the public servant you are and the many
lives you've impacted and saved, but I'm most especially proud
because you're my nephew.
Thank you for the many plot ideas you've provided just talking
about life at the fire station and for generously sharing your
paramedic medical expertise.
This book wouldn't have been possible without you.*

AUTHOR'S NOTE

BROTHERS IN SERVICE—THROUGH THICK & THIN is a work of fiction. Any resemblance to actual events or persons is entirely coincidental. While details regarding firefighting efforts and medical treatments have been thoroughly researched, any errors in procedural descriptions included in the book are entirely my own. Thank you to the brave first responders, fire and police, who work to keep us safe each and every day.

BROTHERS IN SERVICE

THROUGH THICK & THIN

HE DIDN'T FIT. No matter how hard he tried, Riley Sullivan just didn't fit. With the ambulance siren wailing overhead, he tried one more time to make room for his long legs in the cab's jump seat. He never thought riding in an ambulance would be this uncomfortable.

"How ya doin' back there, Sully?" Jeremy Ennis, the ambulance driver and one of Riley's best friends, asked with a grin. Jeremy craned his neck to catch Riley's eye. "Doin' okay?" he asked, a little louder this time to be heard over the blaring siren.

Riley frowned his answer. It was the same sarcastic grin Riley remembered from high school. Jeremy always had a smile and a positive attitude, no matter what was going on. It was really rather annoying. Why couldn't Jeremy be grumpy, at least once in a while, like everyone else?

Jeremy looked much the same as he had in high school, a little more filled out than the gangly wide receiver Riley had thrown passes to, but still, the same. A square jaw, thick brown curly hair, cleft chin, and deep green eyes currently gleaming with mischief and pinning Riley from the rear-view mirror.

Riley, Jeremy, and the third of their trio, Cade Marshall, had been inseparable and as close as brothers since middle school. They had even managed to stay close when each had gone their own way for college. Riley couldn't imagine life without either of them.

Even though he'd initially been thrilled to be assigned to the same fire station as Jeremy, Riley was reconsidering his original enthusiasm. With Jeremy as the lead paramedic Riley had been assigned to shadow his first few weeks, Riley was beginning to realize what a difference two years of seniority meant. Riley had always considered himself the leader of their group, so this was going to require some adjustment.

While Riley had gone to college in preparation for law school, per his father's plans for him, Jeremy had gotten a full-ride football scholarship. But that ended his junior year when he'd suffered a career-ending knee injury. Jeremy had taken it hard, especially since losing the scholarship meant he'd had to drop out of college. But in typical Jeremy fashion, he hadn't let it keep him down. After hearing Riley talk about the fire department since middle school, Jeremy checked into the possibility of becoming a firefighter. He worked hard, rehabbed the knee to meet the physical requirements, and passed the written exam and was loving—and thriving—as a firefighter.

Riley was jealous of Jeremy for having already been with the fire department for two years. If Riley had had his way, he would have joined right out of high school, but he'd promised his dad to get a college education. While his dad thought Riley would join the family law firm, Riley had always known the fire service was his calling.

Now, Riley felt like he was starting from behind. But he was determined to work hard, learn the ropes, and be the best he could be at his new job.

While Jeremy, and then Riley, had gone into the fire service, Cade had followed members of his family into the police force. Riley wouldn't get to work as closely with Cade as he did with Jeremy, but he was glad their paths would still cross.

"Yo, Sully. Doin' okay?" Jeremy repeated.

Hitting another large bump, Riley grimaced as his knee hit a hard edge—again. He rubbed his knee and gritted his teeth. "I'm doing great. Just drive."

"Whoa, what's this? The rookie's mouthing off on his first day on the job?" Ethan Walton, the second paramedic asked, feigning wide-eyed shock.

"Knock it off, Walton," Jeremy said with a grin. "Sully's green. He'll learn the chain of command soon enough."

The two looked at Riley, exchanging knowing grins.

Jeremy and Ethan continued their conversation about the upcoming high school football season. Riley hoped they wouldn't bring him into that conversation. He'd rather not talk football with Jeremy. Memories still lingered from the championship game their senior year. Memories he'd rather forget.

Riley looked between the two, wondering what the chain of command remark meant but dismissed it. He had too many other things on his mind to worry about it. This was his first shift on duty and his first official run as a paramedic—albeit as a trainee—but he was happy just to be here.

Riley was jerked suddenly from his reverie upon hearing his name.

"Walton, Sully was our high school's star quarterback. You'll have to ask him about making the play offs," Jeremy said with a mischievous grin, catching Riley's eye once again in the rear-view mirror.

Riley cringed, and his eyes narrowed. He'd *really* rather not talk about football with Jeremy. Four years later, it was still a sore subject. As the siren continued to scream overhead, Riley's mind went back to the final game of their senior year. He'd made a bad decision that night, and that decision had cost the team the state championship. But also on that Friday night, Jeremy and Cade taught him what true friendship looked like.

TEN SECONDS WERE LEFT in the game; enough for one last play. The Abernathy Bobcats had gotten to the 40-yard line, thanks to an end run by Cade, but with so little time on the clock, they had no choice but to throw a pass. The opposing team knew it too.

The Bobcats were down by three, so a touchdown would win it. Riley had taken the snap. He stepped into the pocket, looking down field for his wide receivers. Jeremy was open on the 20 with nothing but open field into the end zone, but Jeremy had uncharacteristically dropped two passes earlier in the game, which caused Riley to hesitate. He finally threw to Brady O'Connor, a hotshot freshman who'd come open in the center of the field, but he'd been open only for an instant. One of the defenders deflected the ball just as the buzzer sounded.

Riley would never forget the expression on Jeremy's face as he turned and looked at Riley. Jeremy, Cade, the team—everyone—had ignored him on the somber walk back to the locker room. Riley hadn't blamed them.

After the game, Riley closed his eyes, face in his hands, elbows on his knees and sat, alone, on the cold bleacher. He didn't hear the footsteps approaching until he felt the weight of someone sitting down beside him. He turned to look.

It was Jeremy.

Riley's shoulders sagged even further.

"What are you doing sitting out here all by yourself, Sully?"

Several long seconds ticked by before Riley answered.

"I'm trying to figure out how to make up to one of my best friends for my poor judgment. I'm trying to figure out how to make up to the rest of the team for blowing the game that cost them the state championship. I'm trying to—"

"Would you just stop already?" Jeremy interrupted irritably.

Riley cocked his head and looked at Jeremy.

Jeremy shrugged nonchalantly. "You take things way too seriously, Sully. It's a football game. Sure, it was a game we all wanted to win. And sure, you blew it." Jeremy heaved a big sigh and finally smiled. "In the end though, you know … really, it's just a football game. It's no fun to lose, but it's not the end of the world either."

"I tell you what's the end of the world," another voice chimed in as Cade plopped down on the other side of Riley, causing the bench to bounce. "The end of the world is not eating. I'm starving."

Jeremy leaned out and catching Cade's eye, sliced his hand across his throat, mouthing "shut up."

Cade raised his arms in mock surrender. "What? What did I say?"

Jeremy rolled his eyes at Cade and slapped Riley on the back.

"Come on. Get over it. It's history now. And besides, we're all kinda hungry," Jeremy said. "Playing football in subfreezing weather will do that to you."

"Now you're talking!" Cade stood quickly. "Come on, Sully."

Riley lifted his head and looked first at Jeremy's beaming face and then Cade's eager one.

"I can't believe you guys are even speaking to me."

Jeremy stood and pulled Riley to his feet. "It's too cold to rehash what's over and done. Besides, for a lunkhead, Cade is right. We're all hungry."

Riley ran his sleeve under his nose and shook his head dejectedly. "You guys should have gone ahead without me."

Jeremy moved to within inches of Riley and poked his finger in Riley's chest. "*You* are team captain. *You* are our leader, and the team doesn't go anywhere without its leader. Get over yourself, Sully. Be the leader we all look up to and respect. No football game is going to change that."

Riley shook his head. "You guys are unbelievable."

"Yeah, we're unbelievable. We're also hungry. Now come on," Cade said, jumping off the bottom stair onto the gravel.

THE AMBULANCE HIT A large rut, jolting Riley harshly back into the present. Four and a half years later, he was a rookie with the fire department, riding in the jump seat of the ambulance Jeremy was driving. Riley looked out over the hood as the ambulance flew past cars pulling to either side of the road at their approach.

He took a deep breath as the ambulance turned a corner and pulled to a stop in front of a small, wooden house, its white paint peeling and chipping. Riley hoped he was ready for this.

Jeremy shut the siren down with a loud squelch but left the lights flashing.

The three piled out into the warm air tinged with the tiniest hint of fall. Riley stepped out of the way as Jeremy and Walton opened compartment doors and grabbed medical bags and equipment with practiced efficiency. They both handed a bag to him to carry. He fell in behind them as they made their way up the walk, its cement crumbling with age, scraggly bits of dead grass dotting the dusty, small yard. The dark navy of their uniform shirts and pants absorbed the sun's rays and sweat broke out on Riley's forehead.

Jeremy looked over his shoulder. "This is your first run. Stay close, but stay out of the way until we know what we've got."

Riley gave a quick nod before a little lady dressed in a thick cotton robe and wearing slippers threw open the glass door, gesturing to them urgently.

"Hurry! Please hurry!" she gasped, turning and hurrying back inside.

They stepped inside, following her down a narrow hallway. Upon entering the cramped space, Riley felt its heat immediately. The strong scent of ointment and camphor permeated the air. The hallway opened into a small living room. Sunlight filtered in through a picture window, its heat adding to the already stifling air. The room's carpeted floor was cluttered with newspapers and magazines while the side tables held empty food containers. A large orange cat watched pensively from its perch on a stool on the far side of the room.

All business, Jeremy and Walton moved quickly to a man lying in the room's lone recliner. His face was chalky white, his eyes closed, and his chest heaving erratically. Beads of perspiration glistened on the man's forehead and upper lip. He tried to open his eyes, hearing Jeremy and Walton kneeling beside him. Walton took the man's wrist and took his pulse as Jeremy pulled out a stethoscope and placed it against the thin t-shirt the man wore. Riley dropped the bags he'd been carrying close to Jeremy and Walton, then stepped out of the way.

"Tom," the woman said, hovering nearby, twisting a handkerchief in her wrinkled hands. "His name is Tom Bertram," she repeated anxiously.

Jeremy nodded, indicating he'd heard her. "Tom," Jeremy said softly as he continued to work. "Can you hear me? Can you tell me how you're feeling?"

Mr. Bertram mumbled an incoherent reply.

Riley had moved to just inside the doorway, watching as the lady edged closer to the recliner. A few inches further and her robe would be brushing the bags holding the medical equipment, and she'd be in the paramedics' way.

"Sullivan, would you assist Mrs. Bertram to a seat?" Jeremy said, indicating with a nod to a chair several feet from where they worked.

A bit unsure of exactly how to assist Mrs. Bertram, Riley reluctantly took the little woman awkwardly by her shoulders, and as best as he could, gently steered her away from the recliner. He placed himself between her and where the paramedics were working. He could tell things weren't going well.

"Is he going to be okay?" the woman asked, her voice trembling as she looked up at Riley.

Riley saw raw fear on her face. He didn't know what to say.

"He's all I've got . . . ," she said softly, straining to see over Riley's shoulder.

Upon the engine's arrival, two of the firefighters brought a gurney through the front door. Its rubber wheels rolled rhythmically down the hallway in the tense quiet, coming to a stop just inside the living room. As they moved Mr. Bertram gently onto it, careful of the IV tubes, Jeremy and Walton suddenly tensed as they looked at the monitor. From where he stood, Riley could tell that the screen showed asystole rhythm—a flat line.

Stepping to the side of the gurney, Walton worked quickly and methodically, performing the standard procedures Riley remembered from his recent training. Walton began the rhythmic compressions of CPR, counting the cadence softly under his breath. Riley thought he was going to be sick when he heard the man's ribs crack on the third compression. As Walton continued to repeat the process over and over, Jeremy monitored for any perceptible change—a heartbeat, a flutter of eyelids. Something. Anything.

But there was nothing; only the solid flat line that continued to float across the screen.

"There's nothing more we can do," Riley heard Walton say to Jeremy under his breath.

Jeremy's shoulders sagged as they looked in unison to Riley, with Mrs. Bertram on the other side of him, straining to see. She saw their faces. She pushed Riley suddenly with such surprising strength, it nearly knocked him off balance.

"Tom!" she cried, clawing at Riley. Riley looked to Jeremy and Walton, unsure of what to do.

Jeremy and Walton exchanged an almost imperceptible nod and stepped away from the gurney. They moved with calm deliberation toward Riley and Mrs. Bertram.

Riley suddenly felt the tautness in Mrs. Bertram begin to relax as she saw Jeremy and Walton moving toward her. Reaching her side, they spoke in low, gentle tones, each putting an arm around her. Eyes focused on her husband, she took a shaky breath and clasped her trembling hands. She began walking unsteadily toward the gurney as they each cupped a hand under her elbows to steady her.

The pensive tick of a large clock hanging on a side wall filtered through the still, warm air, its cadence the only sound for several hushed moments. Mrs. Bertram stood quietly, looking into the still features of her husband. Tears streamed into the wrinkles carved into her face. She bent and kissed his forehead, patting his cheek gently and taking one of his hands in her own. She stared into his face with such love Riley felt uncomfortable, like he was an intruder witnessing such an intimate moment.

Unaware, Riley had taken several steps backward, an unconscious attempt to distance himself from the scene in front of him. He felt a burgeoning sense of unease, accompanied by a new and uncomfortable tingle of alarm. He had a growing sense he didn't belong. Not in this place, and maybe not even in this job.

This job wasn't just fighting fires. This job was meeting people's needs at the basest level, and with the very real-life scene he was witnessing, he wasn't sure he could do it. He'd heard the words of caution from the instructors about what they would encounter and how what they saw would take its emotional toll, but Riley had sloughed it off. The technical stuff and the medicine were the hard stuff; but now, he wondered about the human side of the equation. The instinct, the intuition to know what to do, how to help a family member in a situation like this—that was something else altogether; something he hadn't really planned on. He wanted to fight fire. But now, he thought, he should have paid more attention to what the instructors had said. Was it possible, after all of his dreams and the excitement of going through the academy, that this job might just simply be out of his league?

Uncertainty, a new and unfamiliar sensation, pinned Riley where he stood, looking on as a spectator while Jeremy and Walton consoled the new widow. Riley had never experienced, or even seen, life like this before. Always self-assured and confident, he now felt clumsy and unsure of himself and how to process what he'd just seen. He suddenly felt exposed, his reliable self-confidence melting away.

He ran his fingers nervously through his hair, took a deep breath, and released it slowly. This job was going to demand more of him than he'd dreamed of or bargained for. Had he made a mistake? Had ten years' worth of anticipation been eliminated by one run on his first day?

Caught up in his thoughts, Riley shook his head.

"You okay, Rookie?" Walton asked, looking at Riley as he and Jeremy gathered their equipment.

"Yeah, I'm fine," Riley answered with a slight shrug. Really, he was anything but fine.

ON THE WAY BACK to the station, Jeremy eyed Riley in the rear-view mirror. Riley was staring out the side window. He'd been quiet since leaving the Bertrams'. Jeremy knew a fatality was rough, but for one to happen on the first call of your first shift? That was especially tough.

Jeremy appreciated Walton's effort to break the oppressive quiet in the cab with his banter, but Jeremy broke in when there was an opening.

"Sully?" Jeremy said, catching Riley's eye in the rear-view mirror.

Riley stiffened upon hearing his name.

"Yeah? I mean, yes sir?" Riley said, sitting up.

"If you ever need to talk about something that's happened, something you've seen, something you feel uncomfortable about having seen—anything like that—there are people you can talk to. Including me. I want to make sure you know that. It's nothing to be embarrassed about. We deal with some pretty tough stuff. It's always better to talk it through with someone."

Riley nodded solemnly, looking at Jeremy in the mirror.

"Thanks, Jeremy."

Before Riley could say anything further, dispatch broke in with a call for an unknown injury to a child, 235 Barlow Street.

Jeremy sped up, giving Riley one more quick glance before flicking on the lights and siren. Walton acknowledged receipt of the call as Riley sat up straighter and took a deep breath.

A few short minutes later, Jeremy squelched the siren as they pulled into an upscale residential neighborhood. A few houses down the street, they spotted a young girl standing on the curb, waving frantically. Jeremy stopped the ambulance, leaving the lights flashing. The girl started talking to Jeremy as soon as he got out and followed him around the ambulance to where Riley and Walton were pulling their bags and equipment.

"It's my brother. He fell from a tree," she was saying, gasping for air.

"Can you take us to where he is?" Jeremy asked calmly, already starting toward the house.

"He's in the backyard." The girl took off with Jeremy, Walton and Riley right behind.

She led them through a side gate into a lush backyard that held several large trees and a kidney-shaped swimming pool. Lounge chairs dotted one side of the pool and a long table sat underneath the shade of two bright umbrellas.

They followed the sound of crying coming from the far side of the yard. A young woman sat on the grass, cradling a small boy in her arms. He was holding his right arm tightly, his face red and splotchy from crying.

The young woman looked up, relief evident on her face when she saw them approaching.

"What happened here?" Jeremy asked, kneeling down beside the small boy. "It's too nice a day to be crying. Can you tell me where it hurts?"

Sobbing, the boy shied away from Jeremy, protecting one arm while burrowing his face in his mother's lap.

The mother looked at Jeremy. Tears streaked her cheeks, her eyes welling with fear and uncertainty.

"What's his name?" Jeremy asked softly.

"Oliver. We call him Ollie." She sniffed and brushed some of Oliver's hair from his sweaty forehead as the little girl who had directed them dropped to her knees beside her mom. "This is Samantha," the mother said, putting an arm around the girl's trembling shoulders.

"And your name?" Walton asked the mom.

"Meredith. Meredith Winters." Blinking, a tear fell, and she swiped at it with the back of her hand.

"Mrs. Winters, if you'll move to the side and give us a little room, I think we can have this young man feeling better shortly."

Jeremy moved toward him, but Ollie grabbed at his mother and screamed. She gave Jeremy an apologetic look and leaning over, began talking in Oliver's ear in low, soothing tones. The boy, still holding onto his mother, began to relax as she eased him gently toward Jeremy.

"Oliver," Jeremy began conversationally while he began a gentle examination of the boy's shoulder and arm, "have you ever seen a fire truck up close?"

Ollie sniffed and shook his head slowly, eying Jeremy suspiciously.

"Would you like to?" Jeremy went on. "There's one parked outside your house right now."

Oliver's eyes grew round as he looked at Jeremy.

"Sully, would you pull a splint, gauze, and a sling for me please?"

Walton, who had begun to unzip the bag, looked at Jeremy in surprise. Jeremy gave a slight nod in Sully's direction. Understanding, Walton stood and stepped aside for Riley to take his place.

Riley knelt beside the boy, who was looking at him wide-eyed, as Jeremy carefully felt along the boy's arm and up to his shoulder.

Jeremy turned to Mrs. Winters. "It looks like a dislocated shoulder. Painful, no doubt, but easily remedied. It'd be better to do X-rays at the hospital, so we'll give him a light painkiller and take him there, if that's okay."

Mrs. Winters nodded vigorously as Walton relayed the needed facts to Medical Control. After quickly receiving the dosage amount, he passed the information to Riley, who prepared the syringe and medication.

After administering the medication, Riley began situating the splint. He placed a sling under Ollie's arm, wrapping it once around his body to hold the arm close and as immobile as possible. While Riley worked, Jeremy talked to Oliver, keeping him distracted. Riley sat back and looked at Jeremy, who nodded approval.

Mrs. Winters glanced back and forth, from the house to Oliver, as they were finishing up

"My husband is on his way home and should be here any minute and—"

At that instant, the back door flung open, and a young man dressed in a suit and tie came running out.

"Ollie?! Meredith?! Samantha?!"

Spying the group, he ran around the pool. Reaching them, he looked first at his son and then his wife, wide-eyed with concern. He dropped to his knees beside them. He stroked Oliver's forehead and put his arm around his wife.

"Hey, buddy," Mr. Winters said, looking at Oliver. "Didn't have your monkey suit on today to climb trees?"

Oliver giggled. His dad grinned before looking anxiously at his wife.

Looking to the paramedics, his eyebrows arched in concern. "How is he?"

"Mr. Winters?" Jeremy asked as the young man nodded quickly. "It looks like Mr. Oliver here has dislocated a shoulder. We've given him a light painkiller but we'll transport him to Abernathy Memorial for X-rays before treatment. Since he's so young, one of you can ride in the ambulance with him if you'd like. The others can follow in a personal vehicle."

Riley watched and listened while he and Walton put the excess supplies away. A few seconds later, Carrier and Grimes came through the gate with the gurney. Mr. and Mrs. Winters hovered attentively nearby, Mrs. Winters with an arm around Samantha, watching as Oliver was transferred to the gurney.

They were a nice-looking family, Riley thought as he stood and reached for one of the bags. He thought of Maggie and his heart leapt. He was looking forward to them having a family like this one day. He smiled to himself. He was supposed to pick up the engagement ring tomorrow.

As Riley walked beside the gurney on the way to the ambulance, Oliver looked up at him and asked, "Are you a real fireman?"

Riley chuckled and answered conspiratorially, "Well, yes. But actually, today is my first day. And how lucky for me that on my first day I got to meet you? But . . . I need your help."

Oliver looked at him quizzically. "My help?"

"Yeah! I need a really good patient to make me look good. Can you help me with that?"

Oliver nodded enthusiastically as they reached the back of the ambulance. Riley nodded and gave him a wink and whispered, "Thank you."

Jeremy grinned at Riley. "Sully, you ride in the back with Oliver and Mrs. Winters. Make sure he stays comfortable. Keep an eye on his vitals and make sure there are no spikes. Use the intercom into the cab if anything comes up."

Riley nodded and stepped inside the box as Carrier and Grimes lifted the gurney into the back.

"Meredith, we're right behind you," Mr. Winters said as Walton assisted Mrs. Winters into the back of the ambulance. She looked back at her husband and nodded as she took the seat across the gurney from Riley.

"You sure are a brave young man," Riley said to Oliver as he adjusted the straps on the gurney so they wouldn't rub Oliver's injured shoulder. "How old did you say you were? I'm guessing around twenty-two?"

Oliver giggled and looked at his mom, who smiled back at him.

The doors banged shut. Riley heard the engine start and felt the ambulance start into motion.

"I'm five," Oliver said and held up the hand from his uninjured arm, his fingers spread wide.

Riley acted shocked, his eyes widening. "What? Are you sure? I thought you were much older, as brave as you are. You must be super tough!"

Mrs. Winters smiled at Oliver. "Thank you," she said, looking up at Riley. "I was so scared. He just looked so little laying there, and he was in such pain. I looked away for a second —just one second —and that's when he fell. I was absolutely frantic. Thank you for taking such good care of him." She bent over and kissed Oliver as he smiled at her.

Riley looked at Oliver and at Mrs. Winters stroking her son's cheek, and he smiled. The day was looking brighter.

R ILEY FOLLOWED JEREMY AND Walton out of the ambulance after Jeremy backed into the bay at the station. It had been a busy day, with a short break in the afternoon. And now they were back at the station. It was close to dinnertime, and Riley was starving.

Station Five, one of the largest stations in Abernathy, housed ten firefighters—two on the ambulance, four on the engine, and four on the truck. It was one of the newer stations in town and had been built to accommodate housing growth at the edge of town. As the growth continued outward, Station Five was now well inside city limits.

The station and its grounds were located on a busy street, with several shopping areas along the same stretch of road, including some big box retailers. The station itself sat back off the street, surrounded by large trees, a small grassy area, and low-cut shrubs. It was a modern, attractive station, and Riley was thrilled to have been assigned here.

While the exterior of the station was red brick, the expansive bay area interior was cinder block painted battleship gray. The bright red accordion-style bay doors folded open and closed to accommodate the truck, engine, and ambulance housed here. The largest of the apparatus—the truck—was situated the furthest from the living quarters, while the engine was parked in the middle and the ambulance was parked closest to the door accessing the living area.

The apparatus were impressive—their red paint gleamed and the chrome sparkled. Riley stopped to admire them longingly. That's where he'd hoped to be assigned. He wanted to fight fires, perform daring rescues, even rescue a cat out of a tree. But not ride the ambulance.

Rookies rotated to each apparatus, and Riley was anxious for his first rotation to either one. Thankfully though, the day had gotten somewhat better since the first run.

"Whew!" Walton said, wiping his forehead with his arm. "What a day!"

"It *has* been busy. But the good news, it's almost dinnertime. I don't know about you guys, but I'm starving," Jeremy replied.

Riley agreed. He was starving too.

"Is it usually *this* busy?" he asked as they walked around to the back of the ambulance.

"Sometimes yes. Sometimes no. You just never know. It's different every shift. That's what keeps it interesting," Jeremy said as Walton nodded.

"But right now, follow me, Rookie," Jeremy said, gesturing with a flick of his hand. "We clean the box and restock when we return to the station and when we have the time."

Jeremy handed Riley a box of disinfectant wipes.

"These are for you. Scrub to your heart's content, my friend. Don't miss a spot. And trust me, we'll be checking," Jeremy said before opening the back doors of the ambulance and sitting down on the bench seat to finish reports. Walton climbed in and started taking inventory of the cabinets.

Riley looked down at the box of disinfectant wipes. His gray eyes flashed the color of steel, then narrowed. Cleaning? He'd gone to the academy for six months. Was all of that just so he could clean according to procedure? Riley took a deep breath and reminded himself he *was* a rookie. He had to learn everything from the ground up but still . . .

Riley groaned inwardly.

"Step to it, Rookie," Walton said, poking his head out of the back of the ambulance. "Another call could come any time."

Riley nodded and walked to the ambulance cab. Opening the driver's door, he pulled a disinfectant wipe from the container and started wiping down the interior surfaces. Nothing escaped Riley's thorough scrubbing as the pungent smell of disinfectant and ammonia filled the air.

Walton's mocking voice startled Riley a few minutes later. "Clean yet?" He stood in the passenger-side doorway, peering over Riley's shoulder.

"It's clean," Riley answered, giving the dash one last swipe.

"We'll see about that," Jeremy said from the driver's-side door.

"What do you think, Walton?" Jeremy asked with feigned severity.

"Hmmm . . . passable for a first attempt I suppose. Always room for improvement, Rookie. Don't forget behind the door handles on the storage cabinets."

Riley bit back a retort. "Of course. I was just about to do that."

Seeing Riley's frustration, Jeremy and Walton exchanged mischievous looks.

Jeremy's phone pinged with a text. He pulled it from his pocket and quickly read the text, which brought a huge grin. Self-consciously, he looked around and quickly typed a response and stifled a smile, slipping the phone back into his pocket.

Riley raised his eyebrows in question, but Jeremy avoided his look.

"Okay, Rookie," Jeremy hurried on, stepping away from the ambulance and walking toward the back of the bay. "Restocking is next. Follow me."

Riley fell into step behind Jeremy and Walton as they walked to a locked storage room at the back. Walton punched in the security code and turned the handle. The cinder block room was square, small and windowless, and chilled with its own air conditioning unit. All four walls held storage shelves which, along with the freestanding shelves in the center, were lined with plastic storage boxes holding medical supplies, each wrapped in disposable plastic packaging.

Jeremy consulted the list Walton had created as they pulled what was needed from various bins. Riley watched closely as Jeremy explained the process.

After pulling the last items on the list, Jeremy thrust the list and full box into Riley's hands.

"Just be sure to put everything in the right place," Jeremy said. He turned his attention to Walton as they walked toward the bay door that led to the station.

"What do think is for supper?" Jeremy asked with a snicker. "Sims is cooking so I'm betting it's spaghetti. I don't think he's willing to try anything else."

"Would you, after what happened last time?" Walton said, chuckling as the door closed behind them.

Riley stood alone in the middle of the bay floor, supply box in hand. Apart from the occasional vehicle passing on the street outside, the silence was deafening. He knew he shouldn't, but he felt abandoned. What happened to the camaraderie he'd heard about between firefighters? What had happened to Jeremy? Riley had envisioned Jeremy showing him the ropes, giving him insights, telling him who was who, what and who to look out for, how things worked. But instead, Jeremy was treating him like . . . well, like a rookie.

Riley chuckled to himself. He sounded like a schoolboy. He humphed and strode toward the ambulance.

After putting the supplies in their labeled places, Riley carefully checked one more time to make sure he'd placed everything correctly. Satisfied, he jumped from the back of the ambulance, his boots hitting the cement floor with a thud. He slammed both doors closed and walked toward the door leading into the station.

The short hallway from the bay opened into the kitchen area on the left and the TV room with its rows of recliners to the right. Another short hallway beyond led to the dormitory bedrooms. The entrance to Captain Jernigan's office was directly across from the hallway to the bay for quick access when needed.

It was quiet when Riley opened the door. But immediately, a cacophony of noise hit him with the force of a monsoon. As Riley stepped into the kitchen, he saw nine firefighters gathered around the large, stainless steel-topped dining table. All four sides of the square table were filled with firefighters, all talking at once, some trying to yell over the others.

Ed Brimly, a grizzled veteran firefighter Riley had met earlier that morning, was at the center of the chaos, scribbling notes on what looked like the back of an envelope. Riley walked up to stand beside Jeremy, who was doing his own share of yelling, trying to get Brimly's attention.

"What's going on?" Riley yelled in the direction of Jeremy's ear.

"We're betting to see who does dishes for the next seven shifts," Jeremy yelled back at Riley. "You'd better get your times down if you want part of the action."

"Times for what?" Riley yelled back, trying to make sense of what was the epicenter of activity.

"The next run," Jeremy yelled. The noise slowed and stopped.

His brows furrowing, Riley's eyes narrowed as he looked first at Jeremy, then at the group.

"Rookie," began Keevin Jernigan, all eyes turning to their well-liked captain, "let me explain. Guys, let me know if I miss anything."

Riley frowned uncomfortably as he saw knowing smirks exchanged around the table.

Captain Jernigan continued. "Rookie, it's like this. We've gotten a run right at dinner time the last three shifts. We're betting—no actual money, of course—to see who gets closest to the time for tonight's run. The one whose time is the furthest from the actual time has to—oh pardon me—*gets* to do the dishes the next seven shifts," he said, chuckling under his breath with a look around the table.

"Got everything you need?" Jernigan asked with a glance over his shoulder to Brimly.

"Yep, Cap. Got it."

"Do we have our winner?" Jernigan asked as all eyes turned to Riley, broad smiles widening on each face.

Riley looked around quickly. "But we haven't had a run—"

Riley realized he hadn't put a bet down either, and being too late, realized this was all by design. He looked at the circle of smug faces.

"Welcome to Station Five A Shift, Rookie and . . . use lots of hot water. We like our dishes *really* clean," Captain Jernigan said, chuckling as he gave Riley a quick slap on the back.

Captain Jernigan took a seat at the table along with the rest of the group. Sims set a huge pot of spaghetti in the middle of the table followed by two large bowls of salad and four loaves of toasted garlic bread.

Riley hesitated but then took the lone spot available, next to Brimly, who glanced at Riley, still chuckling at their prank.

The bay door banged open and Battalion Chief Bentley walked in, surveying the crew at the table as they all stood in greeting.

"Chief Bentley," Captain Jernigan said, "you're just in time for supper. There's an extra seat somewhere. Guys, give Chief Bentley some room."

Brimly scooted toward Riley, nearly pushing him off the edge of the bench seat.

The captain asked for a blessing and the food was passed around the noisy table. Riley, as the rookie, was last to receive the food. He took a small portion and ate sparingly, even though there was enough for seconds. He glanced around the table as the group ate enthusiastically and chatted.

"How's the new station?" Jernigan asked Bentley, forking in a rounded spoonful of spaghetti.

Bentley nodded and swallowed his bite. "It's great. Still getting settled in and working out the kinks in a new facility, but it's getting there. How about here at Five? Anything noteworthy?"

"Got a new rookie. Sullivan, introduce yourself," Captain Jernigan said as all eyes turned toward Riley.

Riley cleared his throat and laid his fork on his plate. "Riley Sullivan, sir. Graduated the academy a couple of weeks ago, assigned to Station Five A Shift. Excited to be here."

Bentley eyed him closely for several uncomfortable seconds. "Welcome to the AFD, Sullivan. You're with a good crew. Captain Jernigan is one of our best."

Murmurs of agreement were heard around the table.

"You guys go way back, don't you?" Hayward, the one introduced to Riley as the engine's driver, asked, directing his question to Jernigan.

"Oh, yeah. You might say that," the captain said with a chuckle, looking at Bentley and exchanging a knowing look. "I knew the chief here when he was a lowly lieutenant. He's come a long way, and I don't just mean in rank."

"I'll take that appraisal," Bentley agreed, taking a drink of tea and setting the glass back on the table. "We were at the Deuce—that's Station Two for those who might not know. That was a great crew too. Hart, Canfield, Hedrick, the Cap here and—"

"Andy Garrett," Captain Jernigan finished for him with a somber look. Silence hung in the air, no one sure what to say as the two men looked at each other solemnly.

Bentley cleared his throat and went on. "We lost Garrett to cancer after he was exposed to carcinogens in a major fire. He was an outstanding firefighter and a good friend. They sure don't make them like him anymore, do they Jernigan? Present company excepted, of course," Bentley added looking around the table.

"No, Chief. No, they don't," Jernigan replied, looking at his plate and pushing his spaghetti around aimlessly for a few minutes before taking another bite.

Conversation resumed gradually until about halfway through the meal, Captain Jernigan said, "Hey, Rookie. Did I mention you're cooking next shift?" He took a chunk of bread and sopped up some spaghetti sauce on his plate.

Riley's head snapped up. "What?! Me? Cook?" he blurted without thinking.

A few muffled chuckles came from around the table.

"Yes, you. We have some finicky eaters, but I'm sure they'll fill you in on what and what not to serve. Guys, feel free," he said, gesturing with his fork.

"No ham," the one called Hayward, the engine driver, said around a mouth full of spaghetti.

"No green vegetables and no salads!" said a firefighter with a deep clefted chin, whose plate was mounded over with spaghetti. He pointed with his fork to the two salad bowls on the table and glared at Sims. "Can't abide green stuff. Meat, bread, and potatoes will do just fine."

"And don't even think about sandwiches, Rookie. The last rookie who served sandwiches for their first meal ended up cleaning toilets for an entire month," said another.

Jeremy looked down, hiding a smile. They were really giving Riley the treatment. He hazarded a sidelong glance down the table. Knowing Riley as well as he did, he could tell Riley was uncomfortable. Jeremy shoved a fork full of spaghetti in his mouth before biting off some garlic bread. He felt bad for Riley, but he couldn't step in and help him. This was what every rookie went through. Riley was going to have to swim on his own to gain the respect of the crew. That's what he and everyone else had had to do.

It had only been two years since Jeremy was a rookie, and he remembered what he'd gone through all too well. Being a rookie wasn't easy, and he was thankful that time in his career was in the past. Being a rookie was exhausting and at times embarrassing, but it was a rite of passage for any firefighter. From arriving at the station before anyone else to make coffee and tea to cleaning the bathrooms each shift and even to the time he'd had to mop the entire bay when someone 'accidentally' tracked mud across the floor, it had been grueling.

Jeremy took a bite of salad and looked around the table. Everyone was having fun at Riley's expense. But then again, they didn't tease those they didn't like. Even though Riley didn't realize it right now, and he'd probably find it hard to believe if Jeremy tried to explain it, the guys were paying him a huge compliment with their ready acceptance of him.

RILEY STOPPED TRYING TO remember all the requests, the likes, the dislikes. The best solution was to find something he *could* cook. Up until now, the most he'd ever cooked was spreading peanut butter and jelly between two slices of bread. The one time he'd tried to fix macaroni and cheese, the pasta had come out tough and the cheese lumpy.

But then a thought snagged, and it was pure inspiration. Maggie. She was a great cook, and Riley was sure she'd be glad to give him a cooking lesson or two.

The spaghetti bowls were passed one last time and scraped clean of every strand of pasta. Riley noted that not a single run had come in during the meal. He made his way around the table, gathering dishes and taking them to the sink to wash after the majority of the firefighters had headed toward the TV room. Riley sighed quietly. Life as a firefighter—at least as a rookie firefighter—wasn't exactly one exciting adventure after another.

As he started to put the dishes in the dishwasher, the tones sounded. The dishes rattled as he hurriedly put them in the sink and rushed to follow Jeremy and Walton to the ambulance. As the dispatcher continued relaying information about an accident with an overturned vehicle, Riley folded himself into the jump seat. Jeremy and Walton quickly followed, climbing into their seats and simultaneously slamming doors and buckling their seat belts. Lieutenant Cochran's voice came over the radio, acknowledging their response as the red lights began circling the walls and the sirens started. The ambulance pulled out first, followed by the engine.

Riley's heart raced as he anxiously looked through the windshield. He soon spotted a swath of flashing emergency lights several blocks ahead. His adrenaline was pumping. He was not sure if he was ready for whatever lay ahead, but he *was* ready to find out.

Cade Marshall, doing his best to stem his frustration, stood with his hands akimbo, watching his partner, Bart Crawford, circle the overturned vehicle while berating the victim.

They had just finished setting flares around the accident scene while officers from the first arriving cruiser directed traffic. The victim was upside down, held tightly in place by his seat belt. He was blubbering, slurring his words, and clumsily trying to get free.

"Can it, Gorretti." Crawford mocked the man sarcastically as he bent down momentarily to look inside the car before continuing his verbal attack as he circled the vehicle. "You're not going anywhere but jail. This is the second pile up you've caused this month," he said loudly with a mocking laugh.

Cade grimaced. He and Crawford had arrested Gorretti several weeks ago after he was the cause of a major wreck. Gorretti hadn't been injured, but he had been driving while intoxicated. Crawford berated Gorretti in front of the other citizens involved in the accident and in front of other responding officers. Cade was surprised there had been no disciplinary proceedings after several citizens expressed concern over Crawford's conduct.

Crawford's reputation was well-known in the ranks and hearing his comments now to Gorretti, the other two officers looked over their shoulders and frowned at Crawford, but gave Cade a sympathetic glance.

Cade ran his fingers through his brown hair and tried not to roll his eyes as he looked away in embarrassment. He'd been partnered with Bart Crawford for almost a year. It had been a very long, very trying year. He was tired of Crawford's sarcasm and the way he treated people, himself included.

He tried his best not to let Crawford get to him. But there were times, like this shift, when things between them had been exceptionally strained. Crawford had decided to stop for something to eat at a place he knew Cade didn't like. Even though Cade was hungry, he'd elected not to eat. Enjoying himself at Cade's expense, Crawford had made an obnoxious show of eating slowly and loudly in the cruiser while Cade had no choice but to sit and listen.

Cade had tried bringing a couple of meals from home but was derided mercilessly by Crawford, not only to his face, but loudly to other officers at the end of shift. The times they'd gone into a fast-food restaurant to eat, Cade embarrassedly listened to Crawford belittling employees, enjoying the fear he'd caused. Numerous times, Cade had waited until Crawford was back in the cruiser before making an excuse to go back inside and apologize to the workers.

Being a police officer and serving citizens of the community was honorable work. Cade wanted the police force to be looked to with respect and as having integrity but also knew citizens needed to be treated with respect.

Cade had joined the police force to proudly continue his family's legacy of policing and community service. He'd breezed through the academy, absorbing every detail and working hard to perfect the physical training. He had anxiously awaited his first partner assignment with assurances from his dad that he'd get a great partner. The Marshall family was well-known, and everyone vied to have a family member as their rookie to train, in light of the family's stellar reputation.

Cade's first partner had been exactly the type Cade had hoped to have. James Walsh was a veteran, a by-the-book officer who knew and respected Cade's father and grandfather. Cade had learned and matured steadily under Officer Walsh's tutelage, but six months later, much to Cade's disappointment, Officer Walsh was promoted and transferred to the detective division. Cade was hopeful he'd get another strong partner to finish out his rookie year.

But to his dismay, Cade's new partner was Bart Crawford.

"This is a chance to see the kind of cop you *don't* want to be," Cade's dad had told him, encouraging him to look on the bright side. "Take this in stride and learn from it. You already know what you're doing, and you've got a good head on your shoulders. Stay true to yourself and who you are. You'll be fine. And who knows, you might even have a positive influence on him."

Cade had laughed when his dad said that, and it only became more ironic the longer he was partnered with the guy. Cade wasn't having an impact of any kind that he could tell, except to be a verbal punching bag when no one else was available. Cade was more than ready for another partner, but his dad continued to encourage him to ride it out and not make waves. "Something will happen when you least expect it," he'd said, giving Cade's shoulder a squeeze. "Just be patient."

While they waited for the paramedics and ambulance to arrive, Cade took notes and measurements for the accident report to keep himself busy, ignoring as much of Crawford's diatribe as possible.

Distant sirens drew closer. As dusk fell, Cade could see the emergency lights approaching. He knew Jeremy was on duty today but hoped it would be another station responding. As badly as Crawford treated everyone else, he treated firefighters worse. And since Crawford had found out Jeremy and Cade were friends, he didn't let up.

Cade watched as the ambulance pulled up, the siren ending as it came to a stop. He groaned. Jeremy was driving, and when Riley piled out behind Jeremy, Cade stiffened. He heaved a sigh and walked around to the other side of the vehicle. All Cade could do was hope Jeremy had warned Riley about Crawford and that nothing would be said about the three of them being friends. It could make life rough. Not just for Jeremy and Riley, but for him too.

J EREMY BRAKED THE AMBULANCE to a short stop several feet from the overturned car. He killed the siren. The engine pulled at an angle to the ambulance, giving them as much safe space away from oncoming traffic as possible. Jeremy and Walton quickly climbed out. Riley followed as deftly as he could.

"So, what's your problem today, Gorretti? You do nothing but cause trouble for yourself and everybody else," a gruff, disembodied voice was shouting at the car's lone occupant as the three began pulling out their medical bags, and the engine crew began pulling extrication equipment. The car, a late model four-door sedan, rested on its top, slightly rocking. The asphalt was still radiating heat from the afternoon's sun. They could see the lone occupant of the car hanging upside down, the seat belt holding him solidly in place. The windshield's shattered glass covered the roadway, inches away from the man's head.

As they walked toward the wrecked vehicle, Riley could hear the man inside crying and blubbering incoherently. The person on the other side of the vehicle bent over, and Riley could see him clearly through the opening where the passenger window would have been. The only word that came to Riley's mind when he saw the man was 'thick.' The man's neck was solid and wide in diameter, just like his head. And from what Riley could see of his form, he had a beefy torso. Riley sucked in a sharp breath when he realized the man berating the crash victim so cruelly was wearing a police uniform.

Hearing Riley's reaction, Jeremy caught Riley's eye and did a slight shake of his head, He wouldn't say anything just yet. While they waited for the firefighters to stabilize the car and remove the victim, Riley was surprised to see Cade walk around from the back of the car. He didn't speak, but gave a solemn nod in Riley and Jeremy's direction before coming to stand by them to watch the extrication. Cade planted his hands on hips, his feet set apart as he glared, watching the work being done. Riley could see and feel the frustration radiating from Cade.

Riley tried to get a read on what was going on. Jeremy obviously knew something about Cade and that other officer. Cade, the normally easygoing, laid-back guy, was wound tight. His eyes, which were usually glinting with mischief, were dark and brooding. His muscular frame was rigid with irritation. He was running his fingers through his hair.

Riley started to step over and say something to Cade, but Jeremy made a slight move to stop him. Riley tried to catch Jeremy's eye, but Jeremy didn't acknowledge him. Whether on purpose or not, Riley wasn't sure.

The verbal abuse from the other officer continued as firefighters skillfully worked to safely remove the victim. The belligerent officer moved around to the side of the car where the firefighters were working. Only after Cade stepped between him and the firefighters did his tirade slow.

"What's the problem, Marshall?" the gruff officer smirked, looking at the firefighters with obvious disdain. "Are you afraid I'll offend your little firefighter friends?"

Riley saw Cade stiffen and sensed the tension rise among the firefighters simultaneously.

"Officer Crawford, why don't we tone things down?" Cade said with as much force as he dared.

"Oh yeah?" the officer retorted, turning on Cade with a withering look. "How about I . . ."

Whatever Officer Crawford was about to say was lost as the last efforts to free the victim were completed, and the extrication team stepped back to make way for the paramedics.

"Excuse us," Jeremy said, elbowing his way past the officer. "We have a victim to treat."

Crawford humphed as he moved, but he only moved slightly.

Riley tried to catch Cade's eye, but Cade looked away and followed Crawford to where other officers were working traffic control.

Riley assisted Jeremy and Walton where he was needed. He couldn't help but be impressed with their professionalism as they treated the victim who reeked of alcohol. His injuries were light considering the severity of the crash, and it didn't take long to prep him for transport.

"You're up front with me, Sully," Jeremy said. Walton gave Jeremy a questioning look as he climbed into the back of the ambulance.

Jeremy's cab door slammed closed as he started the siren and buckled his seat belt. He didn't speak until he had maneuvered past the police officers and pulled onto the freeway, picking up speed quickly.

Without looking at Riley, Jeremy said, "Not a word. Don't say a word about this to Cade. If he says something, that's fine. Just don't you be the one to bring it up."

"Who was that guy? What's his problem?"

"That's Cade's partner, Bart Crawford," Jeremy said with a frown and sideways look at Riley. The headlights of cars in the opposite lane played across Jeremy's solemn face.

"His partner?" Riley asked, incredulous. "I thought . . ."

"You thought he had a great partner and loved being a police officer? Well, that's what Cade wanted you to think. I mean it was true at first. He *was* excited when he graduated from the academy and his first few months on the job. But then his partner was promoted and transferred to another division. And some higher-up partnered him with Crawford. Cade has been miserable ever since. I don't know how he's lasted this long," Jeremy said, shaking his head. "His dream has always been to be an officer. You know that."

Riley nodded distractedly. "Yeah, I know. I remember we tried our best to talk him into being a firefighter. But his family's police legacy was just too strong. You think he might be rethinking things now?"

"Don't bet on it. He spends a lot of time with us at the station but still swears he wants to be a cop. Just not with that guy as his partner."

"Guys, I hate to break in on memory lane, but this guy is puking his guts up back here. Are we getting close?" Walton's voice came over the speaker.

"Pulling in now. The rookie's on his way back to help," Jeremy said, giving Riley a wicked grin.

Riley grimaced and shook his head as he opened the door. Cade had always dreamed of being a police officer, and Riley hated to think this one rogue officer was making things so miserable for him. If there was anything Riley could do to help, he would. Cop or no cop.

RILEY DRUG HIMSELF TO his SUV the next morning. It was a busy night. Three calls were medicals and the fourth was a medical but only after the police had calmed a domestic dispute before they could enter. He gave a half-hearted wave to Jeremy as Jeremy pulled out of the station's parking lot, a huge grin plastered on his all too cheerful face. How could Jeremy be so bright and chipper after the calls they'd had throughout the wee hours of the morning?

Riley stifled a yawn and looked at his watch. 6:38 a.m. He'd drop by his apartment for a quick shower and then check in with Winston Forbes, a longtime friend and Riley's high school guidance counselor. Riley had been intending to stop by and see Winston's new business, Electronix Doc, but just hadn't had the time. Today seemed like a good day to do that and maybe they'd have an opportunity to talk. They'd talked occasionally by phone, while Riley was away at school, but Riley missed visiting with Winston face to face. Winston had supported Riley's decision to go to college and join the fire service. Riley wondered what Winston would say now if he knew Riley was having doubts.

Revived after a hot shower and power breakfast with strong coffee, Riley pulled into Abernathy's old downtown district that in recent years had been revitalized into a popular and trendy location. A narrow, brick-paved main street was lined on both sides with charming, old-fashioned store fronts. Intermittent planters along the sidewalks were filled with flowers and greenery, bringing a colorful and fresh feel to the area. Spotting Electronix Doc's storefront with it's eye-catching but tasteful neon sign, Riley found a nearby spot and parked.

He pushed open the door to the shop to find Winston himself at a round glass table, intently studying a phone and conversing with the owner sitting across from him.

Looking up and seeing Riley, Winston broke into a wide grin. "Hey, stranger! Take a look around. We're wrapping up here."

Riley smiled his acknowledgment and took his time perusing the colorful space. Riley admired the area with its bright, upscale, and modern color scheme and grinned. Winston had never been one to follow convention too closely. It all looked so very Winston. From the tasteful blue industrial carpeting on the floor to the broad diagonal slashes of neon green and bold blue across stark white walls, the atmosphere was crisp and upbeat. Two clear acrylic conference tables were on one side of the room with a couple of modern but comfortable-looking chairs at each. Displays of electronics and accessory products were on the opposite wall behind an acrylic transaction counter. Riley casually strolled around the room, taking everything in as Winston wrapped up with his customer.

"Joe, we'll get started on this right away," Winston said as he stood and walked to the transaction counter, phone in hand, the customer following. "We're a little backed up, but we'll get it back to you, good as new, in no time. I've filled in the work needed and cost if you'll just complete your contact information. Of course, if the cost comes in under the estimate, you'll get the lower amount. We'll either give you a call or shoot you a text as soon as it's ready."

"Appreciate you, Winston. It's good to have a dependable local electronics store with good service instead of having to send our pieces off to these big tech companies," Joe said, shaking Winston's hand.

"It's truly my pleasure, Joe. We'll see you soon. And tell Beverly hello for me."

Joe turned, giving Riley a friendly nod as Riley sidestepped out of his way. Joe opened the glass door and joined the growing number of pedestrians on the walk outside.

"Riley Sullivan. You're a sight for sore eyes."

Riley turned back as Winston rounded the counter, walking toward Riley, a wide smile on his slim face, his hand extended. He gave Riley a firm handshake and clapped him into a loose hug with a slap on the back.

"Winston," Riley said with a smile of his own. "It's great to see you."

"How long have you been in town?" Winston asked, waving Riley to one of the glass conference tables.

Riley winced.

"Well, I actually got back in April after graduation. But then the fire academy started right away and . . ."

"Ah, I see," Winston nodded knowingly.

Riley shifted uncomfortably. "Sorry, I . . ."

Winston held up a hand and grinned, stopping Riley mid-sentence. "Just messing with you. I knew when you got back, and I know how busy the academy has kept you. I'm just glad you found your way in today."

"So, Dad's keeping you in the loop, huh?" Riley asked with a slight tease and frown. Riley looked around appreciatively. "This place looks awesome."

Winston gave a slight shrug and stood as he followed Riley's gaze around the room. "Yeah, I don't see your dad often. But as old friends, we make sure to stay in touch. But come on. You ain't seen nothing yet. Follow me."

Riley's mouth dropped open when he followed Winston into the back area of the shop. The space was large and well lit. Various types of electronics and tools were scattered on bright stainless-steel tables with enormous dome lights over each workspace. There were doors on one wall leading to what looked like an office, conference room, and a break room, and the back wall held a larger version of the Electronix Doc logo, back lit with brilliant white light.

"This is my happy place," Winston said with a pleased grin. "I've invested pretty much everything I've got, but I think I'm going to see a great return. At least it's looking promising."

"I can certainly see why," Riley said, taking his eyes from the crispness of the stainless-steel and bright lights to study Winston's beaming face. Even though Winston was already retired when Riley met him in high school, he hadn't seemed to age a day. The scope of this workspace was a testament to Winston's forward-thinking, upbeat attitude. Riley felt like a bumbling hulk with his brooding doubts compared to the positive energy Winston radiated. Winston was slim, his olive complexion a contrast to his lightly graying hair, his arms gesturing proudly about the room as he gave Riley a tour.

"This is amazing," Riley was finally able to interject when Winston paused for breath. "I can see why you're so proud, and you obviously enjoy it. This would definitely be a great space to work in every day. You are certainly a man of many talents and from the looks of this place, business must be good."

Winston chuckled. "That's an understatement. Business is booming. It started out as more of a hobby than a career, but technology is here to stay. As much as we'd like for it to be perfect, it's certainly not. And it's always changing, which keeps a tech guy like me happy and in business. Repairs are still a big part of Electronix Doc, but installation demand is growing too—flat screen TV's, stereo systems, home movie theaters. You name it. I've got five guys working for me now. They're all out on installs this morning but most will be back this afternoon to work on these repair projects." He gestured with a wave of his hand. "And I need to add this one to the list," he said, moving to an electronic pad to enter information for the phone in his hand.

Riley walked around the room, picking up some of the intricate tools and studying the electronic pad on each table with the project's details. Winston glanced up and studied Riley. Something was bothering him. Winston could tell.

Laying the phone aside, Winston walked over to a low table and sat in one of the side chairs.

"What's up? You didn't just wander in today."

Riley followed, and as he sat, his shoulders slumped. He leaned his forearms on his legs and dropped his head into his hands.

"I think I've made a mistake," Riley said, his voice so low Winston barely heard.

"Mistake about what?" Winston asked gently. "You haven't let that pretty girl get away, have you?"

Riley sat up with a slight grin. "No. I was actually getting ready to propose. But now, I'm not so sure about . . . other things."

Winston leaned back, a concerned furrow between his brows.

"The fire department?"

Riley nodded. He knew Winston was the right one to come to.

"Well, how did training go at the academy? I've heard that the academy is where you figure out if the fire service is the right fit for you and you for it. If you've finished the academy, don't you have the hardest part behind you? Or are you saying you're having second thoughts about law school? Your dad sure would be thrilled."

Riley leaned back, slumping in his chair. He groaned.

"I can tell you right now, I don't see law school in my future. And the academy was great. Everything I'd always dreamed it would be. But the first shift . . ."

Riley trailed off, reliving the death of the man yesterday morning. He blinked and shook it off. "There was a fatality my first run as a paramedic, and I . . ."

Winston leaned forward. "And what, Riley?" he asked softly.

"I watched Jeremy and the other paramedic work on the man until there was nothing else they could do. The man's wife was looking for me to give something I didn't know how to give. The thing is, both Jeremy and Ethan, the other paramedic, they knew. They knew how to comfort her, the things to say, the things to do . . . I just stood there feeling like a total idiot."

Riley stood and started pacing.

"And then at the station, Jeremy treats me like a . . . a rookie." Riley, hearing himself, stopped, grinning slightly before he went on. "Look. I can understand that from the other guys. But from Jeremy? He's supposed to be one of my best friends. Shouldn't he be giving me some tips or back up or something? He just threw me to the wolves. And, I'm supposed to cook dinner next shift. I've never cooked a thing in my life. I'm going to see if Maggie will give me a couple of crash course cooking lessons, but what else can I do?"

Riley stopped pacing and looked at Winston, who was watching and listening with a huge grin on his face.

Riley jammed his hands into his pockets in frustration.

"What's that smirk about?" he asked gruffly.

"Riley, my boy, it's been one shift. One day. You're just getting started. A fatality is tough, no question, but how many of those kinds of calls have Jeremy and the other paramedic been on? This was your first. Don't you think they had the same feelings you're experiencing when they started? You're way too anxious. You've got to give yourself some time to learn and adjust. Did things improve any throughout the rest of the day?"

Riley rubbed the back of his neck and looked at Winston. "Well, there *were* others. And I assisted. I guess I even took the lead on some—per Jeremy's instruction, of course." Riley hesitated, thinking about Oliver and the thanks he'd gotten from Oliver's mother. "I guess, maybe—I did do a little bit of good yesterday. You could be right. Maybe I'm expecting too much right now." Riley shrugged, feeling a little foolish.

Winston chuckled. "That's more like it."

Riley paused. "But ... then there's Jeremy. I thought he was a friend. But at the station and around the other guys, he acts like he hardly knows me."

"Riley, whether you realize it now or not, Jeremy is doing you a favor. Do you think any of those other guys had a friend on the inside who made things easy for them? I highly doubt it. So why do you think you're entitled? I'd be pretty miffed if I saw a rookie getting special treatment or shortcutting something I'd had to work to obtain."

Winston stopped and studied Riley.

"You've wanted to be a firefighter as long as I've known you, Riley. I can't imagine you giving it up after just one shift. But then, that's entirely up to you."

Winston stood and walked to the door leading to the break room.

"I do better thinking over a cup of coffee. You?"

Riley nodded and absent-mindedly followed Winston.

"Seems I recall that you like tinkering with electronics," Winston said. He pulled two clean mugs from the dishwasher and poured coffee from a half-full decanter.

Riley slid into a chair at the table.

"Yeah, I do. They still fascinate me. It's amazing how quickly things change and how they're a part of everything we do these days. I still enjoy tinkering around when I have the time," Riley said, taking the steaming cup from Winston.

"Well, I was thinking," Winston said and took a seat, "did you mean what you said earlier? About this store being an amazing place to work?"

Riley gave Winston a long look over the edge of his mug as he took a sip.

"Are you offering me a job?" he asked with a widening grin.

"I am," Winston nodded. "We definitely need the help. I realize it'd have to be around your shift schedule. That is, if you decide to stay on as a firefighter, of course. But as I said, business is booming. I sure could use the help."

"Well, that sounds great. I'm in," Riley said, temporarily forgetting his concerns about firefighting. He stood and extended his hand to shake on the deal. "Finding a job that would work around my shift days has been on my to-do list. This is better than I could have imagined. When do I start?"

"How about right now?"

J EREMY SAT IN HIS truck, the motor idling. The good humor he'd felt when he'd left the station had evaporated with the text from his father.

Jeremy, headed to the shop. I'll meet you there.

The shop was where Jeremy came to decompress after a shift. It was *his* sanctuary where he could work his stress out by feeling the hard sturdiness of wood in his hands as he methodically crafted it into whatever the wood wished to reveal. His dad coming there, first thing in the morning, meant only one thing—he wanted to continue the conversation Jeremy had walked out on a couple of days ago. Jeremy half-chuckled to himself. His mom probably put his dad up to coming. She couldn't stand having tension or disagreement of any kind in the family.

Jeremy turned the key, opened his truck's door and stepped into the early morning air.

The door to the shop stood ajar, his dad's pick up already parked next to where Jeremy had parked. He stuffed his hands in his pockets and, scuffing the toe of one boot, walked toward the door.

"Son," his dad called from the back of the shop.

Jeremy flipped the light switch and the overhead neon lights blazed on with their familiar hum.

"Dad," Jeremy replied, not looking in his dad's direction, but making his way around the room, turning machines on to warm up.

His dad rarely came to the shop anymore. He had been a mechanic and had used the shop to work on engines before turning it over to Jeremy.

"I hope you don't mind. I went ahead and made coffee. I thought you might like a cup," Mr. Ennis said, holding a mug up.

"Yeah, thanks. I'll be there in just a minute."

After putting off the inevitable as long as he could, Jeremy walked to the back of the shop where the coffee maker was and poured himself a cup. He then walked casually to where his dad sat at the workbench in the center of the shop.

"You've got some nice stuff going here," his dad offered hesitantly, with an appreciative look around.

"You think so?" Jeremy asked, surprised.

His dad gave him a reproving look. "Well, I wouldn't say it if I didn't mean it."

Jeremy sighed. "What brings you out this morning?"

"You. Your mother and I didn't like the way things were left the other night. We . . . I . . . thought we should clear the air and come to a better understanding."

"I think I do understand," Jeremy replied curtly. "You think I need to find something more structured. I may not be setting any records, but I'm doing what I enjoy and what I'm good at doing. Can you not give me the space to do what *I* want to do and just let it go?"

Charles Ennis eyed his son closely and waited several seconds before responding. "Jeremy, listen to someone who has been around the block a couple of times. You're doing 'okay' selling a few pieces of your stuff here and there, but if you're serious about Allie and thinking about getting married, you need to think about a steadier income to supplement what you make at the fire department. That's all. Your mom and I just encourage you to think about it."

Marry Allie? Jeremy had stopped listening at that point. Is that what everyone was thinking? Is that what Allie was thinking? Though he did feel something different with her, he hadn't allowed himself to think that direction—he couldn't.

Frustrated, Jeremy slammed the coffee cup down on the work bench and sloshed hot coffee onto his hand. "Geez!" he said, grabbing a nearby rag and swiping at his hand.

Jeremy took a breath. He shook his head before taking a sip from his now half-empty cup as his dad continued talking. Jeremy wasn't going to marry anyone. He wasn't going to need a business or an income. How could his dad not believe what Grandpa Mars had told him? How could he not know and take seriously what Jeremy was facing? Jeremy had tried to bring it up several times, but his dad refused to even discuss it.

Jeremy stood abruptly, stopping his dad mid-sentence.

"I appreciate it, Dad. Really, I do," Jeremy said. He picked up the leg of a Windsor chair he was working on. He turned to one of the pieces of equipment in an attempt to cut the conversation short.

To appease his dad, he added, "But, I'll think about it. I promise. I know you're just looking out for me."

Mr. Ennis eyed Jeremy with a speculative eyebrow raised. He set his coffee cup on the workbench and rose.

"Okay, son, okay. You've definitely got the Ennis stubborn streak in you. But just remember, your mom and I are always here if you need us."

He patted Jeremy on the shoulder and walked slowly to the door.

Jeremy stood rooted for several seconds, staring at the chair leg in his hand. He turned and was about to say something just as his dad pulled the door closed behind him.

Jeremy sighed. He didn't mind having the Ennis stubborn streak, but there were other things about being an Ennis he'd gladly give up.

Jeremy sat back down on the stool, cradling the unfinished chair leg in his hands. He began to relax as the familiar smells of fresh-cut wood, coffee, and paint stain floated in the air around him, soothing him as they always did. But then, thoughts of the inevitable future he faced crowded in. Frustrated, he stood and walked to the coffee maker and refilled his cup.

Taking a sip of coffee, he thought about talking to Riley or Cade, or both, about his situation but quickly dismissed that idea. If he thought what Grandpa Mars had told him was crazy, they would think not only that the idea was crazy, but that he was too. He absently shook his head as he paced the narrow space.

Jeremy knew Grandpa Mars loved him. He would never have told Jeremy what he believed to be Jeremy's future if he didn't wholeheartedly believe it. No matter how implausible the whole scenario sounded to him, Jeremy trusted Grandpa Mars completely. It was his future, and it was up to him to face his own mortality and what was coming.

H E'D GOTTEN OFF SHIFT late, but he'd made it, and the constant thump of basketballs coming from the gym was like music to Cade. The basketball gym had come to feel like his home away from home. He loved playing football, but he loved being a youth league basketball coach ten times more. He was looking forward to spending the evening with the great little guys on the Roadside Market Roadrunners team.

He stood courtside, watching his team of nine-year olds shooting baskets as a warmup. They had already completed a run through of their team drills, and Cade, grinning to himself, had caught the opposing coach watching intently.

After several minutes, Cade blew his whistle and circled his finger in the air, a signal to gather around. As the last of the rosy-cheeked boys bunched into the circle, their eager faces looking up at him, he gave them a firm nod and smiled the encouraging "coach" smile he'd received from his coaches growing up.

"Men," he started, and they all beamed. "We've got a tough opponent today, but I'm not worried. Are you worried?"

There were firm head shakes from each boy.

"No, sir!" one little boy exclaimed loudly. The others chimed in just as loudly.

"That's what I like to hear!" Cade said, struggling to hide his own eagerness. He could feel his competitive spirit firing up. This was Cade's second year coaching these boys. Their record last season was a dismal three and twelve. But so far this year, they were thirteen and one, and if they won this game, they'd be top seed in the year's end of season tournament. Cade was incredibly proud of these boys, not just for the huge turnaround in their record, but for how hard they'd worked and come together as a team. Cade had received the coach's usual share of the parents' comments and suggestions, but when the team kept winning, and the parents saw how the team reacted to Cade's coaching, they'd backed off, leaving Cade to do his thing. He was loving it.

Cade stuck his hand in the middle of the circle and twelve little hands piled on top.

"Men, you're winners," Cade began. "Remember that. And keep doing what you've been doing because you're good. I mean, you're really good. And that other team," Cade motioned with his head toward the other side of the gym. "They don't stand a chance against the Roadrunners."

Heads bobbed in excited agreement.

"Runners on three," Cade said and looked each player in the eye. "One. Two. Three. Runners!"

They all shouted and threw their hands in the air. The bleachers were full of proud, boisterous parents who leapt to their feet, cheering loudly. Cade couldn't help but beam as he turned toward the court.

As he turned, he thought he saw a familiar figure at the edge of the bleachers and did a double-take. No, that couldn't be possible, he thought. When Cade looked again, no one was there. Funny, that guy looked a lot like Crawford, but . . .

The buzzer sounded, drawing Cade back to the game which passed in a blur. Roadrunners were up by ten in the first half and didn't look back.

RILEY WALKED OUT THE door of Electronix Doc a little after five, feeling more upbeat than when he'd walked in that morning. Maybe he *was* being too hasty about the fire department. There were some good moments on his first shift after all, and he'd know better what to expect next shift. His biggest problem was figuring out what to cook for his first dinner.

He glanced at his watch as he slid into the driver's seat. Perfect timing to stop by Jeremy and Cade's and see if they might want to grab a bite before he went over to Maggie's. He hadn't gotten to see her much lately and felt bad. He'd promised to call her, but the time had gotten away from him. She'd understand.

He put the SUV in reverse and started to back out when his phone rang. It was his dad.

Riley groaned.

"Hey, Dad," Riley said, answering reluctantly on the fourth ring.

"Son, just checking. Are you coming by the house or are you going straight to the Club?"

Riley frowned.

"I'm sorry. What?"

His dad took an exasperated breath. "The firm dinner at the Club tonight. Your mother told you about this a few days ago. From the sound of this conversation, looks like we'll be meeting you and Maggie at the Club. 6:30. Don't be late."

"Dad, wait. I don't know anything about this—"

The phone went dead.

Hitting the steering wheel with the palm of his hand, Riley let out a frustrated rush of air. A firm dinner was his dad's way of thanking the staff for their hard work on a big case. His dad expected Riley, his sister, Allie, and their mom to join him in showing their appreciation. The staff did work hard, no question, but why tonight? Riley's good mood disappeared. At least he'd get to see Maggie, he thought, as he dialed her number.

The phone rang several times before it went to voice mail. Strange . . . Maggie usually picked up quickly. She was probably still at the store. She worked in retail but on the administrative side. She was getting off soon so even though it wasn't his norm, he left a voicemail when the tone sounded.

"Hey, Mags. Sorry not to have called today. I've got a new job. You'll never believe who I'm working for. Can't wait to tell you. I wish we could have had a quiet evening but evidently, Dad has a company dinner planned at the Club for 6:30. Can I swing by and pick you up about 6:15?"

As he hung up, Riley noticed a voice mail indicator. He tapped the button and heard a formal voice say, "Mr. Sullivan, this is Giles with Butler Brothers Jewelers. The sizing of your ring is complete. It will be ready for pick up at your leisure. Good day."

Riley grinned. Maggie's ring. It was finally ready. He'd been side-tracked with so many things lately, he'd just realized a month had already passed since he'd left it to be sized. He needed to start in earnest on plans for the proposal he'd been envisioning for months. No matter what else might come along, Maggie was the one sure thing in his life, and this proposal had to be absolutely perfect to show her how much she meant to him. He was looking forward to seeing her tonight and couldn't wait for when he'd come home to her every night.

Riley pulled into the parking lot of his complex and dashed inside his apartment. He hurried through the living room with a scant glance at the few pieces of furniture and bare walls. He probably should do something to make this place a bit more comfortable, but he'd think about that later.

He rushed through a shower and threw on some khakis, an open collar white shirt, and a navy-blue blazer to meet the Club's dress code requirements. As he dressed, he checked his phone for a message from Maggie. Nothing. That was really strange.

He called and got her voicemail again. He left another message letting her know he'd meet her at the Club around 6:30.

Twenty minutes later, Riley pulled under the portico of the Abernathy Country Club's main club house, coming to a stop at the valet stand.

The Abernathy Country Club sat at the edge of town and with the distance from city noise, the soft silence felt soothing. Riley took a deep, slow breath as he stepped out of his SUV. It was a beautiful late summer evening, and he breathed the fresh air deeply.

The clubhouse sat atop a slight rise overlooking the lush golf course with the carefully manicured green of the eighteenth hole ending beneath the club's patio balcony. Soft landscape lighting accented the brick building with its cement capstones over each window and Corinthian columns at the entry to the main clubhouse as well as the portico where Riley stood.

"Good evening, Mr. Sullivan," Todd, the valet, said as he held Riley's door.

"Mr. Sullivan? Really?" Riley clapped Todd on the back.

"Your dad just arrived," Todd said with a knowing look and nod toward the driver's side door.

Riley nodded, understanding. His dad was formality to a fault.

"No dings, no dents, no—"

"Damage, I know," Todd grinned as he pulled the car door closed and drove away.

Riley took his time, waiting for Maggie. He casually looked around the Club's well-appointed lobby as he entered. Wealth was notable everywhere.

One had to be invited in order to join the Club. And when Ballard and Jane Sullivan had received their invitation years before Riley was born, they'd accepted immediately. As partner of one of the city's new leading law firms, Ballard Sullivan thought it only fitting to be a member of such a prestigious social organization. Riley had come here often growing up, but while he enjoyed playing the golf course, the pretentious atmosphere of the club and self-absorbed attitude of its members had always felt stilted and hollow.

Riley paced the black and white checked marble floor in the lobby, circling the large wooden table in the middle of the room with its oversized vase filled with exotic flowers. A sparkling chandelier hung over the table, its crystals sending shards of twinkling light across the room. Large landscape paintings hung in ornate frames over leather sofas and chairs grouped into conversation areas on plush rugs around the edges of the room. Heavy carved doors led to the formal dining room while another led to the more casual grill and bar. Another door led to the patio balcony that overlooked the eighteenth green.

There was no sign of Maggie. Riley hesitated, glancing at his watch again. His family was probably already in the dining room. It was 6:45, and it wasn't like Maggie to be late.

With one last look around, Riley headed toward the dining room's door just as his dad walked out. Their eyes locked. His dad frowned and jerked his head toward the dining room before going back in. Riley's phone buzzed with a text message from Maggie.

Can't make it tonight. Dinner tomorrow night at the Club? 7:00?

Disappointed, Riley sighed. Now, the evening looming ahead suddenly looked even longer.

Sure thing. Look forward to seeing you then.

He hit "send" and slid the phone into his pocket.

Riley walked into the dining room and began making his way toward his mom and sister, engulfed by staff members along the way. His dad's assistant, Marian, was the first to reach him, giving him a sympathetic look before embracing him in a short hug. One person after another shook Riley's hand, but no one would meet his eye. Riley dutifully thanked each of them for being such loyal members of the firm's law family and for their hard work.

He finally reached his mother and took his seat next to his sister, Allie. An empty chair to his side had been meant for Maggie, which made him miss her even more. Curiously, there was also an empty chair on the other side of Allie. Who was that for?

"He hasn't told you, has he?" Allie asked.

Riley looked at her, confused. "Who? And told me what?"

Allie shook her head slowly. "Dad. He didn't tell you what this dinner is about?"

Riley looked from his sister's face to those seated at the tables around them, who all seemed to be looking at him with something akin to sympathy.

What was going on? Riley felt suddenly anxious.

"No . . . Dad hasn't mentioned anything. Why is everyone looking at me that way?"

Before Allie could answer, Douglas Swanson, the other partner in Sullivan and Swanson and their dad's close friend, stood with a champagne glass in his hand and tapped it gently with a fork to get everyone's attention.

This was different. His dad usually made the opening toast.

"Dear friends, family, and colleagues. On behalf of the Sullivan and Swanson Law Firm, thank you for coming this evening. Tonight is a night of celebration, and it's one I've long dreamed of. I raise my glass in proud toast to my son, Lyle, who is following in my footsteps. Having successfully completed law school, he will sit for the bar in the spring. He's now officially an intern with Sullivan and Swanson. To Lyle!"

Riley's face burned hot and he gulped a quick breath.

Crystal champagne flutes clinked, followed by a silence, as everyone took a sip and resumed their seats. Low murmurs of table conversations began rippling around the room. Riley slowly set his glass on the pristine white linen tablecloth. He could feel his father's glare boring into him from where he sat down at the table. Much to the disapproval of his father, Riley had decided to enter the fire academy instead of following his father into law. It had been an unspoken—but well-known—contest between the firm's two partners as to whose son would be the one to achieve that goal.

Riley had no idea Lyle had already graduated and was working for the firm, and his father had certainly made no effort to forewarn Riley of the announcement tonight. Riley's father had made it clear to anyone who would listen that he fully expected Riley to fail at being a firefighter and then he'd have no choice but to join the firm, where he belonged. Riley had promised himself months ago, and now, again tonight with renewed conviction, that he couldn't, he wouldn't, give his father the pleasure of seeing him fail.

Remembering the censuring look he'd gotten from his father when he told him he'd submitted his application to the fire academy, Riley looked everywhere but down the table where he could feel his father's glare.

RILEY DIDN'T HAVE TO look. He remembered that look all too well as his mind drifted back to the showdown in his father's office last December.

Riley exhaled slowly, as the "Thank you for submitting your application," notification popped up on the screen. He'd actually done it and submitted his application to the Abernathy Fire Department. He had been monitoring the hiring process the last three years and knew the timing couldn't be more perfect. He would graduate college and just two weeks later, he'd start the fire academy. The notice said only fourteen spots were available, and the competition for an open academy spot was always fierce. He wasn't worried. He was ready.

His phone dinged. It was a text from his dad, asking Riley to meet him in his office in an hour. It was Christmas break of Riley's college senior year and looking at the stack of law school applications he'd pushed to the side of the desk in his old room, Riley had a pretty good idea what this summons was about.

An hour later, Riley approached Marian's desk who had worked for his dad as long as Riley could remember.

"Marian! It's great to see you. How are you doing?"

"Riley! Welcome home! You're just as handsome as ever," she said as she stood and gave him a hug.

"You always make me blush," Riley teased, causing Marian to blush herself.

"Stop that, Riley Sullivan," she said with a playful shove and chuckle. "Your dad is finishing up a call. It will be just a minute."

"No worries," Riley said and took a seat in the guest chair across from Marian. Before he'd even settled in, the large door behind Marian opened, and his dad stepped out.

"Riley, you're actually on time."

Riley winced and bit his tongue. His dad enjoyed goading him.

Ballard Sullivan was a tall, imposing man. Riley had gotten his dad's dark wavy hair, but his dad's hair was now graying slightly at the temples. He was distinguished and could be willfully intimidating. He certainly had the intimidation part down. Riley had known for quite some time this confrontation over the fire academy was coming, but it was still quite daunting to go against his dad.

"Hey, Dad."

Riley glanced at Marian and winked reassuringly as he passed her desk.

Riley followed his dad into his office and closed the door behind him. He took a seat in one of the leather guest chairs across the massive desk, where his dad was seated.

He came unceremoniously to the point.

"Son, it's your senior year and time to start thinking about which law school you will be attending."

There it was. For years, Riley had been anticipating this moment. And now that it was here, all of his well-rehearsed plans and logical reasons for going into the fire service evaporated under the withering stare of his father.

"You have a bright future ahead of you, son," his dad went on. "Your grades have been outstanding so I have no doubt you'll have your choice of the most prestigious law schools in the country. I would suggest you take a look at—"

"Dad," Riley interrupted before his dad could launch into an opening argument typical of the forceful litigator he was.

Mr. Sullivan paused and looked at Riley expectantly, but Riley hesitated, his thoughts scattering.

"Well, Son. Did you have something to say?"

Steeling his resolve and knowing his plans—*his* plans—Riley sat straighter, his conviction returning.

"Sir, I'm pretty sure we've talked about this before, so you know I'm not going to law school."

Mr. Sullivan visibly tensed.

"I'm going into the fire service," Riley continued. "As a matter of fact, I . . ." The words died on his lips when he saw the anger building on his father's face.

Hands clasped tightly on his desk, his mouth taut in a disapproving line, Mr. Sullivan leaned forward, bringing his full intimidation to bear on Riley.

Riley knew he was waving the proverbial red flag in front of a bull. For as long as he could remember, his dad had talked about Riley going into law and taking over the practice one day. Riley had considered the prospect with dread—the stuffy law books, the high stakes courtroom theatrics, the long hours at the office dissecting old law cases. None of it was even remotely appealing.

That was until he'd gotten a firsthand glimpse of firefighters working a large warehouse fire one day in middle school. Riley had dreaded what seemed to be his certain fate—always being tied up with a case, distracted, and constantly irritated about something. What a contrast to watching firefighters battle the warehouse blaze! It had left an indelible impression. Not only had the firefighters worked well together, but they helped each other too. Riley had heard their good-natured ribbing and seen them smile as they worked, their teeth white in their soot-covered faces. From that afternoon, Riley knew the fire service was his calling.

"Riley," his dad started again, yanking Riley back to the present. "You have been raised with the expectation of your taking over this practice one day. Since you were born, I have dreamed of the day we would work side by side, and you continuing the legacy I've worked so hard to build. You are my only son, the one carrying my name, and it is your responsibility to continue the high standards of Sullivan and Swanson into the future."

Riley knew he had to tread carefully.

Riley took a deep breath. He looked his dad squarely in the eye. "I appreciate everything you've worked so hard to build, Dad. I truly do. But my calling, as it has been for years, is the fire service. I *am* going to be a firefighter. I submitted my application this afternoon."

Riley watched the color drain from his dad's face and braced himself for the explosion, but it never came.

His dad studied Riley closely, his expression unreadable, but his eyes glittered with fury. Ballard was formidable, even in the best of times, so Riley could only imagine the storm brewing behind the fierce eyes trained on him.

Riley returned the look, refusing to show any type of weakness. The only sound was murmured voices from the other side of the door.

After several very long minutes, his dad took a deep breath and exhaled slowly.

Riley's heart rate jumped a notch.

"Well, Son, it seems you have made up your mind. You had mentioned this ridiculous idea a few times, but I never dreamed you were actually serious. You are meant to do great things, not sit around a fire station eating all day. I've seen them on my way to and from work. They sit in lawn chairs in front of the station drinking coffee in the morning, and they're still there in the evening drinking who knows what."

Riley had to hide a smile. He knew that station well. It was where Jeremy worked. Jeremy had given him the grand tour last week and introduced him to the other guys. It was an impressive bunch. Riley hoped he might be assigned there when he completed the academy but that was a long shot and a long way off.

"Dad . . ."

His dad went on, ignoring Riley's interruption. "You seem determined to follow through with this farce, therefore, I must adjust my plans accordingly. As you are so intent on joining the fire service, you may do so at your leisure. Mark my words though. You. Will. Fail. I will keep the office next door ready for you. You'll come to your senses as soon as things get a little rough."

He looked away from Riley and picked up a law book and folder off his desk. He placed them in front of him, seemingly dismissing Riley.

Riley sat stunned at the ease with which his dad dismissed him, his plans, and his dreams, all while being confident in Riley's failure. Riley's first instinct was to storm out and slam the door, but instead, he gripped the arms of the chair, willing himself to stay in place, and refusing to give his dad the satisfaction of knowing he'd gotten to him.

"Dad," Riley said in as even a tone as he could muster, "that office is going to stay empty. It's going to be empty tomorrow, next week, next month, next year, and for the next lifetime. I'd hoped you would support me in following my dreams. *My* dreams, not yours."

Before Riley could continue, his dad broke in.

"We seem to have nothing further to discuss. You have declared your intentions with no discussion. I feel inclined to do the same."

Riley swallowed hard. "You're right. There's nothing further to discuss."

He stood and had his hand on the doorknob when his dad spoke again, breaking the stony silence.

"You'll live to regret this decision, Riley. The office next door will be yours, mark my words, but don't expect it to be easy for you when you have to crawl back."

Riley opened the door and walked out without looking back. He'd made his decision. It was the right one.

"RILEY? YOU HAVEN'T HEARD a word I've said," Allie said, jerking him back to the present. She buttered a roll and took a bite as she studied him. "Don't let him get to you," she said, waving the roll in the direction of their father. "He's still proud of you somewhere . . . deep down. I mean way down." A mischievous grin edged up her face.

"You're a lot of help. Thanks." Riley shook out his napkin as one of the finely uniformed waiters placed a plate of salad in front him. "Eat your roll."

Allie grinned wickedly and popped the rest of the roll in her mouth.

Riley picked up his fork and glanced down the table at his father. He and his partner, Douglas Swanson, seemed to be in serious conversation.

Mr. Swanson appeared to be gloating while Riley's father looked very unhappy.

BALLARD SULLIVAN WAS AS near a snarl as he'd ever come when talking to his partner, Douglas Swanson.

"Gloating does not become you, Doug," Ballard said between clenched teeth.

"Ah, but it sure feels good," Douglas said with a satisfied sigh and mocking grin.

"It's not over yet," Ballard said, picking up his champagne flute and swirling the liquid. "Not near over," he repeated, almost to himself.

The hum of conversation from the tables around them drifted across the room, accompanied by the occasional clink of silverware against china. Waiters in crisp white jackets and creased black pants, continued to move between the tables, clearing finished salad plates and delivering silver-domed entrees. Other servers, white towels draped over one arm, moved among the diners pouring either white or red wine to accompany their entree of choice.

Ballard swirled the remaining champagne in his glass before taking a final sip but was too distracted to taste it. He looked down the table and for several minutes watched Riley talking to Allie. He drummed his fingers absentmindedly on the edge of the table, the thick linen muting the sound. He shook his head. Riley was such a fine young man. Ballard had worked so hard, dreamed so big for both of them. This should be his and Riley's night, celebrating—not Doug and Lyle Swanson's.

Thirty years ago, when he'd started his one-man practice in a cramped rented office, he'd worked sixty hours a week, sometimes more, to make a name for himself and his firm in Abernathy. And he'd built a solid reputation.

But it had come with sacrifices. He and Jane had only been married a short time and being newlyweds, his long hours at the office and sleepless nights before trials hadn't been easy for Jane. She'd made her own sacrifices for the firm. And now Riley had callously turned his focus from his family and away from his professional responsibility to play at being a firefighter. Ballard shifted in his chair and frowning, picked up a fork and stabbed some lettuce from the salad in front of him.

He had even gone as far as having business cards printed for Riley along with new letterhead that included Riley's name as a junior partner. The office next door remained, and would remain, ready for Riley to move in at any time. While the firm's security and financial arrangements needed to be considered, what he was most upset about was not having father/son time with Riley, and the opportunity to share his love of the law with his son. It was hard to admit just how disappointed he truly was and how much he'd been looking forward to Riley being in the office. Even though Riley's actually joining the fire department had come as a blow, Ballard still refused to believe Riley would truly be happy there. Ballard wasn't giving up. He was still committed to convincing Riley of the error of his ways. It was just a matter of time.

"I hear Riley has started with the fire department," Douglas said smugly, breaking in on Ballard's thoughts. Leaning over and glancing at Riley, he returned his bemused look to Ballard. "Seems to me it's looking pretty certain."

"If you'll remember, I was the one who started this firm thirty years ago. And I brought you on as a junior partner years later," Ballard said, leaning close to Douglas. "You can't imagine I'd actually turn ownership and running of things over to you, now do you?"

"A bet's a bet, my friend. Unless you've forgotten the little wager we made," Douglas said with a cocky look. "Let me refresh your memory. We said whichever son passed the bar and became junior partner in Sullivan and Swanson first would guarantee 51% controlling ownership of the firm to his father. Do you recall?"

"Of course I recall. But a wager made on the golf course after a few beers isn't legally binding," Ballard retorted hotly.

"Ah, but I believe we shook hands on it. For gentlemen such as you and I, I'd call that binding."

"Again, after a few beers and impeded judgment…"

"Let's not spoil my son's evening. What do you say, Ballard? This can be discussed in due course. But in the meantime, I'm looking forward to having my son join me at the office. Perhaps you can visit your son at…the fire station?"

Douglas Swanson turned away, joining his son and wife who were already in conversation with several staff members.

Ballard tamped down a frustrated retort before turning and glaring at Riley, who happened to look up at that instant. Their eyes met and held. Ballard couldn't keep his disappointment from showing. He was so very proud of Riley and the fine man he'd become, but he also saw his dream of having Riley as a partner slipping away.

A waiter set Ballard's entree in front of him and removed the silver dome, releasing a plume of steam. Ballard slowly picked up his knife and fork and began to cut his fillet.

He almost regretted the hurt look he saw cross Riley's face, but with the firm at stake, he had to be resolute. Riley had to change his mind about practicing law—and soon.

Riley DROVE UP THE sweeping drive that led to the front of the Abernathy Country Club for the second time in two evenings. He had been looking forward to seeing Maggie all day, and the evening ahead promised to be much better than the one last night. Riley smiled as he tapped his pocket holding the engagement ring, safe and secure in its box.

Riley had driven straight to Butler Brothers Jewelers after work. When the jeweler opened the ring box and the ring's diamonds caught the light, Riley's breath hitched. The ring was even more beautiful than he remembered. Maggie was going to love it. He just knew it. He paid the clerk who carefully secured the ring in a velvet box which he then placed inside a black cardboard box with the jeweler's logo on top. It was ready for Riley to pop the question.

He was still trying to decide exactly how he was going to propose. He wanted it to be really special, something romantic, and certainly memorable. He'd entertained the idea of recruiting Jeremy and Cade to show up on her doorstep and whisk her away to somewhere special to both of them. He'd be waiting for her there. He'd also considered a simple walk on a chilly fall day in the city park, where they'd spent so much time growing up and where they'd shared their first kiss. He'd surprise her by dropping to one knee at the swings and proposing. Or, should it be something more formal? He just couldn't decide, but he knew the right time and idea would come.

Maggie saw Riley as soon as he stepped into the doorway. Hawkins, the maître d', pointed in her direction, and Riley flashed a smile when their eyes met. Her heart skipped a beat as it did every time she saw him—the same way it had since grade school. He'd been her hero since fourth grade when a bully tried to take candy from her after she'd received a perfect score on a spelling test. The bully had grabbed the candy out of her hand at recess, but Riley had grabbed the candy back and handed it to her before pushing the bully down. Riley had gotten in trouble, but the smile he gave her told her everything was okay. Riley was her hero then and was still her hero now.

Even though they'd managed to stay close while attending different colleges, since finishing and returning to Abernathy, things hadn't gone quite the way Maggie imagined they would. Maggie was happy to have secured a full-time management position at the department store where she'd worked throughout high school. Already familiar with the store, it was a simple step to move into the management role of overseeing the store's marketing program. She excelled, loving the job and the work it entailed.

Riley, in the meantime, had been more focused on the fire department than spending time with her. He still called, just not often. They went out occasionally, but it was more often just grabbing take out and spending a few hours together before Riley had to get back to study during the academy.

Having some extra time had prompted Maggie to think about her own professional plans and goals. Opportunities were opening up for her at work, and her boss had let it slip a couple of weeks ago that she was being considered for a promotion, but it would involve her moving to Dallas. She hadn't mentioned any of this to Riley—there hadn't been an opportunity. The offer had come through, and they'd been pushing her for an answer.

She'd dreamed of marrying Riley for as long as she could remember. She loved Riley with her whole heart and had always known Riley was the one—the only one—she'd ever love or fully trust. She wanted to give her heart to him, but now, things were...different. She just wasn't sure if he felt the same way about her.

As hard as it had been, there was no more wondering what to do. She'd made her decision.

She watched him approach, his disarming good looks attracting the eye of every woman in the room. His wavy dark hair was cut short on the sides but longer on the top, with the familiar stray lock falling across his forehead. He made a quick swipe, putting it back into place. His gray eyes, with their chocolate brown flecks, were trained on her as he moved across the room. He waved greetings to a few others in the dining room who called out to him and slapped one waiter on the back in greeting as he passed.

This was Riley's element. He'd grown up with wealth, just as she had, and he wore it easily, nonchalantly. But now, there was something different about him. Something simmering just beneath the surface. It was something she couldn't explain, and she wasn't sure Riley was even aware of it. Maybe it was because he'd struck out on his own and followed his dream to become a firefighter.

Mr. Sullivan had asked her to talk to Riley when Riley first mentioned going into the fire service. He'd told her she had more influence over Riley than anyone else, but she knew better. She had some influence, yes, but Jeremy and Cade's opinions mattered most to him.

Reaching their table, Riley leaned over and gave Maggie a soft kiss on the lips, his eyes softening as he looked into hers. Maggie looked tired, he thought, but as beautiful as ever. Dressed impeccably, as always, she wore a summer dress with a light sweater. Her long blond hair fell over her shoulders, her blue eyes seemed overly bright, and her cheeks glowed hotly. Despite her casual outward appearance, though, she seemed on edge.

Maggie, as always, was thrilled by Riley's touch, but tonight, she could only manage a hesitant smile in return.

A slight frown line creased between Riley's brows.

Riley sat in one of the soft leather chairs and rolled it to the table. He smelled of a fresh shower and soft musk cologne. So familiar. So Riley.

Riley eyed her with concern as he picked up his menu. "You okay?"

Maggie cleared her throat. "Yes. I'm fine. Don't mind me. It's just been a day."

Riley studied her closely for a few more seconds before turning back to his menu. "I would have picked you up, you know. No need for you to drive out here by yourself."

Maggie nodded thoughtfully before her eyes drifted down to her lap. "Oh, I know. But it would have put you out of your way. And since the Club was my suggestion, I thought I'd save you the trip."

"I never mind going out of my way—or anywhere for that matter—for you, Mags," Riley said without hesitation. He put his hand over hers and looked her in the eye.

Maggie's eyes widened as she met Riley's unwavering gaze. She automatically started to take his hand that rested on top of hers, but then she caught herself and stopped.

A flicker of uncertainty crossed Riley's face but before anything could be said, Joel, their waiter, approached carrying two sparkling waters, their standard order.

"Joel, my man. How's it going?" Riley asked as Joel set the goblets on the table.

"I'm doing well, Mr. Sullivan. Thank you for asking."

Riley narrowed his eyes and scowled playfully. "Joel, I think we're on a little better terms than that. Let me ask you again. How's it going?"

Joel relaxed and grinned. "Things are great, Riley. How's the firefighting biz?"

Riley laughed. "Now that's more like it. The firefighting biz is . . . busy. You know, any time you want a tour, all you've got to do is drop by the station."

"Yes, sir. I might just take you up on that one day." Joel gave them both a broad smile before turning to wait on another table.

Maggie took a sip of water. Laying her menu on the table, she placed her trembling hands back in her lap. She already knew what she was going to order; not that food mattered.

Riley focused his glance back to her. "I missed you last night. The dinner was, shall we say, interesting. Good ole Lyle has graduated law school and started at the firm. I'm really in hot water now," Riley said with a frown and light shrug.

Maggie fingered the corner of her menu but made no reply.

Casting a questioning look Maggie's direction a couple of times, Riley finished studying his menu before laying it down and taking a sip of water.

Maggie watched him, trying to memorize everything about him—the way he chewed his lower lip as he read the menu, the way the same unruly lock of dark hair always fell across his forehead, the strength in his square jaw, the soft furrow between his brows, his gray eyes, and his soft lips.

She yearned for things to stay the same. She wanted to stay here with him, but she didn't see that working out. They had both changed, or were changing, and after so many years together, their worlds and their dreams seemed to be pulling them apart just when they should be bringing them together. No, things weren't the same, and Maggie had reconciled, or was trying to reconcile, herself to that fact.

"I'm so sorry to have missed it," she said, attempting a teasing tone but failing. "I know how much you hate those dinners even without the added pressure from your dad."

Riley studied Maggie closely before taking her hand and softly rubbing his thumb across the back.

"What is it, Mags? What's wrong? You're not yourself tonight."

Maggie looked down and wadded her napkin in her free hand.

Riley bent his head close to hers. "You wanted to come to the Club, and you haven't wanted to come here in a long time. Second, you won't let me pick you up. And now, you sit here looking like you've lost your best friend. What's going on? You know you can talk to me."

Maggie swallowed hard and pulled her hand gently from his. The surprised look on his face caused her to wince.

"Riley, I—" She began to speak just as Joel walked up to take their order.

She hurriedly named something. And after Riley gave his order, he turned back to her with even more concern.

"You're worrying me, Maggie. What is it?" he asked, an edge creeping into his voice.

Maggie cleared her throat and began, "Riley, you know how much I care about you—"

Before she could go any further, Riley leaned back in his chair, the color draining from his face.

"You know how much I care about you," Maggie started again, not daring to look at him. "But I'm not sure where our relationship is headed. I'm not sure we want the same things anymore. You've made your career decision, and I'm happy for you—I truly am. But that leaves me unsure of where I fit into your life. Or even *if* I fit any longer."

Riley leaned forward and opened his mouth to say something, but Maggie forged ahead.

"I don't know that we have the same goals in life any longer. So, I've had to make some decisions. I've done well at the department store, and it's been noticed by some of the corporate managers. They've approached me with a promotion. I've accepted. I'll be moving to Dallas in two weeks." She said the last detail in a rush, afraid if she didn't say it quickly, she wouldn't be able to say it at all.

She looked down and picked at the white linen tablecloth, waiting for Riley to respond. When he didn't, she looked up and saw such a stricken look on his face, she felt a sudden stab of guilt.

RILEY HADN'T SEEN THIS coming. At all. He sat stunned, not sure how to collect his thoughts enough to form a reply.

"Maggie, I . . . I don't know what to say," he finally managed. "I thought the path we were taking, we were taking—together. When we talked about graduating college and coming back here, I thought it was for us to be together."

Struggling, he paused several seconds before he could continue.

"I think I can appreciate, probably more than anyone, wanting to pursue a career. I just didn't think you'd want one that would take you away from Abernathy . . ."

He trailed off and looked down.

After several uncomfortable minutes with no response from Maggie, Riley went on. "But, if you're sure this is what you want and what will make you happy, then I'm behind you 100%. I only want what will make you happy, Maggie, I always have. Just please be sure. I can't imagine being here—being anywhere—without you."

"Really? Are *you* sure?" Maggie snapped, wanting—no *needing*—him to tell her he loved her.

"All that has occupied your mind since our junior year in college was the fire service, passing the exam, making one of the open slots, the academy, where you'd be stationed, and on and on and on. Do you hear what I'm saying? I didn't hear anything about me or *our* plans in there anywhere, do you? I have a life and a career I'd like to pursue, too. I thought I knew what we wanted and I thought it was together. But now, I'm not sure if that's what you *truly* want any more."

Maggie picked up her fork and pushed the salad around on its plate that had arrived at some point. Riley poked at his salmon without taking a bite.

Riley grasped for something...anything. It seemed his world was falling apart just when he thought everything would be coming together. Though he was now a firefighter, his father was disappointed in him and now Maggie was leaving.

Riley looked down and said softly, "Please, don't go, Maggie. Please. Can't we talk about this first before you pack up and move? I'm sorry we haven't talked more lately. And yes, that's on me, but give us a chance to talk about this, about us more. I need you, Maggie. I need *us*. Don't you?"

When Maggie finally looked at Riley, she could see the depth of emotion in his eyes. But there was something new. Was it uncertainty? He'd never been unsure of anything in his life. What was he unsure of now? Her? Them?

She needed more from him. She needed him to decide, to commit to her. She needed to hear him say he loved her. That was what she had been waiting for and *really* needed. She thought she knew how he felt about her, but she couldn't go on assuming—and waiting. She had to know.

But Riley didn't say anything else. He just stared at her, his eyes round with worry, with fear.

She couldn't do this. She'd made her decision. Maggie took a deep breath, picked up her purse and stood.

"Goodbye, Riley." She kissed him lightly on the cheek and squeezed his shoulder gently before walking away. She didn't look back.

AFTER MAGGIE LEFT, RILEY sat and stared. He wasn't sure how long. He finally put his hand inside his jacket and felt the velvet box holding the ring he'd picked up that afternoon. He sighed a long, deep, painful sigh. Somehow, he managed to sign the tab Joel had left earlier and then stood to leave, but had to put his hand on the table to steady himself. The imbalance of his life felt like it was physically bearing down on him. He turned and slowly walked out of the Club, his confident demeanor gone. As Riley waited for the valet to retrieve his SUV, he jammed his fists into his pockets and looked up into the night sky.

The alarm buzzed at five the next morning, but Riley didn't need it. He hadn't slept much. And when he did, nightmarish dreams invaded his sleep. He kept seeing Maggie on the gurney like Mr. Bertram, the man who had died his first shift. Jeremy would look at Riley and say, "There's nothing we can do." And Riley, his legs like lead weights, tried to get to Maggie, but was held back. When he called out to her, his words were garbled and unintelligible. He jerked awake several times, his heart pounding

In another dream, he and the other guys were in the station's kitchen. He was trying to cook while the crew laughed at him. Jeremy stood to the side, laughing with the rest of them and had just tossed something to Riley when the alarm buzzed.

Riley ran his fingers through his already tousled hair as he laid in bed, staring at the ceiling. He could almost feel a physical weight bearing down on him as he rubbed his bare chest with a fist. He pushed the sheets aside and sat on the edge of the bed, head in his hands for several minutes before taking a deep breath. He stood and walked resolutely to the shower. Riley Sullivan was not a quitter. He'd figure things out at the station and then he'd figure out how to get Maggie back. That's all there was to it.

RILEY WALKED INTO THE station at 5:45 a.m., armed with a grocery list, recipes, and determination. He went right to work, making sure the fuel gages on the truck, engine, and ambulance were at or above the minimum three-quarter tank full. He pulled his bunker gear from the storage area and stowed it in the compartment in the ambulance, just in case. He sighed and gave the gear a quick pat. Someday he'd be out there.

Several of those already around the table mumbled a "good morning," as Riley strode into the kitchen forty-five minutes later. Some were eating, some were reading a newspaper, but all were drinking the "required" fire house coffee. You weren't deemed a true firefighter unless you could make *and* drink the stout brew. Riley had been drinking his coffee strong, with no cream or sugar, for the past couple of years just so he'd be ready.

He checked the sink for dirty dishes. As the rookie, it was his responsibility to make sure any dirty dishes were washed and stowed before the start of the shift. He'd just put some tea bags in water and popped it in the microwave to brew the mandatory pitcher of tea when Captain Jernigan came into the room.

"Good morning, gentlemen. And Rookie," Jernigan said with a grin. Jeremy sauntered in a few steps behind him.

"Good mornings" went around the room as Riley turned to the dishwasher and began unloading the clean dishes.

Jeremy had a teasing comment on his tongue, but after a glance at Riley, he did a quick double take. Something was up, and it couldn't be good. Riley looked terrible.

Oblivious to Riley's mental state, the others started peppering Riley with questions as he closed the dishwasher door and waited in front of the microwave for the tea to finish brewing.

"So, Rookie, you've had a whole two days to decide. Which of us do you like best?" Derek Hayward, the engine's driver, asked with mock sincerity. "It's important to us that we get your thoughts."

Riley, his back to them, hands fisted on his hips, turned slowly and assessed each face staring back at him with suspiciously pious sincerity. First, there was the truck crew, with easy-going Captain Keevin Jernigan as the officer. He was the father figure to the entire station, dependable and a firefighter's firefighter. Ed Brimly, who sat next to the captain at the table, eyed Riley speculatively over the rim of his cup. Next to Brimly sat Walt Sims, whose reputation as a terrible cook was well-known, a reputation Riley didn't want to replace. Last of the truck's foursome standing just inside the door and grinning was Tanner Jones, whose twangy accent and old-fashioned sayings were the source of ongoing commentary.

Lieutenant Cochran, the officer on the engine, was typically quiet and unassuming. He sat silently at the table, watching and listening. Next to the Lieutenant was Derek Hayward, the driver and engineer who'd started this whole exercise. Next was Greg Grimes, who Riley knew he had to be nice to since Grimes had volunteered to go to the grocery store with him. The fourth man on the engine, Josh Carrier, was the last rookie before Riley. Carrier still seemed a bit unsure of himself. Jeremy and Ethan Walton leaned against the cabinet sipping coffee, waiting. All looked at Riley expectantly.

"Well, let's see," Riley started tentatively after taking another look around the room. He really wasn't in a joking mood. But since they'd asked, he'd play along. He crossed his arms over his chest and leaned against the counter. "This isn't much of a selection, but if I'm supposed to make a choice, I'd have to go with . . ."

"I'm sorry. What did he just say?" Walt Sims asked with feigned shock. "Gentlemen, I think we've just been insulted."

Mumbles of agreement went around the table, as well as appreciative nods at the rookie's spunk. Jeremy nodded, hiding his own approval, as Riley turned to remove the measuring cup of brewed tea bags from the microwave.

"For clarification," Riley started, turning back around, but stopped short when the tones sounded.

"Engine Five, Med Five. Medical Response. 1402 Warfield. Repeat Medical Response 1402 Warfield."

Those on the engine and ambulance stood, exchanging glances with the truck crew, who remained seated.

"See you in a few," Lt. Cochran said as he stood and took a sip from his cup.

The doors were already rolling up as they pulled on bunker pants and grabbed their coats off the engine doors. Hayward, the driver, pulled himself into the driver's seat and started the diesel engine as the others climbed on board.

Walton climbed into the ambulance's driver seat as Jeremy grabbed the passenger seat and Riley the jump seat. Jeremy glanced over his shoulder at Riley. "Lead paramedic switches every other shift. It's my man Walton's turn this shift."

Nodding, Riley looked up from buckling his seat belt when Jeremy went on. "4-1-1 on this call. Mr. Thornton is one of our regulars. Sometimes he needs help getting up and other times he just needs some company."

Walton nodded. "He lost his wife a couple of years ago. And besides a nurse who's there part-time, he lives alone. He gets lonely."

Riley nodded. He wondered, yet again, if this job was the right fit for him.

Riley thought he heard the ding of a text on someone's phone. He checked his. Nothing. But he saw Jeremy look at his phone and grin. He typed something quickly back and then stowed his phone in his pocket. Curious, Riley wondered who could be sending texts that would make Jeremy grin such a goofy grin? Could he be seeing someone? Riley dismissed the thought. Jeremy would have told him and Cade if he were.

A few minutes later, Walton turned a corner and slowed, the engine pulling up behind them and both sirens winding down.

The four from the engine climbed out of the cab and waited while the paramedics pulled their standard gear and walked to the house.

Riley walked behind, carrying what was dubbed the "ambulance in a bag." The house was an inviting, mid-size brick home, with nice landscaping on a wide well-treed residential street. Evidently accustomed to a fire engine and ambulance being on their street, neighbors walking their dogs or watering their lawns exchanged waves with the firefighters.

Walton knocked on the front door. Without hesitating, he opened the door and walked in. "Fire Department, Mr. Thornton."

"Mr. Thornton?" Jeremy called as the three walked into the entryway.

"I'm in the bedroom. Back here," a soft voice answered.

Walton and Jeremy, with Riley close behind, walked down the hall. Walton stopped at the open door at the end.

"Mr. Thornton, what's up?" Walton asked with a slight tease in his voice.

"I'm so sorry," Mr. Thornton said, laying on a large bed, fully enveloped in a heavy coverlet. "I thought I could make it up this morning, but my legs aren't quite cooperating."

"Not to worry," Jeremy replied with a smile. "We haven't seen you in a while so we're glad to be here. Let us help you."

Walton and Jeremy eased the covers back and helped Mr. Walton turn to sit on the edge of the bed. Mr. Thornton was a thin, wiry man, mostly bald with wisps of soft gray around the bottom of his head and one large tuft which stood up on the top. His bony hands were lined with blue veins and his skin was paper thin. But what caught Riley's attention most were Mr. Thornton's eyes. They were sharp and sparkled with obvious pleasure at having some company.

After sitting for several seconds, Mr. Thornton looked up and spotted Riley.

"Who is that with you?" he asked, raising a shaky finger and pointing at Riley.

Riley, determined to be more proactive, walked forward.

"Riley Sullivan, sir. New rookie at Station Five."

"Rookie, huh?" Mr. Thornton said with a slight wheeze and smile. "It's a pleasure to meet you. I'm sure you'll be seeing more of me. I hope these guys are treating you right."

"Sully and I are old friends," Jeremy added with a look toward Riley. "We played football together in high school."

"Is that so? Were either of you any good?"

"I was, sir," Riley said quickly. "Can't say so much for Ennis here."

"Rookie talking smack, Ennis. You're going to have to set him straight," Walton grinned.

Mr. Thornton chuckled, enjoying the banter.

"Do you feel like trying to stand now?" Walton asked as he and Jeremy moved to either side of him.

Mr. Thornton nodded. He grunted as Jeremy and Walton pulled him gently to his feet, using the lift maneuver Riley recognized from paramedic training. They placed his walker in front of him and stepped back as he pulled on a robe over his t-shirt and pajama pants.

"You boys are the best. Can't thank you enough."

"Totally our pleasure," Jeremy said. He gathered the bags they'd brought in with them. "Would you like us to hang around a bit to make sure all is well?"

"Oh no. I know you boys have bigger things to attend to than me. I'm fine. And besides, Joanne will be here soon. That nurse makes an awesome brownie."

He led them out of his room and down the hallway, pushing his walker steadily ahead of him.

"If any of you guys ever have a craving for some great brownies, drop by. I'll make sure Joanne always has a fresh batch ready, just in case."

"You've got yourself a deal," Riley heard himself answering.

"I look forward to it then, Rookie," Mr. Thornton said with a wave. He watched them walk down the front steps.

Riley turned and waved again to Mr. Thornton with a smile. He walked to the ambulance and placed the bag in its compartment. He had a feeling he'd be back soon for a visit.

T HE AMBULANCE AND ENGINE backed into the bay, the rumble of the diesel engines reverberating around the cinder block walls. The air brakes hissed and then the bay was suddenly quiet when Hayward and Walton killed the engines.

"Just a few things to tidy up on the box," Jeremy said as Riley climbed out behind him. "I imagine you have some grocery shopping to do. What's for supper?"

"Uh uh. No hints and no sneak peeks. You'll find out when everybody else does," Riley said, trying his best at a smile.

Jeremy glanced at Walton walking toward the back of the bay before coming up beside Riley.

"What's going on? You act right but you look like hell."

Riley's shoulders slumped. He turned away from Jeremy to brace his arm against the ambulance.

Jeremy took a step closer and put a hand on Riley's shoulder. "I don't think I've seen you this upset since you lost the championship game for us."

Riley shook his head with a smile. "What a pal. Thanks for bringing that up."

Walton walked back past them with a curious glance as he headed toward the station door. Jeremy waved him on before turning back to Riley.

"Seriously, man, what's going on?"

Riley turned slowly and slumped against the ambulance.

"Maggie broke up with me last night."

Jeremy took a step back.

"What?! You can't be serious. I thought you bought a ring and—"

"Had it in my pocket. Ironic, huh?"

"So, what's the deal? What did she say?"

"She said something about not being sure if we had the same goals anymore, and she wasn't sure where the relationship was headed. And other things I don't remember."

"Well, did you tell her you had a ring? That you were going to propose?"

"I couldn't very well ask a girl to marry me when she was in the middle of breaking up with me, now could I?"

Jeremy came and slumped against the ambulance beside Riley. "Wow. Never saw this coming."

"Neither did I," Riley said. "And to add to it, the dinner at the Club the other night was to celebrate Lyle Swanson graduating law school and starting at the firm."

Jeremy let out a low whistle. "I guess that means your dad's turned up the heat, then."

"That's a bit of an understatement."

The station door opened as members of the truck crew, bantering among themselves, came through, headed toward the truck.

Riley nodded stiffly to them before straightening and starting toward the station door.

"I've got a meal to cook. I'd better make that trip to the grocery store."

"Sully. Hang in there, man."

Riley acknowledged Jeremy with a nod and wave but kept walking.

The trip to the grocery store had been quick and fairly easy. Grimes knew his way around the store and was a big help with the shopping. There were even a few dollars left over from the food kitty everyone donated to each shift. Riley was thankful there had only been one or two quick medical calls, and the engine and truck each had one run. Overall, it had been a quiet day.

Riley started early so dinner would be ready at the prescribed five o'clock dinner hour. Some of the guys made a trip through the kitchen during the afternoon to get a drink from A's refrigerator or to grab a snack, but they mostly left Riley to his own devices. He had no idea how this was going to turn out, but he could honestly say, with no reservation, he was giving it his all. He only hoped the end result would bear that out.

He carefully slid the chicken into the oven, breaded with the mixture he'd made from the recipe he'd gotten from his mom. He'd even greased the foil so the chicken wouldn't stick as she'd advised. He then started on the mashed potatoes and green beans. He'd gotten frozen rolls to bake along with a cake and some ice cream for dessert. Things seemed to be under control.

Thirty minutes after putting the chicken in the oven, he opened the oven door to check. He thought he'd smell it cooking but hadn't yet. A dread started creeping over him. He reached into the oven and touched the pan lightly. It was cold. The entire oven was cold.

Riley looked at the clock and immediately panicked. It was 4:50. Not nearly enough time for the oven to heat and bake the chicken by five.

He slammed the oven door closed and turned quickly when he heard footsteps behind him.

"What's up, Rookie?" Grimes asked, grabbing a glass from the cabinet. "You look like you've seen a ghost."

"I...I..."

Grimes cocked an eyebrow. "Something wrong?"

Riley gulped. "The chicken isn't cooked. The oven isn't on. I *know* I turned it on."

He turned around and started fumbling with the pan as he pulled it out of the oven.

"Calm down, Rookie. Did no one tell you when the engine or truck have a call, the oven shuts off automatically? It's a safety measure so there's no risk of it being left on while we're out of the station." He looked at his watch. "Yep, truck just got back from a gas investigation about twenty minutes ago. I bet that's what did it."

Riley ran his fingers through his hair. "What am I going to do? I've got five minutes to have dinner on the table."

Grimes patted Riley on the back. "No worries! We've got this. We'll just fry that dude. Everybody loves fried chicken."

Riley had no clue about the first thing to do to fry chicken, but Grimes seemed pretty confident about what to do. Grimes pulled a couple of skillets from the stockpile of pans and started heating grease while Riley gathered the chicken and readied it to fry. The grease heated quickly, and Grimes began dropping pieces of chicken into the skillets as firefighters started wandering in and sitting at the table.

"Dinner's at five, Rookie," Brimly said, filling a glass from the freshly made pitcher of tea on the table.

Riley gave him a quick glance over his shoulder but kept handing chicken pieces to Grimes. Riley grew concerned seeing the confused look on Grimes' face as Grimes pushed the chicken around in the popping grease.

"What? What is it?" Riley asked in a hushed voice.

"Not sure, but this isn't looking quite right," Grimes whispered back, poking at a piece of chicken turning a weird yellow rather than golden brown.

Derek Hayward and Tanner Jones walked over for a closer look. Riley cringed. These guys were always loud, which meant there was no way to keep the impending disaster under wraps.

"What is that?" Hayward thundered. He scowled and almost shouted. "Not sure that's edible."

"Sit down and shut up, Hayward," Grimes replied, his face flushed red. "It'll be ready when it's ready. And you'll eat it, or you won't. Your call."

Curious, more firefighters gathered behind Riley and Grimes, freely voicing opinions, suggestions, and unhelpful comments.

Captain Jernigan, the last one to enter the kitchen, walked to the stove where five firefighters hovered, all talking at once. As the crowd parted, he looked at the skillets on the stove.

"What's that supposed to be, Rookie?" he asked in a dead-pan voice, a glint in his eye.

"It was supposed to be baked chicken, sir, but the oven turned off, and I didn't know it. So we thought we'd fry it instead. It's not looking too promising," Riley added in a quiet voice.

"Grill it. That's always the answer. Somebody fire up the grill and somebody start scraping this mess off the chicken. I'm hungry, and I don't want to eat at midnight," Jernigan said. He took a seat at the table before pouring himself a glass of tea.

Bodies scrambled as some stepped onto the patio and started the grill; others speared the chicken with forks and started scraping breading off. Riley was everywhere, helping with the grill and then helping scrape the chicken before carrying it to the patio.

Thirty minutes later, ten firefighters sat silently around the table, staring at the platter in front of them of what used to be chicken, along with soggy mashed potatoes and cold green beans.

Riley could only stare in frustration and disappointment.

"Well, I believe this will go down in station history as one of its most memorable meals. Hayward, ask grace please. I think this meal's going to need it," Jernigan said with a thin trace of humor.

As soon as grace was said, the food was passed. Chicken pieces were speared with vigor, and the potatoes unceremoniously plopped onto plates. The frozen rolls were still frozen, so there was no bread.

As the first bites were taken, chewing stopped almost immediately.

"This is awful!" Brimly said, gagging, before gulping a mouthful of tea.

"Ketchup. We need lots of ketchup," Jernigan said, trying not to grimace with a cold mouthful of potatoes.

Jeremy kept quiet, his head down, feeling for Riley. He was never going to live this down. Everyone was hungry, and the food money was spent.

Grimes plopped two big bottles of ketchup on the table just as the tones sounded.

It was a structure fire. Everyone pushed their chairs back when Station Five was named. As everyone started toward the bay, Riley noticed Jeremy pull his phone out. He sent a quick text before slipping the phone back into his pocket and buckling up.

THE STRUCTURE FIRE ENDED up being an electrical short with a cursory follow up inspection, so it wasn't too long before everyone returned to the station. Leaving everyone in the bay, Riley walked slowly to the kitchen with dread but stopped mid-step as he entered. On the table were seven large pizza boxes, and the heavenly smell was unmistakable. But how?

No. He wasn't going to question this gift.

He quickly cleared the table of the disaster of a dinner and pulled out plates and some soft drinks from the refrigerator as everyone filed in.

The captain stopped short, the rest of the crew bunching up in a semicircle behind him.

"Well, well, well. What do we have here, Rookie?" Captain Jernigan asked, obviously delighted.

"I believe they call it pizza, sir," Riley said with a flourish toward the table. "Bona appetit!"

The crew descended on the table. Chairs were hurriedly pulled out as everyone reached over each other to get a slice of their favorite. They ate as if they hadn't eaten in weeks, talking and joking around mouthfuls of pizza. The cake and ice cream were then brought out, and Riley became an instant hero.

"Rookie, don't know how you did it, but kudos to you, man," Jones said in his undeniable twang, rubbing his belly as he leaned back in his chair.

"Yeah, I wasn't looking forward to hearing my gut growl all night," Hayward said with a good-humored snicker.

Riley eyed Jeremy suspiciously as Jeremy talked and joked with the guys. Riley had the strong suspicion the meal was thanks to him. Pisa Pizza had been one of their hang outs in high school and the new owner was a friend.

Riley looked around the table at the nine firefighters, some lean-ing back in their chairs, a toothpick between their teeth, others talking good naturedly while others reached for another soft drink or glass of tea.

Riley smiled to himself; he might have just experienced some of the fire service brotherhood today. No one had gotten mad about the chicken and his disastrous attempt at dinner. Instead, everyone pitched in and tried to make it right. The men around the table were good men; men who had your back when it was needed. They looked out for each other, and they'd looked out for him today. That was a good feeling. And for tonight at least, life as a firefighter was looking up.

A LLIE'S HAND FELT SO good in his. Or was it his hand felt so good in hers? Jeremy wasn't sure, but one thing he did know—he was falling for Allie Sullivan. And hard.

It seemed weird in a way. He'd known Allie almost her entire life. She was Riley's little sister but being with her—like they were now— he'd never seen this coming. He almost, *almost*, felt guilty for not having told Riley yet, but Allie had wanted to wait. They hadn't decided exactly when, but they were going to tell him soon. Riley had a lot on his mind right now; he didn't need to add one of his best friends dating his little sister to the list.

"Pretty night, isn't it?" Jeremy asked softly as he pulled Allie a bit closer. They'd been walking along one of the city's nature trails for a while and the late afternoon light was turning to dusk.

Jeremy smiled down at Allie, and his heart flipped. He almost forgot to breathe when she looked up at him and smiled.

"Yes, it is. The cool breeze feels wonderful," she sighed contentedly.

"Are you hungry?" Jeremy asked a few minutes later, as they continued their slow stroll.

"Actually, I am. Do you have something in mind?" Allie replied, resting her head against his arm.

"Well, I've got everything to grill burgers. Come back to the apartment and we'll grill. Cade is coaching his youth basketball team in a game tonight, so he won't be back for hours."

Allie smiled up at Jeremy. "That sounds wonderful! I'll help."

An hour later, Allie set her empty plate on the coffee table and leaned back on the sofa to find Jeremy's arm already waiting to place around her. Jeremy pulled her to him as she scooted closer.

"You are a grill wizard, Jeremy Ennis," Allie said. "That was an amazing hamburger. Where did you learn to grill like that?"

"Why, thank you, ma'am," Jeremy chuckled. "Grilling is a staple at the station. You pretty much have to learn by default or be harassed without mercy. It's kind of a self-preservation thing."

Allie laughed softly. "You guys have a good time at the station, don't you?"

"Yeah, we do. But part of it is the need to blow off steam. Things get a little intense sometimes."

He didn't want to elaborate. And he was glad that Allie didn't press him.

"Speaking of blowing off steam," Jeremy said with a grin. "Your texts sure brighten my day. I love hearing from you, any time."

Allie smiled as Jeremy took her hand and wove his fingers with hers.

"I heard about Maggie. That was definitely a surprise," Allie said with a frown.

"Yeah. The last shift was a tough one for Riley."

Jeremy suddenly sat up and looked at Allie. "Oh my word, Allie! I don't think I ever thanked you for getting those pizzas to the station last shift. You were a life-saver. The life you saved being Riley's, of course. After the day he'd had, those pizzas were a welcome sight."

"Besides Maggie, how's Riley doing? I haven't talked to him in a while," Allie asked as Jeremy leaned back and continued playing with her fingers.

"Well, he *is* a rookie you know, but he's actually picking things up quickly. Being a rookie is never fun, but being at the bottom of the pile is where everyone starts. You grow from there."

Allie let out a low whistle. "Wow, the bottom of the pile is not Riley's style. I bet he's having a hard time with that."

"He'll be fine. Sully's a natural leader. He'll find that level sooner or later. But you know what?" Jeremy asked, pulling Allie to face him. "Even though Riley's my friend, I don't really want to talk about him right now."

"Oh no?" Allie asked with a knowing grin.

"No," Jeremy said as he ran the back of his fingers down Allie's cheek.

"Well then, just what would you like to talk—"

Allie never got to finish her question. Jeremy's lips found hers. He kissed her softly, brushing his lips across hers several times. He leaned back and looked at her, smiling softly as he pulled her close and kissed her again, more intensely.

Allie melted into his arms and kissed him back, running her fingers through his hair as he stroked her long hair with his free hand. Being here, with Allie, felt so good, Jeremy thought. It was exactly where he wanted to be.

The apartment door banged open. "Do I smell burgers?"

Cade strode in, tossing a gym bag inside the entry.

His eyes grew round when he saw Jeremy and Allie on the couch kissing.

Jeremy groaned and Allie blushed.

"Oh hey guys, sorry," Cade said, turning quickly into the kitchen. "Carry on like I'm not even here."

"Talk about rotten timing," Jeremy grumbled loudly.

"I said I'm sorry!" Cade called back. Jeremy and Allie laughed as they scooted a few inches apart.

"Yeah, there's burgers. Help yourself," Jeremy said, grinning at Allie, continuing to finger her hair.

"I thought you had a game tonight," Jeremy said, putting his arm back around Allie and taking her hand.

"We demolished the other team, so it was a quick game. Sorry, I should have checked before I came barging in." Cade came out of the kitchen and started down the hall carrying a plate loaded with two burgers and a mound of chips. "I'll eat in my room. Carry on."

Allie couldn't help but laugh when Cade's door closed.

Jeremy looked at her with a grin, his eyes twinkling. "Now, where were we before we were so rudely interrupted?"

Allie smiled playfully and whispered, "I think we were just about here." She leaned in close as Jeremy's lips once again found hers.

J EREMY SUDDENLY REALIZED HE'D been staring at the wood in front of him for several minutes, sander in hand, poised above the flat surface. He'd been thinking about Allie. It seemed like she'd been on his mind a lot lately. And no wonder, he thought, as he smiled to himself.

Her blue eyes danced when she smiled, which she always seemed to be doing. Her smile seemed to be contagious; it made him want to smile. The soft blush on her cheeks made him think of how soft her skin felt beneath his fingers and how warm her lips had been when he'd kissed her last night. His fingers itched to glide through the silkiness of her long blond hair again.

Stop. What was he thinking?

He shook his head, lowering the sander and began sanding again in earnest. He'd started this table before last shift and was anxious to see it take shape. He needed to focus on his work. He'd been surprised to receive orders for some wood pieces lately. It seemed his work was being noticed and friends were referring others to him. He enjoyed crafting pieces from wood, but he'd never thought people might actually buy them.

As the wood began to smooth, Jeremy's thoughts went back to the conversation he'd had with his dad a few days ago here in the shop.

His dad thought Jeremy was anticipating marriage with Allie. Jeremy flinched. That conversation had him thinking about the consequences of his actions. If his parents thought he and Allie were headed down the marriage path, was Allie thinking the same thing?

His birthday was coming up, which meant he should put a stop to things with Allie really soon. Grandpa Mars' revelation before he died had derailed Jeremy's plans, but Jeremy was having a hard time letting go. He didn't want to put a stop to things with Allie. She'd become an important part of his life, every day and in every way. He wasn't sure if he could handle being without her.

But then, he thought, that wasn't being fair to Allie. Was it right for him to selfishly put him wanting to be with her over how she would feel when, according to Grandpa Mars' warning, Jeremy's days were numbered and he wouldn't be around anymore?

Jeremy stopped sanding and groaned in frustration. This was all so unfair! Why him and why now? He understood why his grandfather hadn't told him sooner, but now, things in his life were really falling into place. He was reaching his stride at the fire station and with Riley coming on board, things were even better. And then, most importantly, there was Allie and everything she was coming to mean to him. She meant so much more than he could have ever dared to imagine.

But no. This was getting him nowhere. He had to call things off with Allie. Soon. But the question was, how soon?

Jeremy was pulling cold soft drink cans out of the refrigerator that evening when Riley barged through the apartment door with bags of wings and fries. He dumped them on the kitchen counter.

"Remind me to lock that door," Jeremy said over his shoulder as he turned with the two cans in hand.

Riley shrugged as he started pulling food from the bags. "Where's Cade?" he asked with a glance around. "I thought it was the three of us tonight."

"He texted. He'll be a bit late. He's wrapping up basketball practice with his team. They're winning, and he's pumped," Jeremy said through a mouth full of fries. "Looks like you're stuck with just me for a while."

"Well, I've done worse, and I've done better," Riley said, popping open a can and taking a long drink.

"Yeah, love you too," Jeremy said, grabbing a plate full of food and heading to the living room where a football game was already on the TV.

"I'd ask if we should wait on Cade, but looks like you've got other plans," Riley said, bringing his own loaded plate into the living room and sinking into the leather sofa.

"Humph," Jeremy grunted. "Every man for himself, I say."

The two ate in companionable silence, watching the game, with neither having a clear team favorite. Several minutes later, the apartment door banged open, and Cade strode in, a huge grin on his face.

"What smells so good?" he asked as he dumped a duffel bag on the floor. "I'm starved."

Jeremy gestured to the kitchen with barbecue sauce-coated fingers. "See? Told you. We were right to go ahead. There will be nothing left once he's made his first round."

A few minutes later, Cade came into the living room carrying a plate rounded with food in one hand and two cold drink cans in the other.

Cade plopped down into the overstuffed leather recliner. And after setting the cans onto the table, he dug into the food on his plate.

Riley and Jeremy watched with amusement.

"Food's not going anywhere, Cade," Riley said with a grin.

Cade looked up. "Huh?"

Riley and Jeremy laughed.

"What Riley is trying to say is that you don't have to rush," Jeremy interjected. "Your food's not going anywhere. Believe me, I've seen safer bear attacks. I can't speak for Riley, but I know I'm not dumb enough to try and take it away from you."

Cade eyed them suspiciously but then grinned as he picked up his drink. "Not sure why I put up with you two. But hey, I'm here to cheer up a friend who just lost his girl. Heard about you and Maggie," Cade said, gesturing to Riley with his can before taking a drink. "Really sorry. Thought if anybody'd make the trip down the aisle, it'd be you two."

Cade took another bite of mac and cheese as Riley turned and glared at Jeremy.

"I thought this was just a hanging out thing. I didn't realize it was a feel-sorry-for-Riley party," Riley said, standing and walking to the kitchen. "Maybe I'd better head out."

"Sit down, Sully," Jeremy said as he relaxed into his chair. "This *is* a hanging out thing. Nothing like relaxing, eating a few wings and watching football."

"I hate to admit it, but I have missed hanging out with you two knuckleheads," Riley said, coming back into the room and reclaiming his seat, and setting a bag of cookies on the table for dessert. He eyed Cade, who was still devouring his food.

"Have you not eaten in a month or something?" Riley asked.

"This is the first I've eaten all day," Cade said, gulping down a mouth full of chicken and then grinning. "First, I drew some extra time on shift with a different partner, thank goodness, and then had practice this evening. Since we're the number one seed in the tournament next weekend, we're practicing hard this week. And I think with the way they're playing, we stand a good chance—a really good chance—of winning it all."

Riley and Jeremy grinned at Cade's enthusiasm and obvious pride.

Already knowing, but wanting Cade to tell Riley, Jeremy asked, "Tell me again. What was the team's record last season compared to this season?"

Cade beamed. "Last season the Roadrunners were three and twelve. This season we are fourteen and one. Those little guys are sure playing their hearts out."

Riley realized he hadn't seen Cade smile—really smile—in a long time. It was good to see it.

"I think that might be due to their coach . . . maybe?" Jeremy said, grinning and looking between Cade and Riley.

"Cheers to Coach Marshall," Riley said, as he and Jeremy held their cans aloft. Cade grinned as he lifted his own can.

The three finished their meal and sat back comfortably, putting their feet on the coffee table.

The satisfied look on Jeremy and Cade's faces reminded Riley of the same look on faces of the station crew after devouring the pizza that had mysteriously appeared.

Riley reached into his wallet and pulled out several bills and placed them on the coffee table near Jeremy.

"What's this?" Jeremy asked, eying the bills.

"What I owe you for the pizza the other night," Riley said, leaning back.

"You don't owe me anything," Jeremy said, pushing the bills back toward Riley with the heel of his sock.

"You saved my bacon is all," Riley said, pushing the bills back toward Jeremy.

Before Jeremy could push them back again, Cade reached over and picked them up and let out a low whistle after counting them.

"That must have been a lot of bacon," Cade said, placing the bills back near Jeremy's foot.

"He bought pizza for the station after my meal flopped," Riley said with a grimace.

"Oh? I haven't heard about this. What happened?"

"Nothing," Jeremy said, standing and heading to the kitchen.

"Maybe nothing to you, but it was a lot to me," Riley called after him. Riley turned to Cade, "My first attempt to cook for the station didn't turn out too well. Little did I know, the oven turns off as a safety measure, so thirty minutes after the truck had a call, I checked and the oven is off and ice cold. My chicken hadn't cooked. At all."

Jeremy walked in with two fresh soft drinks and sat one down in front of Riley.

"You should have seen the guys trying to help," Jeremy said, plopping down on the sofa. "First they were going to fry it. When that didn't work, the Cap told them to grill it. Not a good idea either. It was dry as a bone, the mashed potatoes were soggy, and the green beans were ice cold. It was a disaster with a capital D."

Cade looked between the two of them and started laughing.

"Well, it wasn't *that* funny, especially at the time," Riley said with a grin. "But when we got a run at the most opportune moment possible, pizza was waiting for us when we got back." Riley looked at Jeremy. "Come to think of it, just how did you order pizza? I was with you the whole time. You never made a call. But come to think of it, you did send a text ..."

"Come on. A genius doesn't reveal his secrets," Jeremy said with a chuckle.

"I don't know any genius," Cade said. "How did *you* do it?"

Jeremy shot Cade a quick look but then sighed dramatically. "I texted Allie on the way to the bay. She ordered it, and the rest, as they say, is history."

Riley sat up. "Allie. As in my sister, Allie?"

Jeremy shifted a bit on the sofa and didn't quite meet Riley's eye.

"Aw, you know I've known Allie as long as I've known you. It's not a big deal. She and I have just gotten better acquainted the last few months."

"Better acquainted?" Cade asked, choking on a swallow of his drink. "Is that what you call her hanging out over here several evenings a week?" Cade shook his head. "And that doesn't even count the 'official' dates."

"What?" Riley bolted up. "You're dating my sister and haven't told me? Either one of you?"

"I think it's probably because of what you're doing right now," Cade said, looking at Riley and trying not to laugh.

Riley ran his fingers through his hair before sitting back down.

"How long?" Riley asked, doing his best to keep an even tone.

Still not meeting Riley's eye, Jeremy mumbled, "A few months."

"A few months?" Cade scoffed. "Try almost a year."

"A year?" Riley gritted out with a glare at Jeremy. "And all this time neither one of you ever thought to tell me? I thought we were friends."

"We *are* friends, Riley," Jeremy replied hotly. "And that's exactly why I haven't told you. It didn't start out as dating, honest. We ran into each other one day and just started hanging out. The more time we spent together, though, things began to change. Then it became a lot more than friendship."

"A lot more, huh?" Riley said stiffly, glaring at Jeremy.

Jeremy cleared his throat nervously and went on. "You were finishing college and then busy with the academy and coming on board at the station. And time just went by and then there just didn't seem to be the right time to tell you. I mean, then everything with Maggie and —"

Tense silence hung in the air for several minutes before Riley nodded pensively. "I didn't think about it at the time, but there was an empty chair by Allie at the firm dinner the other night. That was meant for you, wasn't it? Allie wouldn't say."

Jeremy looked uncomfortable. "Yeah, I was supposed to be there, and we were going to tell you then. But, well, she found out the dinner was to announce Lyle's graduation and starting at the firm. She knew you'd have enough to deal with without me being there to complicate things. So we decided to wait. Sorry, Sully. I . . . well, we, should have told you sooner."

Riley sat down and nodded slowly. "Yeah. You should have."

Jeremy sensed Riley was calming down. "And really, we're just hanging out more than anything."

Cade nodded sagely. "I guess what I walked in on the other night then was 'just hanging out' huh?" he asked, doing air quotes.

Jeremy's eyes narrowed as he shot Cade a glare. He looked sheepishly back to Riley. "Well, we do a little bit of, you know ..."

Riley gave Jeremy a hard look. "You're messing around with my sister and leading her on? So should I come to the logical conclusion that this is leading to something more serious?"

Jeremy sighed. "Sully, you don't understand ..."

"Then enlighten me."

Jeremy studied the floor, then looked at Riley. "I like Allie, a lot. And, I'd probably be thinking marriage soon, but Riley, I ... I don't think I'll be getting married to her or anyone."

Jeremy heaved a heavy sigh, looking first at Cade before looking back to Riley. "I've never told anyone this, not anyone. So you both have to swear to keep this between the three of us."

Jeremy hesitated for several moments, looking anxiously between Riley and Cade who were leaning forward expectantly.

Jeremy straightened and took a step back. "You know, on second thought, I probably shouldn't say anything. Let's just forget about it. I've been thinking, and actually, it's probably best if I just break things off with Allie."

Jeremy's face was ashen with tension evident on his face.

Riley's anger was building, and he felt himself losing control. Too much had happened in the past few days. He couldn't stop himself. He pressed on.

"You're telling me you guys have been together for almost a year and now, you're going to just break it off? Just like that? You can't just break up with someone without a good reason, Jeremy. Do you have a good reason?" Riley almost shouted, Maggie's face flashing before his eyes.

"You guys are my best friends," Jeremy replied softly. "I love you two like brothers, but you'll think I'm a lunatic if I tell you. This is hard enough, so you'll just have to trust me on this."

Looking to Riley, Jeremy said, "I'll talk to Allie and let her know it's best if we stop seeing each other. It wouldn't be right to lead her on. I care for her too much to do that."

"Wait a minute, Jeremy," Riley said, standing. "You can't do that to her without a good reason. And I haven't heard one yet."

"Actually, it's really none of your business," Jeremy replied somberly.

Cade looked uneasily between Riley and Jeremy as they stood locked in a tense glare.

"Yeah. You're right. It's none of my business," Riley said and reached for his keys. "My apologies. I was just trying to look out for my sister. And a friend that I trusted."

Riley turned and stalked to the door without looking back.

"Come on, Sully. Don't—"

Jeremy was cut off by the door's slam.

Cade let out a breath and slumped back in his chair, staring at Jeremy in confusion.

ALLIE SAT CROSS-LEGGED IN front of the big screen TV in the final yoga position of her workout. Her willowy frame had moved easily through the routine as she'd felt herself relaxing. She brushed back a stray wisp of blond hair that had come loose from its ponytail. Yoga was the best way she'd found to de-stress after a hectic day, even if today she'd gotten out of her last class early. Her senior year of college hadn't been as bad as she'd thought it might be after getting an apartment of her own. It wasn't that she didn't enjoy her roommates, but the constant hubbub of activity could be tiring and distracting at times. Allie loved to come home to her own quiet retreat.

She stretched one last time and then stood. She had just begun to roll up her yoga mat when her phone dinged with the tone indicating a text from Jeremy. She picked up her phone off the bar.

You home?

I'm home. Just finished a workout.

Can I come over?

Allie hesitated and frowned. Jeremy knew tonight was the weekly Sullivan family dinner. But no matter when or the reason, Allie was always glad to see Jeremy. She had been taken totally off guard when their relationship turned romantic. Jeremy was one of Riley's best friends, and she'd known him most of her life. It wasn't until one day, when they'd accidentally run into each other at a local restaurant, that he suddenly looked different to her.

Jeremy was no longer just one of her brother's annoying friends, but he was a guy—a really good-looking, thoughtful guy. Amazingly, he seemed to see her differently too. They'd gone on a few casual dates and then started seeing each other several times a week. Each time they kissed goodbye, Allie could hardly wait to see him again. She was well on her way to falling in love, and from every indication, Jeremy seemed to feel the same. She smiled thinking of him. It seemed thinking of Jeremy always made her smile.

No matter the reason for coming over, she was always happy to see him.

Absolutely! Give me fifteen to shower.

Jeremy texted a thumbs up emoji back.

Allie flew through a shower and was just sweeping her hair into a loose bun when Jeremy knocked.

She opened the door with a flourish and stood on her toes to give him a kiss. But instead, he walked past her into the apartment. Puzzled, Allie frowned and closed the door.

Jeremy turned, a pained look on his face. He looked tired, as if he hadn't slept.

"Jeremy, what is it?" Allie asked, concerned, as she took a step toward him.

Jeremy hadn't said anything since walking in. He turned away from her and ran his fingers through his hair.

Growing even more perplexed at this uncharacteristic behavior, Allie came up behind him and put her arms around him. He seemed to relax and put his hands on top of hers. After several long seconds, he turned to face her and taking a step away, he took her hands in his.

"Allie," he began, his hazel eyes boring into her green ones, "I hope you know how much you mean to me and how much I've enjoyed our time together. But I think it's best . . . it's best if we stop seeing each other."

Allie dropped her hands from his and took a step back, first disbelief, then panic sweeping through her.

"What are you talking about?" Tears already brimmed in Allie's eyes, threatening to spill over. "We have a really great thing going! At least I thought we did."

"Yes, Allie, we do. We absolutely do," Jeremy said. He jammed his hands in his pockets.

"Then why are you doing this, Jeremy? We enjoy each other's company, we are comfortable together, we like the same things, laugh at the same things. You even put up with my crazy whims." Allie paused and when Jeremy didn't say anything, she went on.

"Remember when I wanted to go swimming last spring and the temperature was barely above fifty? You swam right along with me and then we drove to the Coffee Grind and got the largest and hottest black coffee they had and sat with our teeth chattering, drinking coffee and laughing at ourselves. Remember?" Allie stopped and swiped at tear, waiting for Jeremy to say something, anything.

"What about all of the personal, the private things, we've told each other? There are so many things I've never told anyone but you—only you—. Was I wrong to trust you? To trust in what I thought we shared? I didn't think so then. But tell me, Jeremy, was I?"

"Allie," Jeremy finally sighed, "I think you're the most amazing girl I've ever known. And I really mean that. We have had some wonderful times, and you make me happier than I deserve to be. But it's just . . . well, it's just complicated. Please don't ask me to explain it anymore. Just trust me when I say, I'm thinking of you in doing this. I want you to be happy and—"

"What do you mean thinking of me? What if my being happy means being with you?"

Jeremy looked at her, a pained look on his face.

Allie took a steadying breath. She wasn't going to panic. They could and they would talk this out.

"Jeremy, I don't know what's happened or what you're thinking, but let's not do anything drastic. Let's talk about this. We care about each other, so I think we owe each other at least that much. Wouldn't you agree?" Allie's voice sounded shaky and nervous in her own ears.

"Allie, I'm sorry but this is the way it has to be. Riley helped me see—"

"Riley? What does he have to do with you and me? Did he pull the protective big brother card? He's my brother, Jeremy, and your friend, but what we have is between us and no one else. Including Riley."

"Allie, please listen. It's not like that. He just helped me see that I'm being selfish. I'm not being fair to you when I know—"

"When you know what? What is it that you know, Jeremy? Please don't be cryptic with me."

A tear spilled over in spite of Allie's best attempt to hold them back, and Jeremy winced as if in physical pain.

"Tell me what's going on. Help me understand why you're doing this," Allie begged, her eyes swimming in tears.

"Allie, I'm sorry . . . I'm so sorry but this is for the best. You'll realize that someday. Allie . . . I . . ."

Jeremy reached out to hug her, but Allie stepped away, fighting off the tears she couldn't hold back much longer.

"Whether you believe me or not, this upsets me just as much, maybe even more, than it does you. I wish I could explain more but . . ."

Jeremy trailed off and hung his head. "Well, I'd better go."

Jeremy hesitated, looking at her with profound sadness. Allie couldn't bear it, and she had to turn away. She heard Jeremy sigh heavily, and then the door opened and closed softly. She collapsed onto the sofa. Unable to hold the tears back any longer, she cried, as if her heart were breaking, which she knew it had to be.

What had Riley said that would cause Jeremy to do this? After several minutes, she caught her breath and swiped at her cheeks, anger quickly replacing the hurt. She'd get to the bottom of this. And there was no other way except to ask Riley face to face.

MAGGIE LOOKED AROUND AT the chaos that was her new apartment. Furniture was mostly in place. Mostly. Everything else was in total disarray. The blank white walls, the stacks of boxes, and the piles of clothes in stacks around the room were almost overwhelming. There was a starting place somewhere. It was just a matter of finding it.

Maggie sighed and sat on the only place available, the corner of the sofa. Everything around her looked familiar but, just like her, totally out of place in these new surroundings. She was excited about starting her new position, but it just didn't seem right not to be sharing everything with Riley.

She looked at her watch. 6:20 p.m. She wondered what he was doing. It was Saturday night, but she wasn't sure if he was on duty. He'd called and texted several times the week after she'd broken things off, but it had been several days since he'd tried to contact her again. Maybe she should have at least called him before she'd left. But no, hearing his voice would have weakened her resolve. She would talk to him again, at some point, but she just couldn't. Not yet.

She stood and made her way to the bedroom. She'd need to clear a space to sleep tonight. Her dad and brother had taken care of setting up her bed, so she just needed to find the sheets, pillows, and comforter. No small matter in this mess.

She picked up the remote where her dad had left it and turned on the TV to have some noise. She needed to remember to thank her brother and dad for getting the electronics and Wi-Fi set up and working. Riley had always been her "go to" with technology and had made her dorm room, and eventually, the house she shared with some sorority sisters, the envy of everyone with the latest and greatest in electronics.

She had just started putting the bottom sheet on the bed when her cell phone rang. It was in the living room. As she hurriedly sidestepped boxes and bypassed other items scattered across the floor, she hoped it might be Riley. If it were, she'd decided on the way to the phone, she'd talk to him. She hadn't realized just how much she'd miss him.

When she looked at her phone, it was her dad.

"Hi, Dad."

"How's it going, Kiddo?"

"It's going fine. I'm just trying to sort a few things out."

"A few?"

"Well, I guess a lot."

Maggie tried a light chuckle and then sighed.

"What's wrong, Maggie? You don't sound happy. I thought you'd be excited," her father said softly.

"I *am* excited. At least I'm trying to be," Maggie said. "It's just…just…Dad, did I make the right decision?"

There was a long pause. "Maggie, honey, only you can know for sure. As far as a career, I would say you had to follow this opportunity and see where it might lead. But as far as you and Riley goes? Well, only you know your heart and what you and Riley are to each other. If it's meant to be between the two of you, it will find a way. If it's not, then you'll know that in the end too. There's no definitive answer. If there was, it sure would be a lot easier, wouldn't it? Unfortunately, there's not. You're in Dallas now. You've got a great new apartment and you're starting an exciting new job on Monday. After that, just let things play out and see what happens. That's the best I've got. I hope it helps, Magpie."

Maggie smiled into the phone, hearing her dad's nickname for her since she was little. He'd said she talked constantly, just like a little magpie.

"It's exactly what I needed to hear, Dad. You're the best. Thank you. I'll give you and Mom a call Monday evening to let you know how the first day goes."

"Sounds good. But you know, if you need us, we're just a call away. We love you, and you're going to knock their socks off Monday."

"Thanks, Dad. And thanks again to you, Mom, and Cory for all the help moving. I'll have you guys up for dinner in a couple of weeks when I'm all straightened out so you can see the progress."

"We'll be looking forward to it."

"Maggie! Maggie!" Maggie could hear her mom in the background.

"I think your mom wants to talk to you, Magpie."

Maggie could hear the grin in her dad's voice.

"Love you and talk soon."

"Love you too, Dad," Maggie said as her mom got on the phone.

"Maggie dear, you okay? Everything going alright? Do you need anything?"

Maggie chuckled. "I'm fine, Mom. I'm putting the sheets on the bed right now."

"Good, good. I left the grocery list on the kitchen counter. You've got the bare necessities right now but—"

"Thanks, Mom. I've already added things to the list since you left and will go to the store tomorrow. I'll be all set up before you know it.

I told Dad I want to have you guys up for dinner in a couple of weeks so you can see the progress. I'll give you a call Monday evening after my first day. How does that sound?"

"Sounds lovely, dear. You know we love you and want the best for you."

"I know, Mom. I know. Love you guys. I'd better get busy. We'll talk Monday."

Maggie hung up and walked back to the bedroom and started tugging on the sheet. The old saying "she'd made her bed and now she'd have to lie in it" went through her head. So true, she thought, on so many levels.

THE QUIET HUM OF the domed lights in the work area and the low drone of voices from the store front were the perfect back-drop for Riley to concentrate on the laptop repair he'd begun about an hour ago. He was the only technician working in the shop. All of the others were either on installs or had the day off.

Riley looked up when the door to the store area suddenly swished open, and Winston hurriedly came in. He barely gave Riley a nod before ducking into his office. Riley shrugged and turned back to the laptop. A few minutes later, a usually unflappable Winston approached Riley's workbench.

"Winston, is everything—"

"Riley, sorry to cut you short, but I need your help."

"Well, sure," Riley said, turning to Winston with concern.

"James just called from the O'Brien's house. He and Martin are working on their home theater install today."

Riley nodded. He'd heard about this particular install. Everyone at Electronix Doc had. The O'Brien's were a wealthy Abernathy family who had ordered an extremely large and complex system and asked that it be installed on a rush basis for a reason that hadn't been shared with the staff. It was a very big job for Electronix Doc, and Winston had been babysitting the details every step of the way.

Winston hurriedly went on. "Martin was just called away for a family emergency, leaving James there to finish this up alone. You and I both know that these types of installs are impossible for one person to do."

Riley nodded, already knowing where this was leading.

"Would you like for me to head over there and help him?" Riley asked, laying his tools down and standing.

Winston's face relaxed immediately. "Yes, Riley, please. I know we're backed up in the shop, but I just called a couple of technicians who are off today. They're not available until tomorrow, and we promised this job would be finished this afternoon. All that's left to do is some of the fine-tuning. James just needs some help to wrap it up and make sure everything is in perfect working order."

"No worries," Riley assured Winston, clapping him on the back. "We've got this."

"Thank you, Riley. I'll text James and let him know you're on the way."

Friday night was the traditional night for the Sullivan's weekly family meal. Of course, Riley's mom had reminded him when she'd called that afternoon. She'd caught Riley in the middle of the theater install.

"Mom," Riley said, "I can't tonight."

"No excuses. We're eating at home instead of the Club. Be here at 6:30. We're having one of your favorites . . . lasagna! See you in a bit." She hung up quickly, probably to keep him from saying no.

He barely made it to his parents' house by the appointed 6:30 hour, only to find that his sister wasn't there yet. He and his parents had just sat down at the table and were exchanging small talk when they heard the front door bang open. A few seconds later, Allie stormed into the dining room, her eyes puffy and red.

Riley groaned.

"What'd you say to him?" Allie asked in low, angry tones as she rounded the table, heading toward Riley. "What did you say?"

Riley stood and started toward Allie, who backed away from him as tears began to stream down her cheeks.

Riley's parents looked on in alarmed confusion.

"What's going on?" Ballard asked, standing as Jane went to Allie and put an arm around her.

Looks of hurt and confusion flashed between the four.

When no one responded, Ballard said, "I'll ask again. Will someone please explain what's going on?" He looked from Riley to Allie and back to Riley.

Riley reached for the back of his chair, gripping it tightly as he looked down, studying the plush rug intently.

"He talked Jeremy into breaking up with me," Allie choked out as she continued to cry. "That's what's going on. How could you, Riley? How *could* you?!"

Ballard and Jane turned accusing looks on Riley in unison.

"Son?" Ballard asked, his eyebrows arching, punctuating the question.

"I didn't even know they were dating until last night," Riley said, taking a deep breath and looking up. "Jeremy said something about texting you to order pizza for the station, and I asked when you two got so familiar, and that's when it came out you guys were a thing and—"

"So it made you mad we didn't tell you, so you took it upon yourself to tell him to break it off?" Allie said, dropping into her chair and taking the tissue her mother offered.

"No! That's not what happened." Riley ran his fingers through his hair before resuming his seat. He looked imploringly between his parents and sister.

"Yeah, I was upset you guys hadn't told me, but then one thing led to another. He said it'd be best that he break it off with you but I told him he couldn't do that without a good reason—a real good reason—and he couldn't give me one. It got kinda heated and I left. We're not exactly speaking right now."

Riley looked down and began to absentmindedly play with his silverware.

"Then he doesn't care about me," Allie said in a weak voice, slumping in her chair.

Riley stood and came to kneel in front of Allie, taking her hands in his.

"Quite the opposite, actually. He said he cares for you a great deal, and I believe him. I honestly don't know what it is. He said something about not marrying anyone, ever. I don't know what he's gotten into his thick head, but I'll do everything in my power to find out. I didn't think he'd really break things off. Truly. Let me talk to him. Okay?"

Allie looked up at Riley, studying him for several seconds and then nodding dejectedly.

"You may still think of me as your little sister, Riley, but I've grown up. And I care for Jeremy. I really do. I didn't realize just how much until I had to think of being without him. *Please* find out what's going on."

"I will do my best, sis. I promise."

Riley squeezed her hands before releasing them. He stood, looking from his dad to his mom.

"I'll try to talk to him and find out what's on his mind," he assured them.

"Thank you, son," Ballard said as everyone took their seats. He handed his plate to Jane for her to serve the lasagna. "We've always been fond of Jeremy, and Cade too of course, but even more so the last few months. It does a parent's heart good to see their daughter being treated so well. Perhaps while you're at it, you can straighten out whatever went wrong between you and Maggie."

Riley tensed as he handed his own plate to his mother, then slumped at the reminder.

"One thing at a time please, Dad. And besides, I always thought you had higher aspirations for Allie than marrying a firefighter," Riley asked with a hint of sarcasm.

"Well," Ballard said and reached for his tea glass, "they have a tendency to grow on you."

Riley smiled wryly to himself. It was a small but positive step. He'd take it.

After giving Allie a few minutes to compose herself, Ballard asked the blessing.

Riley passed the basket of garlic bread to his mom before forking in a hearty bite of the lasagna. He was going to kill Jeremy or at least seriously maim him. Riley was allowed to mess with his sister but no one else could. And no one, not even Jeremy or Cade, could get away with making her cry. Riley was determined to get to the bottom of whatever was bothering Jeremy. And once he knew what it was, he'd straighten it out, one way or another.

As he enjoyed the steamy rich goodness of the pasta, clinks of silverware on china and his family's voices drifting around him in conversation, Riley sat deep in thought. It seemed everyone's life had been going well until he'd come back into the picture. And now, one by one, things were going wrong with his family, his friends, and at work. He said he'd straighten Jeremy out, but actually, Riley felt like he needed someone to straighten *him* out.

RILEY LOOKED AT HIS watch. It was Saturday, 6:27 p.m. He was on the couch, alone in his apartment. A movie was on the big screen TV he'd just installed that day. It was his first big purchase for his apartment, and he cared absolutely nothing about what was on the HD screen he'd so scrupulously researched before purchasing. He was trying to get just one thing out of his mind. Maggie.

And then, there was Jeremy and Allie. It had been a week since Jeremy had broken up with Allie. Riley had tried to talk to him about it several times, but Jeremy avoided him if at all possible and cut short any conversation when Riley tried to bring Allie up.

Meanwhile, Riley had to field Allie's multiple texts and calls, as she constantly asked if he'd talked to Jeremy. Riley had to be careful. He knew Jeremy and knew if he pushed him too hard, Jeremy would shut him out completely. And that wouldn't help anybody.

Riley understood Allie's feelings and frustration all too well. He knew what it was like to have the person you love walk out of your life with no real explanation. He knew what it was like to lose that close connection, that camaraderie you'd shared with someone special. He knew what it felt like to be alone without being able to look forward to seeing that special person, to sit across from them at a meal, to hold their hand. Riley knew. At least he could try to do something to help Allie, but it had to be at the right time and in the right way.

What could he do to help himself? he wondered for the thousandth time. He'd lost track of the number of times he'd called Maggie the first week after she'd walked out of the Club. By the second week he'd gotten frustrated and had stopped calling altogether. He'd wondered if maybe he should have been more patient, but this afternoon, he'd learned there was no need to wonder any longer.

Since Jeremy had been avoiding him all week, Riley was surprised when Jeremy had called that afternoon. When Jeremy asked if Riley had heard Maggie had moved, he'd gotten mad. Well, it was more like poorly contained fury. Riley realized even though there was a reckoning coming for Jeremy because of Allie, Jeremy really was a good friend to have taken the verbal outburst Riley had unleashed on him during that call.

Riley put one arm behind his head and stared at the blank walls and at the ceiling above his sofa. It was one thing for Maggie not to take his calls or return his messages, but it was something else entirely to leave town without the courtesy of a goodbye. If she cared that little about him after all the years they'd been together, maybe her leaving *was* for the best. He didn't really believe that, but it was the best he could do in a last-ditch effort to make himself feel better. It wasn't working.

RILEY AND JEREMY WORKED side by side in an uneasy silence as they conducted the routine morning inventory and check of the ambulance. After Walton's transfer to the engine, medical calls were the only times Jeremy and Riley had been alone together since Jeremy had broken up with Allie. Even now, Jeremy was avoiding eye contact.

Jeremy slammed the back doors of the ambulance closed then walked to the front where Riley sat in the passenger seat, checking the computer logs. Jeremy paused. Riley looked up.

"You need something?" Riley asked, looking back to his notes.

"No. All's good. Everything is set in the box."

Jeremy shuffled his feet but didn't leave.

Riley stopped and looked at Jeremy.

"Well? You got something to say?"

"Uh ... well, I was just wondering how Allie is doing."

Riley set the iPad on his lap and looked at Jeremy through narrowed eyes. "My sister has not had a great week, if you know what I mean."

"Yeah, well, I haven't had a great week either if it matters," Jeremy said, scuffing his boot on the concrete floor while holding onto the side mirror mount.

"Well, since you're the one who created the situation, you can also be the one to remedy it, you know," Riley replied, trying to sound understanding.

Jeremy hung his head but still didn't walk off.

Riley climbed out of the cab and steered Jeremy to a couple of chairs at the side of the bay.

"Come on, Jeremy. You know you can talk to me. Lord knows I've laid enough on you through the year—hell, even in the past couple of weeks. I hate seeing you and Allie so miserable. And don't think you're going to escape my wrath. No one makes my sister cry and gets away with it."

Jeremy shook his head sadly.

"I didn't mean to make her cry. I did what I thought was best, for both of us. I knew she was upset, but I didn't think—"

"Well, maybe that's the problem. You didn't think. Or maybe you're thinking too much. I don't know what it is, but I do know you're both unhappy. Can't you tell me what's got you so spooked about a serious relationship? And with my sister of all people?"

When Jeremy looked at Riley, the haunted look in his eyes surprised Riley.

"What is it, Jeremy?" Riley asked in a softer tone. "You know you can tell me. We've always been able to talk to each other."

Jeremy slumped over, his elbows on his knees, and his head cradled in his hands.

"You wouldn't understand. You'd think I was crazy. And you'd probably be right."

"Guys! Hey! What's happening?" Cade asked as he bounced through the bay door, a wide grin on his face.

Riley groaned inwardly.

Jeremy quickly jumped to his feet and cleared his throat. "Nothing. Just the morning routine. What are you doing here? Didn't you just get off duty? I thought you'd be in bed by now."

Cade frowned as he looked between Riley and Jeremy. "You guys look like something's up."

"Hey! Looks like the station mascot is in the house. Welcome, Sheriff!" Grimes said as he crossed through the bay. "Got a fresh batch of donuts on the kitchen table, Officer."

Cade laughed sarcastically. "You think you're funny, Grimes?"

Grimes grinned and continued toward the engine as Derek Hayward, the driver, and Josh Carrier, the other firefighter on the engine, came through the door and followed a few seconds later.

"What are you guys up to?" Jeremy asked.

"Cap asked us to do some hose testing this morning, and we thought sure, why not?" Hayward said with a grin.

"Yeah, I'm sure it was 'sure, why not'," Jeremy chuckled, turning back to Cade as the guys walked off.

"Hey, I'm headed to the apartment, but I was hoping to talk to you guys," Cade said with an eager smile. "An opening has just been posted for a campus resource officer at the high school. I'm thinking about applying but wanted to see what you guys thought first. Do you think I should? Or do I even stand a chance?"

Before Riley could say anything, Jeremy slapped Cade on the back. "That job's got your name all over it. Go for it and don't look back."

Cade grinned and then looked at Riley. "What do you think, Sully? You agree?"

"I couldn't agree more," Riley said. "Do it."

The perfect opportunity to get Cade away from that partner of his, Riley thought.

Cade's grin broadened, but then he sobered quickly. "Seriously, do you guys really think I stand a chance? There will probably be more highly qualified officers applying. It's a long shot, really. And if Crawford finds out, well . . . there'll be hell to pay."

Cade raised a good point. With Crawford's disposition, that was a very real possibility. Jeremy and Riley studied Cade. His excitement was palpable and there was no doubt about his enthusiasm for the youth work he'd been doing. It was definitely worth taking the chance.

They glanced at each other and nodded. Several seconds ticked off the large clock on the bay's wall and several cars drove by when Jeremy finally said, "I still say go for it. Your experience coaching youth sports teams, working with the youth leagues? All of that plays in your favor. They'd be crazy to go with anybody else."

Riley nodded his eager agreement, pointing to Jeremy. "What he said."

Cade's broad grin returned. "All right then. I'm doing it. Wish me luck."

Cade turned to leave, but Jeremy called him back as he reached into his pocket and dug something out. He gave it a quick glance, then placed it in Cade's hand.

Cade and Riley looked to see what it was as Jeremy pulled his hand away.

"Your lucky rabbit's foot?" Cade asked, incredulous. "I can't take this. Your granddad gave this to you. You've had it since we were kids."

"Yeah, I know," Jeremy said a bit wistfully. "But I've gotten all the magic out of it that's meant for me. Now it's time for it to turn its charm on you. I want you to get this job."

Jeremy looked at Cade intently. "And apart from how great you'll be at it, you've got to get away from Crawford."

Riley studied Jeremy as he talked to Cade. Jeremy swore he'd never part with that rabbit's foot. It was something special between him and his grandfather, and he'd held on to it all these years. He even fought another kid on the playground over it. With his grandfather's recent passing, he had become even more attached to it. For him to give it up now, well, for some reason it made Riley uneasy, and he could tell Cade felt the same way.

"Jeremy, seriously, I can't take this," Cade said, trying to hand it back to Jeremy. But Jeremy backed away, hands in the air.

"Nope, it's all yours. Come on, Rookie, we've got work to do," Jeremy said to Riley. "Keep us posted."

Jeremy turned and walked to the door leading to the station. "Oh, and there really are donuts in the kitchen, Officer. Just saying."

Cade waved Jeremy off as he and Riley exchanged a puzzled look.

Cade frowned and carefully placed the rabbit's foot in his pocket before he turned to leave.

Riley turned and followed Jeremy, unsure and even more concerned than ever at what could possibly be on Jeremy's mind.

IT HAD BEEN AN unusually quiet shift, with only a couple of medical calls and a few simple runs for the engine and truck. Grimes had cooked a delicious dinner, and Riley did the kitchen clean up with Hayward and Sims pitching in. The majority of the crew filled recliners in the station's TV room watching a movie while others were in their rooms reading or just taking it easy. Evidently, the movie wasn't holding the interest of some of the others, as he could hear snoring over sounds of the movie. Riley grinned. He was thankful they had separate bedrooms. And with the late hour, he knew it wouldn't be long before most would be heading off to bed.

He stood and helped himself to a glass of milk and a couple of cookies from the batch someone had dropped off that afternoon. He pulled his phone out to check messages as he popped a cookie in his mouth. His phone rang, Allie's name popping up. Riley shook his head and sighed.

"Hey, sis."

"Hey, Riley. Hope I'm not calling too late." Allie's voice sounded tired and strained. It made him feel bad.

"No. You're fine. Did you have a good day?"

Silence met his inquiry.

"Sorry. That was a dumb question," Riley said with a grimace.

"Yeah, it kinda was. Any luck today?"

He hated the hope in her voice, knowing he was going to disappoint her.

"Well, he did ask about you this morning."

"He did? What did he say?" There was excitement in Allie's voice.

"He just asked how you were doing, and I told him you haven't had a great week. He said he hadn't either." Riley sighed. "I told him he could remedy the situation. But about the time he was about to say something, Cade barged in, and he clammed up."

Allie sighed. "Oh Riley, what am I going to do? I've texted and called, but he doesn't respond."

"Sis, it really has me puzzled. I tried to broach the subject with him a couple more times today but with no luck. He just shuts down," Riley said. "Don't worry. I'll keep trying. He's stubborn, but I am too."

"Thanks, Riley. Keep me posted. Please."

"You know I will. I promise. Good night."

"Good night," Allie said.

Riley could hear the heavy dejection in her voice. He sighed before popping another cookie in his mouth.

Lieutenant Cochran wandered into the kitchen and opened the door to A Shift's refrigerator, spilling light into the dimly lit space.

"Rookie," Cochran said, leaning against the kitchen counter and taking a long drink from a cold bottle of water. "I heard you're pretty good with electronic stuff."

Riley laid his phone down, looking at Cochran. "Yeah, I work for Electronix Doc doing electronic repairs as a second job. Installs, that kind of thing. It's been a hobby of mine for a while too."

"I'm curious. Have you ever worked with drones?"

Surprised, Riley shook his head. "No, not yet, but I'd love to. The configurations are endless on those things."

"I've been reading up on them," Cochran said eagerly. "I hear the fire service is starting to use them for all kinds of situations. They'd be interesting to learn more about."

"I've heard the same thing. I'd love to know some specifics too," Riley said, putting the last small bite of cookie in his mouth and washing it down with the remainder of his milk.

"I've got a friend at Admin who might know more. I wonder if the higher ups in Abernathy are thinking about using them. I'll check and see what he's heard or knows. I'll keep you posted."

Cochran took another drink of water as he walked back to the TV room.

Riley had heard Cochran was into amateur technology. It was always good to find someone with similar interests.

Riley was rinsing off his glass when the lights blazed on and the tones sounded. The dispatcher's voice came across the intercom: "Engine Five, Med Five: Medical Emergency, Spend Less Grocery, 125 North Commerce."

Riley headed toward the bay, just ahead of the others coming from the TV room and bedrooms. Jeremy, who had been in his room, slid into the driver's seat of the ambulance as Riley slid into the passenger seat, and they buckled their seat belts. Flipping the lights and siren on, Jeremy pulled out ahead of the engine as Lieutenant Cochran acknowledged their response to dispatch.

The mega grocery store was a few short blocks from the station, and Riley barely had time to enter the needed information into the on-board computer before Jeremy killed the siren and pulled up to the front of the store, the engine right behind them.

A police squad car already sat in front of the store, its lights flashing. With the late hour, the parking lot was almost empty, but the few patrons entering and exiting watched curiously as Riley and Jeremy pulled their gear from the ambulance's storage compartments and walked into the store. Lieutenant Cochran and Carrier were a few steps behind.

The manager met them and led them to the deli section of the store where a scattered ring of onlookers loosely circled a man on the floor, unconscious and slumped against one of the deli display cases. Cade and Crawford stood between the man and the curious onlookers, with Crawford loudly ordering the group to move aside. Jeremy and Riley made their way through.

Jeremy looked up and eyed the circle of faces as he knelt beside the still figure. "Does anyone know this man?"

There were only negative head shakes in reply.

Riley noticed partially opened food packages scattered about and felt, as well as heard, the crunch of what must be crackers beneath his feet and knees as he joined Jeremy kneeling beside the unconscious man.

The man was extremely pale and shivering uncontrollably as they carefully removed his suit jacket and rolled up his sleeve to administer an IV. Riley could tell the man's suit and the fine cotton shirt he wore were expensive, and the man's loafers were the same fine Italian leather Riley's dad often wore. The man was mumbling incoherently, and when Riley looked at the thermometer, it read 103 degrees.

The engine crew walked up with the gurney as Jeremy and Riley finished prepping the man for transport. Crawford made one last motion to the onlookers to stand back before cockily sauntering to where the store manager stood, watching Riley and Jeremy work.

Riley, along with everyone else standing nearby, heard Crawford's comments to the store manager.

"It's obvious this man was stealing food. I recommend pressing charges," Crawford said smugly.

Startled, Riley took a quick look at the store manager as he and Jeremy lifted the man onto the gurney and began placing a blanket over him.

The store manager hesitated. "Well, I don't know. No harm, actually. His behavior was just a bit erratic so we thought it best to call for help."

"Yes, yes. You did the right thing," Crawford said in a condescending tone that made Riley's skin crawl. "But still, you can't let even one of these lowlifes steal or else the word will spread. Soon, you'll be inundated and robbed blind before you know it. Pressing charges is a simple process. I'll be glad to start the paperwork for you."

Watching out of the corner of his eye, Riley could see Crawford standing near the store manager and blocking their exit from the deli area, his posture intimidating. Cade stood a few feet away, looking uncomfortable.

The patient moaned and tried to move, but Riley patted him assuringly on the shoulder before turning to gather their equipment. Riley began to follow the firefighters rolling the gurney toward the exit, but he hesitated, hearing Crawford continuing to badger the store manager to press charges.

Before he could stop himself, Riley turned to the store manager. "Sir, I'll be happy to pay the cost for any food damaged or eaten by this man. He is ill and probably had no idea what he was doing. If you'll figure up the cost, I'll be back tomorrow to pay you."

Jeremy stopped in his tracks beside the gurney and turned to stare at Riley, his lips twitching. Cade turned away, trying to hide a grin of his own. The store manager broke into a relieved smile.

Crawford, however, scowled darkly at Riley, his face turning an ugly shade of red.

"Stay out of this, Firefighter Sullivan," he spat out, glancing at Riley's uniform to get his name. "This is police business."

"Not anymore, Officer Crawford," Riley said, making a show of looking at Crawford's name badge in return. "I believe it has been resolved."

Riley turned to the store manager. "I'll see you tomorrow morning, sir."

Riley caught up to Jeremy as they maneuvered back to the store's entrance and followed the gurney out through the automated doors.

"What did you just do?" Jeremy asked, shaking his head.

"Saved a sick man from having vindictive charges filed against him by an overbearing excuse for a police officer," Riley said, following the gurney into the back of the ambulance. "Got a problem with that?"

Jeremy shook his head and grinned. "Not at all."

"SULLIVAN! IN MY OFFICE," Captain Jernigan said as soon as Riley and Jeremy entered the kitchen after returning from the hospital.

Riley turned to Jeremy, raising his eyebrows in a question.

Jeremy shrugged and followed a few steps behind Riley, stopping just outside the office door.

"Sullivan, I got a call from Officer Crawford with a complaint. He said you interfered in official police business on the run to Spend Less. What happened?"

The captain dropped his glasses onto the desk, adding them to the scattered papers, pens and an empty coffee mug on a stained coaster already there. The office air was dry and smelled of old coffee and disinfectant.

The captain eased back into the desk chair, his index finger tapping his lips as Riley recounted his version of events from his chair across the desk.

When Riley got to the end of the story, he added, "Sir, I could tell this man was not homeless or a lowlife. His clothes were too expensive. He was just very ill and probably totally unaware of what he was doing. It would have been wrong to file charges without getting more information first and giving him a chance to tell his side of the story. Charges can still be filed, but Officer Crawford was trying to push the store manager into doing it even though the manager was obviously reluctant."

After several seconds, the captain nodded and leaned forward.

"I appreciate the sentiment, and you looking out for someone who couldn't help themselves. But try to keep any direct encounters with Officer Crawford to a minimum. He's trouble, and he can make trouble for you. I don't want that for you. Or for me. Paperwork stuff, you know." The captain shrugged, trying to hide a smile as he waved his hand dismissively. "Now get outta here."

Riley stood to leave but the captain stopped him.

"And Rookie? Keep up the good work."

Riley grinned. With a nod, he walked out of the stuffy office and into the cool hallway, nearly running into Jeremy.

"Well?" Jeremy asked anxiously.

"Well, what?" Riley replied as he walked toward the kitchen.

"What did he say? Did Crawford call him?" Jeremy asked, keeping step with Riley.

Riley stopped suddenly and turned, Jeremy nearly plowing into him.

"Yeah, Crawford called and *tried* to make trouble. But Cap set him straight. He did tell me to be careful. He said Crawford could cause me trouble. I mean, I don't want to make trouble for me or for Cade."

They silently eased into chairs at the kitchen table, deep in thought.

The kitchen was quiet except for the muffled noise coming from the TV and the refrigerators humming.

"I'll do my best to stay out of Crawford's way. Not just for my sake but for Cade's sake as well," Riley finally said in a hushed voice.

"Don't worry about that," Jeremy interjected. "Cade can take care of himself."

"Oh, I know he can," Riley quickly agreed. "I just don't want it to come down to that."

IT HAD BEEN A quiet night at the station. Only two minor medical calls. Riley couldn't say as much for the work at Electronix Doc. Winston had been right when he'd said business was picking up. Riley had all the work he could handle on his days off from the station.

He had run by Spend Less first thing this morning and paid the manager for the food loss from the sick man the night before. And he'd been hard at work since. It was the end of the day, and Riley glanced quickly at the iPad to see if any additional calls had come in while he'd helped another technician install a home theater system. The install had gone smoothly, and they'd finished early. Since it was already late afternoon, Riley was glad to see the schedule was clear.

Winston had told Riley if nothing else came in after he helped with the install, the rest of the afternoon was his own. Deep in thought, Riley turned onto a residential street that looked familiar for some reason. He was looking back and forth to either side of the street when he noticed the small park on the right. When he looked to the left, he recognized Mr. Thornton's house. He'd only approached it from the opposite direction, from the station. There had been a few more morning calls to Mr. Thornton's for one thing or another since their first meeting. He was such a nice man, Riley thought, to be so lonely.

A sudden idea popped into Riley's head. He made a quick U-turn and parked in front of Mr. Thornton's house. He had nothing going for the rest of the afternoon and a nice visit without having to rush back to the station sounded nice. Maybe Mr. Thornton would enjoy some company.

Riley approached the front porch and was surprised when the door suddenly swung open. A woman wearing a fierce scowl stood with a broom in one hand and her other hand fisted on her hip.

"Whatever you're selling, we don't want."

Riley stopped, caught off guard.

"I beg your pardon? I'm not selling anything. I just—"

"You're not sneaking by me, mister. Turn around and leave the way you came."

"But—"

"I said—"

"Joanne, who is it?" Riley heard Mr. Thornton's voice.

"Some salesman, but he's leaving," she said with a pointed glare at Riley.

Mr. Thornton came to the door and peered over Joanne's shoulder.

"Mr. Thornton, it's Riley Sullivan, sir. From Fire Station Five?"

"Riley!" he said with a huge smile. "Come in. Joanne, this is one of the nice firemen who comes by and helps me when you're not here." He shuffled away from the door using his walker and motioned for Riley to follow.

Joanne looked sheepishly at Riley as he stepped around her, giving her a wide berth.

"Sorry. We get salesmen all the time trying to take advantage of Mr. Thornton. I'm a little overprotective, I guess."

Riley looked at her, still a little uncertain, but Mr. Thornton was motioning him into the living room.

"No worries," Riley replied with a hesitant smile. "Mr. Thornton is lucky to have someone like you looking out for him."

She smiled self-consciously, but pleased.

"Joanne," Mr. Thornton called from the living room. "Would you please bring us a big plate of your wonderful brownies and some iced tea or lemonade? I've promised these boys some of your delicious brownies if they ever stop by."

Riley smiled. He'd forgotten about the brownies.

"What a pleasant surprise, young man. It's such a pleasure to have a visitor," Mr. Thornton said as Riley took a chair across from him.

Joanne hurried back and set a large plate of brownies on the coffee table. Riley's mouth watered just looking at the thick layer of chocolate frosting swirled on each one. Joanne returned shortly with a pitcher of lemonade and two glasses filled with ice, leaving everything for Mr. Thornton and Riley to serve themselves.

"Brownie?" Mr. Thornton gestured, taking one for himself and relishing a big bite.

Riley grinned and took one as well after pouring a glass of lemonade for each of them.

The brownies definitely lived up to Mr. Thornton's endorsement. And after a few pleasantries, Riley found himself reaching for another, much to Mr. Thornton's delight.

"Just about the best brownies I've ever had, except for my sweet Martha's," Mr. Thornton said, taking a long drink of the tart lemonade. "Don't mind Joanne. She's been my day nurse for so many years, I've lost count."

He moved closer to Riley and whispered, "She's a bit bossy, but don't tell her I said that."

"I heard that!" came Joanne's teasing voice from the kitchen.

Riley chuckled. "I admit, these are some of the best brownies I've ever had too." With a satisfied sigh, Riley relaxed into the overstuffed chair, taking an occasional sip of lemonade.

The living room had a large picture window that overlooked the front yard that was currently dappled with shade from the large oak tree in the yard. They sat facing the window, a small table with the brownies and lemonade between them. Riley hadn't noticed the room before on their calls. But now, he could see that the space was rather small with comfortable but sparse furnishings. He relaxed further into the chair, happy to be here and to see a bright smile on Mr. Thornton's face.

Conversation flowed easily. Riley told Mr. Thornton about his second job at Electronix Doc, a bit about life at the fire station and even about his disastrous first meal. They laughed about it together, Mr. Thornton laughing until he had to wipe tears from his eyes.

"I haven't laughed that hard since I can't remember when," Mr. Thornton said, catching his breath. "I'm not laughing at you, mind you, but I can just picture it all."

"Oh no offense taken. Believe me, it certainly wasn't funny at the time, but it's good to laugh about it now."

"It's good to laugh when you can. I'm sure you see other things you'd rather not have seen."

Riley nodded thoughtfully. "Yes, sir. I'm still new but already..."

His mind drifted back to his first run. Shaking himself out of the bleak reverie, Riley smiled at Mr. Thornton. "There are some really good things about being a paramedic too."

"Oh? Such as?" Mr. Thornton held out his glass to Riley for a refill.

"Such as making a new friend."

Mr. Thornton beamed his pleasure. "Riley, you have no idea how happy you've made me, stopping by today. But being such a fine young man, I bet you've got a sweet young lady waiting for you."

A shadow crossed Riley's face and his smile faded.

"Oh dear. Something amiss in the young lady department?" Mr. Thornton asked, eying Riley.

Riley nodded.

"It might help to talk about it, son," Mr. Thornton said gently. "I'm a good listener. And I might even offer up some advice. Not sure if it'd be any good, but I'm willing to listen and try."

Riley took a deep breath and swirled the remaining lemonade in his glass.

"Well, okay, but you'll have to remember you asked," Riley said with a half-hearted attempt at humor.

"All ears. Lay it on me."

Riley grinned in spite of himself, then exhaled slowly. "Her name is Maggie."

Riley's face softened when he said her name, and Mr. Thornton tried to hide a grin. He could tell Riley was in love.

"We met in grade school," Riley went on. "We've been together ever since. Well, until just about a month ago. I had just gotten the ring and was ready to propose, but before I could ask her, she broke up with me and moved to Dallas. She said she wasn't sure there was anything left between us or how she fit into my life anymore."

Riley paused and sighed dejectedly. "She said I've changed since I joined the fire service, but I don't know why she thinks that, and I didn't have the chance to find out exactly what she meant. She got a promotion at work, which required the move, so she was gone in less than two weeks. She didn't talk to me about how she was feeling, anything about the job, or really, anything else. She just accepted the job and moved. I couldn't believe it. I still can't believe it!"

Agitated, Riley stood and began to pace.

"I've tried to call her repeatedly, but she won't pick up or return messages. I don't understand what happened, I really don't. I love her and want her back, but I don't know what to do or, if anything I tried would even work." Riley paused and took a deep breath. "Any words of advice, Mr. Thornton?"

Riley sat down in his chair and shrugged, looking at Mr. Thornton expectantly. "This is the first time I've really talked to anyone about it."

Mr. Thornton rocked gently in his chair, studying Riley and stroking his chin thoughtfully. "Have you told her how you feel? I mean, laid all of your cards on the table? She might just need to hear you say you love her."

"Well, sure I've told her! Many times."

"Okay. Name one time that stands out in your mind," Mr. Thornton queried with surprising directness. "Where were you? Was it spontaneous or a special occasion? Were you specific about your feelings? What was her reaction? You know, what are some details?"

"Oh, I don't know," Riley said with an evasive shrug. "It's hard to pick just one time."

Mr. Thornton continued to rock, studying Riley with a knowing nod. "Ah, I see."

"What do you mean you see?" Riley asked, a bit exasperated.

"I think I understand why Maggie left."

Riley sat back, puzzled. He could hear the muffled sound of a motorcycle going by and a lawn mower starting up next door as he looked, perplexed, at Mr. Thornton.

"What do you mean you understand why she left? How could you possibly understand? You've never even talked to her!"

"True, true," Mr. Thornton replied calmly. "But if you can't easily name a single time, you said the words 'I love you' to Maggie, odds are you never did. Or if you did, it wasn't anything to write home about. Take it from a misty-eyed, old romantic—a girl likes to know, and hear, with no doubts or ambiguities, that she's loved and treasured. I speak from experience.

"I assumed a lot after my Martha and I had been dating for a while. I thought I had her snagged, so I backed off and just coasted. This was nearly one of the biggest mistakes of my life. I got my eyes opened in a hurry when I heard she'd gone out with a guy named Floyd Weber. I can tell you, that motivated me into taking some quick action. I told her exactly how I felt about her, dropped down on one knee and proposed right then and there. I didn't have the ring yet, but there was no way I was going to let her get away."

Mr. Thornton smiled, reminiscing. "I worked three jobs to buy her the ring she wanted, and it was worth every second. And after all of that, do you know what she told me?" He paused and chuckled. "She said she knew all along we were going to be together. She just needed me to figure it out and do something about it."

Riley watched Mr. Thornton's face light up as he talked about "his Martha," but watched his smile fade as a faraway look came into his eyes.

"She's been gone for almost three years now. I don't know how it's possible, but I miss her more every day. There is one thing I know for certain, young Riley. I sure am looking forward to seeing her again." He chuckled. "Even though she'll probably fuss at me for eating too many brownies." He gave the near empty plate a mischievous glance.

Riley's troubled look turned into a grin.

Mr. Thornton looked at Riley earnestly. "Riley, son, you may have had a close relationship with Maggie in the past, but before it goes to the next step, that girl may just need to be convinced of your feelings.

You have some serious work to do if you truly love her and want her back."

While Riley looked at this kind old gentleman, his thoughts spun through the countless times he and Maggie had been together. He couldn't recall a single time he'd ever told her that he loved her using the actual words. Surely he'd openly voiced his feelings, his love and affection, and even his admiration for her. Hadn't he? He thought everything about their relationship demonstrated vividly how much she meant to him and how deeply he felt about her. Because he did love her, very much. He knew how he felt, and he'd assumed—incorrectly, so it seemed that she would be able to know it too. Riley turned a troubled look to Mr. Thornton and met his studious appraisal.

"Ah, it seems I might be right," Mr. Thornton said with a gentle smile.

Riley nodded wearily. "Yes, sir. I think you are. I just never—"

Mr. Thornton held up a hand to stop Riley. "Don't look back, son. Look forward. And decide how you're going to win Maggie back. You can do it. I have a feeling Maggie feels the same about you, but just like my Martha, she needs you to figure it out first and do something about it."

Riley could hear doves cooing as early evening started to darken the room. The tree's shadows were lengthening across the lawn when Joanne came in to close the window blinds and switch on a lamp on the side table.

Riley stood. "I'd best be getting on, but I've really enjoyed our visit."

"I have too, Riley. I hope you'll come back."

"And I promise not to treat you like a door-to-door salesman," Joanne said with a toothy grin.

Riley chuckled and smiled. "Well, I'd like that. But just one thing . . ."

He paused and looked between the two of them, then pointed to the lone brownie left on the plate. "I think we'll be needing some more brownies."

Mr. Thornton and Joanne both laughed.

"You can count on it," Joanne said as she picked up the plate, offering the remaining brownie to Riley.

Riley started toward the front door, brownie in hand, followed by Mr. Thornton shuffling behind him with his walker.

"I'll see you soon, sir," Riley said, extending his hand which Mr. Thornton shook with a surprisingly strong grip.

"I'm counting on that, Riley."

Riley made his way down the sidewalk, glancing back once to see Mr. Thornton wave before he turned and shuffled back inside.

Riley felt better than he had in days. He would make sure Maggie knew how he felt. First step? He'd remind Maggie of what they'd shared and the fun they'd had together. Riley smiled as he got into his SUV and started the engine. He had a plan.

T HE LAST RAYS OF sunlight slanted through Maggie's office windows as she sank wearily into her chair. This week seemed to stretch on forever. Thank goodness it was Friday. Except for the fact she had to work tomorrow. The first marketing campaign she'd worked on wasn't quite ready for its Monday client presentation, which meant working over the weekend.

She was the newest one on the team. And while she appreciated the confidence shown in her, she felt like she was in over her head. Maggie ignored the clock and the fact that it was Friday night and had just opened the first email when her phone dinged with a text.

It was Riley.

Heading home from work and thought of you as I passed The Creamery. Your favorite is salted caramel and mine is rocky road. Rather apropos right now.

Miss you, Mags. R.

Maggie's lips quirked in a soft smile. There were so many special memories of that ice cream shop. Maggie remembered the afternoon Riley came over after school when he'd gotten his driver's license and first car, enveloping herself in the moment.

"Mags," Riley's excited voice came over the phone. "You busy?"

"What's up?" she asked, holding a fashion magazine in front of her.

"Come outside and find out."

"You're at my house?" Maggie asked, sitting up.

"You'll have to come outside to see," Riley said, chuckling as he hung up.

When Maggie threw open the door, she saw Riley in the driveway. He was smiling broadly as he leaned casually against a brand new, white Camaro, its hood and trunk lined with black racing stripes.

Riley motioned with his hand. "So, what do you think?"

"It's awesome!" Maggie said with a broad smile.

"Want to go for a spin?"

"Absolutely!"

Riley held the passenger door open as Maggie slid into the black seat, inhaling the smell of leather, as Riley closed the door and came around to the driver's side.

"So, what do Jeremy and Cade think about your new car?" Maggie asked, as Riley drove.

"They haven't seen it."

"They haven't seen it?" Astonished, Maggie turned to look at Riley.

He shrugged lightly. "Nope, not yet. I wanted you to see it first."

"I thought first cars were really big deals to you guys."

"Oh, they are, but they'll have plenty of opportunities to see it. I just wanted you to see it first," Riley answered, cutting his eyes to Maggie and grinning.

Pleased, Maggie turned to look out the window, smiling.

Riley pulled up in front of The Creamery Ice Cream Shoppe, one of their favorite places.

"Ice cream, Miss Rawlings?"

"I'd be delighted, Mr. Sullivan."

After getting their waffle cones filled with salted caramel and rocky road ice cream, Riley drove the few blocks to Old City Park where they'd played as children. It was still a favorite haunt.

They walked to the swings, the late afternoon sun warming them as they gently swung, enjoying their ice cream in silence.

"Today has certainly been a big day," Riley said at last. "It's been kinda like a rite of passage."

"Yeah, it has," Maggie agreed thoughtfully. "You're lucky. I can't wait to get my driver's license. I mean, *and* my first car.

"It's only a couple of months if my calculations are correct," Riley said with a teasing glance. Maggie smiled and returned his teasing look.

Riley drug his heels in the sand to slow his swing. Reaching over, he took hold of the chain holding Maggie's swing and pulled her slowly toward him.

Riley was so close, Maggie could see the soft brown flecks in his gray eyes and smell his soft musk cologne. The sun put rich glints in his dark hair, and her breath hitched being so wonderfully close to him.

"As I said," Riley said in a soft voice, leaning toward her. "It's been a big day. I got my driver's license and a new car. But it's sharing it with you, Mags. That's what makes it an especially big day for me."

Surprised, Maggie stared at him wide-eyed. She could feel something about to change between them. Something she'd been waiting and hoping for.

Riley pulled Maggie closer and kissed her gently at first and then with more intensity. It was their first kiss, and he wanted her to know she was so much more to him than a friend.

When their lips finally parted, they looked closely into each other's eyes for a long, sweet moment and smiled before Riley pulled Maggie even closer, and they kissed again.

Maggie, her heart pounding wildly, kissed Riley back, her hand clasping his. Something *had* changed between them, and she never wanted this moment to end.

"WELL, THAT'S SOME SMILE, Maggie. Penny for your thoughts?"

"Connor! I didn't hear you walk up," Maggie said, nervously clearing her throat and sitting up in her chair. She laid her phone face down on the desk.

Her boss, Connor Matthews, stood in her office door, watching her with a teasing grin as he looked from her phone to her blushing face. Handsome, with dark blond wavy hair and vivid bottle-green eyes, he was Vice President of the Marketing Department. And from what Maggie had heard from others around the office, he would be quite the catch. Evidently, he thought so too.

Even though Maggie tried to treat him as her boss, she found herself treating him more like a friend. He was a brilliant marketer and great teacher, and she enjoyed his company.

Connor walked in and made himself at home, plopping down in one of the guest chairs in front of Maggie's desk. "I came by to get your take on the meeting," he said, reaching for a miniature chocolate bar from the jar on Maggie's desk.

"Well, I think they have a point about it not reaching the right demographic. We're close. But as you know, that little bit can make a big difference."

Connor nodded solemnly as he ate the chocolate.

"You're right, of course," he said, reaching up for another chocolate bar. "But the question is, which direction do you take it and exactly how far do you go?" He shrugged and moved to the edge of the chair, leaning forward to put his elbows on Maggie's desk.

"Look, I know it was a long meeting and there's a lot to go over before the follow up meeting tomorrow. Sorry about having to work Saturday, but we're on a strict deadline. I've got an idea, kill two birds with one stone so to speak. How about we discuss this over dinner? It's still early, so we have plenty of time to eat and talk strategy too. It *is* Friday night after all. You up for it?"

Connor stood, looking at Maggie expectantly.

"Well, I don't know. That meeting did run long, but I . . . I've just got so much to do."

"Maggie," Connor said, leaning over her desk and looking her in the eye, "It's 6:30 on a Friday night. That's not early. Besides, I'm the boss, and I'm hungry. Come on. We'll get more than enough done over dinner, so you'll have time to work on your other stuff tomorrow."

He headed to the door but stopped and turned to see if Maggie was following. He raised his eyebrows expectantly.

Maggie sighed, then smiled indulgently before taking a last look at her computer screen and shutting her laptop.

"Okay then," she said with mock irritation. "Where are we going?"

A victorious smile flashed across Connor's handsome face. "How does Italian sound? And I'm not talking pizza."

"That sounds wonderful," Maggie said, grabbing her things.

She followed him to the door as he stepped aside, allowing her to go first. She looked up at him and smiled. The text from Riley was forgotten. For the moment.

RILEY YAWNED. 6:00 A.M. was early. He was just starting to put the first sheet on his bed when Jeremy stuck his head in the door.

"Come on. Cap wants to see us."

"What's up?" Riley asked, pulling the sheet tight and tucking the corner in.

"I'm not a mind reader. I suggest you follow me and we'll both find out."

Riley rolled his eyes and followed Jeremy across the station. He was still being frustratingly evasive about the conversation they needed to have.

A Shift was just getting underway, with most of the crew assembled in the kitchen. The strong aroma of the coffee he'd put on earlier filled the air. Riley had been too busy to get a cup then, but he sure wanted a cup now. This probably wasn't the best time for a side trip, however.

Cap's office was a nice-sized space used by each shift commander. Captain Jernigan sat at the desk that occupied the center of the room, his head bent toward the computer screen, his glasses perched on the end of his nose. Papers and scribbled notes were scattered across his desk. The start of each shift was always hectic for command staff, as they made sure all firefighter and paramedic slots were filled across the city.

Jeremy knocked as he and Riley walked in and sat in the two guest chairs.

Jernigan held up a hand up. They realized he was listening to someone on the office's speaker phone.

"Got it, Chief. Got it," Jernigan said, typing something onto the keyboard. "Do you need anyone from Five?"

"No. I think these adjustments will do it. Thanks, Keevin." They recognized Chief Bentley's voice on the speaker.

"You've got it, Chief. Let us know if you need anything."

"Copy that. Later."

Captain Jernigan disconnected the call, then finished typing something. He turned to Jeremy and Riley, sweeping his glasses to the top of his head. He looked tired and strained for such an early hour.

"Gentlemen. Let's get straight to it. I have a change in assignment for both of you. Ennis, you are now on the engine as its senior firefighter. Carrier is moving back to the ambulance."

Riley's heart sank. Jeremy was moving to the engine. That's what *he'd* wanted to do since joining the department. To make matters worse, Carrier had been the station rookie until Riley's arrival. Riley braced himself to hear that Carrier was going to be senior paramedic, and Riley would now report to him.

Instead, Jernigan turned to Riley. "Sullivan, you are now senior paramedic on the box. Carrier needs a bit more training, and you've proven yourself a capable paramedic. Of course, I'm sure this exceptional proficiency only came about because of the great leader you've had to emulate in Mr. Ennis here," he said, with a nod in Jeremy's direction.

"That's certainly the way I see it, Cap," Jeremy quickly agreed, feigning seriousness.

"Are these changes just for today, sir?" Riley asked, with a glower at Jeremy.

"Nope. These changes are effective immediately and for the foreseeable future. And another thing, Sullivan. I want you to start boning up on the engine and truck. Not sure when it's going to happen, but we're going to start rotating so everyone works all the apparatus at one time or another. We're looking for a balance of experience, so if the time should ever come, everyone will be equally prepared."

"Yes, sir!" Riley said, trying not portray too much excitement. "I'll be ready."

The captain studied Riley for several seconds. "Yes, Sullivan, I have no doubt but that you will be." Turning to Jeremy, Jernigan said, "And Ennis, I thought you were going to test for lieutenant? I haven't seen your name on any testing lists."

"Well, Cap...you see," Jeremy uncharacteristically faltered. "I...uh."

"I strongly encourage you to test, Ennis. You would make an outstanding lieutenant."

"I agree," Riley added. "You should."

Jeremy shot Riley a responding glare.

"I'll think about it," Jeremy lamely replied and stood. "Anything else, Cap?"

"Nope, that's it. But gentlemen, be aware. These changes in assignment are not made lightly. While I completely agree with them, they come at the directive of Battalion Chief Bentley. As I said, the work you've done has not gone unnoticed. Keep it up," Captain Jernigan said, turning back to the computer. "Now, go on. Annoy somebody else."

Riley stood as Cap bent his head toward the computer screen and swept his glasses back to his nose. Both Riley and Jeremy grinned and mumbled, "Thank you, sir," before leaving.

They walked in silence until they got back to Riley's bedroom door. Riley put a hand on Jeremy's arm and pulled him into his room.

"I'm more than ready to be a firefighter, but I don't think I'm ready to be lead paramedic," Riley said, tousling his hair and pacing. "I appreciate their confidence but I don't know."

"You're ready," Jeremy said. "You're more than ready. I've put a good word in for you as have others. The only thing you're missing is confidence, and you're gaining in that department too. You've just got to believe in yourself."

Surprised, Riley stopped and stared at Jeremy.

Jeremy sighed and ran his fingers through his hair. "Sully, I've thought about this a lot, and I don't want to make you mad, but you're still letting that one run on your first shift dictate your confidence level. I wish you could see what I see, what others see, when you're with a patient. You're good—very good—at what you do, whether you choose to believe it or not."

Riley's brow furrowed as he shook his head. "Hold on, I haven't let that affect—"

Jeremy held a hand up, stopping him. "Sorry, buddy, but you have. You couldn't wait to get to the station for your first shift. But then, there was a rough run, and two months later, you still say you have no confidence. That's not the Riley Sullivan I know. Yes, a fatality of any kind is always rough, but you can't let one instance continue to dictate your outlook or how you do your job."

Jeremy paused again and sighed. He looked at Riley for several seconds before continuing. "You know, this is just like it was with you and that high school championship football game. You zeroed in on one play and moped around like the entire season had been a bust when actually, the leadership you showed all season was far more important than a state championship could ever be. Give yourself a break and have confidence in the skills and abilities everyone else can see. Got it?"

Jeremy stopped pacing the small bedroom space and pinned Riley with a direct look.

"Got it?" Jeremy repeated.

"Well, sure I guess," Riley replied.

Jeremy huffed in frustration. "I ought to knock sense into that thick head of yours."

"Yeah? I could say the same for you."

Jeremy stopped mid-stride and closed his eyes, his breathing quickening.

"We're not talking about me," he finally said.

"Maybe we need to," Riley replied.

Jeremy stared at the white, textured wall where three framed prints of large fires in Abernathy hung over Riley's bed. "There's nothing to talk about. Let's just drop it, okay?"

Jeremy walked to the door but stopped and turned when Riley cleared his throat. "Wait. What's up with the lieutenant's exam? I thought you would've taken it a long time ago. You are way more than ready to be an officer."

"Maybe but . . ." Jeremy shrugged but didn't make a move to leave.

After a few minutes of awkward silence, Riley hazarded, "Allie is still asking about you."

Jeremy straightened from where he'd leaned against the door frame. "Don't, Sully." Jeremy turned to walk away. "You just don't understand."

"But Jeremy," Riley pressed as Jeremy paused.

The tones for a medical call suddenly echoed through the station and the bay.

Jeremy looked up, listening to the announcement. "That's you. Good luck with Carrier," Jeremy said, looking relieved as Riley brushed past him. "I have a feeling you're going to need it."

Jeremy hadn't been wrong. It had been an unusually busy afternoon with one medical call after another, and Carrier had been all over the place. He'd trained with another department and couldn't remember the order Abernathy paramedics performed procedures. Riley reminded him continually, expecting something to be handed to him or something done a certain way. But instead, Carrier waited for Riley's directions, or he'd fumbled getting medications or supplies from their bags, slowing their response. Riley could tell Carrier was trying, but things just weren't clicking.

THEY RETURNED MIDAFTERNOON AFTER dropping their latest patient at the hospital and sat across from each other at the kitchen table gobbling down leftover tacos for lunch. Microwaving the tacos certainly hadn't done them any favors.

The engine crew was in the kitchen getting meat ready to grill for dinner. Jeremy was providing running commentary and lending unwanted instruction.

After taking a long drink of iced tea to wash down the last bite of taco sticking in his throat, Riley leaned back in his chair and pulled out his phone.

It's been a wild day. But never too busy to think of you, Mags. I miss you. R.

Riley scrolled down and reread the past several texts he'd sent to Maggie. He hadn't received a single reply in return. He sighed and reread the text he'd just typed before hitting send and slipping his phone back in his pocket.

The tones sounded with another medical call but this time at the naming of the address, Riley froze as he rose from his chair.

"What is it?" Carrier asked, looking at Riley.

Riley shook his head and quickly started toward the bay door ahead of Carrier.

As Riley pulled out ahead of the engine, Carrier started relaying directions.

"No need for directions," Riley interrupted. "I know where I'm going. That address is my dad's office."

RILEY'S MIND WAS RACING as fast as the ambulance was. Who was needing emergency medical help? Had something happened to his dad? To Marian, his dad's assistant? Riley knew all of the staff.

He was driving a bit erratically, but Carrier, bless him this once, hadn't said another word.

Riley squelched the siren as they came to an abrupt halt in front of the imposing two-story brick building that housed Sullivan and Swanson Law Offices. Riley and Carrier jumped out and grabbed their equipment bags. They strode quickly up the wide, sweeping steps to the ornate wooden door as the engine pulled up behind them.

Janice Murphy, Douglas Swanson's assistant, jerked the front door open as Riley reached for the handle. The frantic look on her face was replaced by surprise upon seeing Riley.

"Riley! Oh my goodness, I almost didn't recognize you in uniform! Please hurry. He's upstairs."

"Who is it?" Riley asked as he and Carrier followed Janice down the main hallway to the building's single elevator.

"It's Douglas . . . Mr. Swanson," she corrected as the elevator doors closed behind them. "Your dad tried to help him, but he just got worse so fast." Her voice caught. "We weren't sure what to do."

"You did the right thing to call 9-1-1," Carrier assured her.

The elevator doors opened to a throng of anxious staff gathered outside the main conference room door.

"Excuse me. Please make way," Riley said with nods to those who caught his eye, their surprise evident when they recognized him. Riley stepped through the conference room door to find Douglas Swanson prone on the floor and in obvious distress. His dad, Marian, and Lyle, Douglas' son, were on their knees on the floor around him, anxiously trying to help.

Riley's dad looked up, hearing them enter. Riley had never seen his dad look scared or flustered before, and seeing that now on his father's face surprised Riley.

"If you'll please move aside," Carrier asked, motioning them back as Riley set his gear down beside Mr. Swanson.

Riley gave Marian a fleeting smile as she stood and patted him on the shoulder.

Riley's dad moved to the side but stayed close.

"What happened? And how long ago?" Riley asked as he began his examination.

"It was about twenty minutes ago," his dad said. "Doug, Lyle, and I had been back from a late lunch meeting for about ten minutes and had started another meeting in here when Doug said he was feeling a bit off. He said he was fine, but then he'd started breathing heavily and was pulling at his tie. He said he felt like he was choking. He tried to stand but then collapsed. We loosened his tie and unbuttoned his collar while Marian called 9-1-1."

"Is he having a heart attack?" Lyle asked anxiously.

Riley spared a quick glance at Lyle to acknowledge he'd heard the question but didn't answer. Riley thought he recognized the symptoms but wanted to confirm. "What did he have for lunch?"

"Lunch?" his dad asked, surprised.

"Yes. Anything he doesn't normally eat?"

"Well, the client served a selection of salads with different meats. Doug had seafood if I remember correctly."

"What kind of seafood?" Riley pressed as he opened a bag with medications.

Riley's dad looked to Lyle. "Do you remember what he had?"

Lyle hesitated. "Crab. He had crab. I remember because he hadn't had crab salad before and wanted to try it."

Riley nodded. Exactly what he'd thought. Mr.Swanson was having an anaphylactic reaction to shellfish.

In spite of the oxygen Carrier had administered, Mr. Swanson's struggle to breathe was growing worse. His face, lips, and eyes were now swelling and at an alarming rate.

Riley reached into the bag where they carried their drug supply and pulled out a container of epinephrine and inserted a needle, drawing the drug out quickly. He then inserted the needle just under the skin on Mr. Swanson's forearm.

"Carrier, start an IV with diphenhydramene."

While Carrier busily pulled the supplies and prepared to insert the IV, Riley continued watching for a response to the drug he'd administered. Mr. Swanson's breathing had eased slightly but then tightened up again after only a moment or two. Riley immediately administered more of the epinephrine.

He was relieved when he began to see a more positive response, as Mr. Swanson's breathing eased.

The group, including Riley's dad, watched the entire process with rapt attention. The tension in the room eased when Mr. Swanson's breathing started to loosen.

Riley and Carrier had begun preparations to transport him when Mr. Swanson took a strained but deep breath. He tried to open his eyes, which were still only slits, as the swelling was receding slowly. He peered first at Carrier and then turning his head, looked at Riley, taking in Riley's uniform with a quick glance.

"What happened?" he managed as he weakly held his hand up and looked at the IV.

"You had anaphylaxisa—a severe allergic reaction to shellfish," Riley stated in a matter-of-fact tone.

At that moment, Jeremy and the Engine Five crew came through the conference room door with the gurney, rolling it between the large leather conference chairs and a credenza, maneuvering as close to the patient as space allowed.

"We've administered epinephrine and diphenhydramene, which has helped with the swelling and constriction of your airway, but we need to get you to the hospital," Riley said, moving to make way for the gurney.

"There's no need for the hospital," Douglas spluttered. "I've got work to do. We're in a meeting."

Grimes and Carrier lifted Mr. Swanson onto the gurney and covered him with a blanket before pulling the straps into place.

"Dad, you're going to the hospital," Lyle stated firmly, stepping to the gurney's side. "Don't worry. We'll save some work for you."

Focused on Mr. Swanson, Riley didn't think about Jeremy being there until he glanced up and intercepted a glare his dad was sending in Jeremy's direction. Riley could tell it bothered Jeremy, but Jeremy simply moved toward the door before Riley's dad could say anything.

"Lyle, we're taking him to Abernathy Memorial. We'll meet you there," Riley said quickly as he zipped up the last bag and stood.

Lyle nodded and moved to follow them.

Gathering the bags, Riley started to follow the gurney and other firefighters when his dad spoke.

"Riley."

Riley turned and was surprised to see what he thought might be admiration in his dad's eyes.

"Thank you, son."

Riley gave a small smile and quick nod before turning to follow the gurney. Lyle followed, a few steps behind.

RILEY PONDERED THE INTERACTION with his dad as he walked to the back of the ambulance. He began placing the medical bags in the storage compartments as Jeremy oversaw the loading of the gurney carrying Mr. Swanson into the ambulance.

Closing the door as Riley rounded the back of the ambulance, Jeremy leaned close so only Riley could hear. "I was right again."

"About what?" Riley asked, shoving the last bag into its compartment and heading toward the driver's door.

"About you. That couldn't have been easy. First day as lead and in front of all those people you know? Especially your dad. But you handled it like a pro. Good job."

"I . . . well . . . I'm just glad it went well. And hey, sorry about that with my dad." Riley indicated the second floor with his chin.

A dejected look crossed Jeremy's face, but he still shrugged good-naturedly and turned to walk to the engine.

Riley tried not to smile at what Jeremy had said but couldn't help it as he climbed in and started the siren.

ALLARD STOOD AT THE door of the conference room. He watched the receding back of his son as Riley wove his way through the staff that had gathered, acknowledging their numerous pats on the back with a simple nod. The Abernathy Fire Rescue logo emblazoned on the back of Riley's shirt seemed to lay claim to him, mocking Ballard with its possession.

He looked over his shoulder at the spot on the floor where his longtime friend and business partner, Douglas Swanson, had lain, the scene replaying vividly in Ballard's mind.

Douglas hadn't been able to breathe and had struggled for each precious gasp of air. Ballard and Lyle had done what they could, but thank goodness for Marian's presence of mind to call 9-1-1.

It seemed like it had taken forever for help to arrive, and when it did, it had been Riley. Ballard shook his head and stroked his chin thoughtfully, remembering Riley's uniform, the medical bags he carried, and his son's air of command. Watching Riley work, Ballard had felt like he was seeing Riley, *really* seeing his son for the first time.

When Douglas had begun breathing easier, Ballard remembered exhaling in relief and looking again with wonder at his son, who handled the situation so calmly.

Ballard was amazed. No, he was stunned. His son had just saved his partner's life. As he did, he'd brought a calmness that permeated the entire room.

When Douglas had objected to going to the hospital, Ballard was glad Lyle had stepped in to handle his father's objections. Was *he* like that? Ballard wondered. Was work above everything else for him, even his health, and had he been guilty of wanting the same for Riley? If so, after what he'd just witnessed, he'd been very wrong.

"Rather impressive, wouldn't you say?" Marian asked as she came to stand by Ballard, watching Riley and the others turn the corner and out of sight.

"Hmmmm?" Ballard asked, distracted by his thoughts.

"I said that was pretty impressive. You should be proud. Riley just saved Douglas' life."

"Oh, yes . . . of course. I am . . . I am very proud." Ballard cut a quick glance toward Marian and cleared his throat.

He *was* proud of what he'd just witnessed. He'd thought Riley would get the fire service out of his system and come to realize he belonged at the firm, but Ballard realized now he might have misjudged Riley.

He felt a new feeling swirling around inside. He wasn't quite sure what it was—sadness, loss? Maybe it was a newfound pride and understanding of his son. Whatever it was, the feeling was strong and growing stronger.

T HE NEXT EVENING, RILEY sat at his workstation at Electronix Doc. The workday had long since ended, but working with his hands helped him think. And he had a lot to think about.

Time was passing, and he still hadn't been able to get Jeremy to talk to him. He was trying not to pressure him, but Riley hated seeing Allie so gloomy and out of sorts. It was the complete opposite of her normal outgoing and sunny self. He and Jeremy had been alone together several times in the ambulance, but the right time never seemed to come for that kind of conversation. Riley had contemplated several different ways to try and start the conversation but none he thought would work.

Riley was musing over yet another approach when he noticed Winston turn off his office light and start toward the door.

"Riley, what are you doing here so late? I thought everyone was long gone." Winston strode over and put a hand on Riley's shoulder.

Riley straightened and stretched his back.

"This old stereo has me intrigued. I want to get it crooning again," Riley said, looking up at Winston with a slight shrug. "I just have a thing for old vinyl, you know?"

"As do I. As do I," Winston said, taking the stool next to Riley's. He leaned over to get a closer look at the section where Riley was working and let out a low whistle.

"Now that's some antique technology. I haven't seen vacuum tubes in years," Winston said, lowering his glasses and leaning over to get a closer look.

"And luckily, all are intact. The problem seems to be the wiring," Riley said, holding up some frayed wires connected to the console. It will take a little bit of time, but these can definitely be replaced, and then we should be in business."

Winston leaned back and gave Riley an appraising look.

"You've really got a real knack for this, Riley. I'm sure glad to have you on board."

"Thank you. I'm glad to be here," Riley said distractedly.

"Something bothering you, son?" Winston asked, his brows furrowing with concern.

Riley sighed. He set his tools down and turned to Winston. "Yes, there is. And actually, it may be something you can help me with. Do you have just a minute or two?"

"I've got nothing but time," Winston said, leaning an elbow on the worktable. "What's up?"

"You know Jeremy Ennis, one of my best friends from high school, right?"

Winston nodded. "Of course I do. Seems like there were three of you, right? Cade Marshall was the third in the trio."

"That you are. Great memory!"

"I'm not in my dotage yet I'll have you know," Winston said with mock severity.

"That never crossed my mind," Riley said with a chuckle. He quickly switched to a more somber tone. "I found out a few weeks ago that Jeremy and my sister, Allie, had started dating while I was away at school. But he broke it off with her suddenly and says now he probably won't get married—ever. When Cade and I both press him on it, he gets defensive and clams up.

"I really don't understand it, and Jeremy absolutely won't talk about it. And believe me, I've tried. I haven't pushed him, but I've tried to bring it up several times. He just says we'll think he's crazy and says nothing. From what Jeremy said before and from what Allie has said, they are really crazy about each other so none of what he's said or done makes sense."

Riley took a breath and picked up one of the tiny screwdrivers laying on the workbench and began twirling it between his fingers. The soft hum of the florescent lights buzzed overhead.

"I promised Allie I'd find out what Jeremy has on his mind, but I'm getting nowhere. Do you have any suggestions?"

"And you have no idea what it could be?"

"None. I wish I did. And another thing. Though it may sound silly, this is really out of character for Jeremy. He gave Cade his lucky rabbit's foot. I know that may not sound like a big deal, but his grandfather gave that rabbit's foot to him way back when he was just a kid. Jeremy swore he'd never part with it. But out of the blue, he gave it to Cade for good luck on a job interview. It's even stranger because it was something special between him and his grandfather. And his grandfather just passed away a few months ago. I'm coming up empty for an explanation, and my sister is about ready to explode," Riley sighed, shaking his head.

Winston studied Riley, who seemed lost in thought, before standing. He jammed his hands in his pockets and started pacing slowly.

Riley watched him for several minutes before Winston finally came to a stop and climbed back on the stool he'd just vacated.

"This is quite a mind bender. I can see why it's bothering you. It sounds like there's something deeply troubling Jeremy, and it's something so deep and so personal he's reluctant to talk about it—even with his two best friends. Riley, I honestly don't think you're going to get Jeremy to talk about it until he's ready. It probably won't hurt to ask him once in a while, but it's better for it to come from him voluntarily. I know that's not what Allie wants to hear, but I believe patience will have its own reward in this case. Just give him a little more time."

Riley nodded. "I was kinda thinking along those same lines, but it's good to hear you think the same. I can't blame Allie for being impatient, but this is all so unlike Jeremy. I know he has to have a good reason, but he's sure not making things easy right now."

Winston nodded thoughtfully and stood. He patted Riley on the back and turned to leave.

"Don't work too late, son," he said as he started toward the door. "We can see how that stereo croons tomorrow."

Riley chuckled. "Yes sir, but I plan to have it working before I leave tonight. Thanks for listening and for the advice."

"Not sure how much good it was but sometimes a second opinion can help confirm what you're already thinking. See you tomorrow," Winston said over his shoulder. He paused and turned as he got to the door.

"Riley, whatever is bothering Jeremy, it may be that he's just afraid to say it out loud. Sometimes the things that scare us the most are the things that are the hardest to talk about."

Riley stared at Winston for several long seconds before Winston finally walked out, quietly pulling the door closed behind him.

Riley sat deep in thought for several minutes, realizing that statement summed Jeremy up over the past few weeks. Not afraid—Jeremy was never afraid—but haunted; haunted by something only he knew. But what could that be?

Riley stared at the stereo and its pieces on the worktable in front of him. Why couldn't life be as simple as putting pieces back together so everything worked again? That's what Riley wanted. He wanted things back together and working again—he and Maggie back together, Jeremy and Allie back together, and a partner or a new job, or even both, for Cade. The most frustrating thing was that all of it was totally out of his control. For him, nothing could be more frustrating.

He picked up his tools and started replacing the stereo's frayed wiring as his mind continued to turn. What seemed like a short while, but actually two and a half hours later, Riley plugged the stereo in and dropped a record onto the turntable. He placed the needle carefully onto the record and suddenly, Andy Williams' smooth voice rolled out of the speakers in perfect, rich stereo.

Satisfied, Riley smiled and leaned back, crossing his arms on top of his head. At least that was one thing he could put back together again.

CADE PULLED INTO THE gym's parking lot. He had arranged for the Roadrunners to play a scrimmage tonight against a team a year or two older to give them some intense competition in preparation for next weekend's tournament. He'd invited Jeremy and Riley to the tournament, and they'd promised to come, as long as they weren't on shift.

Cade was still trying to figure out what was going on with Jeremy. His moping around was getting worse, and it felt out of character for him. He and Riley were both trying to talk to him, but nothing was getting through. They weren't giving up.

Cade brought his mind back to tonight's game. The Roadrunners' practices had been going really well, so he was anxious to see how they fared playing a little older team. These little guys were working hard, and Cade had been looking forward to this all afternoon. No matter the kind of day he'd had with Crawford, these guys' enthusiasm and excitement always re-energized him.

Cade sat in his truck, downing the quick meal he'd grabbed on the way and was checking emails when his phone buzzed with a text. When he opened it, his heart sped up. It was from HR.

Officer Marshall, we have reviewed your application for the high school resource officer position and would like to schedule an interview with you and the school's principal. Please respond with which of the following times on this date work best for you. Congratulations. I look forward to hearing back from you at your earliest convenience.

He quickly checked his calendar for the August 17th date, which was just a few days away. He was happy to see that he was actually off duty that day. He picked the last time slot available, hoping to be the last and most memorable candidate. He texted HR back with his availability and selected time and then breathed a happy sigh when he received their confirmation in return.

He did a silent fist pump as an excited smile spread from ear to ear. He cleared his throat and tried to get serious, but the smile just wouldn't go away. He shrugged. Oh well, he had a lot to be happy about.

He swallowed the last bite of his burger and was about to open his truck's door when he saw a truck that looked a lot like Crawford's pull into a parking space a few rows over. Curious, Cade waited to see who got out.

When Crawford stepped out, Cade's mouth dropped open. He watched as Crawford scanned the lot as if making sure no one was watching before striding quickly toward the gym's side entrance.

Cade waited until Crawford had entered the gym before getting out of his truck and retrieving his gym bag. Cade entered the front door as he usually did and breathed in the smell of stale sweat, popcorn, and rubber. The squeaks from tennis shoes on the court and the thump of basketballs bouncing or hitting backboards made a welcoming cacophony of noise. He walked to the bleachers where some of the parents and boys were already gathered. He bantered back and forth with them while waiting for the rest of team. Cade scanned the gym a few times looking for Crawford. But he never saw him again that night.

The game had been surprisingly intense. While the Roadrunners didn't win, they didn't lose by much. Cade was pleased at how well they'd played against the older boys. It definitely boded well for their chances against boys of their own age in the tournament.

Cade's team followed him back to the bench and gathered around him, after shaking hands with the other team at center court. He could tell they were disappointed.

"Men," he began, "we might not have had the highest score tonight, but your outstanding effort throughout the entire game—the *entire* game—was a major victory. The tournament coming up is our opportunity to show everyone that the Roadrunners are in the house! Right?"

"Right!" the team shouted back, their sweaty faces starting to brighten.

"Listen closely, Runners." Cade lowered his voice to draw the team closer.

"I'm excited not just about the tournament, but I'm excited about how each and every one of you have practiced hard and worked hard to get here. You, gentlemen, are what it's all about. I am proud—*very* proud—to be a Roadrunner!"

Cade stuck his hand in the middle of the circle, their hands piling on top.

"Runners on three. One. Two. Three. Runners!"

AFTER GETTING HOME THAT night, Cade texted Riley and Jeremy:

Got an interview. Tuesday at 4.

He chuckled when they both immediately responded with cele-bratory memes and thumbs up emojis.

Cade grabbed a drink from the refrigerator and plopped down on the sofa. He took a deep breath and ran his fingers through his hair. He was excited about the upcoming interview but nervous too. Possible interview questions went through his mind as he began to formulate potential answers. He tried not to get too excited as his mind drifted to the opportunities being a campus resource officer might bring. From counseling troubled students to improved safety measures for the entire campus, the possibilities seemed endless. He was ready to get started. But first, he had to get the job.

He pulled Jeremy's rabbit's foot out of his pocket and rolled its silky fur between his fingers. He put his arm behind his head and leaned his head back, thinking about Jeremy's moodiness and wondering at its cause. He also thought about Riley feeling down after Maggie's move. His friends were having some hard times right now. But then sometimes, life was just hard. He saw enough of that on the streets.

Cade sighed and picked up his can from the coffee table and took a drink. He missed the three of them hanging out and hoped everything could, somehow, be resolved soon—for everyone's sake.

JEREMY HAD BEEN DRIVING around aimlessly for most of the morning after getting off shift. He had met his mom for lunch, her trying to pick up where the conversation in the shop with his dad had left off, but Jeremy steered it away to more neutral topics. The concerned look on her face throughout lunch had bothered him. He'd never been good at hiding things from his mom.

After lunch, Jeremy was left at loose ends for the rest of the day. He'd spent a few hours at the shop but couldn't really get into any of the projects he had going. He unlocked the apartment door and flipped on one of the lights. The apartment was empty and quiet. Cade was coaching his basketball team and wouldn't be back until later. Jeremy attempted a grin. He hoped those boys survived Cade's rigorous training for the tournament. The faint rumble of a bass that one of the neighbors was playing drifted through the apartment wall.

Jeremy threw his keys on the side table with a clang and then plopped unceremoniously onto the sofa and rubbed his temples. That glare from Mr. Sullivan across the conference room last shift was still bothering him. Not that it wasn't warranted. He knew it was certainly deserved, but Jeremy just wished things were different. He really liked Riley and Allie's parents. He should tell them, he thought for the thousandth time, and get them to understand. Especially Allie. He really needed them to understand, especially when he could feel the impending gloom of Grandpa Mars' prediction bearing down.

The TV was supposed to be his only company for the night, and it wasn't even on. The big black box mocked the darkness of his mood from the wall. There was no one to hang out with tonight. Riley was with his family for their weekly dinner together. Jeremy could just imagine how that conversation was going.

Jeremy sighed and leaned back, putting his hands behind his head, closing his eyes and setting his feet on the coffee table. He missed Allie. He really missed her. The evenings were lonely without her. She always knew what to say to get his mind off of a rough call or she would bring over one of his favorites for dinner or text him during the day with a just saying hi or thinking of you. She could always make him laugh, and right now, he needed a good laugh.

Being with the guys and at the station was helping more than they'd ever know. The station was the only place he didn't really feel alone, even though he shared an apartment with Cade. Happy-go-lucky, go-with-the-flow Cade. Jeremy was envious. The only time Cade seemed down was when he came off a shift with Crawford. Jeremy grunted. That would put anyone in a bad mood.

Out of habit, he felt in his pocket for his lucky rabbit's foot, but his pocket was empty. He missed that too, but he'd done the right thing giving it to Cade. Cade just had to get that job.

He felt a little hungry, but not enough to get up and fix something or even order something to be delivered. He just felt like sitting here. The longer he went without Allie, the more uncertain of things he became. Was the situation really as hopeless as his grandfather had said? He wished he'd been wiser and had had more of his wits about him to ask important questions when his grandfather told him what lay ahead. But now, it was too late.

Jeremy picked up his phone but laid it back down on the sofa. Allie would be at her parents' place. And besides, he couldn't just call her out of the blue, not after breaking up with her. He regretted having to do that more than anything, but he'd done it for her sake, and now, he had to be strong about it. He hadn't meant for them to date. It hadn't started out that way, but it had somehow evolved. And, after he'd realized he'd fallen in love with her, it was too late.

His stomach physically clenched at the thought. For a so-called tough guy, he felt the unfamiliar prick of tears. Life didn't feel fair, and this fact was becoming all too clear.

His mind wondered, and he must have fallen asleep because the next thing he knew the apartment lights were on and Cade was banging around in the kitchen.

"What time is it?" Jeremy asked, picking up his phone and trying to make out the time.

Cade rounded the corner, a sandwich in one hand and can of soda in the other.

"It's nine. What are you doing sitting here in the dark?" Cade asked, taking a bite of his sandwich as he sat down. He studied Jeremy as he chewed.

"Guess I fell asleep. How was practice?"

"Awesome! They're going to be great in the tournament. I just know it."

Jeremy nodded and yawned.

Cade took a drink from his soda. Placing it on the coffee table, he leaned over and looked at Jeremy closely.

"What gives, Jeremy? You've been moping around for weeks now, ever since you broke up with Allie. If you didn't want to break up with her, why did you? And if it was a mistake, fix it! I have it on good authority she's just as mopey as you are. And for some reason I can't understand, she's still crazy about you."

He leaned back and took another bite of his sandwich, his eyes locked on Jeremy.

Uncomfortable, Jeremy looked away. If Cade was offering him advice, he *was* a basket case.

"It's complicated," Jeremy began.

"Yeah, you've said that before. So explain it to me then. I'll listen slowly."

Jeremy rolled his eyes and stood.

"I'm hungry," he said as he headed to the kitchen.

"There's not much left," Cade said around a mouthful.

"Then I think I'll just go to bed," Jeremy said, walking into the hallway.

"It's not going to go away, Jer," Cade said, standing and moving between Jeremy and the hallway, forcing Jeremy to look at him. "Whatever is bothering you, it's only festering, and it won't get better until you meet it head on or talk about it with somebody. Riley and I are your best friends. You know you can talk to us about anything. We want to help."

Jeremy's shoulders slumped. "I know, and I appreciate it, but I just don't want to talk about it. Maybe soon, but not yet."

Cade nodded, then moved aside to let Jeremy pass. "I'll be asking again, you know."

Jeremy acknowledged the statement with a glance and walked down the hall.

Cade went back to the living room and turned the TV on as he plopped into his chair.

Jeremy lay down on his bed, wide awake, noise from the TV drifting in through the door. He had way too much time to think. Too much time to dread the inevitable.

RILEY STUDIED MR. THORNTON worriedly. He didn't look good. His breathing was quick and shallow. Mr. Thornton wiped his mouth with his napkin before laying it beside his still mostly full plate. Riley set his iced tea glass on the table, catching Joanne's worried look as she cleared their plates.

"Great dinner, Joanne," Mr. Thornton said.

"Thank you, Mr. T."

"I have to admit," Riley added, "I don't think I've ever tasted better fried catfish, and the hush puppies were definitely the best I've ever had."

"It's Mr. T's favorite meal so I fix it a lot. Practice makes perfect as they say," she said. She looked down at Mr. Thornton's plate. "But Mr. T, you sure didn't eat very much."

Mr. Thornton waved her away as she continued clearing the table.

"Well, I think your cooking has reached perfection. And thank you for the dinner invitation. This evening is a special treat," Riley said, draining the last of his iced tea.

"Young Riley, we enjoy having you," Mr. Thornton said as he stood, pushing his chair back and reaching for his walker. "Let's have dessert in the den."

Riley stood and pulled the walker close for Mr. Thornton and then followed him to a room toward the back of the house. The den was small, with a fireplace on one wall and two worn but inviting overstuffed chairs in front of it, a small table between them.

"Have a seat, Riley. That fire feels good to these old bones."

The fire popped and crackled loudly as if to reply.

Coffee cups rattled as Joanne carried in a tray with two cups and a thermal pitcher of coffee. Riley took the second chair and reached to pour, handing a cup to Mr. Thornton, who blew on his coffee then took a tentative sip.

They sat quietly in front of the fire for several minutes, Mr. Thornton coughing periodically. Joanne brought in plates, with a large slice of fresh-baked apple pie and dollop of ice cream on each. Mr. Thornton took a couple of bites before setting his plate on the table between them. Riley ate his pie and ice cream as Mr. Thornton uncharacteristically stared silently into the fire.

"Mr. Thornton," Riley asked, putting his empty plate on the table. "Are you okay?"

Mr. Thornton started, seemingly surprised Riley was there. He looked over and nodded.

"Having a little hard time breathing tonight, Young Riley, but all things considered, doing pretty well."

Riley sipped his coffee and looked away from Mr. Thornton for a moment and took in the comfortable room. Ornately framed pictures of a smiling couple in various locales, their ages progressing from young to elderly, graced the fireplace mantel. Richly stained bookcases lined another wall, their shelves filled with finely bound volumes along with a scattering of paperbacks. A worn afghan lay across a footstool in front of a chair in one corner, a basket filled with balls of yarn, two knitting needles stuck in them, beside it. A glass display case stood on the wall opposite the bookshelves, but it was the Christmas tree in the corner, next to the case, where Riley's eye stopped. It was only half decorated—a few ornaments here and there but nothing else. It was early September.

When he looked back, he caught Mr. Thornton watching him. Embarrassed to be caught staring, Riley shifted uncomfortably.

"Sorry, sir. I didn't mean to stare but your Christmas tree caught my eye."

Mr. Thornton nodded slowly, his voice drifting into a sad tone.

"We were decorating the tree that night," he finally said. "My Martha and I. That was the night she had a heart attack. Right over there."

His thin finger pointed shakily toward the corner where the Christmas tree stood. "The paramedics tried, but they said it was a massive attack. She was gone only a few minutes after she collapsed. Worst night of my life."

Mr. Thornton stared back into the fire. "I just haven't had the heart, or the will, to pack the ornaments away or take the tree down. It was the last thing Martha and I got to do together. I figure if I want to leave it up as it was that night, that's okay. What do you think?"

Riley cleared his throat. "Mr. Thornton, if it brings you comfort, then absolutely, leave it where it is. I see nothing wrong with it."

"Thank you, son. Hearing you say that does my old heart good." Mr. Thornton beamed.

"Joanne!" he called out, startling Riley. "Young Riley here agrees with me about the tree. What do you think of that?"

Joanne came in, putting her hands on her hips and pinning Riley with a teasing look.

"Did he, now? Why am I not surprised?" she said with a low chuckle before straightening a pillow at Mr. Thornton's back. "I knew you'd be recruiting his support as soon as you adjourned to this room. I think Mrs. T would be fussing at you for leaving it up but then I also think she'd be mighty touched by the reasons why. You are a cantankerous soul, but still a dear."

She laughed as Riley and Mr. Thornton chuckled with her.

"How are things going with your gal? Have you talked to her yet?" Mr. Thornton asked, turning to Riley.

Riley groaned. "No, sir. Whenever I think I've got enough time off between the station and Electronix Doc, I'm asked to help with an install or someone is needing a shift covered at the station. Something always seems to come up. But I have been sending her texts letting her know I'm thinking of her. I figure that's a good first step, right?"

Riley grimaced. His excuses and reasoning sounded feeble in his own ears.

Mr. Thornton eyed Riley closely. "Well, seems to me if you really loved that little gal, you'd *make* the time to go, one way or another."

Riley started to protest but then stopped. He knew Mr. Thornton was right.

"I'm just speaking from my perspective, Riley, which is quite a few years older than yours. I know you'll go when the time is right. Just don't let fear stop you."

"I never said I was afraid," Riley protested, more strongly than he'd intended.

"Ah, I can see that," Mr. Thornton said, raising his hands in surrender before a coughing fit seized him. Riley started to get up, but Mr. Thornton waved him off. After a few minutes, Mr. Thornton went on, his voice weaker. Riley leaned forward, straining to hear.

"I just encourage you not to wait too long, Riley. If you love her as you say, you don't want to risk losing her to someone else. I bet she's really pretty and pretty girls always attract young men. It's like bees drawn to nectar."

Mr. Thornton stopped talking, his breathing labored. He studied Riley thoughtfully for several long seconds before turning his gaze to the fire. Riley's glance went back to and lingered on the photos of the smiling couple on the mantel before his gaze drifted to the fire as he sat deep in thought.

Focused, Maggie and Jenna Jacobs leaned over Maggie's desk, studying a set of marketing campaign storyboards. This particular campaign was coming together really well and their animated discussion was succeeding in bringing the last pieces together.

"I'm loving this, Maggie!" Jenna said, lifting one of the boards and scrutinizing it closely. "I think we're going to knock this one out of the park." She laid the board back on Maggie's desk as Maggie nodded with a broad smile.

"I couldn't agree more. I think this is some of our best work yet." Maggie didn't add that this was the type of work she'd been hired to do and wanted to do. It felt good to finally work on something familiar and that she felt confident doing. Connor had insisted she work mainly on specific high-end campaigns that focused on products she didn't know or hadn't even heard of. It made planning an appealing marketing program extremely difficult. It didn't put her work in a positive light, and her frustration was building.

Satisfied with the first board, Maggie and Jenna were moving to the second when an obviously frantic Connor darted into the doorway. He stopped short when he saw Jenna as both ladies looked up.

"Connor?" Maggie asked, straightening. "Is everything okay?"

Almost breathless, the usually composed Connor said, "No. No, it's not. Klondike just called. They want to meet in two hours."

"What?" Maggie exclaimed, taking a step back. "We're not supposed to meet with them for another two weeks. We've got preliminary research done but nothing concrete. And certainly nothing solid enough to present. Can't you postpone the meeting?'

Connor's face turned a mottled red. "Don't you think I asked?" he huffed. "They said it has to be today. They have a high-level executive who surprised them by coming in and since he's leaving the country for a month, he wants to make sure this campaign is off the ground before he leaves."

Jenna looked wide-eyed between them. "Is there something I can do to help?" she asked breathlessly.

"Yes, please. Go tell Josh we need him in here asap to start pulling as much together as possible. And then get everyone on the campaign team in the conference room. We need all hands on deck," Maggie said, starting to pull files.

Jenna rushed past Connor on her way out.

"Conference room in ten," Connor said as he turned and hurried back down the hall.

Two hours later, Maggie was cramming everything she needed into her briefcase.

"Ready?"

Connor stood in her office doorway, anxiously shifting back and forth. He was impeccably dressed, and his usually stoic but handsome face was creased with worry.

"Just one more minute." Maggie grabbed her phone, pushing it down into the side of her briefcase before picking up her purse.

"Ready," she said, almost breathless. Since Connor was rarely this uptight, Maggie was flustered as he hovered nervously at her door.

"Great," Connor said as they hurried down the hall to the reception area and the front doors just beyond. Maggie was practically running to keep up with him.

The team had done amazing work in the two hours they'd had, but the determining factor of success was always the client presentation. Maggie tried to take a deep breath. She had her work cut out for her to calm Connor down on the drive to the client's office.

"We'll review the presentation on the way over. It's good, but I thought we had time to do a few more tweaks. You're my back-up so I'm counting on you for the details," Connor said over his shoulder.

Maggie's breath caught. "I thought Josh was coming. He did the majority of the research," she said breathlessly as she hurried beside him.

"No," Connor snapped. "I mean, I need him at the office to work on another big project that just came up. It's you and me on this." Connor pushed the glass door open for Maggie.

Maggie turned to the receptionist. "We'll be back in a couple of hours."

"No, probably not," Connor corrected. "We'll be back midafternoon at the earliest."

Maggie was puzzled. This meeting shouldn't take that long, but Connor was the boss, and this was an important client meeting so of course, she had to defer to him.

"We need to hurry, Maggie. We're going to be late," Connor said, rushing her toward the parking garage as the lobby doors swung closed behind them.

RILEY HATED THE CITY, with its cramped downtown streets and even more cramped parking garages. After too many one-way streets and wrong turns, he'd finally found the address for Maggie's office building Jeremy had gotten for him from Mr. Rawlings. Riley found the underground parking garage and after making several frustrating circles through four levels, finally found an empty space to park.

Riley was anxious to see Maggie but wondered if she would be glad to see him. Taking a few deep breaths, he grabbed the flowers he'd brought off the seat and headed toward the bank of elevators.

Ignoring the countryside rolling by on either side of the highway, Riley had used the two-hour drive to think. He'd already decided what he was going to say and then rehearsed it. He'd never had to think about what to say to Maggie before. Conversation had always flowed so easily between them—at least until the past several months. He had to take ownership of that fact.

Riley realized now, he'd gotten so busy with the fire academy and then joining the department, that he'd practically ignored Maggie. Or even worse, taken her for granted. He knew he loved her and wanted to spend the rest of his life with her, but Mr. Thornton was right. Riley needed to tell her that and make his feelings plain.

Stopping on the first floor to check the directory, he found the floor he needed and waited for another elevator. Several women exited the elevator when it stopped, some eying Riley appreciatively. Oblivious, he waited, clutching the bouquet tightly. He was the only one to step onto the empty elevator. After punching the button for the floor he needed, he took a few more deep breaths, bouncing on his toes as the elevator quickly rose.

Stepping off the elevator, Riley looked quickly to his left and then to his right and saw the double glass doors of Mantovia Marketing. A large, curved receptionist desk with a white marble top was just inside. The well-appointed lobby to the right with its richly upholstered chairs, upscale artwork, and stylish accessories was impressive.

The doors swished open and the receptionist looked up to see Riley approaching. The practiced smile on her lips quickly gave way to a genuinely warm and welcoming one when she saw him.

"Good morning," she said in a smooth voice, her eyes sliding to the flowers Riley held. "How may I help you?"

Riley cleared his throat. "I'd like to see Maggie Rawlings please."

A slight frown furrowed the receptionist's brows.

"I'm so sorry. Maggie just left for a meeting out of the office. We don't expect her back until later this afternoon."

Riley's smile faltered as his heart sank.

"Oh," he managed, trying not to sound as dejected as he felt.

"I'd be glad to give her a message or you can leave one for her if you'd like."

"That'd be great," Riley said, laying the flowers on the counter. "Do you have a pen and paper I could use please?"

She handed a pen and a few sheets of paper to Riley, and he stepped to one end of the broad sweep of the counter, trying to think of what he should say.

While Riley stood deep in thought, a lady came from an office beyond the receptionist area and waited while the receptionist took a call.

"Brenda, have you seen Connor?" the lady asked the receptionist when the call was over. "I have some contracts he needs to sign before end of day."

Before Brenda could answer, another lady walking up overheard the question.

"He's not here. He and Maggie just left together—again."

Riley's ears pricked up as he heard Maggie's name, but he tried to act as if he hadn't overheard the comments.

"Those two spend more time together than I spend with my own husband," the first lady said. "You think they've got something going on outside the office too?"

"I wouldn't be a bit surprised. It's no secret Connor is giving her a lot of assignments a more tenured person should be handling. But hey, he's the boss."

Brenda, looking between Riley, struggling to maintain a look of calm disinterest among the ladies intent on their gossip. She quickly interrupted. "They've left for a meeting at Klondike's and said they'd be back midafternoon." She brought attention to Riley with a jerk of her head.

The group belatedly noticed Riley and the flowers laying on the counter.

Riley's eyes narrowed and his face grew hot at the whispers and stifled giggles he overheard as the group scattered. Wanting to leave as quickly as possible, Riley hurriedly wrote, *Miss you. R.*

He folded the note and placed it among the flowers before handing the pen back.

"Would you please make sure these get to Maggie?" he asked, handing the flowers to the receptionist.

"Of course. I'm sorry about that," she said, taking the flowers with a nod toward where the other ladies had disappeared.

"No worries. Thank you."

Riley pushed open the glass door with a strong shove and punched the elevator button quickly several times, waiting impatiently. Several of the ladies had returned quickly to the front desk as he left, many watching him with open curiosity. He'd thought the elevator must have gotten lost but the bell finally and mercifully dinged, announcing its arrival. The doors opened.

He couldn't leave this building or get out of Dallas fast enough. What had he been thinking?

IT WAS A LITTLE before five when Maggie pushed the button for Mantovia Marketing's floor as Connor loosened his tie. He'd insisted on going to a late lunch for which Maggie had had no appetite.

The meeting had gone terribly. She'd fumbled several requests from Connor for data Josh had compiled but she'd had no access to prior to the meeting. While Josh had graciously emailed everything to her, the sheer volume kept her from being able to provide what Connor had requested in front of the clients. She sighed quietly as the elevator rose. She'd tried to convince Connor to let Josh come to the meeting, but Connor had firmly said no.

When the elevator doors opened, they stepped onto their floor and Connor reached to open the glass door.

"Take a few minutes and then let's meet in the conference room in fifteen," Connor said as he unbuttoned the top button of his shirt. "We need to work on this while everything is still fresh." He didn't stop but continued walking down the hall toward his office. He didn't look back or wait for a reply from Maggie.

Exhausted, Maggie walked into her office. Connor was not pleased with how things had gone, and neither was she. She appreciated the opportunities Connor was giving her, but she wasn't ready for some of these higher-level meetings that he insisted she attend. She'd tried to tell him many times, but he didn't seem to listen.

The flowers in the middle of her desk caught her eye immediately. Setting aside her briefcase and purse, she picked them up and held them close, smelling the intoxicating aroma of the pink roses—her favorite—plentifully scattered among the other flowers. A piece of paper caught her eye, and she pulled it out, laying the flowers aside.

Miss you. R.

Maggie's breath caught, and she sat down heavily in her chair. Riley had been here.

She groaned at a quick knock on her door. She needed at least a few minutes away from Connor.

Looking up, she was surprised to see Brenda.

"I wanted to make sure you got the flowers okay," Brenda said with a small smile. "I'm sorry you missed the guy who brought them. He was really nice."

Surprised, Maggie asked, "Why are you apologizing?"

"Not apologizing exactly. He just looked so disappointed," Brenda said. "I felt sorry for him."

Speechless, Maggie looked at Brenda blankly.

"Well, have a good evening. I'll lock the front door," Brenda said. She was gone before Maggie could reply.

Maggie picked up the flowers and held them close again. Riley had come. Suddenly, not interested in spending another minute in the office, or with Connor, she cradled the flowers in one arm, picked her purse up with the other and walked quickly out.

CADE WAITED IMPATIENTLY IN the lobby of the high school principal's office, his right leg pumping nervously. He knew he was the fourth and last candidate to interview. He looked around while he waited. The principal's office looked much the same as it had when he, Riley, and Jeremy had been in school. Everything looked a little older and a bit more worn, understandably. The large wood counter attested to years of use with its scratches and nicks. It held baskets of papers, stacks of fliers, and copies of the school newsletter. It even held a couple of black and gold pom poms, which probably belonged to the girl he could hear talking in an office a few doors down the hall to his left. From the conversation, it sounded like she was talking to the school's cheerleader sponsor about plans for the upcoming year.

The walls held several pieces of framed artwork painted by some of the better art students over the years. A large flat screen hanging in one corner, currently showed blank schedules and an interactive map with teacher's names and a color code for each so that a teacher's location could be determined in real time. Cade nodded appreciatively. That was a new security measure, and he made mental note. The school's black and gold colors were used generously throughout the office. A new school year was an exciting time, expectations and excitement always ran high, and Cade could tell everything was gearing up.

He took a breath and shifted in the uncomfortable, wooden chair. He grinned to himself, thinking what it had felt like sitting in this same spot not too many years ago when he'd been in trouble. When they'd *all* been in trouble.

As football team captains and representing the team, they had sat in this very office their senior year. The team had painted the football goal posts of their arch nemesis, the Crandall Cavaliers, a patchwork of obnoxious neon colors. It was an annual challenge. Whoever won the yearly rivalry game got to paint the other team's goal posts in colors of their choice. Unfortunately for the Abernathy Bobcats, that particular year was when the principals of the two schools had decided to crack down on the tradition. As a result, the entire Bobcats team had to work after school to buy the paint and then another couple of after school sessions to paint the posts back to their official white. Cade grinned. It had been worth it though. The picture of the team beneath their goal post artwork was awesome and had made it into both towns' newspapers.

The door to the principal's office finally swung open, and Principal Whitman strode out, extending his hand to Cade.

"Officer Marshall, please come in."

Cade smiled and stood, shaking Principal Whitman's hand firmly.

"Good afternoon, Mr. Whitman. I appreciate this opportunity."

Principal Whitman gestured for Cade to follow him to his office then closed the door behind them.

"Take a seat, Officer," Principal Whitman said. He seated himself behind the large oak desk Cade remembered from the last time he sat in this spot. Mr. Whitman had added some personal touches but the office still looked basically the same as it had for years with its half-dead ivy plant on the window sill, the filing cabinets with more files stacked on top than likely inside, and the scattering of notebooks, sheets of paper, and post-it notes of all colors scattered in an array on the desk. A small banker's lamp was centered at the top of the desk, its small circle of light pooling on the worn wood.

"We appreciate your interest in the resource officer position with Abernathy High School. Let's get straight to it," Principal Whitman said. "I want to get past the typical information on a resume. Tell me about yourself and why you're interested in this particular position." He sat back, steepling his fingers in front of him and waited for Cade to respond.

Cade shifted nervously in his seat and cleared his throat.

"Well sir, I am a born and raised native of Abernathy. I attended public schools in Abernathy and attended Abernathy Senior High, where I played on the varsity football team."

"I understand you were quite the athlete," Principal Whitman interrupted.

Surprised, Cade paused for a second and grinned slightly before continuing. "I loved playing football, sir. I was the starting running back my junior and senior years. We lost the championship game my senior year, but we had quite a run at it. There's nothing like team sports to build friendships and to learn how to work with others to reach a common goal," he said fervently, feeling suddenly inspired.

Principal Whitman nodded slowly and studied Cade.

"Officer Marshall, why do you want to be the school's resource officer? I think this job might get to be a little dull for someone young like you just starting their law enforcement career."

"Oh no, sir," Cade quickly interjected. "I don't think being responsible for the safety and wellbeing of the campus could ever get boring. In addition, I think my younger age will help me relate to the students better, and I will hopefully provide a relatable role model."

"I see," Principal Whitman said solemnly. After a lengthy pause, he went on. "Officer Marshall, why do you think you are more qualified than the other applicants for the position, and what is something distinctive you would you bring to the role?"

Cade had a feeling that both of these questions might be asked, and he'd thought at length about how to answer. With the other highly qualified candidates vying for the position, how he answered would be crucial.

"Mr. Whitman, as I mentioned earlier, I'm a native of Abernathy. Members of my family have served this community in law enforcement for over thirty years. And though I'm very proud of my legacy, I want to serve my community and I want to serve in a way I feel my talents are strongest. I played football for Abernathy High School with my two best friends who are still my best and closest friends. I applied for this job thanks to their encouragement."

Pausing to take a quick breath, Cade continued.

"I coach youth sports leagues, sir—football and basketball. Nothing makes me happier than seeing a team come together, whether it's to win a game, learning how to work together, or just having fun. Those are things they'll be able to take with them and use the rest of their lives. I'm happy to say the teams I've coached have been successful. Sure, they've been winning, but more importantly, they've learned teamwork. To be even a small part of helping students achieve their potential and instill confidence and desire to go higher and farther than they dreamed possible? That, sir, is why I want this job."

Cade sat back. He'd unconsciously moved to the edge of his chair in his enthusiasm.

Mr. Whitman looked at Cade steadily and then leaned forward in his chair.

"I realize this is not typically how things are done, but when I see something that's so obviously right, I move on it. What kind of notice do you need to give your commanding officer?"

"Sir?" Cade asked, unsure of what he'd heard.

"I need to know when you can start. You're exactly what we need on this campus, Officer. The new school year is getting underway, and I want you in place."

Cade sat up quickly, excitement coursing through him.

"I'm not sure, but I can find out and let you know right away."

Principal Whitman stood and with a broad smile, extended his hand. "Welcome to Abernathy High School, Officer Marshall. We're excited to have you join us. I'll introduce you to my assistant before you leave. She will be your contact going forward. Officer Lane, the current on campus officer, who is retiring, agreed to stay on a few weeks to go over the duties, responsibilities, and routines with his replacement. Emily will set that meeting up between the two of you as well. Any questions before we get things rolling?"

Mr. Whitman paused and retracted the hand he had extended with a stricken look on his face.

"Officer Marshall, my apologies. It seems I've made a huge mistake."

Cade's stomach clinched. "Mistake, sir?"

"I'm getting ahead of myself. I'm going on about a start date, and I haven't even asked if you'd like the job. Do you want the job, Officer Marshall?"

Cade laughed and stood, a huge smile spreading across his face as he shook the principal's hand.

"Yes, sir. Without a doubt I want this job. I'm excited to get started, and I look forward to working with you."

"Likewise, Officer. There's a lot for you to do and learn in a short period of time so let's get a start date nailed down as soon as possible."

Principal Whitman walked to the door and opened it, following Cade into the front office.

"Ah, Emily. Good. Glad you're back. Let me introduce you. Emily, this is Cade Marshall, our new on campus resource officer. We need to coordinate with PD to get the process and paperwork started to bring him on board. Officer Marshall, this is Emily Tucker, my assistant."

Principal Whitman was talking, but Cade wasn't listening. He was focused on the incredible brunette whose beautiful blue eyes were now trained on him.

Her eyes sparkled when they met his. Her cheeks turned rosy with a blush as Cade continued staring until Principal Whitman completed the introductions.

"Officer Marshall?"

Startled, Cade cleared his throat, reddening when he noticed the principal trying to suppress a grin.

"It's nice to meet you, Ms. Tucker," Cade finally managed, addressing the beautiful young woman.

"It's totally my pleasure, Officer."

Cade studied Emily as Principal Whitman gave her instructions on the meetings to schedule and other details Cade should have been making note of. Whatever information he didn't remember, he thought, would be a wonderful excuse to call her.

"Any questions?" Principal Whitman asked, addressing them both.

"No, sir," they responded in unison.

"Very well. And Emily, you'll need to notify the other applicants. But wait to hear from Officer Marshall first to confirm he has made the needed arrangements on his end. We don't want to cause any problems with his commanding officer."

"Thank you, sir. I appreciate that," Cade said with a nod.

Cade turned to Emily. "It will probably be tomorrow before I can talk to the sergeant, but I'll let you know as soon as possible. And you can call me Cade."

"And you can call me Emily." She smiled bashfully. "I look forward to hearing from you."

Cade nodded and made it out the door, managing to look back at Emily only once before the door closed between them. He was in the parking lot before letting loose a loud and very unprofessional whoop. He caught stares from the few people in the parking lot, but he didn't care. Cade was so happy, he thought he was going to bust wide open.

He found himself looking forward to talking to Emily again. Suddenly, tomorrow seemed a long way away. And then to top everything off, he'd gotten the job! Somehow the smile on his face managed to grow even broader.

Cade glanced over his shoulder to see Emily watching him from the office window. She was smiling and gave a quick wave. He waved back and walked to his truck with a noticeable spring in his step.

RILEY PULLED UP IN front of his apartment a lot earlier than he'd expected. His phone dinged with a text.

C and I are grabbing a bite. Join us?

Riley sighed. He needed a distraction.

Sure. Where?

Max's in 30.

RILEY WAS WAITING AT a table when Jeremy and Cade filed in.

"You look like hell," Cade said as he swung a leg over the back of a chair and sat down.

"And a fine hello to you too," Riley growled out in reply, his fingers curled tightly around a half-empty chilled mug.

Jeremy and Cade exchanged a look as they settled into their seats.

Max's was a holdover hangout from their high school days, a favorite of their high school set. It had the best and greasiest burgers in town. New owners had added a selection of beers, which had eliminated the high school crowd. Country music, with an occasional rock and roll classic, belted out from the old juke box. Neon signs decorated the walls and time-worn tables and accompanying wooden chairs were scattered across a scratched linoleum floor. It was familiar and comfortable.

Even knowing what they'd order, the three studied their menus in silence. The din of the music was a convenient excuse for unnecessary conversation. After they gave their orders to the server, Jeremy turned to Riley. "You got back early. How did it go?"

"Got back from where?" Cade asked as he dipped a cheese stick in ranch dressing. "You guys don't tell me anything."

"Dallas," Jeremy said flatly with a quick look at Cade.

"What'd you go to Dallas for?" Cade asked, receiving another withering look from Jeremy.

"That's where Maggie moved, you blockhead," Jeremy said, thumping Cade on the arm.

"Oh, right. Sorry, Riley," Cade mumbled with a mouthful.

Riley sighed and leaned back in his chair. "She wasn't there."

Jeremy studied Riley knowingly. "There's more. What happened?"

Riley shrugged and leaned forward. "She'd just left for a meeting with a guy named Connor. From what I overheard, they're spending a lot of time together."

"Ah, come on. Don't get wound up. That doesn't mean anything. Who is this Connor guy anyway?" Jeremy asked, taking a sip of his drink.

"Beats me," Riley said with a dejected shrug. "I think I've blown it. I should have proposed a long time ago and now . . . well, who knows. Looks like she may have moved on."

Cade laughed out loud. "Maggie? With another guy? No way. Absolutely no way."

"Things can change, and quickly. Sometimes things are out of our control," Jeremy added, looking between them both, suddenly very somber. "Sorry, Riley, but don't say it's over until you know something for sure. You never know."

Even though he wasn't hungry, Riley took a huge bite of the burger the server had just placed in front of him to avoid having to make a reply.

Cade looked between his two morose friends as they ate slowly in contemplative silence. These two used to be a lot more fun. He was just glad they'd gotten past their disagreement over Allie or at least they'd called a tentative truce and just weren't discussing it. Cade took a bite of his own burger.

"Guys," Cade said after swallowing and taking a long swallow of his drink.

"Yeah?" Jeremy answered distractedly, swishing some fries around in a puddle of ketchup.

"I'd like to share some good news," he said, trying but failing to hide a growing smile.

Riley and Jeremy looked at each other and then at Cade.

"You got the job!" Riley exclaimed.

"Well, yeah but—"

"But what?" Jeremy interrupted. "Did you get the job or not?!"

"Well, I'll tell you if you'd both shut up," Cade chided.

He looked between them and waited, purposefully drawing the suspense out.

"Come on, Cade!" Jeremy said, rolling his eyes.

Cade took another bite of his hamburger and chewed slowly, enjoying the distraction this was proving to be for his friends.

After taking another sip of his drink and swallowing, Cade wiped his mouth slowly.

Riley and Jeremy threw their napkins on the table and leaned back in their chairs, crossing their arms, half-hearted irritation on their faces.

"Okay, you guys ready?" Cade asked with an innocent smile.

"For Pete's sake, Cade! Spit it out. Don't make us have to wring it out of you!" Riley said, trying hard to glare. Cade was enjoying this way too much.

"Well," Cade finally said, "My interview was today. I met with Principal Whitman. Would you believe the furniture is still the same since we were there? Pretty amazing."

"Cade, you are trying my patience sorely, and I don't have much to begin with," Riley said, waving a french fry threateningly in Cade's face. "Trust me. We don't care about the furniture in the principal's office."

"Oh, well okay then," Cade said with a wicked grin before going on. "We had a very nice visit. He asked me why I wanted the job, why I was more qualified than the other candidates. Blah. Blah. Blah. All the usual stuff."

"So you think you did well then?" Jeremy asked.

"Yeah, I think it went really well," Cade replied, trying to suppress a grin.

"Did they say when they'd let you know?" Riley asked.

"No. No they didn't say," Cade said and took another bite of his burger.

Jeremy sighed in frustration. "Cade! You should have asked!"

"There was no need," Cade said, unable to hide his excitement any longer.

"Well, why not?" Riley asked, almost coming out of his seat.

"Well, because they offered me the job on the spot, and I took it," Cade said with a smug grin.

Riley and Jeremy exchanged dumbfounded looks and collapsed against the backs of their chairs before bursting into excited congratulations and slapping Cade on the back.

After Riley ordered another round, they held their mugs aloft and offered a toast to Abernathy High School's new campus resource officer.

Cade couldn't stop smiling.

They exchanged smiles and a few more toasts before a happy silence settled over their table.

"Oh, and guys," Cade said, looking between Riley and Jeremy with a sparkle in his eye, "I met a girl."

RILEY LOOKED UP FROM his grocery list, hearing the door from the bay bang open. A grimy engine crew filed through on the way to their quarters to clean up. Jeremy brought up the rear, looking especially doleful. It seemed to reflect Riley's own mood. Jeremy spared a glance for Riley but kept walking, his head down. It was back to the real world today after celebrating with Cade last night, but it didn't look like things were going well for Jeremy.

The ambulance had been released earlier from the house fire the engine crew had just wrapped up. The call had come just as A Shift came on duty, which portended a busy day. Riley looked back to his list. He'd cooked several times now and was getting better every time. Tonight was a new but what appeared to be an easy recipe—hamburger casserole.

He stuck the pencil's eraser between his teeth and unconsciously started chewing on it, staring at the list and trying to remember what else he needed. After returning from the house fire, it had ended up being a surprisingly quiet morning for the ambulance but that could end any time, so he needed to wrap it up and make the grocery store run.

Carrier came through and stopped to look over Riley's shoulder at the grocery list.

"Don't forget ice cream," Carrier said, popping the last bite of a Pop-Tart in his mouth.

"Not sure we've got the funds for that, but I'll keep it in mind," Riley grumbled, adding it to the bottom of his list.

He was tired. He was grumpy. Riley wasn't exactly sure why he was feeling so down this morning. Maybe he'd expected too much after leaving the flowers for Maggie yesterday on his disappointing trip to Dallas. He'd thought, or rather hoped, he might at least hear something from her. But nothing. She really must have moved on or didn't care. He sighed.

One by one the crew filed through the kitchen while Riley finished his list, some snagging something out of A Shift's refrigerator while others just passed through.

Grimes stopped at the table and looked over Riley's shoulder.

"What's for dinner, Rookie?" Grimes asked, grabbing an apple from a bowl on the table and taking a large, loud bite.

Grimes was the youngest of the engine crew, having become a member of the fire service right out of high school. He was an avid golfer, and Riley had taken him to the Club a couple of times to play a round on their days off.

Riley sighed and without looking up said, "Hamburger casserole."

"Ah, that sounds awesome," Grimes said sarcastically and took another loud bite of his apple.

"Do you mind?" Riley asked irritably.

"No, I don't mind hamburger for dinner but thanks for asking. Hey, Sims! We're having hamburger casserole for dinner. Sounds like one of your specialties. Do you mind?"

Sims stopped halfway through his trip from the bedroom area to the TV room with a puzzled look on his face.

"Mind? Why would I mind so long as I'm not cooking?" he said and continued on his way until Grimes gave a quick jerk of his head toward Riley.

Picking up on Grimes' signal, Sims walked over and sat at the table across from Riley. "What's for dessert?" he asked and took a long swallow of water from the ever-present water bottle he carried.

Trying to hide his growing irritation, Riley gripped the pencil harder. "Ice cream. Is that okay?"

"Jones, Rookie's making hamburger casserole for dinner and ice cream for dessert. Do you mind?"

Tanner Jones, the country boy with the twang, walked over slowly and stood beside Grimes to look at the list over Riley's shoulder.

"Well, seems to me like we need a bit more than hamburger and ice cream," he drawled, sending a grin over Riley's head to Sims.

Riley sighed again. "There's more, guys. I promise. Now would all of you just please—"

"Is this a congregational meeting?" Brimly bellowed as he walked toward the table from the bay. "We've got work to do, gentlemen."

"Yes, sir," the group answered, but no one moved.

He threw his hands out, with an expectant look.

"We're helping the rookie here with his grocery list," Grimes said, indicating Riley with his head. Brimly studied the group as they all looked at him expectantly.

Looking from Grimes to Riley and then at each of the others, he picked up on what they were doing and nodded knowingly.

Joining in, he said, "Well, first things first, as they say. We'll help you with your list, Rookie, so *every*one can get back to work. What does everyone want? Grimes?"

"Now wait a minute," Riley said, his irritation now in full bloom.

"It's my turn to cook, and I get to pick what I'm cooking, not you guys. Are we clear?"

Everyone froze, and the kitchen went silent. Uncertain looks were exchanged over Riley's head. Riley tensed before putting his head in his hands.

The captain walked in and surveyed the group for several long seconds.

"Do we have an issue here?" he demanded, looking from man to man. "I'm sensing some irritation from the station rookie. Mr. Sullivan? Is there a problem?"

"Sorry, sir. No problem. I'm just working on my grocery list and seem to be getting a lot of unsolicited help."

Brimly caught the captain's eye and gave a head jerk in Riley's direction, just as Riley looked up to see the exchange.

"Ah, I see," Captain Jernigan said, stroking his chin. "The rookie needs our help deciding what's for supper. After the chicken debacle, I'd steer clear of chicken if I were you, Rookie."

Each man was grinning as Riley looked around the circle. He realized that in their own goofy way, they were trying to lighten his mood. Touched, Riley looked down and worked to clear his throat.

"Let's give the rookie some space," Jernigan said. "Sullivan, let us know if you need any more helpful suggestions."

"Thanks, Cap. I'll do that."

After everyone had wandered off, a freshly showered and much cleaner Jeremy eased into a chair across from Riley.

"They mean well."

"Oh, I know, and it's appreciated," Riley said. "I must have really been a bear for it to be noticed."

"Yeah, but be glad they didn't give you the hose treatment," Jeremy said with a slight grin. "Before the ambulance got back from the last one, I got a hosing down while cleaning the engine. Guess my bad mood was getting the better of me too."

"Sorry I missed that," Riley said with a low whistle.

Jeremy rolled his eyes and stood as the tones sounded with a medical emergency.

RILEY HAD JUST PULLED two casserole dishes and a sauce pan out of the cabinet when the station's doorbell rang. Expected to answer the door as the rookie, Riley tossed the kitchen towel on the counter and headed toward the front door, but hearing Tanner and Sims' voices, he knew they'd already answered it. He started pulling ingredients out of the refrigerator for the dinner's casserole.

Tanner stuck his head around the corner. "Rookie, you have a visitor."

Puzzled, Riley laid the hamburger meat he'd started to unwrap on the counter and wiped his hands on a dishcloth. He headed toward the lobby area but finding it empty, he followed voices to the TV room. Standing in a semicircle of firefighters, a tall immaculately dressed man stood, chatting amiably.

Seeing Riley in the doorway, Captain Jernigan extended his hand. "Here he is. Sullivan, this gentleman is here to see you."

Riley walked over, the others making way for him.

"Riley Sullivan?" the man asked, extending his hand.

"Yes, sir. It's a pleasure to meet you," Riley said, looking puzzled.

"Franklin Bradford, Riley. My name is Franklin Bradford." He took Riley's outstretched hand and shook it firmly.

Riley studied him closely. He looked familiar, but Riley couldn't quite put his finger on why. The man was tall and slender with short, neatly combed hair. His teeth showed white against his tan skin. The suit he wore was obviously expensive, and his shoes were an expensive brand as well.

"Mr. Sullivan, you may not remember me, but I remember you."

"Spend Less," Riley said, looking directly at the man and smiling broadly. "You look a whole lot better than the last time we saw you."

"I should hope so," Bradford said. "I was really sick. It took several days for me to come to myself in the hospital, and when I did, I started hearing your name, what you did, and how I came to be there. So, I wanted to come by and extend my sincerest thanks. But I also understand, I may owe you some money."

Riley tried to wave him off.

"You don't owe me a thing, Mr. Bradford."

"Franklin, please."

"Sure, Franklin. But really, you don't owe me a thing. I'm glad you've recovered but really, I was just doing my job."

"I beg to differ. You see, I own a manufacturing company, Bradford Strategies, if you've heard of it?"

Lieutenant Cochran let out a low whistle. "You *own* Bradford Strategies?"

Bradford turned to him, pleased. "Indeed, I do. I take it you've heard of it?"

Cochran smiled excitedly and turned to Riley. "Bradford Strategies is one of the largest drone manufacturers in the country. I've got a catalog, and you wouldn't believe everything they offer."

Bradford smiled broadly at Cochran's enthusiasm and knowledge of his company. "I appreciate that. Glad you're familiar with us."

Bradford turned back to Riley. "You see, from what I've heard about what happened at that store, the police wanted to file charges. If they had, it would have seriously hurt my reputation and the chances of Bradford Strategies opening the manufacturing plant we're hoping to open here in Abernathy. I was here on a location scouting trip when I developed an infection that finally got so bad, it totally incapacitated me that night, as you well know. If it hadn't been for you stepping in, there would have been a lot of repercussions."

Riley was stunned, as were the rest of the guys, at what could have happened and its implications for the entire city. Surprised looks were exchanged between them as everyone stood in shocked silence.

"Wow, I don't know what to say," Riley stammered.

"Nothing for you to say," Bradford said jovially. "That's what I'm here to do. First of all, here's some cash to cover whatever it was you paid the store on my behalf."

Bradford handed Riley a stack of bills that Riley took reluctantly after receiving an approving nod from Captain Jernigan.

"Thank you, Franklin," Riley said. "This will go in the food kitty so everyone can enjoy."

Franklin nodded approvingly. "And I've decided, based on the exemplary treatment I received, that I didn't even know I was receiving," joked Franklin with a chuckle, "I'd like to do something for the Abernathy Fire Department. I've taken the liberty of checking with Chief Harrison on what might be most beneficial, and he indicated the department is considering the use of drones. I'd say between Bradford Strategies and the Abernathy Fire Department, it's a perfect fit. The chief and I are working through the details, but depending on what he says the department's greatest needs are, I will be donating at least two of each type of Bradford's finest to the fire department for its use."

Low whistles and nods of appreciation went around the circle.

"And, if you guys know of anyone who might be interested in working specifically with the drones, I bet Chief Harrison would be interested in talking to them. These are cutting edge units, and I think they'll be able to provide a lot of assistance and possibly even save some lives. That's the goal."

"We'll certainly pass the word," Captain Jernigan said, uncharacteristically nervous. "We don't know how to thank you. But just know everything you're doing is greatly appreciated."

"Actually, it's my thanks to all of you for your service and what you do every day. I admire each of you." He shared an appreciative look with each firefighter. "But now, I'll be on my way. Riley, thanks again for stepping in the way you did that night."

Mr. Bradford turned and walked to the front door, Riley going with him. He extended his hand and shook Riley's firmly.

"Mr. Bradford—Franklin—please. You don't owe me any thanks. It's us who should be thanking you. We appreciate the opportunity you're providing to put the latest and greatest technology to use serving the community."

Mr. Bradford smiled. "You're a credit to the profession, Mr. Sullivan. I'm grateful it was you that came to my rescue the other night."

"Me too, sir. But now, I guess I'd better get to work. It's my night to cook and the guys get restless if dinner is late."

They both chuckled.

"Go feed them, Mr. Sullivan. It's a pleasure to meet you and this time be in my right mind."

Riley saw him out the door and walked back to the kitchen, shaking his head.

RILEY HELPED CLEAR THE table as Grimes and Hayward loaded the dishwasher. The hamburger casserole hadn't turned out too badly.

He'd actually received a compliment or two—not that anyone was actually paying attention to the food. Conversation had centered around drones, what could be done with them, how other departments were using them, their cost, their range, and speculation on what might have happened should charges have been filed against Franklin Bradford, and on and on.

Lieutenant Cochran, already well versed on drones, couldn't stop talking about the possibilities. As he talked, his face lit up like it was Christmas come early. Riley figured Cochran would probably be talking to the chief about his interest in working with the drones when the time came.

The clanging of the dishwasher signaled the end of kitchen clean up as Riley heaved a large trash bag onto his shoulder. Mulling over the events of the evening, he trudged to the trash bins in the back of the station. He heaved the trash bag into the bin as his phone dinged with a text. He pulled it out of his pocket, its screen lighting up the evening.

The flowers were lovely. Thank you. M.

CADE POPPED THE LAST bite of his sub sandwich in his mouth and wadded up the paper before turning to the sound of slurping. Crawford had just finished an Italian sub, replete with meatballs and lots of marina sauce and was noisily draining the last of his drink. It was annoying, but Cade wanted to see if he might generate some conversation and find out what Crawford was doing at the gym the other night.

"So, Crawford," Cade began with a nervous edge in his voice. "Do you like sports? I played on the high school football team here in Abernathy. I was a running back. How about you? Did you play any ball?"

Crawford's eyes narrowed as he turned a sour look Cade's direction.

"What are you blathering about, Marshall? Is this an interrogation?"

Cade tried to chuckle. "No. No interrogation, sir. I was just trying to make conversation."

Crawford humphed and scowled. "Why don't you try to focus on work instead." Crawford slurped his soft drink one more time before handing the empty cup to Cade.

Cade quietly sighed and gathered the rest of the trash from their dinner. Maybe he'd try again another time.

CRAWFORD HAD GONE INTO a coffee shop about midnight to get them both a cup of coffee. Cade stayed with the patrol car, but all was quiet. His thoughts turned to Jeremy. He puzzled over, again, what had happened to make Jeremy so gloomy. The only thing out of the ordinary was Jeremy's grandfather, his father's father, passing away a few months ago. That had seemed to rattle Jeremy, but he'd seemed to have gotten past it, or at least until the conversation with Riley about Allie. That seemed to have started Jeremy into a downward spiral that neither Cade nor Riley could figure out or pull him out of, even though they'd both tried talking to him. As hard as it was, they'd just have to wait Jeremy out.

Crawford tapped on Cade's window and handed in a cup of coffee before coming around to the driver's door. After Crawford slid behind the wheel, the radio suddenly crackled and the inboard computer lit up:

Code 10-148, 16th and Fernwood, Bottle Top Bar & Grill. Patron altercation. Time out 12:17.

Cade acknowledged receipt of the call as Crawford sped the car into a U-turn, kicking the siren and lights on. It was just a few short blocks to the bar's location, making Cade and Crawford the first on scene. Cade groaned to himself when he saw an ambulance and fire engine pulling up right behind them. If Cade was lucky, they'd be from a different station since Jeremy and Riley were on duty. He was hoping everyone's paths wouldn't cross again so soon after the Spend Well incident.

That hope was short lived when Riley got out of the ambulance and Jeremy out of the engine a few seconds later.

Stepping out of the patrol car, Cade could see the altercation had moved outside of the bar with about fifteen bar patrons engaging in an all-out brawl. One victim was down but trying to get to his feet. Some stepped over him or fought around him while others trounced him with kicks and punches to his stomach and head.

Cade pulled his billy club from his belt and started walking confidently toward the throng, but Crawford put an arm out, holding him back.

"Wait for back-up. There are too many for us to go in alone," Crawford said, his breathing heavy.

Cade looked at him wide-eyed. "But sir, there's a victim down and getting pummeled. He's going to be in much worse shape if we wait, not to mention injuries to those still fighting."

Riley and Carrier walked up and stood by Cade, medical bags in hand, ready to move in.

"We're waiting for back-up," Cade said, turning to Riley.

"You're what?" Riley asked, incredulous. "There's a guy getting his guts kicked in. I don't think he's going to appreciate our waiting."

Jeremy and the other three firefighters from the engine strode up, stopping beside Riley and Carrier, waiting expectantly for the okay to move into the melee.

Crawford, hearing the exchange between Riley and Cade, turned and looked at Riley, his eyes narrowing.

"You." It was an accusation, not a statement.

"Officer Crawford," Riley replied coldly.

"If you don't like the way police conduct business, Fire Boy, why don't you do something about it?"

Cade looked between Crawford and Riley as a beer bottle crashed at their feet. What was taking the other patrol cars so long? This was spiraling out of hand quickly, and he wasn't thinking only of the bar brawl.

"Okay, we will do something about it. Carrier, with me," Riley said as he shouldered his bags and started walking toward the fighting, broken glass crunching beneath his rubber shoes.

Jeremy and Cade's eyes widened as they exchanged shocked looks. Lieutenant Cochran, a determined look on his face, motioned for Jeremy and the others to follow.

Seeing the paramedics and firefighters approaching, the closest group of fighters suddenly stopped fighting, unsure of what was happening. Riley went straight for the victim on the ground as the other brawlers, surprised, scattered or stopped to see what was going on.

Cade, with a quick look at Crawford, followed the firefighters and joined the protective ring they'd formed, their backs inward, to shield Riley and Carrier while they worked on the victim.

Some light scuffling continued, but enthusiasm for fighting had lost its momentum.

Carrier elbowed his way back through the protective ring of firefighters and made his way to the ambulance, retrieving the gurney and wheeling it through the circle.

Officer Crawford hadn't moved. His hands were fisted on his hips, his face a deep shade of red, his eyes narrowed slits as he looked on.

A second police cruiser, a second ambulance, and another fire engine pulled up, the officers and firefighters hurrying toward the scene. The police officers slowed for an instant, looking confusedly between Crawford and the firefighters encircled amid what appeared to be a waning fight. While newly arrived paramedics checked some of the patrons for injuries, Riley and Carrier loaded their victim onto the gurney and prepared to leave.

Cade started assisting the newly arrived officers in securing the scene, glancing nervously over his shoulder at Crawford. Fury radiated from Crawford like heat from a furnace. He still hadn't moved, the tension building to a crescendo around him.

As Riley and Carrier began to wheel the victim toward the ambulance, Crawford stalked toward them quickly, moving to intercept them. Cade saw what was happening and moved as quickly as he could, trying to get there first. Breathless, he came to a stop just short of where Riley and Carrier were lifting the patient into the ambulance.

After Carrier got in the back, Riley turned rigidly and gave Crawford a scorching glare. Crawford stiffened and started toward Riley.

"Everyone needs to cool down," Cade said, stepping between them and putting his arms out, holding both Riley and Crawford at bay.

"Get out of my way, Officer," Crawford said, glaring at Riley who stood on the other side of Cade, tensed and ready for a physical confrontation.

"No, sir. This needs to end right here. Everyone is okay. The victim and scene have been secured. Any irregularities should be addressed later, not here, not now, not like this," Cade said.

Jeremy hurried up, looking anxiously between them all.

Riley relaxed his stance. "Sorry. You're right, Cade. Besides, we have a victim to transport." Riley stepped to the front of the ambulance and got in. Cochran banged on the doors, signaling Riley to pull out. As the ambulance pulled out, Cochran came up to where Crawford and Cade stood.

"Officer Crawford, I have a feeling we'll be discussing this incident in more detail," the lieutenant said, accosting Officer Crawford with a glare. "Even though the process was a bit out of the norm, I assure you, the paramedics acted in the best interest of the victim and to deescalate the situation. That will be in my report."

"Men," Cochran motioned the other firefighters standing nearby back to the engine. Jeremy hesitated briefly, giving Cade a questioning look, before following them.

Surprising Cade, Crawford turned to him. "That firefighter—Sullivan? He called you Cade. Not officer, not Officer Marshall, but Cade. Seems like I've heard that a friend of yours just joined the fire department. Firefighter Sullivan wouldn't happen to be that new member now, would he?"

Cade swallowed hard. His answer, a truthful answer, might mean trouble for Riley, and with Riley being new, it could hurt him with the fire department.

"I'm waiting, Marshall," Crawford growled out.

Cade sighed then looked defiantly at his partner.

"Yes, sir. Riley and I have been best friends since middle school. I know him, and I know he wouldn't do anything but what he thought was in the best interest of someone needing help. You can file anything you want to file. Riley is new and has a lot to learn. But what Riley did, while out of the norm and dangerous, as the lieutenant said, probably saved that man's life. If that gets him in trouble, then we're all in the wrong profession. Excuse me, sir, we have some prisoners to transport."

Cade walked away as Officer Crawford was left standing, his mouth agape.

RILEY'S BREATH CAME FAST and shallow. He was absolutely livid. And deep down, he was afraid he'd just done irreparable damage to his fledgling career with the fire department. What had he been thinking? Never before in his life had he charged in anywhere without thinking. And tonight, he could have gotten a lot of people hurt or worse.

He pulled into the ER and after slamming it in park, ran around to the back and opened the doors to help Carrier.

Megan Jefferson, one of the ER nurses typically on duty the same days as Riley, joined them at the back of the ambulance as the gurney was lowered. Unlike him, she always seemed to be cool under pressure.

"Abrasions, contusions, and possible internal injuries," Carrier said quickly as they wheeled the victim inside.

While Carrier continued to the exam room with the nurse and victim, Riley got back into the ambulance. Gripping the steering wheel until his knuckles turned white, he rested his head on his hands.

What had he been thinking?

An approaching siren brought Riley to himself, and he quickly moved the ambulance to one of the designated parking spots. He went inside and made his way to the computer to enter the report.

He acknowledged several of the nurses with a quick nod then focused on the screen. Carrier appeared at his side a few minutes later.

"He's all squared away, Sullivan. I'll double check our supplies," Carrier offered hesitantly and then hurried off when Riley didn't respond.

Riley closed his eyes and pinched the bridge of his nose before sighing.

"Rough one?" Megan asked, concern on her face as she approached.

Riley straightened and turned toward her.

"A bit, but I'm afraid I made things worse."

Megan frowned. "How could you make things worse?"

Riley gestured toward the exam room. "He was injured and down in the middle of a brawl. I just charged in. I didn't think about the danger I was putting everyone else in. They followed me in and now . . ."

Riley ran his fingers through his hair and shrugged. "Now, I may have just ended my 'brilliant' career with the fire department."

He heaved another heavy sigh and turned back to the computer.

Megan sidestepped a gurney being hurriedly wheeled past the workstation before putting a gentle but firm hand on Riley's arm. An announcement came across the intercom as chatter and loud laughter from the waiting room blended with the general hum of the emergency area's nurse's station. Forcing him to look at her, she leaned close.

"Riley, the victim you just brought in is presenting with multiple broken ribs and possible internal bleeding. I have a feeling if you hadn't charged in when you did, we'd be notifying his family of their loss. I wouldn't rush to assume your career is over. If you need anyone to testify at a hearing or whatever else might happen, please let me know. I will be happy to inform them of the victim's condition when you brought him in. Your actions may have very well saved his life."

Riley felt the tightness in his chest relax for the first time since he'd found himself kneeling beside the victim in the bar's parking lot.

"Thank you, Megan," Riley said with an embarrassed shrug. "Maybe I was overreacting a bit."

"I don't see that you have anything to worry about, Riley. You'll be able to justify your actions easily."

"Well, we'll see. There's one police officer who's not going to make it that easy."

Carrier walked up, looking between the two of them expectantly.

"Ready to roll when you are," Carrier said. He turned toward the doors, supplies in hand.

"Right behind you," Riley said as he submitted the report.

Megan started to walk off, but Riley called her back.

"Thank you, Megan. I needed someone to talk some sense to me. I appreciate it."

Megan smiled. "Happy to help, Riley. Be safe."

Riley forced a smile as Megan started toward the exam room. Broken ribs and possible internal bleeding? Maybe his rash action was justified.

THE RIDE BACK TO the station was made in silence. Carrier didn't say a word until Riley backed the ambulance into the bay and shut off the engine.

"That was one of the bravest things I've ever seen," Carrier said as he turned and looked at Riley. "Not one of the smartest, but definitely one of the bravest."

"Thanks, Carrier, but let me apologize. I put your safety at risk. I was only thinking about getting in there to help that guy, not about what that might mean for everyone else."

"It all worked out fine, but I'm not sure how the brass is going to see it. Especially with Bart Crawford involved."

"Yeah. To be honest, I'm worried about that too."

Riley opened his door, climbed out of the ambulance and not stopping to do the mandatory cleaning, walked resolutely to the station door. He didn't slow down once inside.

He passed the kitchen and saw that the table was filled with firefighters, which was unusual for the wee hours of the morning. Their silence was an ominous sign. Riley walked straight to Captain Jernigan's office and knocked.

"Come in."

Riley opened the door and stepped inside. Seated in the chairs across from the captain were Lieutenant Cochran and Jeremy, all three grim-faced.

"Sullivan, we've been waiting for you. Pull up that chair," the captain said, motioning to a chair against the back wall.

"Let's start with the condition of the victim. What's his status?"

Riley glanced quickly between the three then looked back to the captain. "He has multiple abrasions, contusions, at least two broken ribs, and possible internal bleeding. They were still evaluating him when we left."

The captain leaned back in his chair, steepling his fingers in front of him. "Prognosis?"

"Not certain, but the attending nurse did say if the beating had gone much further, a family notification more than likely would have been needed."

Riley shuffled his feet and looked down, his hands clasped tightly in front of him.

"Lieutenant Cochran here said you took matters into your own hands without waiting for police to secure the scene."

Riley hung his head even lower.

The captain went on. "But, he also said the officer in charge took no action. Instead, he was waiting on back up, whose ETA was unknown. Lieutenant Cochran and Ennis, here as senior firefighter, thought your actions were a bit rash, certainly skirting the lines of protocol. But in this particular case, it was justified, which seems even more so now in light of the victim's prognosis."

Riley hazarded a quick glance at Jeremy, whose attention was focused on the captain, his face strained.

Jernigan continued. "I understand the police officer in question was Officer Crawford?"

Riley nodded.

The captain sighed heavily. "I know we discussed being especially mindful of him after previous encounters. Sullivan, we are here to work *with* the police, not against them. And we certainly don't want to antagonize them. I understand Crawford is problematic for everyone so it's not entirely your fault, but this can't happen again. I want to make myself perfectly clear on that. I'm sure we'll be hearing something from PD, and we'll cross that bridge when and if it comes. But let me emphasize something."

The door opened suddenly. Chief Bentley stepped inside, closing the door behind him.

The four already in the room stood.

"Evening, uh morning, Chief," Captain Jernigan said, moving from behind his desk. "Please have a seat."

"Not necessary, Jernigan, but thank you." Bentley moved inside the room and sat on the corner of the desk nearest Riley.

"Sullivan," the chief said, eying Riley closely. "I understand there was an incident tonight involving police, where you didn't wait for the scene to be secured before entering. Is that correct?"

"Yes, sir," Riley answered.

"I've heard from Sergeant Dickson at PD. Now, I want to hear your version."

Riley recounted the events as factually as he could remember them, including the prognosis of the patient Nurse Jefferson had provided.

"Lieutenant? Firefighter Ennis? Do you corroborate the events as Firefighter Sullivan just relayed them?"

Both nodded simultaneously. "Yes, sir."

Chief Bentley nodded solemnly. He stood up, his head bent and his hands gripped tightly behind him. He paced a few steps and then back to the edge of the desk.

"Sullivan, I'm sure the good captain here has been schooling you on the importance of protocol and procedures. As you know full well, firefighters are not armed, so to enter an unsecured scene puts lives at risk. I understand there are circumstances when it's necessary to bend these policies and procedures. But only bend them slightly. And only in extremely rare instances. Those rare instances have also been related to experienced firefighters whose judgment has already proven to be sound and reliable. You've been with the department how long, Sullivan?"

"Two months, sir," Riley managed, barely able to breathe.

It felt like all of the air had fled from the room.

"Two months?" Bentley said, pausing a few seconds. He and Jernigan exchanged a solemn look.

"Well, Mr. Sullivan," Bentley said, looking steadily at Riley. "In your short time with the department, you have certainly made your presence known. While that's not always a good thing, it doesn't necessarily mean it's always bad either."

Bentley paused, seeming to weigh his next words. He returned and sat on the edge of the desk nearest Riley, his chief's badge catching the light with his movement. He quietly studied his clasped hands for several long seconds.

Riley could feel sweat trickling down the back of his neck. He tried to swallow, but his mouth was excruciatingly dry. His heart was pounding loud enough he was sure everyone in the hushed room could hear it.

Bentley sighed and looked at each person in the room before his eyes came to rest on Riley.

"Mr. Sullivan, while this type of conduct or behavior is not condoned, it seems, after hearing from all perspectives, in this particular instance it was justified."

Riley's breath quickened.

"There will, of course, have to be a formal investigation, but that will be a mere formality. But Mr. Sullivan, let me make it very clear, this can't happen again. Period. I've heard about the previous altercations between you and Officer Crawford. They stop now. He's not the best representative of the badge, and I don't want him to be the cause of our losing an outstanding paramedic because said paramedic can't keep his cool. We clear?"

"Yes, sir," Riley managed to get out around his pounding heart and short breaths.

"Now, gentlemen, I'd like to speak to Captain Jernigan alone. You are dismissed."

Cochran, Jeremy, and Riley filed out of the captain's office.

The door closing behind him, Riley leaned against the wall outside the captain's office, his cheeks scorching hot and his hands trembling. He jammed his hands into his pockets and took a deep breath.

Jeremy placed a hand on Riley's shoulder with a quick pat and followed Cochran to the kitchen.

Riley couldn't face them all. Not yet. He turned in the direction of the bedrooms, his head down, but then he stopped. No, he was going to have to face them sooner or later. They worked in the same station after all. Best to get it over with.

Riley turned and walked purposefully to the kitchen, his head high.

They were all still in the kitchen. The only change was Sims at the counter pulling out pans to start breakfast. At the sound of Riley's voice, they all turned.

"Gentlemen," Riley said, "I owe each of you an apology."

"An apology for what?" Hayward asked as he pulled plates from the cabinet. "Do you know what he's talking about, Grimes?"

"I have no clue. How about you, Sims?" Grimes said, standing and pushing his chair under the table. "The only apology I think we've got coming is for what is supposed to be breakfast."

They all chuckled and gave Riley a nod before resuming their conversations.

Unsure of what to do, Riley blinked in surprise and didn't move.

"Oh, Rookie," Sims called, holding out a large saucepan, "you're peeling potatoes for hash browns. Get over here. We've got to do something to keep you busy and out of trouble."

Riley couldn't help the laugh that escaped him. He relaxed, and his shoulders slumped with relief. What a great group of guys, he thought, smiling to himself.

BATTALION CHIEF BENTLEY TOOK the chair Lieutenant Cochran had just vacated.

"Well, Keevin. Besides all the official mumbo jumbo we're going to have to do, what are your thoughts?"

Captain Jernigan leaned back in his chair. "Sullivan is an outstanding paramedic and a model rookie. The only problems seem to be when his path crosses Crawford's. Seems he got the better of Crawford on a previous incident, and Crawford hasn't forgotten. Crawford doesn't like to be bettered or challenged. You know that."

Bentley nodded. "I know. I know. For the life of me, I can't figure out why Dickson doesn't do something about him. Not my call, of course, but Crawford sure can make things difficult."

Bentley hesitated and shifted slightly, the chair creaking with the movement. "Actually, he reminds me of me in my younger days. I was a bit difficult back then."

He raised an eyebrow, daring Jernigan to reply.

Captain Jernigan grinned. "You know what? You're right. The only difference is that you realized how your conduct affected people and mended your ways. I'm not sure Crawford ever will."

Bentley nodded thoughtfully. "I was lucky. I had Andy Garrett tormenting me but he did inspire me to change. Who knows? Maybe Crawford will have someone to inspire him one day, and he'll change."

"Garrett inspired all of us in one way or another." Jernigan said, seeming to be lost in thought before adding wryly, "As for Crawford, though, we can only hope."

Bentley chuckled and stood. Walking to the door, he put his hand on the handle before turning back to face Jernigan. "Is it true that everyone followed Sullivan in with no hesitation?"

Captain Jernigan did his best to suppress a smile.

"Yes, sir. That's what I've heard from multiple personnel that were on scene."

Bentley nodded thoughtfully. "There's something to be said for that, isn't there?"

"Yes, sir, there certainly is," Jernigan replied, a gleam in his eye.

"Keevin, I tell you what. Move Sullivan over to the engine for a few shifts. Let's see how that goes. If it goes well, we'll see about making it permanent. Do you think he'll mind being pulled from the ambulance for a while?"

"Sullivan has been wanting on the engine since his first shift. He's going to be thrilled."

"This should not be construed as a reward or bump up. Make sure Sullivan is fully aware of that fact. In light of what happened tonight, he should also be assigned extra duties around the station, as well as the internal courses on appropriate fire protocols and procedures. He needs to be fully immersed in processes and procedures. I want to see scores from those courses on my desk within two weeks. Are we on the same page?"

"Yes, sir. We certainly are," Captain Jernigan said, standing and coming around the desk to shake the chief's hand. "I'll decide who to switch with Sullivan on the engine and then make sure he gets on those courses right away."

"I know you will." Chief Bentley nodded and exited, leaving the door open.

Murmurs of conversation drifted in from the kitchen.

"Gentlemen," Jernigan heard the chief say as he passed through, "have a good rest of shift and stay safe out there."

Jernigan heard the mumbled replies as he sat back down and pulled the computer mouse toward him, activating the screen. He accessed the departmental training library on his computer. He quickly pulled up the courses Bentley had indicated he wanted assigned to Sullivan.

Jernigan selected the courses on leadership, command presence, situational awareness, and problem solving. He registered Riley for each one.

Across town, Cade cringed as he sat outside Sergeant Dickson's office, listening to Crawford rage. He'd been going strong for over thirty minutes while Cade had only heard short, murmured responses from the sergeant. Tonight had not been one of Officer Crawford's finer moments, but it really wasn't worth such a temper tantrum.

Waiting, Cade slumped in his chair and absentmindedly thumbed through his phone, acknowledging the occasional officer that stopped at the nearby vending machines.

The door suddenly opened and Crawford stormed out, giving Cade a glare as he stalked down the hall. Sergeant Dickson emerged a few seconds later and motioned wearily for Cade to come in.

"Have a seat, Officer." Dickson eased back into his chair and ran his fingers through his graying hair.

"Well, tonight has been a bit eventful to say the least," the sergeant said with a tired smirk. "How are you handling all of this?"

"I'm fine, sir," Cade replied, unsure if he should say more.

"Officer Marshall, you were there and saw what happened first-hand. I'd like to hear your perspective." The sergeant steepled his fingers and waited, studying Cade.

"Well, sir, I thought the response to the incident tonight would have been cut and dry," Cade said and cleared his throat nervously. "I don't understand Officer Crawford's reaction—or his non-reaction as the case may be. He just gets so . . . maybe the word is belligerent?" Cade said, throwing his hands in the air. "My apologies, sir."

Dickson dismissed the apology with a wave of his hand and indicated for Cade to continue.

"I think he's a good officer at heart, or he could be. I just hate that he thinks the tough bluster and bullying are more effective than being nice. You catch more flies with honey than vinegar as the saying goes."

Cade shrugged and looked down.

"Cade, you're a good complement to him. Just keep doing what you're doing and give him a little space. This is on him. He needs to work this out himself."

Cade nodded. "Yes sir, but about that . . ."

"Yes?" Sergeant Dickson asked with a knowing smile.

"I had planned to tell you at the end of shift."

Sergeant Dickson chuckled. "Let me save you the trouble, Officer. Congratulations on the school resource officer job. I hate to lose you, but you're a perfect fit for that role. You are going to be a big asset to the school."

"How did you know?"

"They asked for an evaluation of your job performance from your commanding officer when they were screening resumes. Yours stood out, and they did a bit more due diligence up front."

"Thank you, sir. And my apologies. I should have told you at the start of shift. The school would like me to start as soon as possible so I can train with the retiring officer."

"I've already talked to HR and they've sent the paperwork. It seems the school is really pushing to get this through. I've given them the date of two weeks from today. That will give us time to assign a new officer to Crawford."

"That sounds great. Thank you, sir. I hope you don't think I applied just to get away from a bad situation. I'm not a coward."

"Stop right there, Marshall. I never entertained that idea. Your work with the youth teams is well known, your age is a huge benefit to the school for relatability, and your involvement with sports while in school is a big plus. You're an exemplary officer and have already served with care and distinction. I have no doubt you'll diligently serve the school as you have here. No, they've made a very wise choice. Are you pleased?" Sergeant Dickson asked with a smile.

"Yes, sir. I'm very excited. I can't wait to get started and gear up for the school year."

Sergeant Dickson nodded. "Principal Whitman is a personal friend. When he called and asked for my thoughts as he reviewed applications, I told him they wouldn't find a better or more qualified officer for that position than you. You're going to be the shot in the arm that program needs."

Cade's chest swelled with pride and excitement at the praise.

"Thank you, sir," Cade said, beaming.

"Now, don't let me down, Officer Marshall," Sergeant Dickson said with a teasing glint in his eye.

"I won't, sir. I plan to give it my very best."

Cade stood to leave.

"I have no doubt. And keep me posted. I want to know how things go," Sergeant Dickson said as he shuffled papers on his desk. "Oh, and don't worry about the next two weeks with Officer Crawford. I wasn't the only officer who recommended you to the school."

Cade sat back down. "What?"

Sergeant Dickson chuckled. "I'm still learning that there's a lot more to Bart Crawford than first meets the eye. He's impressed with your work with the youth basketball league. He said your little team is top seed in an upcoming tournament."

"Well, yes but how did he know?"

"He was intrigued with what you are doing and has been spending time at the gym. He was afraid you'd feel inhibited if you knew he was there, so he's stayed out of sight. Don't let him know I told you, but I can tell from the way he talked that he really enjoys being there. I don't know how he found out about your application, but when he said something to me about it, he asked if it would be possible for him to put in a good word for you too. I think working with you might be cracking Officer Crawford's shell. What a nice surprise it would be to discover that there really is a nice guy underneath all the bluster."

Cade nodded, still stunned. It sure would be a nice surprise, he thought.

CADE PICKED UP THE paperwork on his way out the door that morning to start his exit process. The transition was underway and with his last day set, he needed to notify the school of his availability to start. That meant he needed to call Emily.

Cade smiled, and it occurred to him as he drove to the apartment after shift, he could just go by the school and tell her in person.

An hour later, he pulled into the parking spot in front of the admin building and had to laugh at himself. He was more nervous about seeing Emily than he'd been for his interview.

He took a deep breath and opened the door from the hallway into her office. When she saw him and smiled, his nerves vanished. It made him happy just seeing how pleased she was to see him.

EMILY TURNED, HEARING THE door open, and when she saw it was Cade, her heart flipped. He was absolutely adorable. His short blond hair was a bit curly on top and shorter on the sides, and his eyes were a brilliant shade of green that reminded her of a mountain lake. He was a good height and extremely well built. He was a police officer, after all, she told herself.

She knew she was blushing but couldn't help the big smile that spread involuntarily as she stood and met him at the counter. She wondered how someone she just met could have such an affect on her.

"Cade," she said, her eyes sparkling. "I wasn't expecting you."

Cade hesitated. He'd only thought of getting to see Emily but hadn't thought of an excuse for showing up in person so decided to go with the truth. "Well, I could have called, but I thought it would be nice to actually see you than just talk to you on the phone. I hope you don't mind?"

"Oh, I don't mind at all. It's actually great to see you," Emily said, her smile growing even brighter. "Is everything squared away with the police department? They know you're leaving and have set your last day?"

Emily walked to her desk and pulled a file before walking back to the counter where Cade waited, watching her every move.

"Yes. That's what I wanted to tell you. My last day is two weeks from yesterday, so I'd like to start the next Monday if that works for the school."

"Mmmm..." Emily said, looking between the papers and consulting a calendar. "It looks like that Monday is September 11th. Yeah, from everything I'm seeing here, that works great. Officer Lane is here until the end of the month so you will have a little over two weeks for him to show you the ropes. How does that sound?"

Cade realized that Emily had just asked him something he needed to respond to, but he couldn't get enough of just looking at her—her dark hair, her soft complexion, her long, dark lashes and her brilliant blue eyes. He'd never seen anything so lovely or something he wanted to touch so badly.

"Cade?" Emily asked again.

Blushing, Cade gave a start and cleared his throat. "My apologies. What did you say?"

Emily blushed in return, realizing he'd been staring at her. "Your start date? Monday, September 11th, will give you two weeks with Officer Lane. Does that sound like enough time to train?"

"Yes. I think that should be plenty of time. I'm already a police officer and a graduate of this school, so I think I've got the basics down," Cade said with a grin.

"You certainly do," Emily agreed with a small giggle.

Cade hesitated. He wasn't ready to leave, but then he didn't have any other business to conduct either. A bell rang, and Cade looked at Emily, puzzled.

"They're installing new software for the bell system to make sure it goes off at the right time," Emily offered as explanation.

"Well, if my calculations are correct," Cade said, glancing at his watch. "That sounded like the lunch bell."

"Oh?" Emily laughed. "Does the lunch bell sound different than the other bells that ring throughout the day?"

"Well, I've always thought it sounds a bit happier than all of the other bells," Cade teased with a wink. "And since it is lunch time, or at least close to it, would you like to grab a bite? I know all the nearby hangouts to get you back before the next bell." Cade smiled and raised his eyebrows in question.

His smile did funny things to her stomach. There was no way she was turning him down.

"That sounds great. I only have forty-five minutes, so we'd better get a move on." She came around the counter to join Cade as they walked out the office door.

AFTER SETTLING INTO THEIR booth at Max's, Cade watched Emily as she studied her menu. They gave the server their orders before turning to each other. Cade was suddenly self-conscious, unsure of what to say to the beautiful girl sitting across from him.

Emily smiled nervously.

"Where did you—" Cade began at the same time Emily said, "Do you—"

"Ladies first," Cade chuckled, gesturing for her to continue.

"As they say in the movies, do you come here often?" Emily asked, glancing around at the growing lunchtime crowd. "I noticed you didn't even look at the menu before ordering."

"This place has been around forever. We used to come here during high school and just never stopped coming. It's changed hands a couple of times, but the food stays pretty consistent. I mean, I guess it'd be hard to mess up burgers and fries."

"So, you've been in Abernathy for a while?" Emily played with the napkin dispenser at the center of their table as she glanced up at Cade.

"Born and raised. I went to high school at Abernathy High, and I have to confess, while in school, I became very familiar with the principal's office."

Emily laughed. "Somehow, that doesn't surprise me."

The server placed their drinks on the table before hurrying away. Cade and Emily smiled at each other as they took a sip from their drinks.

Setting his cup down, Cade continued. "And members of my family have proudly served Abernathy as police officers for generations. I am, however, the first campus resource officer in the family. I intend to make them proud."

"And you will," Emily stated firmly, twirling her straw and looking up at Cade shyly.

"Oh? And just how do you know that?" Cade asked with a slight tease.

"I've just got a feeling about you," Emily replied with a teasing smile of her own.

"I'm going to remind you of that when I have to come to the principal's office," Cade chuckled.

"You've got a deal," Emily said.

The server placed a red plastic basket in front of each them. Each basket was lined with red and white checked paper and held a large burger and a huge mound of fries.

Emily's eyes rounded at the amount of food. "Oh my."

Cade smiled as Emily gingerly picked up her burger and took a bite.

"Ummm. This is awesome!" she mumbled, her mouth full.

"Yeah? I'm glad you like it. It's what keeps people coming back. But now, it's my turn for a question. I'm betting you recently moved to Abernathy, but from where?"

Cade waited, taking a bite of his burger and dipping some of his fries in ketchup.

Emily wiped her mouth and fingers with a paper napkin before replying. "I moved here from Fort Worth in the spring. I graduated from college and landed the job at the high school with Principal Whitman. I grew up in Fort Worth, but I've always wanted to live in a smaller town, and Abernathy is a perfect fit. It's still close to home but with the small-town atmosphere I've always wanted. It's everything I've been hoping to find in a new hometown and I've met so many incredible people." She looked at Cade and blushed, then went on quickly. "How did you know I recently moved to town?"

Cade looked closely at Emily. "Well, I am a police officer after all. If you were from Abernathy or had been here for any length of time, you would know about Max's. It's a town staple."

"Oh, I see. It was detective work."

Cade laughed. "Actually, that was a lucky guess. But I am glad. I mean, glad that you moved here."

"Me too. Glad that I moved here," Emily answered, her eyes sparkling.

CADE COULDN'T BELIEVE IT. That had been the fastest forty-five minutes of his life. He and Emily had talked the entire time, never missing a beat, except for a bite of food now and then. She was absolutely amazing. He had her number safely in his phone's contacts, and they'd made plans to talk that evening. He'd told her about Riley and Jeremy and about his youth basketball team and the weekend's upcoming tournament. She said she wanted to come and before he knew it, he'd given her the information on where and times for the games.

Cade happily drummed his fingers on the steering wheel and whistled. He glanced at his watch and smiled. He was looking forward to their call tonight.

RILEY, JEREMY, AND CADE waited for the pizza to be delivered that evening while they watched Thursday Night Football on Riley's big screen TV. Cade had given his basketball team the night off to rest in preparation for the start of the tournament.

Jeremy claimed the overstuffed chair where Riley usually sat, and Cade occupied one end of the couch, so Riley collapsed on the other. Soft drinks sat on the coffee table between them and the TV. Bare walls surrounded them. The sofa, chairs, and coffee table were the only furniture items in the living room. Riley still hadn't taken time to fix the apartment up in any way. It certainly wasn't a priority—not with everything else he had on his mind.

"How long until the pizza arrives?" Cade asked, looking at his watch.

"Fifteen minutes. Game will have barely started so we're good. You guys need anything?" Riley asked, attempting to be the good host his mother had raised him to be.

"Just a pizza," Cade groused good-naturedly.

Riley picked up one of the sofa pillows and threw it at Cade, who just laughed.

"Patience, my friend, will be rewarded," Riley teased.

"Patience in all things will be rewarded," Cade added in a mocking tone.

"Where did you get all of this wisdom all of a sudden?" Jeremy asked, cutting a glance Cade's direction with a cocked eyebrow.

"Well, you know, when being an adult and working with children, one must exhibit wisdom at all times."

Jeremy and Riley looked at each other blankly.

"Come on, guys. I'm practicing my wisdom for when I start my new job. I only have another week and a half, so I need to work on sounding wise for when I speak to the children."

Riley and Jeremy rolled their eyes.

"Hate to tell you, but I don't think the wisdom thing is working for you. Those kids are already in trouble," Riley said, laughing.

The doorbell rang, and Riley stood and headed toward the door. "Pizza's early! Must be our lucky night."

Riley thanked the driver and walked back to the living room, grabbing some paper plates off the kitchen counter on the way. Placing it on the coffee table, Riley opened the box and the pizza's tempting aroma filled the room. They each grabbed a plate and a piece of pizza with the announcers' commentary droning in the background while they ate.

"Exceptional pizza," Cade mumbled, biting into his third piece.

"You say that about every pizza," Jeremy said with a shake of his head.

"I think it's part of that wisdom stuff he's working on for his new job," Riley said, popping the top on another can and taking a drink.

Cade grinned and shrugged nonchalantly. "You guys don't bother me. I'm feeling pretty happy these days. I've got a new job I'm excited about and I've started dating a great girl. Life's looking pretty awesome right now."

Riley and Jeremy exchanged looks. "Did you say dating and girl? As in together? You're *dating* somebody?" Jeremy asked.

"That's right. I'd told you I'd met someone, but I was waiting until we had actually gone out before telling you about Emily," Cade said, breaking into a wide grin. "But I tell you what, if you promise to be nice, I'll introduce you."

Riley and Jeremy looked at each other. Setting their plates on the coffee table, they leaned forward.

"Tell us now," they said at the same time.

"Emily," Cade said again, still grinning. "Her name is Emily Tucker. She's the principal's assistant at the high school. We've talked and we've been to lunch. In fact," he checked his watch again, "I'm going to need to cut out in about an hour. We've got a phone date."

Riley and Jeremy could only look at each other in shock as Cade went on. "I'm going to wait until after the tournament this weekend before asking her out on an official date, but I have asked her to come to the games. If you guys come, you'll get to meet her. She's . . . well, she's pretty awesome."

Jeremy and Riley sat in stunned silence.

"Aren't you guys going to say anything?" Cade asked, swallowing a bite of pizza.

Jeremy absentmindedly picked up his can to take a drink but stopped halfway to his mouth.

"You've got a new job *and* a girlfriend? Both are a bit life-altering. We get you holding out about the job, but didn't you think we'd like to know that you've started dating someone?" Jeremy asked, sounding a bit irritated.

"Sounds familiar, doesn't it?" Riley asked with a pointed look at Jeremy. "Anyway, don't mind him," Riley said, turning to Cade. "I think we're both actually a little jealous."

Cade looked at the floor. "Yeah, that's why I hesitated to tell you about Emily. I know you guys are missing Maggie and Allie. I didn't want to make you feel worse."

Riley picked up the now empty pizza box and took it into the kitchen, returning with more soft drinks and resuming his seat on the sofa.

"Meh, don't worry about us," Jeremy said with a shrug, taking a can from Riley. "We're happy for you. And we can't wait to meet Emily."

Cade's face brightened again. "I can't wait for you both to meet her. She's pretty awesome."

"Yeah," Riley said with a grin. "I think you just said that."

The buzzer sounded to start the second half, but Cade was so focused on talking to his team he almost missed getting the players onto the court. He ran his fingers nervously through his hair as he paced in front of the Roadrunners' bench. They were down by six. They'd never been down by that much going into the second half. The nervous looks on their little faces reflected how his own gut felt. But he couldn't let them know that.

He knew that he shouldn't be worried. This team, as a unit and each individual player, was already a winner in his book. It had been a long and tough road at first, but that had only made these guys tougher competitors. They'd already won three games and now just needed to battle through the next half. They could do it.

He looked into the crowded bleachers to see Emily watching him. She smiled confidently and gave him a thumbs up from where she sat between Riley and Jeremy. A little nervous with that arrangement, he still felt jubilant at how readily they'd accepted her after meeting her for the first time at Friday night's game. Riley and Jeremy had taken off a few hours from their Sunday shift to be here today for the championship game. Cade knew he should count his blessings having such great friends, but he also knew he'd better make sure they weren't telling Emily any wild stories about him.

When the ball dropped for the tip off and the buzzer sounded, Cade's focus narrowed to action on the court. The score went back and forth, the Roadrunners coming to within two points before dropping back by as much as eight points at another point. Noise from the crowd's raucous cheering reverberated around the gym walls. Cade had to yell to be heard, but he still talked to the players the entire time, making substitutions, calling timeouts, or offering words of encouragement to the players as they rotated in and out of the game.

When the clock ticked down to one minute, the Roadrunners were within four points. They were playing tough but the other team maintained their slim lead. Drenched in sweat, Cade felt as if he were playing himself, rasping out instructions as loudly as he could, his voice almost gone. He called a time out and brought the team together in a circle around him.

"Men, I am so incredibly proud of you. You are playing tougher and you're more focused than I've ever seen you play before. It's been an intense game, but you're sharp. You're ready to take this all the way. As it stands now, we need six points—just six points—to put us over the top. Can you do it?"

Twelve tired, but excited, and very determined faces looked back, heads nodding fervently.

"Then let's do it. Runners on three." Cade put his hand in the middle of the circle as other hands piled on top. Cade looked each player in the eye. "One. Two. Three. Runners!"

The boys ran with determination onto the court, and the stands erupted.

When recounting that night later, Riley and Jeremy gave Cade a hard time when Cade said he couldn't remember everything that happened in that last minute. What he did remember was the buzzer sounding and looking at the scoreboard. He'd rubbed the sweat out of his eyes, to read Runners 28, Coyotes 26.

The bedlam after the game, Cade was convinced, must be like after a national championship win. The boys were all jumping up and down and hugging him. He enthusiastically hugged each one back while the stands emptied onto the court. Parents were pounding him on the back, shaking his hand, and hugging all of the boys. It felt like complete happy chaos.

After things settled a bit, the teams lined up and shook hands, the team and each individual player receiving their trophies in a rowdy presentation ceremony. Cade, along with the Roadrunner Market owner, had already been planning a party for the team and their parents, no matter the tournament results. This championship would make the party that much sweeter.

Riley and Jeremy had worked their way through the crowd to shake his hand and clap him on the back before they went back to the station. Crawford had approached him to congratulate him while Riley and Jeremy were still talking to him, and Cade held his breath. Crawford gave Riley a sideways look through narrowed eyes, but the high spirits and excitement wiped out the opportunity for cross words. Cade breathed a quick sigh of relief.

Exhausted but thrilled, Cade talked to every team member and their parents after the game. He congratulated them on how their son played and made sure they knew about the party to come. However, Cade knew the best trophy he could have ever hoped to achieve came true when he saw the boys' eyes shining with the success of their accomplishment. He didn't think he could be any happier until after shaking the last hand, he turned toward the bench to retrieve his gym bag and saw Emily waiting for him, a bright smile on her face.

"Wow! That was some finish, Coach Marshall. You've got to be thrilled! Congratulations," she said as he walked up to her.

"I can't believe you waited so long."

"No way would I leave without congratulating you. You were where you should have been, with those boys and their parents."

Cade laughed. "Yeah, pretty exciting stuff. Those kids are absolutely amazing." He ran his fingers through his sweaty hair. "Geez, sorry. I bet I look a mess."

Emily gave him playful wink. "Oh, I don't know. You still look great to me."

Cade smiled as he leaned over to pick up his bag. Today had been absolutely perfect. He reached for Emily's hand, which she quickly placed in his. They walked out together, their footsteps and voices echoed in unison throughout the empty gym.

RILEY WAS THINKING OF Cade as he traversed the obstacle course at the training facility. It had been two days since Cade's team had won the tournament championship, and Cade still hadn't come down from cloud nine. Riley was happy for him, not just for winning the championship, but for finding Emily. He and Jeremy agreed they really liked her. She was beautiful and had a fun personality. They'd teasingly told her they weren't exactly sure what she saw in Cade, but then she'd surprised them by replying she wasn't sure what he saw in them either. She was spunky. The perfect fit for Cade.

Riley leaned over, putting his hands on knees as his breathing slowed. The obstacle course was still a challenge, but it seemed easier now than it was several months ago. At that point, he'd had to pass it to capture a spot at the fire academy. The course had been daunting then, but as Riley straightened and stretched, he smiled to himself. Now, it wasn't bad at all.

He'd been at the training field each morning the past four shifts with about ten others honing their basic firefighting skills. Most were rookies, like him, who had been working as paramedics the first several months of their tenure while others were there just for the additional experience. Today was the last day, and Riley had enjoyed every second.

While completing the exercises at the training field, Riley was also working his way through the courses Captain Jernigan had assigned in the wake of the bar incident. Jernigan may have been surprised that Riley was actually enjoying them. He'd already been able to apply a lot of the material real time to situations he faced on the ambulance. He couldn't say he was enjoying the other things he'd been assigned, such as re-rolling hoses, cleaning the masks on the self-contained breathing apparatus, or inventorying the medical supplies at least two times per shift.

Riley recognized the extra assignments for what they were and didn't disagree with having to do them. They were assigned to him for a reason. The first reason was to make him think before barging into a situation and the second, but most important reason, was to make him a better firefighter.

An hour later, he walked into the bay of Station Five, his bunker gear in hand from its use at the training field that morning. He walked to the storeroom and hung his gear on his assigned hook.

Lunch had just ended, with a few firefighters remaining around the table, while a couple were in the crew's office, checking email and catching up on reports. Riley had seen others in the bay working on and adjusting equipment.

Riley stuck his head in the captain's office.

"I'm back, Cap."

Captain Jernigan gave him a nod and a quick wave before turning back to the computer screen and conference call Riley could hear over the phone. It seemed that the captain was in a lot more meetings lately and when he was not in a meeting, he was engrossed in paperwork. He also seemed a bit more harried and tired. Captain Jernigan, as always, took things in stride, but his presence and banter were missing when he wasn't alongside the crews.

Riley walked back to the kitchen to grab a bite of any possible leftovers as Hayward wiped down the stainless-steel island, polishing it until it sparkled.

"How'd training go, Rookie?" Hayward asked as he punched the buttons to start the dishwasher. "And please take note. I did the dishes for you. Today and today only."

"Thanks, Hayward. I owe you," Riley said, walking toward A Shift's refrigerator.

"Yes, you do, Rookie. And I collect," Hayward said with a final swipe at an invisible spot. "And training?"

Riley opened the refrigerator door and scanned the shelves. "Today was our last day. I'm ready to rotate onto the engine any time. Hope it's soon."

"Ah, you rookies. All got dreams of fighting the 'big one,'" Hayward said, indicating air quotes with his fingers. "Your time will come. At that point, let's see what you say. I bet it's going to be different than what you thought it'd be."

Riley shrugged. "Maybe. But I'm ready to find out." He reached for a couple of small containers of leftovers in the refrigerator.

"Fair enough," Hayward replied, turning back to the sink. "Sorry, not much left from lunch," he indicated with a wave of the dish towel. "But what's there is yours."

"Thanks," Riley called out to Hayward's back as Hayward headed in the direction of the bay. Riley had just started to open the containers when tones sounded for a medical, and Riley froze. It was Mr. Thornton's address. All of the "regular" calls for Mr. Thornton had been in the morning; never in the afternoon. Riley had a bad feeling as he returned the containers and closed the refrigerator door before hurrying to the ambulance.

Carrier piled in the ambulance as the four firefighters buckled up in the engine. The lights flashed as Riley hit the siren and pulled out. His fingers tapped the steering wheel nervously. Riley's thoughts spun, remembering how little Mr. Thornton had eaten, his cough, and how much frailer he'd been the last time Riley had seen him.

When they arrived and Riley knocked on the door, Joanne's face when she answered betrayed her worry.

"He collapsed after he ate lunch," Joanne began before bursting into tears. She led them down the hall to Mr. Thornton's bedroom. "I called 9-1-1 right away. He looks at me but just stares back and doesn't answer."

"Joanne, we've got it from here," Riley said, patting her arm. "Why don't you wait outside and direct the others back here."

She nodded mutely and stumbled from the room.

Mr. Thornton lay sprawled awkwardly on the floor, his legs at uncomfortable angles beneath him, his eyes staring ahead, blinking occasionally, his mouth open in what looked like an attempt to call out.

Carrier was already pulling what they needed from the bags as Riley knelt beside his friend.

"Mr. Thornton, it's Riley. Can you hear me? We're here to help you."

Mr. Thornton rolled his head toward Riley with great effort and groaned weakly.

Riley proceeded with his examination, trying his best to think of Mr. Thornton as nothing more than a patient, not the sweet, kind man who was his friend.

The AED monitor showed Mr. Thornton to be in V-Fib. Opening his shirt, they applied the paddles and as Carrier said "Clear," Riley hit the button on the paddles. Mr. Thornton's body convulsed, and Riley looked quickly at the monitor. Normal rhythm. They hurriedly prepared him to transport as Riley could hear Joanne leading the engine crew down the hall with the gurney.

Carrier was putting their supplies back in the bags when he glanced at the monitor.

"Sully, check the monitor. V-Fib again."

This wasn't good, Riley thought, doing his best to remain outwardly calm. "Push Epinephrine," he said quickly to Carrier, who was already pulling the medication from the bag.

"Young Riley." Mr. Thornton's weak voice grabbed Riley's attention as Mr. Thornton seemed to come to himself. He reached for Riley's hand. "It's okay, son. Please don't fret over me. This is my time. We both knew it was coming. I'm just so glad you're here."

He gripped Riley's hand weakly.

"I'm going to tell my Martha all about you," he went on, his voice growing faint. "You've been a bright spot these last few months, and I thank you." He stopped to lick his dry lips.

Carrier looked at Riley expectantly, waiting.

Riley held Mr. Thornton's hand. "You haven't enjoyed the visits nearly as much as I have. You have become a very dear friend."

A tear found its way down Riley's cheek, and he clumsily brushed it away.

Mr. Thornton looked intently at Riley and tried to smile. "Things are going to be okay, son. I just know it." He took a labored breath. "Keep faith in your love, Riley. She'll come around."

Riley could only nod, more tears threatening.

"And please tell Joanne thank you for me. Her cooking always reminded me of my Martha's."

A sob from the doorway told Riley that Joanne had heard.

Mr. Thornton sighed softly as his hand went slack in Riley's. As Riley looked to Mr. Thornton's face, he watched as his eyes became fixed, their light fading and slowly going out.

A hush came over the room as Riley sat back on his heels, a gloved hand covering his face, working to get himself under control. He took a deep breath and reaching over, gently closed Mr. Thornton's eyes before he stood and walked quickly out of the room.

RILEY STOOD IN FRONT of the fireplace, deep in thought, watching the pulsing glow of the low embers when he felt a hand on his shoulder.

"Sorry, Sully," Jeremy said. "I didn't know you guys had become friends."

Riley nodded. "We had dinner several times, and the talks we shared were . . ." Riley's voice caught, and he looked away.

Riley wiped at his eyes with the back of one hand. "I'm not being very professional, am I?" he said, straightening. "I need to get back in there."

"They've got it. Take a few minutes."

Riley took a deep breath and looked around the room, his gaze landing on the half-decorated Christmas tree at the same time Jeremy's did.

"What's up with the Christmas tree?" Jeremy asked. "Were they decorating early for Christmas?"

"No," Riley sniffed. "It's been like that for years. Decorating the tree was the last thing Mr. Thornton and his wife did together, and he never had the heart to take it down. Did I tell you he's the one who gave me the recipes I cook at the station?"

Jeremy shook his head as he continued to look around the room. "No, I had no idea. Hey, did he fight in World War II?"

"I don't know. He never said anything about it if he did."

"Look at all of these medals," Jeremy let out a low whistle. "He must have really been something to be awarded all of these."

Riley followed Jeremy's gaze to a display cabinet a few feet from the Christmas tree.

"I never noticed those before," Riley said, amazed. "He sure never said anything about them, and we sat in this room every time after we had dinner." Riley walked over to study them more closely.

He and Jeremy stood side by side, studying the medals and the half-decorated Christmas tree.

"Isn't it odd that I never noticed those medals, and you picked up on them right away?"

"Different perspectives, Riley," Jeremy said softly as they stared at the tree. "We see different things because we're looking through different lens, a lens unique to each of us. What we experience in life influences the lens through which we see things. You picked up on the Christmas tree because you're a romantic. You've got Maggie on your mind. Me? I picked up primarily on the war medals because I'm at war. I'm fighting."

Riley turned and looked steadily at Jeremy. "What are you fighting, Jeremy? Tell me."

"Riley," Joanne's soft voice came from the door.

Reluctantly looking away from Jeremy, Riley turned to see Joanne in the doorway.

"Go," Jeremy said as Riley turned back to him. "It's time that I told you what's going on, so we'll talk later. I promise. But this situation is your priority right now."

Riley nodded and clapped Jeremy on the shoulder before striding to Joanne and enveloping her in a tight hug.

"Are you okay?" he asked.

She nodded mutely, sniffing and dabbing at her eyes. "I'll be okay. He was just such a dear man. I sure am going to miss him."

Riley nodded solemnly. "I am too."

She held out a yellowed envelope.

"He told me he wanted you to have this when he passed."

She held out the envelope, and Riley took it, holding it carefully. "Thank you, Joanne. Do you know what it is?"

"I haven't looked at it. But from what he said, I think it's the letter he wrote Ms. Martha telling her how much he loved her. She kept it in her jewelry box and when he found it after she passed, he kept it with him all the time. It was the thing he cherished most."

Riley remembered seeing something like the envelope in Mr. Thornton's shirt pocket when he visited. He'd just never known what it was. Riley couldn't bring himself to read the letter now, so he carefully placed it in his uniform shirt pocket to read later and re-buttoned the pocket flap.

STANDING AT MR. THORNTON's graveside, Riley shivered in his black suit. The wind had turned cold, and the sky was a steely gray with dark clouds skidding overhead. Mr. Thornton had already made his funeral arrangements and taken care of the few details he'd thought necessary for a simple burial. Riley had asked, with Joanne's permission, if he could add a few things to honor Mr. Thornton.

Riley had first made sure the gray casket was covered with an American flag in honor of Mr. Thornton's military service. He had also ordered the spray of yellow and white flowers centered atop the flag. Their edges were ruffling in the chilly wind. They were the only flowers there. Riley watched as the wind whipped the edges of the flag. He was glad it was fastened down. He wasn't sure why he'd even noticed that.

Joanne, tears on her cheeks, stood to his left, shivering despite her heavy coat. Apart from the funeral home director and minister associated with the funeral home, she and Riley were the only ones there. Riley wished more people were there to honor this kind, sweet gentleman. This kind soul who he had laughed with, whose humor he'd experienced, and most importantly, the kindness and wisdom that Riley had benefited from. Riley felt fortunate to be standing there and to have shared in a small part of Mr. Thornton's life.

After a few moments of silence, the minister looked past them and motioned a young Marine forward, carrying a trumpet. With a nod from the minister, the Marine played "Taps." Riley wanted as much done today to honor Mr. Thornton as possible and was glad he'd made this request as well. The mournful song rang out across the cemetery, its solemn notes swirling around in the wind before being snatched away.

Riley thought about the conversations he'd had with Mr. Thornton and how lovingly he'd talked about "his Martha." They're together now, Riley thought with a small smile. Riley pictured Mr. Thornton's kind face and his infectious smile as they talked in front of the fire, how they'd enjoyed Joanne's confections, and how Mr. Thornton gave advice about Maggie. Riley thought of Mr. Thornton's last moments, his words of encouragement and comfort to both Riley and Joanne. Riley looked at Joanne, tears shining in her eyes, as she stared solemnly at the casket in front of them.

Movement caught Riley's eye, and he blinked hard, twice, to push back sudden tears as Station Five's ambulance, engine, and truck pulled to a stop on the small cemetery road a few dozen yards away. The doors swung open and the A Shift crew piled out one by one. Led by Captain Jernigan and Jeremy, the ten firefighters made their way to stand on the other side of the casket, directly across from Riley and Joanne.

As the minister began his remarks, a car pulled up and parked behind the fire truck. Riley was stunned. His mom and dad emerged and started toward them. Coming to a stop at the foot of the casket, Riley's dad, his mom holding his arm, acknowledged Riley with a solemn nod as they all looked to the minister to continue.

The minister made a few appropriate remarks before asking if anyone would like to share thoughts or comments. Riley looked to Joanne, but she motioned for him to speak. Riley cleared his throat and looked around the group. "Thank you, each of you, for coming to honor James Thornton today. I know he would have been surprised and humbled at the number here. I only met him three months ago, but in those short few months, he became a close friend, and I'll treasure that friendship the rest of my life. I will never forget the delicious dinners prepared by his attentive nurse and friend, Joanne, and how much he appreciated Joanne and her loving care." Riley glanced at Joanne and took her hand and squeezed it as she dabbed at tears with a tissue.

Riley looked back to the casket. "James Thornton was one of the kindest, gentlest souls I've ever known, and the conversations we shared were important then but priceless now. He loved "his Martha," who preceded him several years ago. I can only imagine the joy of their reunion and their happiness at being together again."

Riley hesitated and after a few seconds, cleared his throat before concluding. "Thank you, Mr. Thornton. Thank you for everything. You are loved, and you will be missed."

As THE GROUP OF firefighters stepped away from the graveside, Riley lingered, saying his private farewell, before joining them.

"Cap, guys, thank you for being here," Riley said, shaking their hands. "I had no idea you were coming."

"It was the right thing to do," Captain Jernigan said. "Mr. Thornton has been a regular and a favorite of the station for several years. Nice job on the comments."

"Thank you, sir."

"We'll see you at the station later on?" Jernigan asked as the group began to break up and walk toward the apparatus.

"Yes, sir. I'll be in right around dinner. I appreciate the time off."

Jernigan waved him off before turning and following the others.

Riley turned and looked for his mom and dad. They and Joanne were huddled close together near their cars, bracing themselves against the cold and talking. Riley walked over, the rustle of grass beneath his feet blending with the brush of the dry leaves skittering across the open area, carried by the cold breeze.

"Mom? Dad? I'm glad you guys are here but I didn't think you knew—"

Ballard Sullivan held his hand up, stopping Riley. "I talked to Winston this morning and he told me about your friend and about the service. Our apologies for being late, but after talking with your mother, we decided we wanted to be here, both with you and for you. It sounds like Mr. Thornton was a wonderful man. And it's been our pleasure to meet and visit with Joanne here. I mentioned to her that I have some clients who might be in need of a private nurse, so we're going to see if it would be a good fit for both parties."

Riley glanced at Joanne. She was smiling, looking between Riley and his dad, relief and hope evident on her face.

"Well, you can let them know, they'd be lucky to have her," Riley said, grinning at Joanne. "She is not only an amazing cook, but a wonderfully compassionate, and caring person as well. I'm fortunate to claim her as a friend."

Joanne blushed as she patted Riley's arm. "I can tell you two are related," she said, looking between Riley and his dad with a knowing smile. "You're both certainly charmers."

She gave Riley's arm one last pat before turning to his dad. "I'll look forward to hearing from you, Mr. Sullivan, and thank you again for the opportunity. It was nice to meet you, Mrs. Sullivan."

"The pleasure is ours," Ballard said, as Jane nodded agreement. Joanne turned and started toward her car.

"Riley, honey, you look tired," Riley's mom said worriedly.

"I am tired, Mom, but I'm fine. I'm due at the station later on this afternoon. I'll rest some before I go in." Riley started to walk off but turned and came back and enveloped first his mother and then his father in a tight hug.

"Thank you so much, both of you, for coming today. It really means a lot," Riley said, his voice raspy.

"We didn't know Mr. Thornton, but we know you. And for someone to mean this much to you, they had to be pretty special. We wanted to be here for you," Ballard said with a clap to Riley's back.

"Thanks, Dad. I'll talk to you guys soon."

Ballard opened the car door for his wife and after getting in, they slowly drove off.

Riley looked back to the grave site where the cemetery grounds keeper and crew were beginning preparations to lower the casket into the ground.

"Goodbye, Mr. Thornton. Thank you for your friendship," Riley said softly. "I'll never forget you."

He turned and got into his SUV. The silence and the weight of being alone bore down on him. He wished, yet again, for Maggie.

THE ATMOSPHERE IN THE station was subdued. Riley felt it as soon as he walked through the door that evening. The kitchen was empty and had already been cleaned up from dinner. It looked like everyone was in their rooms. Riley was glad. He didn't feel like being conversational.

He pulled out the half-empty pitcher of tea from the refrigerator and after dropping some ice cubes in a glass, poured tea to the brim. He took a long, slow drink. He started brewing more tea before taking a seat at the empty table.

Carrier came through from the bay and got a soft drink from the refrigerator before heading to his own room. Riley finished the tea once the bags had brewed and slipped the full pitcher into the refrigerator.

Captain Jernigan came through and stopped short when he saw Riley standing at the open refrigerator door. He hoped the news he was about to share would lighten Riley's mood. He'd had to get the paperwork in order before moving Riley to the engine. With Riley's return to the station, the over timer who had been filling in for him today had just left. This would be a good time to let Riley know that it was effective immediately.

"Rookie," Jernigan said as he stepped into the kitchen. He walked to the coffee pot and filled his mug.

"Hi, Cap," Riley said, closing the door and turning toward the captain.

"Can I see you in my office, please?" Jernigan turned, taking a sip of coffee, and walked that direction.

Puzzled, Riley followed.

"Shut the door," Jernigan said as he sat down behind his desk and set his mug on its coaster. Riley hesitantly closed the door and sat in one of the chairs across from him.

"Riley, you've had quite an interesting few months since starting with the department," Jernigan began. "There aren't many rookies who conduct a funeral service for one of our victims or charge into an all-out bar brawl." Jernigan studied Riley, who looked uncomfortable.

"Am I in trouble, sir?" Riley asked dejectedly, his hands clenched tightly in front of him, his shoulders slumped.

"Well, no. You're not in trouble. Unless you think being assigned to the engine is considered a punishment. You will be working with Ennis after all."

Riley's head jerked up, his eyes wide.

"The engine, sir? I'm assigned to the engine?"

"Yes, effective immediately. The overtimer we had in while you were out today was on the engine, and Ennis is doing out-of-class duty the remainder of the shift with Cochran at his girls' ballet recital. Grimes is on the engine the remainder of the shift and then on the ambulance next full shift. This seemed like the perfect time to make these adjustments. I'll let Grimes know the arrangements next. This is a trial run for the next three or four shifts to see how things go. If all goes well, we'll see about making the changes permanent. If not, you'll be back on the ambulance for a while longer. Not a bad thing either way. You're a proficient paramedic, but now, we'd like to see what kind of firefighter you are."

Riley sat back, caught totally off guard, a stunned but pleased look on his face.

"I take it you're okay with this new arrangement?" Jernigan asked, hiding a smile before reaching to straighten the papers in the middle of his desk that he'd been working on.

"Sir? Oh, yes, sir. Thank you. This is great. I've been training and studying hard. I'll do my best," Riley said in a rush.

The captain smiled to himself, glad the timing on this had worked out as it had.

"Alright, alright. Go put your gear on the engine. I'll let you know when it's decided if the arrangements are permanent or if additional moves are needed."

"Yes, sir. And thanks again, sir," Riley said, rising quickly from his chair and walking out with a bounce in his step, leaving the door open behind him.

Riley retrieved his bunker gear and placed it just outside the door on the engine behind Hayward, the driver. Jeremy's gear was already on the front passenger door since he was doing out of class duty as the engine officer for the remainder of the shift. Riley was thrilled, but his happiness was also tempered with the sadness of the day.

Coming in from the bay and sitting back down at the table, Riley sighed. He knew he'd get past the hurt of Mr. Thornton's loss, but he'd been such a bright spot, such a comfort, filling an emptiness Riley hadn't even realized he had.

From habit, he pulled his phone from his pocket and checked his emails. He rolled his eyes at the typical scam emails or advertisements. He wasn't surprised there was no email or text from Maggie, but he was determined to be positive and remain hopeful. He wanted to tell Maggie about his move to the engine, but he wasn't in the mood to send an upbeat text, even with this good news. Not today.

Riley sighed again and stood. Not wanting to stay inside, he walked out behind the station, where a small patio held the station's grill and a weathered picnic table. Even though the wind was cold, the patio was protected so it was comfortable. Riley stepped up on one of the picnic table's benches and sat on the table, swirling the plastic glass in his hand, taking a drink of tea every once in a while as he stared out into the quickening dusk.

A squeak of the back door hinges alerted Riley that someone was coming. He had a feeling it would be Jeremy even before Jeremy sat down beside him.

"Sully," Jeremy stated flatly without looking at Riley.

"Jeremy," Riley replied and took another sip from his glass.

"Nice job today at the service."

"Thanks. I'm glad you guys were there."

Jeremy nodded silently.

"Heard you've been moved to the engine. I know you've been anxious for that to happen so congrats."

"Yeah. I am excited about it, but today just doesn't seem like the day to celebrate."

The silence stretched on for several minutes until Jeremy sighed heavily.

"Sully, I'm fighting demons," Jeremy finally said. "My own demons. You've been asking what's going on, and you asked again the other day at Mr. Thornton's, so it's time I told you. I'm fighting demons and circumstances over which I have absolutely no control."

Riley turned toward Jeremy, his expression hard to make out in the gathering darkness.

"What do you mean . . . demons?" Riley asked, confused.

"Do you remember my Grandpa Mars?" Jeremy asked.

Riley nodded.

"Well, as you know, he passed away four months ago," Jeremy rushed on. "And before he died, he told me something that changed my entire outlook on life. It's why I broke up with Allie. It's why I'm at odds with my dad. It's why—" He paused and looked at Riley, "it's why I haven't taken a promotional exam. It's because I'm not . . . I'm not going to be around." Riley shifted and turned where he could see Jeremy's face, thankful the automatic back parking lot light had just come on.

"What are you talking about?" Riley asked, his forehead furrowed with concern and confusion.

Jeremy clasped his hands in front of him, his head down. He was quiet for so long, Riley wasn't sure he was going to answer.

"There's a "tradition," let's call it, in the Ennis family that I'd never heard until my Grandpa Mars told me about it a few days before he died." Jeremy paused and took a deep breath. "Grandpa Mars was a big researcher, and he especially loved researching Ennis family history and ancestry. Several years ago, he found something that goes back in the Ennis family multiple generations—at least the past hundred and fifty years or so. Evidently, no one in the family had put it all together until he did while doing his research. Whether it's a curse or the cosmos or whatever it is, it's happened like clockwork to every third-generation male in the family."

Jeremy finally turned and looked at Riley. Riley waited anxiously for him to continue.

"You see, for the past hundred to hundred and fifty years, every third-generation male in the family has died before their twenty-fourth birthday. My great grandfather died when he was twenty-two in a farming accident. Three generations before that, my great great great grandfather died from consumption when he was eighteen. And on and on it goes."

Riley continued staring at Jeremy, unsure of what to think or say.

"Don't you see, Sully?" Jeremy said, suddenly standing and stepping off the bench to pace in front of the table. *"I'm* the next one. My great grandfather died, but my grandfather and my dad both lived past their twenty-fourth birthdays. I'm next third generation. I'm looking my mortality square in the face.

"Every time we have a fatality like Mr. Bertram a few months back, I see myself in his place. And Mr. Thornton, actually seeing him pass, I was paralyzed that day. I couldn't move. I was thinking, what's it going to feel like? Where will I be? How it will happen? And today, at his service, all I could think about was, what will people say about me? Have *I* made a difference in this life? Do I have a legacy? What will I be remembered for or will I even be remembered?"

Riley could only continue to stare at Jeremy as Jeremy went on for several minutes, pausing only when he stopped to take a shuddering breath.

Finally, Jeremy looked ruefully at Riley and cocked his head to the side. "I know. I know. You think I'm crazy. But, Riley, it feels so real. It feels immediate. Because Riley, my twenty-fourth birthday is next shift."

Riley stiffened as the immediacy of what Jeremy was saying sunk in. Unsure of what to say, Riley tried to think logically. Maybe they were getting too caught up in this.

Trying to speak evenly, Riley cautiously said, "But Jeremy, take a step back. I think you're getting way ahead of yourself and worrying about things you don't need to worry about so much right now. We all think about what the end will be like—especially working in a dangerous profession—but you can't put your life on hold, waiting for something to happen."

"What happened to members of your family—those are just old wives' tales, unlikely coincidences, or superstition. It's the modern day. Things are more, well, logical. You can't take that kind of thing seriously."

Jeremy stopped pacing and stood in front of Riley.

"Sully, it's held true for hundred and fifty plus years. My twenty-fourth birthday is next shift. What would you think if you were me?"

Riley looked anywhere but at Jeremy as he tried to think of how best to reply. After several moments of profound silence, Riley turned and looked Jeremy in the eye. "You know, I might be thinking the same thing you are, but then I also might be thinking where I'd like to go for dinner to celebrate my birthday. Or I might be deciding where to take my girlfriend on a date the next weekend or how many kids we'd like to have. I hope I'd be thinking there's a whole lot to look forward to in life and not anticipating its end prematurely."

Jeremy stared at Riley as he talked, looking as if he were desperately searching for something in what Riley was saying to hold onto.

"Jeremy, only you can decide how you're going to handle the next few days. But one thing I know for sure. No matter what, don't give up. Ever. Are you hearing me? I mean *really* hearing me? I don't know why, but I have a feeling it's important that you do."

Jeremy stood glued to the pavement, hands fisted on his hips, looking at Riley with a fierceness Riley remembered seeing during football games.

"Thank you, Sully," Jeremy said at last, seeming to come to himself. "I do hear you. But I've thought about this a lot. We've all got our time to go, and I think my time is coming soon."

"Soon?" Riley repeated.

"Yeah. I can't explain it. I just think my time is soon." Jeremy said with a slight shrug. "I've resigned myself to it. But hey, I appreciate you not laughing."

Riley put his hand on Jeremy's shoulder. "No way I'd laugh at you, Jeremy. Well, wait, there was the time . . ."

Attempting to chuckle, Jeremy pushed Riley solemnly away.

"Riley, if something should, you know, happen in the next few days? Would you tell Allie why I called things off with her? I really was thinking about a future for us, together, but I didn't want to lead her on only to have to leave her . . . well, you know . . ."

"Yeah, I know. But I think you're going to have to explain all of this to her yourself. And believe me, as upset as Allie is, I wish you luck with that."

"I only hope you're right, Sully. I won't mind having to plead for forgiveness. I just want to be here and able to do it," Jeremy said solemnly.

Before Jeremy could say anything further the tones sounded, shattering the quiet night air. As Jeremy and Riley hurried into the bay, the dispatcher kept naming equipment for a structure fire. It sounded like the entire department was being called out.

THE LIST OF EQUIPMENT being dispatched continued as Riley stepped into his bunker pants and quickly slipped the suspenders over his shoulders. Throwing his bunker coat on, he jumped into the seat behind the driver, Hayward, who tossed his own bunker coat on the front console. Riley slipped his headphones on after fastening his coat. He mentally began walking through what to do once they were on scene.

He stole a concerned look at Jeremy. After pulling his bunker coat on, Jeremy dropped into the officer's seat across from Hayward. Their conversation replayed in Riley's mind. With Cochran off, Jeremy was serving in a command position for the first time as the engine's officer. Riley could see the muscle clenching and unclenching in Jeremy's jaw as the dispatcher continued.

Grimes fastened his bunker coat, climbing into the seat across from Riley. "Sounds like every station in the city's being called out," he said under his breath, as he slipped his headphones on.

Riley glanced over and nodded solemnly as Hayward shifted the engine into gear, following the ambulance out of the bay. The combined wails of the sirens from the truck, engine, and ambulance bounced loudly off the walls.

Riley's heart was pounding. His breaths were short and shallow. His hands trembled slightly as he grasped his helmet firmly in one hand

and his gloves and hood in the other. He was nervous and excited at the same time. This was his first fire, and it sounded like it was going to be a really big one.

The apparatus flew through the streets of Abernathy in the deepening dusk. Within minutes, Riley could see an orange glow ahead. Everyone sat up at the same time when they saw it. An orange glow still that far in the distance meant this fire had to be huge.

The Belmeade address sounded familiar to Riley. And when they pulled onto the street, Riley realized why. It used to be a warehouse, but was converted into condos. The burning building was the same building that he'd seen on fire all those years ago. The same building that had created his desire to be a firefighter.

His mom had picked him up from middle school that day. She had been in a hurry and wasn't happy when, on their way home, traffic had come to a sudden halt. Streets were blocked off because of a fire at the warehouse. Watching the firefighters as they had worked made a huge impression on Riley. It had literally changed the trajectory of his life. Riley had always been told that he was going to follow his father into law. But after he'd scrambled out of the car that day and rushed closer to watch, his desire and dream of becoming a firefighter had taken hold. And that desire had never wavered.

And now, here he was, the firefighter he'd dreamed of becoming. The enormity of the job and what he was about to do nearly took his breath away as the building came into full view. Riley couldn't help but stare. The building seemed to throb. Flames and smoke billowed from every window. Ebbing in and licking out, the flames looked like a starving beast desperately searching for food.

The various apparatus maneuvered into position. Battalion chiefs exchanged information and began directing those under their command.

While Hayward pulled into the spot directed by Battalion Chief Bentley, Riley watched as firefighters pulled hose off the back of the engines, using the minuteman lay, tying onto five inch and two and a half inch hoses which had been tied onto hydrants. Cross lays and more hose were pulled while ladders were set. Aerial ladders were being raised and swung slowly into place once their trucks were braced and grounded. It was an anthill of activity, but each firefighter was working their assignment with calm and precision. Dozens of firefighters, silhouetted against the orange and yellow of the flames, walked into the building, carrying one of the deployed hose as tenants streamed out, rushing past them.

The air was hot. It seemed to pulse with activity and execution. Smoke, soot, and falling ash blanketed the sky. Billows of smoke blew between the apparatus and the building. Visibility was difficult even at a short distance. The glow from the flames lit the entire area with flickering shadows. Bright floodlights were being switched on, one after another, illuminating the area until it was bright as day.

Grimes had jumped out a few hundred feet up the street to pull and connect hose to a nearby hydrant. As soon as the engine came to a final halt and the air brakes hissed, the three remaining firefighters piled out of the cab. Hayward slipped on his bunker coat and began working the engine's pump panel and gages to start the water flowing. Jeremy and Riley pulled on their self-contained breathing apparatus, cinching the straps tightly in front of them. Grimes quickly did the same when he joined them.

Riley, sweat already trickling down his neck, hazarded a quick look around as fire apparatus continued pulling in and positioning themselves where commanded. The fire ground teemed with firefighters.

After conferring with Battalion Chief Bentley, Captain Jernigan called the Station Five engine and truck crews together behind the truck.

"Gentlemen, we are Attack. We're already hooked up to hydrants so go ahead and pull as much hose as you need. I'll lead one team and approach from Alpha. Ennis, you lead the other and approach from Delta. We're holding a fine line between offensive and defensive so don't hold anything back and stay alert. We have no floor plans for reference. A lot of these units are under renovation, so we'll need to be cautious. Stay in close communication with each other. And Ennis, stay in touch with me. No unnecessary chances."

"Copy that," Jeremy said with a firm nod and a look to Riley, the others nodding their acknowledgment.

The look on Jeremy's face spoke volumes. It conveyed determination, but it was a look meant to convey something, everything. He could hear Jeremy's voice from their conversation not even an hour ago. "We've all got our time to go, and I think my time is coming soon."

Riley's stomach churned. A feeling of dread descended like a cloud. Riley could feel it physically closing in.

"Soon," Jeremy had said. Riley fought the feeling of panic trying to take hold of him.

With a nod to Hayward who turned back to the panel, Jeremy, Riley, and Grimes moved to the back of the engine and began pulling hose.

The Station Five crews made their way to the building, the captain with the truck crew taking the front while Jeremy, with the engine crew, headed toward the side of the building, the charged hose trailing behind them.

The majority of the noise grew muffled as the engine crew followed Jeremy away from the fire ground. Before entering the double push doors they'd located, Jeremy held up a hand, motioning for them to stop and put on the final pieces of their gear. Each slipped on their hood and pulled on their masks, adjusting the straps on the back of their head. Next, they attached their regulator from the air tank to their mask.

As soon as Riley slipped the mask on, it enveloped him in a vacuum of sound. The only things he could hear were his own ragged breathing and radio communications. Successfully donning his gear, Riley pulled on his helmet, cinching it tight under his chin with trembling fingers. Once everyone had pulled on their gloves, they advanced, picking up the fully charged hose, taut with restrained water pressure.

The interior was shrouded in smoke. The darkness was broken only by intermittent pop-up flames that glowed a hazy orange around them. The engine crew followed Jeremy's lead and methodically searched each condo on the first floor. They acknowledged the truck crew as the two teams met in the middle. Ascending the stairs, they began the same process, moving from the back to the front on the second floor. The third condo, one away from where the truck crew had just entered, was different than any they'd seen so far. It was empty, gutted, and appeared to be one of the units currently undergoing a major renovation.

Jeremy cautiously entered the space first, looking side to side as he advanced. The beam from his helmet's flashlight cut small shafts of light into the smoke. Riley followed, a few feet behind, Grimes right behind him. From what Riley could see, the space was twice as large as the other condos they'd searched. An occasional spark or ember drifted by and lit the concrete floor before snuffing out. Glancing to the right, Riley saw several large, unopened wooden crates before he turned, continuing to follow Jeremy.

Radio traffic had just indicated the third floor in their quadrant was heavily involved and beginning to lose structural integrity when Riley saw Jeremy suddenly stiffen. Jeremy whirled to face Riley, his eyes wide. At the same instant, Riley saw what Jeremy had seen.

Directly in front of where the three firefighters stood, a stockpile of cans—paint, paint thinner, turpentine, a couple of air compressors—all with a reflective "FLAMMABLE" on their sides.

"Get out! Now!" Jeremy panted urgently into his radio as he motioned frantically with his hands.

Suddenly, the roof overhead collapsed, a direct hit on the cans. The force of the ensuing blast lifted Riley off his feet, propelling him backward into Grimes, leaving both of them on their back, pinned by debris and portions of the collapsed roof. The cans were replaced by flames, roaring an inferno and hungrily consuming the new fuel, growing quickly.

Stunned, Riley's head rang with the concussion of the blast. He could hear someone who sounded like Captain Jernigan calling on the radio, but he sounded far away. He was calling a mayday. Who is down? Riley wondered. As he tried to move, he realized he couldn't. He was the one down. He tried to focus. And when his mind cleared slightly, his first thought was of . . . Jeremy.

Riley managed to raise his head slightly. From the beam of his flashlight, he finally picked Jeremy out of the gloom and pulsing shadows created by the flames. He was a few feet over, sprawled face down, on top of the crushed wooden crates, his arms and legs dangling limply. He wasn't moving. The chirping he was hearing, Riley realized, was from Jeremy's personal alert safety system.

Riley struggled, trying to call out to Jeremy, but his voice didn't work. He tried, but it was hard to focus and the ringing in his ears made it hard to hear. He tried again, but as the blackness closed in, the last thing he heard was Captain Jernigan's voice repeating, now even further away: "Mayday! Mayday! Multiple firefighters down."

CRAWFORD AND CADE RECEIVED the call about a massive fire midway through their shift and had been dispatched to close the surrounding streets and do crowd control. He knew Riley and Jeremy were on duty. They were here, somewhere. Cade was grabbing some bottled water from the response unit care station located near the ambulance triage area when he heard a loud explosion. All heads turned toward the building as radio traffic slowed then instantaneously jumped. It halted once again and then silence descended when the calls for help came across the air wave: "Multiple firefighters down. Mayday. Mayday. Jernigan, Truck Five, roof collapse, flammable liquid ignited. Three firefighters down: Ennis, Sullivan, Grimes. RIT team to second floor. Heavy fire. Repeat. Mayday."

Cade nearly choked. Jeremy and Riley were down.

Prepared in case of such an eventuality, the RIT team was already on the move, gear in hand. Cade watched as they entered the building. There was nothing he could do to help. All he could do was wait. Frustrated, he began to pace, faster and faster, as radio traffic tracked the rescue underway.

The relentless flames continued to roar, seemingly unabated. Stalwart firefighters continued their efforts while the RIT team began to exit the building at long last. They headed toward the triage area, carrying one firefighter, then another, and finally, the third. Cade made his way closer and recognized Grimes, then he saw Riley and Jeremy. His feet automatically carried him to where the RIT team laid them down, and the paramedics began to work.

"Officer, you're going to have to give us some room," one of the paramedics said as he hurriedly began assembling supplies.

"Oh sorry, sure," Cade said distractedly, but moving only slightly.

"These guys . . . these guys are my best friends," he said to no one in particular. He looked first at Riley then Jeremy. Neither had moved.

The two paramedics working on Jeremy and the other two assessing Riley looked at each other and then at Cade, understanding.

"We'll take good care of them, Officer. Don't worry."

Cade nodded, worried, but knowing he had to move for them to work. After the paramedics had done everything they could—which to Cade looked like a lot—they loaded Jeremy first into one ambulance, Riley into another, and Grimes into a third. Cade wanted to stop and ask how Riley and Jeremy were and the extent of their injuries, but he didn't want to get in the way anymore then he already had.

As the three ambulances began to pull away and their sirens started, Cade watched them, running his trembling fingers through his hair with one hand while his other hand was tightly fisted at his waist. He took a shaky breath and began to pace. As he turned, he saw Crawford walking quickly toward him.

"Marshall, I think you're needed at the hospital. I've made arrangements to have our area here covered. Let's go."

Cade hurried, following Crawford, then out pacing him at a near run to their cruiser. He was not only anxious about Jeremy and Riley but profoundly grateful to Crawford for somehow managing to get him to the hospital.

Early morning light was just beginning to filter through the Sullivan's bedroom windows when the phone rang, slicing through the peace and quiet with urgency. Jane Sullivan glanced at the clock as she sat up, reaching for the phone. 6:03 a.m.

Sudden dread filled her. This couldn't be good news at this hour. Ballard stirred awake next to her as she answered.

"Mrs. Sullivan?" a male voice asked hurriedly.

"Yes. This is Jane Sullivan."

"Mrs. Sullivan, this is Battalion Chief Bentley. Your son, Riley, is in my battalion. I don't want to overly alarm you, but I did want to let you know that we had a major fire incident overnight. Your son, Riley, was injured and has been taken to the hospital. We don't know the extent of his injuries but—"

"Riley? What? How bad? Where is he?" Jane asked in a rush, shooting to her feet and reaching for her husband's hand.

Ballard, now wide awake, took the phone from his wife as he clasped her hand tightly.

"Ballard Sullivan here. I'm Riley's father. What's going on?"

"Sir, this is Battalion Chief Bentley. As I was telling your wife, there has been a major fire incident overnight and your son, Riley, has been injured. We don't know the extent of his injuries, but he listed you and your wife as emergency contacts. I'm sorry to wake you at this early hour but wanted you to know in case the hospital needs information from you, or if they need support in making any major decisions. He's been taken to Abernathy Memorial. Would you like me to send a vehicle to pick you and your wife up and drive you to the hospital?"

Ballard frowned, his heart racing. He tried to give his wife a reassuring look before releasing her hand to pinch the bridge of his nose and squeeze his eyes tightly closed.

"Thank you, Chief, but we can manage. You said Abernathy Memorial?"

"Yes, sir."

"We're on our way."

"Yes, sir. You have my number so please let me know if there's anything you need."

"Yes, thank you," Ballard said, ending the call.

Jane looked at him, her eyes wide. "He's hurt? Did they say how bad?"

Ballard shook his head as he stopped and took his wife's hand, looking her in the eye. "The chief said Riley has been taken to the hospital but doesn't know the extent of his injuries. He did say as Riley's emergency contacts, we need to be there in case they need information or . . . any decisions made. We need to get there."

"Decisions? What kind of decisions?" Jane Ballard gasped, fearing the worst.

"Surgery possibly? There's no way to know. We just need to get there in case we're needed." Ballard pulled his hand from hers and hurried to the closet, pulling clothes from hangers.

Anger, fueled by fear, began to rage in Ballard. "He just couldn't go into a respectable, safe profession like law, could he?" he exploded.

"Oh no! He had to be a firefighter and now look what's happened. I hope he's gotten his fill of it and has had some sense knocked into him in the meantime."

Jane flinched at Ballard's outburst but also understood it was fear talking. Fear for Riley. She felt like she was moving in a dream, though it was more like a nightmare. Riley would be okay. He had to be. She couldn't bear it if...

She couldn't go there, but the look on Ballard's face frightened her. He looked—and sounded—afraid. She hadn't seen him like this before, and it was unnerving. Despite his and Riley's differences, she'd always known Ballard loved Riley. But until this moment, she'd never known just how much.

MAGGIE LEANED BACK IN the leather conference chair, lifting her coffee to take a quick sip. Wrapping both hands around the mug, she glanced over the marketing storyboards in front of her and smiled.

"I like the way this campaign is shaping up," Connor said, catching her smile and returning it with a small wink from across the conference table where he was working on his laptop.

"It's going to be really strong," Maggie agreed as she set her mug back on its coaster. "There's still a lot to do, but with the direction we're headed, it's going to be ready in plenty of time for Tuesday's presentation."

Maggie glanced at her watch. It was already 8:50 a.m. She and Connor had gotten a lot accomplished since their 7:00 a.m. start.

She glanced back up and caught Connor watching her, an undecipherable look on his face. She smiled self-consciously before quickly picking up a storyboard to study. They were working well together, and she enjoyed his company. He seemed to feel the same, but something just didn't feel right.

Maggie startled when her phone suddenly buzzed. She picked it up and glanced at the screen. Cade Marshall. Maggie's brows furrowed. Why would Cade be calling her?

She sent it to voice mail and laid the phone face down on the conference table. Connor glanced at her briefly but then went back to his laptop.

A few minutes passed, and Maggie's phone buzzed again. Maggie picked it up and looked at the screen. Cade again. Now she was curious.

Maggie picked it up and looked at Connor. "Sorry, I think I need to take this." Connor nodded, his gaze lingering on Maggie as she answered and stood, walking a few steps away.

"Hello? Cade?" Maggie asked, her back to Connor. "What's up?"

"Maggie," Cade started, his tone somber.

Alerted, Maggie stiffened. "Cade, what is it? What's wrong?"

"Maggie, we had a big fire last night. Both Riley and Jeremy..." He paused unsure how best to proceed without scaring her.

"What, Cade? Tell me. What is it?" Maggie asked, grabbing the edge of the conference table for support. She gripped it tightly, her knuckles turning white, fearing the worst. Connor sat up, watching the side of Maggie's face.

"We had a big fire last night," Cade began again. "It was massive. It was in The Lofts. You know in the converted warehouse district?"

"Yes, I know. Go on."

Cade explained as briefly as possible what had happened and what he knew of the extent of Riley and Jeremy's injuries.

Maggie's face drained of all color. Her hand flew to her chest as her eyes filled with tears.

"Oh my god, Cade."

"I just thought you might want to know." There was a slight pause before Cade said in a rush, "I've got to go."

"I see. Thank you, Cade. I appreciate you letting me know." Her voice shook as she replied.

Maggie hung up. Resuming her seat, she laid her phone softly on the table. Her fingers were trembling as they rested on top of it. She stared distractedly out the conference room windows.

Riley was hurt. Cade didn't know how badly, but badly enough to be taken unconscious to the hospital. She wanted to be there. But should she go? Suddenly, just how much she wanted and needed to be there hit her full force. She looked at the conference table with files and storyboards scattered across its highly polished top. Connor, their major presentation—she had responsibilities here. But she loved Riley. What if now, she'd never get to tell him that?"

She stared, unseeing, out the conference room windows. Riley's handsome face danced in front of her with his teasing smile and sparkling gray eyes. Her heart clenched. What should she do?

"Maggie?" Connor asked softly. When Maggie didn't respond, Connor said again, "Maggie? Everything okay? You're white as a sheet."

"Oh. I'm fine. I . . . just got some news from home," she said turning to face Connor and swiping quickly at a stray tear.

Connor jumped up and poured a glass of water. Coming around the table, he set the glass near her before sitting down beside her and putting his other hand on her arm.

"What's wrong? Anything I can do?"

Maggie took a quick sip and set the glass on the conference table, her hand trembling.

"Some friends . . . some very good friends were in a big fire in Abernathy. They've both been taken to the hospital. One is in critical condition and in surgery and the other hasn't regained consciousness." Maggie swiped at another tear.

"These must be very good friends," Connor said, observing her closely.

"Yes," she said softly, looking down, "very good friends."

"Do you need a minute before we continue?"

Maggie's head jerked up, her mind reeling. "Continue?"

"Well, yeah. We've lost a lot of time on this campaign, so we've got to shift into high gear. No time to lose."

Maggie could only stare at Connor, trying to remember where things stood before Cade's call.

"Would you excuse me for a minute?" Maggie asked, standing and picking up her phone.

"Sure thing, but Maggie, you know how big this is. We've got to nail it. Let's get through at least the first phase before lunch and then we can tackle the rest this afternoon."

Maggie gave Connor a quick nod that he didn't see. His attention was already back on his laptop.

T HE EMERGENCY ROOM WAS chaotic when Ballard and Jane Sullivan rushed through the sliding glass doors. The waiting room was over-flowing, and the halls to either side of the reception area were lined with occupied gurneys, while others sat on the linoleum floor waiting to be seen.

Ballard steered his wife to the front desk and addressed the frazzled nurse behind it. "I'm Ballard Sullivan. We received a call that our son, Riley, was being brought here. He's a firefighter. Can we find out how he's doing?"

The doctor who had just walked behind the desk and handed something to a nurse, turned upon hearing Ballard's question.

"You're Riley Sullivan's parents?" he asked quickly.

"Yes, Doctor. We were told he's been injured and was being brought here."

"I'm Dr. Austin, the attending ER doctor. Come with me," he said and stepped briskly from behind the nurse's desk. He walked quickly down the hallway to the left.

Ballard and Jane looked at each other and followed, hurrying to catch up as they navigated the busy hallway. Stopping at a door with a large Room 11 sign above it, Dr. Austin opened the door and waited as Ballard and Jane followed him inside before closing it again.

Jane gasped when she saw Riley. He lay unconscious in the hospital bed. He was extremely pale, his lips were parted slightly, a stray lock of dark hair clinging to his damp forehead. One hand was resting on top of the sheet and the other beneath. Oxygen tubes were in his nose, an IV in the arm on top of the sheet, and wires to various nodes attached to his chest looped over the neck of the hospital-issued gown, draping across the sheet, attached to various monitors and equipment giving off a variety of beeps.

Jane put a trembling hand to her lips as Ballard, somber-faced, put an arm around his wife.

"Mr. Sullivan and Mrs. Sullivan, we've run a series of tests and are waiting for the results. Riley suffered some trauma from a close-proximity explosion so there's a chance of some internal injury. We won't know until the tests come back. In the meantime, we'd like to be prepared in case surgery is warranted and need you to sign some forms if you agree."

Ballard tore his eyes from his son. "Sure, Doctor. Whatever you need."

"The nurse will bring the forms to you. Please know this is merely an attempt to speed the process if surgery is needed. If the tests come back showing no internal damage, then these forms are mute."

"Yes, Doc, thanks," Ballard said. "I'm an attorney. I'm aware."

The doctor nodded briskly. "You may stay here with him. I'll send the nurse in."

Jane came close to the bed and reaching over, brushed the stray lock of hair from Riley's forehead. She placed her hand gently on his cheek before reaching down and taking his hand. Tears shown in her eyes as she looked at Ballard as he came to stand beside her. He placed his hands on her shoulders and gazed down worriedly at his son's still form and ashen face.

Allie had texted, letting them know she was in the waiting room and that Jeremy had been injured too. The hospital wouldn't let her come back, but she asked them to please keep her posted about Riley. She promised to do the same when she heard anything about Jeremy.

"WHAT'S TAKING SO LONG?" Ballard grumbled as he paced the small distance between the door and the wall behind Riley's bed that held a variety of monitors and slots filled with medical supplies. A small rectangular window was at ceiling level and allowed a sliver of daylight into the small room that battled with the florescent lighting.

"Shouldn't we have heard something by now?" he went on, rubbing his chin distractedly.

Jane sighed as she rubbed Riley's arm, a worried frown on her face. "Surely, we'll be hearing something soon," she said tiredly. "I still can't believe this."

"Hang in there, sweetheart," he said, leaning over to kiss the top of her head, looking anxiously at Riley's still form. "I'm sure they're doing all they can. And don't pay attention to my grumpiness. I'm just worried, that's all."

AFTER ANOTHER HOUR OF waiting, the same doctor returned with an iPad in hand and a frown on his face. One of the nurses who had been coming in and out, stepped in with him.

"Mr. and Mrs. Sullivan, I have good news. The tests show no internal injury." He tapped a few places on the screen as Ballard and Jane exchanged an alarmed look as he paused. They watched as he took several seconds to read lines on the pad before looking back to them.

"As I was saying, the tests show no internal injuries, which is good news. However, from all indications, he's suffered a severe concussion. I'm a bit concerned he hasn't shown any signs of regaining consciousness but sometimes, that's just the body trying to reset and cope. I want to keep him here for a while longer before moving him to a regular room so we can continue to monitor him closely. I know you've been here for a while. You're welcome to take a break and come back at any time. Nurse Kincaid will be glad to assist you."

"Thank you, Doctor," Ballard said. "I think we could use a break, but one of us will stay with him. Jane, you go ahead and see if you can find Allie. I'll stay with Riley."

Jane nodded. She gathered her purse and stood to follow the nurse and doctor out.

"Oh, Doc," Ballard said, coming to stand close to Jane. "There was another firefighter brought in, Jeremy Ennis. Can you tell us how he's doing? He and Riley are best friends and our families have been close for years."

"Mr. Sullivan, as you're probably aware, I can't share information on another patient's condition. However, I can tell you this: he's been in surgery for a long time."

J ANE RETURNED QUICKLY, BRINGING Ballard a cup of coffee and a hug from Allie. Ballard had been pacing in the small space, eying Riley as he did. There had been no change. Riley still hadn't moved. He hadn't even stirred.

WHAT SEEMED LIKE HOURS later, the door opened and the nurse, who had been in and out of the room all morning, stepped back inside. With a brief nod at Riley's parents, she began checking the monitors on the wall behind the bed but suddenly looked down at Riley then hurried from the room. Riley's dad straightened from where he'd been wearily leaning against the exam room's narrow counter and his mother shifted from the plastic guest chair she had been slumping tiredly on.

When the nurse hurried back in, she went straight to Riley's bedside and began talking to him, encouraging him to open his eyes. Riley's parents clasped hands and moved to where they could see Riley's face. His eyelids were beginning to flutter, and he groaned. They looked hopefully at each other, their eyes widening.

They stepped out of the way as Dr. Austin bustled into the room. He took the nurse's place and began talking to Riley.

Riley's head was throbbing, a slow, steady, mind-numbing throb. What had happened? He couldn't think. He couldn't remember. He felt as if he were coming up from a deep sleep, but he couldn't think of anything except the nagging pain pulsing in his head.

He tried to open one eye, then the other. The bright lights of wherever he was were blinding, and he groaned. He tried to reach up and shield his eyes, but something was weighing his hand down. He frowned, confused, and closed his eyes again.

"Mr. Sullivan?" he heard a soft voice ask.

Mr. Sullivan was his dad. Was his dad here?

He tried to open his eyes again and his eyelids fluttered against the brightness before drifting closed again. He briefly saw a young woman leaning over him. He didn't know her. He felt exhausted and started to drift back into the darkness but heard her voice again.

"Mr. Sullivan, I need you to wake up. Can you hear me?"

The pulsing pain in his head throbbed louder with every word she said. He groaned again and worked to force his eyes open. He succeeded but was only able to peer through small slits before the light became too painful, and he closed them again.

He heard a male voice, more insistent, talking now.

"Mr. Sullivan, it's important that you wake up. Can you hear me? Squeeze my hand if you can hear me."

Riley felt someone lift the hand that had felt so heavy before.

"I need you to squeeze my hand, Riley."

Riley tried to squeeze what felt like a hand clasping his own.

"Good, good. Now open your eyes. I know the light will be bright, but please open your eyes."

Riley tried and finally forced his eyes open, squinting into the light.

"Welcome back. You had us a bit worried. Can you tell me how you're feeling?"

Riley's head throbbed in time with every word said.

"Riley? Can you tell me how you're feeling?" the male voice asked again.

"I . . . my head . . ." He tried to say more, but nothing more came out. He didn't recognize his own voice. It sounded soft and raspy.

His eyes drifted closed again, but he could hear the male voice talking in softer tones to someone else.

Dr. Austin stepped over to where Riley's parents were watching anxiously.

"Mr. Sullivan, he's coming to, but he may respond better to a familiar voice. Would you talk to him? Encourage him to wake up and open his eyes?"

Riley's dad gave a curt nod. Stepping near the bed, he cleared his throat. "Riley? Son? Can you hear me?"

Riley could hear his father's voice coming from somewhere, low and urgent.

"Riley, son. We're here. Your mother and I are here. Can you open your eyes?"

Riley frowned. After several tries, he succeeded in forcing them open. Blurry images of his mother and father appeared, and he blinked until they came into better focus, blurry still, but a bit clearer.

"Dad?" he managed in the same weak voice he didn't recognize.

"Yes, son. Your mother is here too. How do you feel? Can you tell us?"

Riley thought for several seconds, his head still pulsing. "My head hurts."

A face Riley didn't recognize took the place of his parents. "Riley, I'm Dr. Austin. You're in the Abernathy Memorial ER. I imagine your head *is* really hurting right now. You have a severe concussion. But thankfully, no other injuries. It will take a while for the pain to subside, but it will, so try not to worry. We'll get you moved to a regular room in just a little while but for now, just lie still. Your parents are here, and I know they're happy to see you. Can we get you anything?"

Riley tried to move but his entire body hurt, and he winced.

"Just water . . . please," he said.

The young woman in blue scrubs from before held a plastic cup with a straw up to him, placing the straw between his dry lips. He took a couple of short sips before his head dropped back onto the pillow.

He could hear his dad's low and urgent tones and the voice of the doctor, but he couldn't make out what was being said.

His mother's tired and worried face appeared next to him. He could tell her smile was forced.

"Riley, my dear. It's so good to see you awake," she said, a tear rolling down one cheek. She took his hand and held it tightly. "You scared us."

His thoughts began to come together. There was a doctor. What did he say his name was? Riley couldn't remember. And then there was the young woman wearing dark blue scrubs. Didn't the doctor say something about him being in a hospital? He must be. And then, it all came rushing back . . . the fire, the explosion. Jeremy . . .

"Jeremy," he blurted out suddenly. "How's Jeremy?"

He tried to move the sheet off of him.

The conversation stopped. His mother frowned and looked to Riley's dad, who stepped back toward Riley as the doctor came to stand beside him.

"Son," he began solemnly but then stopped.

Riley's eyes widened as he tried to sit up. "No . . ."

The doctor spoke up, gently pressing Riley back onto the bed. "Riley, your friend is in surgery and has been for several hours. There was extensive internal damage. Nothing will be known for a while. Right now, you just need to rest. We'll make sure you know as we know. We do have good news about your other friend, Grimes. He's already been released."

Riley let out a shaky breath. He was glad to hear about Grimes. But Jeremy?

His mother and father exchanged a concerned look as Riley laid his head back onto the pillow and stared blankly at the ceiling.

CADE REACHED INTO HIS pants pocket and pulled out the rabbit's
foot Jeremy had given him a few weeks earlier. He fingered the silky
hair and the small, looped chain at one end. He'd had a feeling, a
sense of dread that day when Jeremy had given it to him and now, this
had happened.

The doors to the ICU unit swished open and Mr. and Mrs. Ennis
stepped out. Mr. Ennis had a protective arm around his wife's shoulders
as she dabbed her eyes with a tissue.

Jeremy had made it out of surgery and post-op and was now in ICU,
but his condition was critical. The grim looks on the doctors' and nurses'
faces when they talked with Mr. and Mrs. Ennis weren't encouraging.

They had just gone in to see Jeremy for the few minutes allotted
each hour while Cade sat alone in the quiet of the small ICU waiting
area, hunched over, his head down.

Seeing them, Cade stood and walked toward them.

"Nothing. No change," Mr. Ennis told Cade, his face drawn and
haggard. "We're going to the cafeteria for some coffee until the next
hour. Would you like to join us?"

"Thank you but no, sir. I'll be here a few more minutes, and then
I'll go check on Riley."

Mr. Ennis nodded and squeezed Cade's shoulder as he and his wife walked slowly out of the waiting area.

Cade looked up as the door to the ICU area opened again and a nurse walked through.

"Excuse me," Cade said, taking a short step toward her. "Do you work in ICU?"

Startled, the nurse stopped short and surveyed Cade. "Yes, I do. Can I help you?"

"Yes, ma'am, please. I have a friend in ICU. Jeremy Ennis."

The nurse's face softened. "Ah, yes. The firefighter."

"Yes, ma'am. He's my best friend, and I know this may sound strange, but could you make sure he gets this?"

Cade held out the rabbit's foot to the nurse. Her fingers closed around it, and she looked up with an understanding nod and smile as she patted Cade's arm with her other hand.

"I'll be happy to. I'll make sure he has it."

CADE MADE HIS WAY to the emergency room waiting area and found Riley's mom and sister sitting together in quiet conversation. They looked up as he approached.

"Any word?" Cade asked, taking a seat next to Allie.

"Riley is awake. They'll be moving him to a regular room soon. Anything on Jeremy?" The desperate look on Allie's face tore at Cade's heart.

"He's still in ICU. Mr. and Mrs. Ennis were just in to see him. There's no change."

Sniffing, Allie slumped back into her chair and brushed a tear away.

"This is all so surreal," Jane said, patting Allie's hand as she looked at Cade."

"Yes, ma'am. It is." Cade cleared his throat and looked away.

"How are you doing, dear?" Jane asked. "You look exhausted. Have you had anything to eat?"

"I'm doing okay. Hanging in there." He gave a wistful smile. "Come to think of it, I guess I haven't. I'd better grab a bite to eat. I'll be back in a little while," Cade said, standing.

"I'll text you with the information when Riley is moved to a regular room," Allie said, standing and giving Cade a hug.

He nodded distractedly, sidestepping a nurse as he headed toward the exit door.

CADE SAT ACROSS FROM Emily, lost in thought. Trying to get his mind off Riley and Jeremy, Emily brought up topics she hoped might be of interest to him, at least for a little while.

"Penny for your thoughts," she finally said after her third attempt to start a conversation.

Cade looked up, a sheepish grin on his handsome face.

"Sorry, I just can't get Riley and Jeremy off my mind. I keep thinking how I could have lost both of my best friends last night. You know the job is dangerous—their job as firefighters, my job as a police officer—but until something like this happens, you just never realize how real that danger is. It's good Riley is going to be okay, but Jeremy . . ."

"You've said you guys have been friends since middle school. How did that come about?"

Cade's face softened, and he grinned. "It's quite an ignoble beginning, especially for me and Jeremy. We're just glad Riley thought we were worth the trouble."

"Well, now you have me intrigued," Emily said with a tease. Putting her elbows on the table, chin in her hands, she leaned forward. "Let's hear it."

Cade chuckled. "Jeremy and I had been messing around after school one afternoon when we came across Riley. We'd all just "graduated" into middle school from sixth grade. We'd seen him at school. I don't know why we remembered him. Maybe it was because he stood out. He looked like a rich kid, you know? We thought he was stuck up.

"We saw him walking home from school and just kinda stood there staring at each other until Jeremy asked Riley if he played any ball. He said he played football and basketball, but then asked if either of us played golf. Golf? Us?" Cade harrumphed with a grin, and Emily laughed.

"He asked if we'd like to give it a try, so we followed him home. His house backed up to a golf course, and he said he liked to hit a few balls from his backyard onto the course. He showed us how but said he didn't hit them too hard so he wouldn't have to go too far to track them down. He made it look easy. But when Jeremy tried it, his ball didn't make it out of the yard or even off the ground. And of course, I saw my chance to one up Jeremy so I stepped up, put the florescent green ball on the tee and then hit it as hard as I could."

Cade shook his head, and Emily winced.

"And did you even hit the ball?"

Cade raised his eyebrows and smirked. "Oh yeah, I hit it alright. Right through Riley's neighbor's window."

Emily gasped. "Oh no! What did you do?"

"Well, we did the only thing we could do. Jeremy and I ran."

"You did what?"

"Yeah," Cade smiled. "We ran and left Riley there to get in trouble and take the blame. Wasn't that a great way to start a friendship?"

"Poor Riley! I would have been furious. What happened then?" Emily asked anxiously.

"Well, we saw him at lunch the next day and asked him what happened. He said the neighbor had offered to replace the window himself if Riley would pay him back by washing cars or doing some yard work for a couple of weeks. Riley was surprisingly cool with it, so Jeremy and I were off the hook."

Cade shrugged before he picked his fork up and took a bite of his now cold enchiladas.

"Please tell me you guys didn't leave it like that with Riley taking the blame and having to do all the work too?"

"Nah," Cade said, taking a chip and dipping it into some salsa before popping it in his mouth. He chewed thoughtfully for a while before answering.

"Jeremy and I talked about it and knew we couldn't leave Riley hanging out to dry, so we showed up at his house the next afternoon. He was pulling grass and weeds from the neighbors' flowerbeds, so we joined him and helped do everything the neighbor lined out."

Cade chuckled. "We found out years later that the neighbor had seen the whole thing and knew exactly who'd hit that ball." Cade blushed. "I still feel guilty about it sometimes."

Emily shook her head and smiled.

"Thankfully, Mr. Pernell, the neighbor, was impressed that Riley was willing to take the blame and do all the punishment. But then, he was also impressed that Jeremy and I owned up to our part in the stunt, even if it was a bit later," Cade added.

Cade leaned back in his chair. "What's fun is that Mr. Pernell became a great friend to all three of us. He'd have us over and we'd sit on his patio, watching the golfers come through, playing the hole behind his house. We'd eat barbecue or hamburgers and just chill," Cade said with a small smile. "Those were good times."

Emily reached across the table and took Cade's hand, smiling reassuringly.

"Please don't worry. More good times are to come. I just know it. And you need to know it too. Keep the faith."

Cade studied Emily, taking in every feature from her soft brown hair and brilliant blue eyes to her rosy cheeks, and the splattering of freckles across her nose. She's as beautiful on the inside as she is on the out, he thought.

He squeezed her hand in return. "Thanks, Emily. I'm a very lucky guy. I have two great best friends, but I find I'm even luckier the past few days."

"Oh?" Emily replied.

"I met you," Cade said, his voice low.

Emily broke into a brilliant smile.

"I feel the same, Cade."

Cade leaned forward and after a conspiratorial look around the restaurant, gave Emily a quick but purposeful kiss.

RILEY'S PARENTS KEPT HIM talking for the next couple of hours until a nurse came in and said they had a regular room ready for him.

"I'm feeling better now," Riley said as he tried to get out of the bed. "I don't think I need to stay."

"Sorry, Mr. Sullivan, the doctor says you do. An orderly will be here in a few minutes to take you to your room."

Riley tried to interject, but the nurse just turned to his parents and continued.

"He'll be in Room 243 if you would like to meet him there."

His parents looked from the nurse to Riley and nodded. They looked tired. He didn't know what time they'd gotten to the hospital that morning, but it must have been early. It had been a long day.

"Mom, Dad," Riley said holding a hand out to his mom, "why don't you guys go home and rest for a while? Looks like I'm not going anywhere."

After a slight hesitation, his dad agreed with a tired smile. "I think we'll do that, son. Rest and we'll be back in just a little while."

Riley did his best to smile as he squeezed his mother's hand. She leaned down and kissed him lightly on the cheek.

"We love you," she whispered.

"Love you too."

It was only a few minutes after his parents left that the orderly came. Releasing the brake on the bed, she rolled Riley out of the exam room and down the hall. Riley looked above him as the ceiling tiles rolled past, his thoughts on Jeremy. Two long halls and an elevator ride later, Riley found himself in a hospital room that overlooked the guest parking lot dotted with a few small trees.

RILEY WASN'T SURE HOW long he'd been asleep when he opened his eyes and looked out the window. The shadows outside were lengthening, and he could tell it was early evening. He frowned as he shifted positions and the bed crackled beneath him.

He heard a soft knock on the door. He turned, expecting to see his parents or a nurse, but instead it was Cade sticking his head in the door. Riley struggled to sit up.

"Hey," Cade said softly, stepping into the room.

"Hey yourself," Riley replied evenly, trying to keep the pain in his head from starting to pulse again.

The florescent light behind Riley's bed put the rest of the room in light shadow as Cade made his way closer.

A grim look on his face, Cade pulled the guest chair next to Riley's bed and eased himself into it. Riley nervously watched Cade's slow, deliberate movements. Cade never eased into anything.

"And Jeremy?" Riley asked, watching Cade's face closely.

Cade sighed. "He was in surgery for a long time and then was in post-op. Now he's in the ICU."

Cade looked down, a pained look on his face as he studied the linoleum floor. "It's not looking good, Sully. They say it's touch and go."

Riley couldn't quite comprehend what Cade was saying. He could only stare at Cade as Jeremy's words from last evening came back to him. *I think my time is coming soon.*

"Jeremy's twenty-fourth birthday is the day after tomorrow," Riley finally said. "He's got to make it until then."

Puzzled, Cade looked at Riley. "Why until then? He's got to make it. Period."

"I know. But he finally told me—just last night—what's been bothering him," Riley sighed heavily, nervously fingering the thin blanket covering him.

Cade sat up and leaned closer. "What? What did he say?"

"He said his grandfather told him right before he passed away that for the past hundred to one-hundred fifty years or so, every third generation Ennis male has died before he turns twenty-four. Jeremy is the next third generation. He's convinced he's going to die before his birthday."

Cade scoffed. "He can't really believe that kind of thing, can he? That's just superstition."

"I thought the same thing, but he's serious. He truly believes he won't make it until then."

Cade looked at the floor, shaking his head. "I'd say he's a lunkhead. But considering the circumstances . . ."

"Nope. Don't go there," Riley interrupted. "He's going to make it. He has to."

Cade took a deep breath and looked back to Riley. "Any word on when you'll be getting out?"

"No, nothing yet. Doctor says I have a concussion, so I have to stay, at least overnight." A few seconds of uncomfortable silence settled between them before Riley asked, "Have you seen anyone else here from the station?"

An orderly tapped the door softly and stepped into the room. Riley could see he was carrying what must have been a dinner tray.

"Dinner, sir," the orderly said. He briskly rolled the table over Riley's bed and set the tray on top. "I'll be back later to pick it up."

"Thanks," Riley said as the orderly quickly strode from the room.

Riley shook his head, lifting the plastic dome from the plate and quickly setting it back down.

Cade rolled his eyes. "Did you hear Grimes was released?"

Riley nodded and tried to roll the table away but couldn't get it to move. He threw his hands up in frustration and then winced with the sudden movement.

Cade eyed Riley, shaking his head. He stood and rolled the table to an open space by the window and sat back down.

"The ER waiting room was pretty full for a while once the fire was finally out enough to release the Station Five crew. They all came straight here, but Bentley sent everyone back to the station when the room got too full. I bet the captain and the guys will be by to see you. They're taking this really hard. I mean Grimes, you, and Jeremy? Cap says he's never had anyone injured on his watch. And now, three fire-fighters at one time? He didn't look too good when he was here."

Big-hearted Cap, Riley thought. He *would* take it hard, even though it was in no way his fault.

"Oh, and Riley, another thing," Cade said, fingering the nurse call button hanging from Riley's bed before Riley reached over and took it from him.

Cade hesitated and cleared his throat nervously.

"This doesn't sound like something I want to know," Riley said.

Cade rubbed his temples with his fingers before looking at Riley.

An eruption of laughter from the hallway drifted in as a group of people passed by the open door.

"I called Maggie."

"You did what?" Riley asked, surprised. "What did she say?"

"She said she understood and thanked me for calling," Cade said, looking sadly at Riley. "Sorry, buddy. I thought she'd want to know."

Momentary quiet had descended in the hall as Riley sighed heavily and closed his eyes. "Apparently she didn't."

A soft voice came from the doorway, "Oh, but I did. I'm glad you called, Cade."

Riley's eyes flew open. Maggie stood in the doorway.

"MAGGIE?" RILEY SAID A little too loudly, wincing as pain shot through his head.

"Riley?" Maggie said with a worried frown as she walked further into the room.

"I'm fine. Just need to take it a little easy," Riley said, closing his eyes and pinching the bridge of his nose.

Maggie looked at Cade.

"Concussion," Cade stated succinctly and stood. "I think this is my cue to leave. I'll be back later."

In a softer voice he added, looking at Maggie, "I'm glad you're here."

"Me too," Maggie said and smiled at Cade as he turned to leave. She nervously turned and saw Riley watching her.

"It's good to see you, Maggie," he said softly.

Maggie came close to the bed and placed her hand on Riley's arm. "How are you? I mean, really?"

"I have a pounding headache, and if I try to sit up, the room spins out of control. But all of that will pass, they say. Overall, I was lucky. Jeremy not so much."

"How is he?"

"I've been out most of the day but from what Cade just told me, he's in ICU. He had a lot of internal damage. Cade said they don't know if he's going to make it."

Unexpected tears suddenly pooled in Riley's eyes, and he looked away, embarrassed to get so emotional.

"Oh, Riley . . ." Maggie said gently. She sat down on the side of the bed and quietly took Riley's hand.

After several minutes, Maggie softly cleared her throat and looked at Riley. He looked so tired, so done in, so vulnerable. She'd never seen him this way, and it made her heart ache.

She struggled to find the nerve to say what she needed to say. She looked at Riley then back to their clasped hands and took a deep breath.

"Riley, I'm so glad Cade called. I have to admit, it scared me. I mean *really* scared me." She glanced up. Riley was studying her, his eyes searching her face.

She paused before pressing on. "When it hit me I could very well have never seen you again, talked to you or held your hand, I couldn't take it."

Keeping her eyes on their clasped hands, she rubbed the back of one of Riley's hand with her thumb. "I felt like I would suffocate if I didn't get here and see you and talk to you myself. Oh Riley, I'm so sorry for leaving as I did. It was so unfair to never give us a chance to talk things through and sort them out together."

After a few moments' hesitation, Maggie asked even more softly, "Do you think we might still have that chance?"

She looked from their hands to Riley's face, anxious for his response and to see the look in his eyes, but then, she smiled softly. His eyes were closed, and he was breathing slowly and steadily. He was sound asleep. She reached up and gently stroked the stubble on his cheek with the backs of her fingers then brushed a lock of his dark hair from his forehead. He frowned slightly but didn't wake up.

Maggie didn't want to leave. She wanted to sit quietly and just be with him. So, she held his hand and watched him sleep.

After a while, a nurse came in and with a little smile at Maggie, checked the readings on the monitors still attached to Riley. Soon after the nurse left, Riley's mom and dad walked in.

"Maggie, dear," Jane said with a huge smile, walking to Maggie with her arms open.

Maggie gently laid Riley's hand at his side, then turned, being immediately engulfed in a huge hug.

"Maggie, it's good to see you," Riley's dad said, hugging her tightly.

The three turned to look at the sleeping Riley.

"I hope you don't mind me being here like this," Maggie said softly, gesturing toward Riley. "He fell asleep while we were talking and I . . . well, I just didn't want to leave."

Riley's parents exchanged an understanding and knowing look.

"Honey, of course we don't mind. We're just happy you're here," Riley's mom said in a hushed voice. She glanced at Riley, love and concern evident on her face.

"My poor dear. He's been through a lot the past few days. Having you here is going to give him a much-needed boost."

A nurse in bright pink scrubs with a coordinating floral headband came abruptly into the room. "Folks, sorry. Visiting hours will be over in about fifteen minutes. Everyone will need to be gone by then."

"I'd like to stay with him if that's okay?" Riley's dad asked as the nurse turned to leave.

"Of course! Let me get a blanket and pillow for you." She turned and was quickly gone.

"Guess we'll be going then," Riley's mom said, turning to Maggie with a tired smile.

Maggie nodded and gathered her coat and purse from a nearby chair.

"Text me when you get home," Ballard said to Jane as he pulled her into a close hug, giving her a quick kiss. "I want to make sure you're home safe."

"I will," she sighed into his jacket as she kept her arms around him a few seconds longer. "I love you," she breathed softly. "Take care of our boy."

"I will. Love you too," he replied as the nurse came in carrying a thin pillow and even thinner blanket. He took them, eying them speculatively but shrugged with a playful grin, giving his wife one more kiss.

Maggie watched their interaction, glancing between Riley's still form and his parents. As Riley's mom took Maggie's arm in her own and steered her toward the hospital room door, Maggie looked back at Riley. She was thankful he was going to be okay, but she still felt a pang of guilt for moving away.

R ILEY WOKE THE NEXT morning, unsure of where he was for a minute until everything came rushing back, at least bits and pieces he
could remember. One thing he wasn't sure about and thought he
might have dreamed, was Maggie being there last night. She'd seemed
so real, but maybe that was just the power of wishful thinking.

Reluctantly, he opened one eye and then the other. The room
was still gray with early morning light. He glanced over and saw his
dad, unshaven and clothes rumpled, scrunched up in the room's guest
chair that doubled as a quasi-bed. Riley knew he couldn't be comfortable. His dad's head rested on a tiny pillow placed against the back of
the chair while a thin blanket was tangled around his legs. Riley was
touched. His dad must have been there all night.

Riley laid his head back and wondered how Jeremy was doing.
He'd always heard the wee hours of the morning were when the body
was its weakest. Riley knew Jeremy was a fighter, but he hoped Jeremy
remembered that somewhere in his subconscious.

Riley knew everyone thought he was the leader of their little trio,
but both he and Cade knew it was really Jeremy. It was Jeremy who
was always the one there to encourage you, to kick you in the pants,
or deliver a strong lecture if warranted. It was Jeremy who seemed

to have a wisdom beyond his years or the insight to know what you needed even before you did. It was Jeremy and always would be Jeremy. Riley realized even more than ever, just how much he and Cade needed Jeremy. Jeremy had to be okay—he just had to be.

The door swished open, and a slice of bright light from the hallway cut into the room. A nurse entered, wheeling a mobile monitoring device. Seeing Riley was awake, she flipped on the overhead light.

"Good morning, Mr. Sullivan. How are you feeling this morning?" she asked cheerily as she placed a sensor on Riley's finger and ran a thermometer across his forehead.

"Better. My head feels a bit clearer at least."

"Well, that's certainly good news. Dr. Austin will be in a little later this morning to see you. I bet you'll be going home sometime today." She continued to work and type things into the laptop she'd brought with her.

Hearing the noise, Ballard stirred and looked around sleepily.

"Hey, Dad. How long have you been here? Did you spend the night?"

Riley's dad pulled the sheet from his legs and sat up in the chair with a grimace.

"Oh, I don't know when we got here last night, but we had a nice visit with Maggie. Did you two make up?"

"So she *was* here," Riley said, his heart beating faster. The nurse cocked an eyebrow when the monitor started beeping quickly. Riley couldn't help the blush that crept up his neck.

Clearing his throat, he turned to his dad and tried to chuckle. "I thought I might have dreamed her being here."

"Well, she was real enough when we walked in last night, and she was holding your hand. We visited for a few minutes, and when it was obvious you weren't going to wake up any time soon, the ladies left, and I stayed to keep you company." He twisted his head from side to side. "Looks like I'll have a couple of cricks in my neck as a reward."

Riley looked at his dad, feeling a warmth in his chest and a new sense of closeness with him. His dad, who never missed work and looked down on those who took time off, had taken time to go to Mr. Thornton's service, had been here with him all day yesterday, and had spent the night in an excruciatingly uncomfortable chair. All for him.

"No, Dad. You have my thanks and appreciation for being such a wonderful dad. That's your reward. That you've been here through all of this, in spite of how you feel about the fire service? Well, it means a lot."

Riley thought he saw tears in his dad's eyes before Mr. Sullivan turned toward the door. "I'm going to see if I can scare up a cup of coffee." He looked to the nurse, who was preparing to leave. "Okay if I get him a cup too?"

"I don't see why not. Except I wouldn't drink too much of that stuff they call coffee in the cafeteria. Oh, and breakfast will be coming around soon. I wouldn't eat too much of that either," she said and made a face as she walked out, leaving Riley and his dad chuckling.

Still chuckling under his breath, Ballard headed to the door but stopped short when he almost ran into Captain Jernigan.

Surprised, Captain Jernigan took a quick step back, looking hesitantly between Riley and his dad.

"Sorry to come so early. Is this a good time?"

"Yes! Of course it is, Cap. Please come in. Captain Jernigan, I'd like you to meet my dad, Ballard Sullivan," Riley said as he moved to sit up.

Captain Jernigan extended his hand to Ballard, who shook it warmly.

"It's nice to meet you," Ballard said. "Riley speaks highly of you, and I assure you he loves working for the fire department."

"Well, sir, he's doing an exceptional job. We're certainly glad he's a part of the crew at Station Five. I think he has a tremendous future with the fire department in front of him. I know you have to be very proud."

"Yes, yes I am," Ballard said, listening to the captain's praise with a thoughtful look at his son.

"But, son, how are you doing?" Jernigan asked, turning to Riley. "These doctors and nurses are tight-lipped, so I'm glad to see you for myself."

Ballard smiled, leaning towards the door. "Captain Jernigan, I was just headed to the cafeteria for some coffee. Give you and Riley a chance to visit. Can I bring you back a cup?"

"That's kind of you, Mr. Sullivan but I won't bother Riley for long. Just checking in. Thank you though."

Ballard nodded. "Riley, can I bring you a cup?"

"I'd love a cup, thanks. And Dad?"

"I know, I know . . . I'll see what I can find out on Jeremy too," Mr. Sullivan said with a quick nod and another shake of Captain Jernigan's hand. "I'll be back as soon as I can."

Ballard slowly walked out of the door, glancing over his shoulder at Riley who seemed genuinely happy to see his captain. Captain Jernigan, Ballard noticed, had called Riley "son." He hesitated for a moment before leaving the room.

"Thanks for coming, Cap," Riley said. "It's great to see you. And the rest of the crew? Grimes? Everyone doing okay?"

"They're all doing great. They're just wondering about you and Ennis. Jernigan shook his head dejectedly. "Well, we're all praying and sending good thoughts his way. And Grimes? I talked to him yesterday.

He's fine. He has a light concussion and will be back pretty quick. You? That's yet to be determined."

"Ah, come on, Cap. I'll be ready, just as soon as I can get out of here."

"I'm afraid you may be out a bit longer, but that decision is above my pay grade. The docs and the chiefs will make that call."

Jernigan chuckled but the laugh sounded forced. "Rookie, you have no idea the red tape this has created. You could have spared a little sympathy for me and saved me all the work."

Riley looked the captain squarely in the eye. "Cap, I hope you're not blaming yourself for what happened. This may not be much coming from a lowly rookie, but it didn't take long for me to figure out that Station Five is a family. You're not just a great leader, but you're a father figure to us all. Each one knows how much you care about each of us, and we, in turn, respect and care about you. We trust you completely and know you'd never send us into a situation you wouldn't go yourself."

"Ah, come on, Rookie." Jernigan smiled and nodded, still a bit solemn.

"We're all looking forward to seeing you back at the station as soon as the docs give you the all-clear," Jernigan went on. "And you know, we haven't had your delicious chicken in a while. Maybe you can cook that your first shift back."

Riley rolled his eyes, as they laughed and shook hands.

"Thanks for coming, Cap."

"Actually, thank you, Rookie."

The captain gave a mock salute and was gone.

MAGGIE SIPPED COFFEE THE next morning as she sat across from her mother and looked out over their backyard, the sun just rising. Maggie could see her mother glancing at her from the corner of her eye as they sat quietly. She knew her mother wanted to ask, but even if she had, Maggie would have had no answers.

She'd thought about it the entire drive from Dallas to Abernathy yesterday. What would Riley think about her coming? Would he be glad to see her? How would he react? The thought had never occurred to her to stay in Dallas. Riley was injured and nothing else mattered.

After Cade's call, she'd just left. She hadn't given Connor much opportunity to object. Her only thought was to get to Abernathy as quickly as possible. But now, she wondered, should she have come? Riley's reaction—or non-reaction as the case had been—had surprised her. She'd expected something more, but it was as if he hadn't known she was there.

"Maggie, honey, what are you thinking? You don't want your face to freeze with that frown," her mother said, studying her daughter, a slight tease in her voice.

"Oh, I'm thinking about Riley," Maggie said with a sigh, setting her coffee mug down. "I love him, Mom. But now, I'm afraid

I've messed up. He may not care about me anymore." She looked at her mother sadly. "At the time, I was frustrated and angry with Riley. I wanted, or needed, him to know what I meant to him. I needed to know that he was committed to our relationship, but all he could think about was being a firefighter. And to be honest, I felt like he was taking me for granted."

Frustrated, Maggie stood and walked to the coffeemaker, pouring herself another cup. She brought the decanter back to the table, refilling her mother's cup as well. When Maggie sat back down, her brows were furrowed in worry.

Maggie ran a finger around the rim of her mug. "What do I do, Mom? I believed at the time I was making the most logical move for my career, but I also made the decision out of hurt and frustration and didn't treat Riley fairly. Now, it's all turned into a big mess."

"How so, dear?"

Maggie sighed and tears welled in her eyes. "My job hasn't turned out to be exactly what I thought it was going to be. I'm not doing what I was actually hired to do and what I'm doing is way over my head. I have no doubt I could learn it all, but in time, not thrown into the deep end at the start. While I want to learn and do more, Connor is pushing me into doing things I know I don't have the experience or knowledge to do just yet. And actually, it's making me look bad. I need the experience first."

Her mother studied her with concern. "Can you talk to Connor and explain your concerns? They obviously know the quality of your work since they promoted you into that position."

Maggie hesitated. She didn't want to tell her mom that she had a nagging feeling, a gut instinct, about her boss. And besides, that wasn't near enough to quit a job she'd worked so hard to get. There had to be something more and she knew what, or who, that was. It was Riley. For her, it always came back to Riley. She sighed and looked out the window.

Her mother looked at her sympathetically. "Maggie, honey, you're obviously not happy. You need to take some time and think about what *will* make you happy and lift this cloud that seems to be hanging over your head."

Maggie couldn't help but smile. "I know exactly what will make me happy."

Her mother smiled. "Riley."

Maggie nodded, tears filling her eyes.

"I think I made the biggest mistake of my life moving away without talking things through with him first. And now . . . he may have decided to just move on."

Her mother smiled and put her hand on top of Maggie's.

"Maggie, Riley cares. I believe he cares very much. Just give him a little grace right now. He's been through a traumatic incident. And besides, a concussion can do funny things to your mind. He may not quite be himself just yet. And then there's his worry and concern for Jeremy. He's dealing with a lot right now so don't rush him into talking about the two of you or the future. There will be time for that, a little ways down the road."

Maggie nodded absently. "I know you're right, but it's hard to wait." She exhaled deeply. "I finally realize my true feelings and have decided what I really want. I'm just anxious to tell him. I can figure the job situation out later."

"Honey, I understand, I truly do. But you'll be much better off waiting. Everything will be okay. I promise. Just take some time to think things through and try to think about things from a different perspective. You might be surprised what other options might be out there."

Maggie knew her Mom meant well, and she was right on most fronts. But Maggie wasn't sure she could wait when it came to Riley. In fact, she knew she couldn't.

RILEY'S HANDS SHOOK SLIGHTLY as he buttoned the last button on his shirt. He didn't like feeling unsure and weak. Even though the doctor had said to expect it to take a couple of days, Riley wanted to be back to normal now.

He looked over to where Cade was stuffing the last of Riley's few things into the overnight bag his mom had brought that morning.

"Is that the way you normally pack?" Riley asked, stepping back and watching Cade skeptically.

"Is that the way you normally look?" Cade shot back. They both chuckled.

"Very mature come-back. Here. I'll finish up so I can hopefully salvage some semblance of order." Riley brushed Cade gently away and began rearranging and refolding his things. Cade took a seat in the guest chair and pulled out his phone.

"I'll walk down to ICU with you," Riley said as he zipped the bag closed.

"Nope," Cade replied, still looking at his phone.

"What do you mean?" Riley asked, irritation in his voice. "I want to see if there's any news on Jeremy."

"As do I. So, this is the plan. I'm going downstairs. I'll find out how he's doing and either text or call you. You'll be on your way home.

And in fact, your mom and dad have gone to get the car and will be pulling around any minute. I hear you get a ride to the door in a wheelchair. Very impressive, really."

"No, that's not the plan," Riley interrupted irritably. "I'm going down there."

"Hey."

Both Riley and Cade stopped mid-discussion and turned as Maggie walked in, chuckling. "I could hear you guys all the way out in the hall. I hope I'm not interrupting anything."

"You're not," Cade said with a grin at the same time Riley said, "You are," with a frown.

"Oh, I see," Maggie said and took a partial step backward.

"Nope. All's good," Cade said with a smirk as he walked to the door. He gave a pointed look to Riley. "I'll be giving you a call."

"Riley," Maggie said softly, looking uncertain.

"Maggie," Riley replied after a few seconds. "I thought I might have dreamed you last night, but my dad said you really were here. And now, I can see that for myself. How are you?"

"I'm fine. But the real question is, how are you?"

"Well, my headache is much better today, and the ringing in my ears is just about gone. Doc was in this morning and dismissed me, so I must be improving. I'll spend a few days with mom and dad and then go back on duty."

Maggie nodded thoughtfully. "Are you headed home now?"

"Yeah. I was told I have to ride out in a wheelchair, so just waiting for that to show up. Cade said my mom and dad are swinging around with the car."

"I'll be glad to drive you home. I'd like to talk."

"Hold on, Maggie," Riley said, turning and eying her with a piercing look. "I am better, but I'm not ready for any kind of serious conversation. Not right now. I've got too much on my mind. My best friend is in ICU, and they're not sure he's going to make it."

Riley looked out the window, then looked down at his hands. "And things . . . serious things have happened while you were gone that you don't know about. And right now, I just need some space."

Surprised, Maggie took a step back. She'd never experienced such pointed directness from Riley.

Riley went on before she could think of how to reply. "We'll talk. I don't know when, just not right now. So, how long will you be in town anyway?"

Maggie felt the last question as a jab and knew she needed to answer carefully. "At least through the weekend. I have a major presentation Tuesday to prepare for but . . ."

"Oh, I see," Riley said. "I may not be able to accommodate my recuperation schedule to your job."

"As I was going to say," Maggie said, her own temper rising, "I will make whatever accommodations I need in order to be here."

Riley stared at her, his eyes narrowing. She knew that look and didn't like it.

"Excuse me, Mr. Sullivan?" a beaming orderly asked, coming through the door with a wheelchair. "Your ride is here. Are you ready?"

Riley turned to the orderly, the dark look slipping from his face and smiled. "Yes, thank you. I'm ready."

Riley picked up his overnight bag and not quite steady on his feet, moved cautiously toward the wheelchair and eased into it with a bit of assistance from the orderly.

"Goodbye, Maggie," Riley said with a nod once he was settled. "And don't worry, we'll talk. Just later."

Maggie began to speak, but the orderly was already wheeling Riley out the door.

She followed them into the hall but then stopped and watched as they disappeared around a corner. Standing forlornly in the middle of the hall, she stared after them, oblivious to those having to sidestep around her.

Riley had never talked to her like that before. Her mom had been right. She probably should have waited. But this was too important. This was Riley. She'd give him some time, but he'd promised that they'd talk. And she'd make sure they did.

RILEY HAD SLEPT MOST of the afternoon after getting to his parents' house but now sat on the edge of the bed in his old room staring at his phone. He had just hung up from talking to Cade. He took a cautious, hopeful breath. Jeremy hadn't regained consciousness, but the doctor had told Jeremy's parents he'd shown some slight improvement through the day. Riley had a feeling if Jeremy could just hang in there until tomorrow morning—his birthday—he'd make it.

Riley took a breath and looked around the room, taking in the familiar things where he'd spent so much time growing up. His mom had been threatening, even before he'd left for college, to turn the room into a craft room or her get-away space. The only evidence of that were the few plastic tubs of fabric and a sewing machine in a carrying case in one corner. In another corner was a foosball table that had seen its heyday when he and Jeremy and Cade had played after school when they were supposed to be doing homework. The bookcase still held his high school sports trophies, but his mom had switched out his football posters for some landscapes and family photos. Riley picked up a picture of him and Maggie off the nightstand. It was the night of homecoming their senior year when they'd been crowned homecoming king and queen. He was in his football uniform and she was in a long, dark blue dress. He sighed and set it back down. That seemed like a long time ago.

His conscience was nagging him. He'd been short with Maggie, but why? She'd come back just because of him, so where was his anger coming from?

He knew, but then had to admit it to himself. She'd walked off and left him. Now that she was back, was he willing to open himself up to his feelings with the looming possibility she'd leave again? Why exactly was she here? Was it just for the weekend to make sure he was okay and then she'd be gone again? Or was she here with something else on her mind?

He'd tried hard not to be too angry when she'd left, even though it had hurt him deeply. She'd left with no warning or hint and gave no opportunity for them to talk things through. He'd missed her and he'd let her know, but she'd given him little to no response. But she was here, so now what?

Riley had just pulled his shirt on and was buttoning it when there was a light tap on the door.

"Come in," Riley called out as he sat on the edge of the bed and began slipping his shoes and socks on. He looked up when he heard his dad's voice.

"Son? Got a minute?"

"Well sure, Dad. Come on in. I'm just finishing up. Mom said dinner would be ready soon. I thought I'd better start getting up and around."

Ballard appraised him as he stepped inside the room and pushed the door softly closed. "Well, don't overdo it after just getting home. You may want to take it easy, at least for a while. We're here to help, so don't push yourself too hard too soon." He cleared his throat and moved to sit on the edge of the bed near Riley.

Riley looked at him, his brows creasing in worry as he turned and faced his dad.

Ballard looked at Riley and put a hand on his shoulder.

"Son, this is a talk I should have had with you weeks ago, and this may be a strange time to have it, but please hear me out before you say or do anything."

Riley looked at his dad suddenly alarmed.

"Dad, is everything okay? Are you okay?"

Ballard held a hand up, stopping Riley. "Hear me out first and then we'll address any questions. Deal?"

"Sure, Dad. Sorry, go ahead."

"Riley," Ballard began as he stood and started pacing, his hands clasped behind his back, a familiar routine Riley had seen him use in front of a jury. "Son, you know how long I've looked forward to your joining me at the office."

Riley groaned inwardly. Was this going to be another "you belong at the firm" speech? It wouldn't be surprising after what had just happened. He couldn't really blame his dad. It would be the typical parents' reaction, and in fact, Riley wouldn't be surprised if this talk was actually his mother's idea.

His dad continued. "Since the day you were born, I've dreamed of our working side by side, building the firm into something more than I could make of it myself. In all of my dreaming and big plans though, I didn't take into account your dreams and what you'd like to do. I may be a bit late, but I'm realizing that now."

He stopped and sat back down beside Riley, looking him in the eye.

"Riley, after seeing what you did for Doug the other day, how calm and confident you were and how you took charge of the situation, and after your walking into a burning building, not thinking about yourself, I see not only you, but myself in an entirely different light."

Ballard stopped and took a breath. Riley was holding his, anxious to hear what his dad said next.

"Son, in spite of the fright you gave your mother and I yesterday, I believe you've chosen your profession wisely. I just wanted to tell you that I'm proud of you and what you're doing."

Riley's eyebrows shot up in surprise as he let the air that he'd been holding out in a rush. He couldn't help smiling as he felt a load lift from his shoulders. The respect he'd always had for his dad, in spite of their differences, grew tenfold.

"The firm will survive, somehow," Ballard went on, and rolled his eyes with a grin. "But you? You're saving lives, Riley. You're serving in a way that makes me so incredibly proud. I'm sure it's not easy—the things you deal with, the things you see, the injuries you suffer. If you ever need to just . . . you know . . . talk, I'm here."

Riley was amazed. This is what he'd been wanting, hoping, and needing to hear from his dad for a long time. He gulped quickly and cleared his throat as his dad waited, looking at him expectantly.

"Dad, you have no idea—absolutely no idea—how happy you've just made me," Riley began. "Thank you. Thank you for understanding. And yes, I'll gladly take you up on your offer of a listening ear."

Riley paused and took a breath. "But Dad, I have to tell you, I had serious misgivings when I first started. Jeremy could tell. He's been a huge support and has helped in ways I didn't understand, or appreciate, at the time. But I do now. He was forcing me to stand on my own at the station and now, I wouldn't have wanted it any other way."

Riley stood and jamming his hands into his pockets, he turned to face his dad.

"I was really questioning my decision when I first started." He looked down and studied the floor for several strained heartbeats, uncomfortable to be admitting the second thoughts and misgivings he'd had.

"The job is more than I ever bargained for—a lot more. And in ways I never imagined. I wasn't sure I was cut out for it. But now, thankfully, I'm starting to feel more confident about it, even after what's just happened."

Ballard nodded gravely. "Son, I'm glad Jeremy has been there for you. He sounds wiser than I've given him credit for. I just regret it's taken me until now to realize all of this. I haven't been there for you as a counselor, an objective listener, or whatever you might have needed, but I promise you, I'm here for you now and will be going forward."

"You know, Dad," Riley said, sitting back down and looking at his dad sadly, "besides Jeremy, I was able to talk to Mr. Thornton and tell him some of what was going on. He was such a good listener." Riley sighed and stared vacantly at a spot on the opposite wall for several seconds before going on. "He may not have had any specific advice at the time, but sometimes it just helped to say things out loud."

Ballard studied Riley thoughtfully.

"I've been trying to process everything. And now with Jeremy, it's just all . . ." Riley stopped unable to go on.

Ballard realized now that Riley was dealing with a lot emotionally, besides the physical trauma he'd just gone through. Placing a hand on Riley's shoulder, he squeezed it trying to convey his understanding.

Ballard took a deep breath. "Riley, son, life is hard sometimes. Really hard. I'm sorry for everything that's taken place over the last few days. After losing Mr. Thornton, facing the unknown with Jeremy, and dealing with your own injuries, it's got to be tough. But know this.

Me, your mother, Allie, we're here, and we support you one hundred percent with whatever you need. We may not be aware of what or when that might be exactly but please promise me you'll tell us. This is new for all of us, but we'll learn how to deal with it together."

Riley nodded thoughtfully, events weighing on him, and unbidden, tears pricked his eyes.

"And Riley," Ballard went on, "just know that starting any new job comes with doubts about the ability to handle it and do it well. Take it from me, when you're dealing with people, their emotions, their very lives, your doubts get magnified. That's not easy either, but nothing like taking care of people in a crisis situation and making split second decisions or running into a burning building."

Ballard paused and looked closely at his son. "No, Riley, I have absolutely no doubt that you're doing exactly what you were destined to do." He chuckled and tried to lighten the mood. "Wow, that actually sounded profound didn't it?"

Riley chuckled too and took a quick swipe at a stray tear or two.

A knock came at the door and Jane peaked in. "Everything okay in here? Riley, are you feeling okay?" She looked between the two and their solemn faces.

"Everything is fine, Jane," Ballard answered, clapping Riley on the shoulder and standing. "Just having a long overdue man to man talk."

Still unsure, she looked between them, then went on. "Well, dinner is on the table and Allie is due any minute. I want us to eat as a family tonight so get a move on."

She closed the door without their saying a word. They looked at each other and grinned, shaking their heads.

"We'd better get downstairs," Ballard said and turned toward the door.

"Dad, thank you," Riley said. "I appreciate this conversation more than you can know."

Ballard grinned and before Riley knew what was happening, his dad clapped him into a tight hug. "I love you, Riley. But I'm warning you, don't pull another stunt like the one the other night. Understand me? My heart can't take it."

Riley laughed and self-consciously rubbed his eyes. "Yes sir, I'll do my best."

Early the next morning, Riley sat on the back patio of his parents' house, drinking a cup of strong coffee. Its warmth felt good against the chill in the air. He looked again at the text message from Cade and looked heavenward. "Thank you, Lord," he thought and closed his eyes.

Mr. Ennis had called Cade, letting him know the doctor had been in to see Jeremy early this morning and was encouraged by steady signs of improvement. He wasn't out of the woods yet, not by any means, but he was holding his own. They had been keeping him lightly sedated but hoped to bring him out of that soon, depending on how he progressed. Tomorrow was Jeremy's twenty-fourth birthday.

Riley's mother opened the door and stepped onto the patio, followed by Maggie a few steps behind.

Riley's heart skipped a beat. Maggie looked beautiful, but apprehensive. He couldn't blame her. He'd been pretty hard on her yesterday. Her blond hair fell softly around her shoulders, lifted slightly by the soft breeze. Her cheeks were a soft pink. Her bright blue eyes were focused unwaveringly on him. It was good to see her, no matter how long she might be in town.

"Riley? Maggie's here. Do you feel like a visit?" Jane asked, eying her son.

Riley's manners kicked in and he stood.

"Of course. It's good to see you, Maggie," he said and gestured to the chair on the other side of the round hardwood table.

Maggie turned and smiled at Jane. She sat in the heavy oak chair as Riley returned to his seat.

"Coffee, Maggie?" Jane asked.

"Yes, please. That would be great, thank you," Maggie replied with a bright smile.

Jane disappeared inside, glancing quickly over her shoulder before closing the door.

Maggie eyed Riley tentatively. "How are you feeling?"

"Much better actually. My head has mostly cleared to where the headache is just a dull throb now. If I can keep the dizziness at bay, I'll be happy."

Silence fell, broken only by Riley's mother bringing Maggie's coffee and a platter of Danish pastries. Setting them on the table, she hesitated briefly before leaving hurriedly.

They sat quietly until they both spoke at the same time.

They laughed softly.

"Please. Go ahead," Riley said.

Maggie smiled bashfully and looked down briefly before raising her eyes and meeting Riley's.

"It's funny. I've thought about it for so long, you know? What I would say to you when given the chance. When I came to the hospital the other night, I poured my heart out to you. Everything I'd so carefully planned to say came tumbling out." Maggie paused and smiled. "But then, when I finally got the courage to look you in the eye, you were sound asleep."

Riley raised his eyebrows. "I fell asleep on you? Oh, Maggie, I am so sorry."

Maggie laughed lightly. "No, please don't be. You did have a con-cussion after all. But now, with you looking at me, I . . ."

Maggie's phone rang. "Sorry, just a second."

Maggie pulled her phone out of her purse and frowned. It was Connor.

She sent the call to voice mail.

"Something important?" Riley asked, taking a sip of coffee and watching her over the rim of his cup.

Maggie's cheeks flushed slightly. "My boss. I'll get back to him later."

Riley studied her as if trying to figure something out.

"Anyway," she said nervously, "what I said the other night is that, I'm glad Cade called, but Riley, it scared me. I mean, this really scared me. When I realized what it all could have meant—never seeing you again, or talking to you, or—"

Maggie's phone rang again. Riley couldn't help a huff of irritation as he sat back in his chair.

Connor again. Maggie frowned and then gave Riley a pleading look as she answered.

"Maggie Rawlings," she said crisply and then waited. "Yes, Connor. I saw where you called, but I'm in the middle of something important. I will need to call you later to discuss. No. It will need to be later. Goodbye." Maggie frowned again before laying her phone on the table.

"Riley, I'm so sorry. There's a big presentation Tuesday and—"

Maggie's phone rang again and this time, Maggie's eyes narrowed and her cheeks blushed crimson with irritation. Riley knew that look. He was glad he wasn't on the other end of the phone right now. He stood to leave to give her some privacy, but Maggie reached over and took his hand, pulling him back down into his chair. Giving him a silent, imploring look, she answered. "Connor, as I said, I am in the middle of something important and will need to call you later." After several seconds of listening, she said, "Okay, fine. Let me tell you this then, I resign."

Riley sat up straight, his eyes wide. Maggie locked eyes with him and gripped his hand tightly.

"Connor, I've told you twice now that I'm in the middle of something important, and I am. I am talking to the most important person in the world to me. And as a hint, it's not you." She looked Riley directly in the eye as she continued. "He and I have a lot to talk about so if you'll excuse me, I need to go. My resignation letter is written. I will email it to you later today. I'll be in later this week, depending on how things are here, to clear out my office. But I really do need to go."

She hung up, and Riley could only stare.

"Maggie, your job! Are you sure?" Riley spluttered.

"As I was saying," Maggie said, cutting him off with a rueful smile. "When I thought I could very well never see you again, or talk to you, or hold your hand, I felt like I was going to suffocate until I could get here and see for myself that you were okay." She reached over and ran the back of her fingers down Riley's cheek.

"Riley, I am so sorry for leaving as I did. I should have told you how I was feeling and given us time to sort things out together. I've come to realize how unfair I've been. I hope we might still have that chance and see where we go from here."

Riley, unaware, had moved to the edge of his chair and was looking deeply into the brilliant depths of Maggie's blue eyes. He took her free hand in his own and held it gently.

"Maggie, you had me when you said you were talking to the most important person in the world to you. I feel the same because I've missed you too. But before we go too far down that path, I have to be honest. Leaving like you did, without a word? That hurt, and it hurt deep. I've never doubted how I feel about you, but I have had serious doubts about how you feel about me. For you to pick up and leave without so much as a chance for a conversation or to say goodbye? I'm just not sure I can pick up and carry on again that easily. I think the trust we once had between us is going to have to be rebuilt."

Maggie hung her head and sighed. "Riley, you're right. I have no excuses. I've been wondering myself why I left like I did. I can only ask for your understanding and forgiveness. Like I said, when there was a chance, I'd never be able to talk to you again, it shook me up badly and made me realize what I *truly* wanted."

"And what is that?" Riley asked softly and leaned forward.

Dappled sunlight filtered through the trees, creating patterns of light and shadow across the patio and across Riley's face as he gazed so intently at Maggie.

Maggie looked up, tears pooling in her beautiful eyes. "I want you, Riley. I want us."

Riley smiled. "I'd like that too, Maggie. Let's work on building back the trust we had between us. Are you willing?"

"Of course, Riley. Of course I am. Whatever it takes."

Riley smiled but then frowned. "But Maggie, what about your job? You just quit!"

"Yeah, I did, didn't I?" Maggie laughed out loud. "And boy, did that feel good!"

Riley laughed along with her but then turned serious. "So, what are you going to do?"

"I have another job already lined up. I'd already planned to quit after this presentation. It's still under discussion, but Riley, there's a chance I might get to work remotely with the new job and if so, I'll be moving back to Abernathy."

Riley's mouth dropped open as he fell back against his chair in surprise. "You *are* full of surprises today, Mags!"

Maggie's heart leapt, hearing Riley use his term of endearment for her. "Only good surprises, I hope."

"So far, so good," Riley replied. He stood and moved to a chair closer to Maggie, taking her hand once again and grinning.

"What's that grin for?" Maggie asked, leaning closer.

"Oh, just thinking. Mr. Thornton was right, and I'm glad he was."

"Who is Mr. Thornton? And what was he right about that puts a grin like that on your face?" Maggie asked, puzzled but smiling.

"How much time do you have?"

BALLARD STOOD WITH HIS arms around Jane. They had been watching Riley and Maggie talk for the past thirty minutes or so. They had exchanged smiles and a nod of approval when they'd seen Riley move to sit closer to Maggie. The two had seemed to relax with each other and become more comfortable throughout the morning.

"Do you think we should tell them it's lunch time?" Jane asked her husband. "They've been talking for hours."

Ballard shook his head and patted his wife's shoulder. "I think talking is what they need right now. But as for me, I'm starved!"

"Well, let's see what we can scare up for lunch then," Jane said. They exchanged a laugh, and as they turned toward the kitchen, Ballard took his wife's hand and kissed her, bringing a blush and soft smile to Jane's face.

EVERYTHING FELT HEAVY. HIS arms and legs, even his body, felt like it was weighted down. He tried to move, he needed to move, but he couldn't. He was drifting. He had a feeling he was supposed to go somewhere, but where? The darkness began to lighten as he felt himself being pulled toward a pinpoint of light directly ahead. He began hearing sounds—beeps, whirs, pulses, rasps.

He moaned and tried to move again but stopped, feeling a jolt of pain. The beeps, whirs and pulses were faster and louder now, and he thought he heard voices. Where was he? If he overslept an alarm at the station, they'd never let him live it down. He moaned again before forcing his eyes open. Everything was blurry and so bright. He quickly shut them again. Where was he? What was going on?

His mind drifted until he suddenly felt like he was choking and couldn't breathe. There was something in his throat, and he began to panic.

"Mr. Ennis. Jeremy, relax. Breathe normally," a soothing female voice was saying.

He felt himself relaxing as he began breathing in and then out slowly. He was drifting off again.

Jeremy felt himself waking up as if from a deep sleep, but somehow, everything seemed out of balance. He tried to open his eyes, and when he did, all he could see was a bright glare. He focused on the ceiling and blinked several times, trying to clear his vision. Unfamiliar white ceiling tiles were overhead. If he wasn't at the station, where was he?

"We're glad to have you back with us, Mr. Ennis, but you sure made us wait a long time," a man wearing a surgical cap and scrubs said, leaning over Jeremy with a smile and eying him closely. "I'm Dr. Cary, your attending physician."

"Where . . ." Jeremy tried to say, but nothing else would come out.

"You're in ICU at Abernathy Memorial. You've actually been here for three days, so that's why we're glad you're awake. You surprised us earlier so we had to put you back out for a few minutes to remove the intubation tube to allow you to breathe on your own. You're still lightly sedated but that's just to keep you comfortable. Can you tell us how you're feeling?"

Jeremy heard what the doctor was saying, but he was confused. What was he doing in the hospital and in ICU?

Jeremy tried to move again but winced with a sharp stab of pain to his midsection.

"Mr. Ennis, I recommend you lie as still as possible. You'll be in ICU for a couple more days so we can make sure all is well, but you've made a huge step forward today. I know things are a bit confusing right now, but try not to worry. Give yourself some time to sort everything out. Rest easy and know you're in good hands. Your parents will be in for a few minutes. They've hardly left the past few days so I know they're anxious to see you."

It seemed he could only stare at the doctor with what must be a dumbstruck look. But that was the best Jeremy could muster right now. He'd have to sort things out later.

Jeremy heard the doctor give what must have been instructions to two nurses in the room before patting Jeremy encouragingly on the shoulder and leaving. The nurses made some adjustments to the monitors, tubes, and wires attached to him, before they too left the room. Jeremy lay there, still a bit groggy, but trying to remember what had happened. He fisted his hands, in an effort to force himself to concentrate, but he felt something in his left hand. He carefully lifted his hand and slowly uncurled his fingers. His grandfather's lucky rabbit's foot was in the palm of his hand.

A NOTHER DAY HAD PASSED, and Riley was even more restless than the day before. He didn't like being treated like an invalid. He felt better—a lot better—and certainly good enough to be out and about, but the doctor had ordered him to rest and not drive for another week. He was still at his parents and being given the royal treatment. He couldn't complain about that, and it was good to eat his mom's cooking, but it still was weird not to be at either the station or Electronix Doc. Winston had told him to take as much time as he needed, and Captain Jernigan had said no work until the doctor's release came through. But Riley was anxious and ready.

With his dad at work and his mom back to being busy with her societies and clubs, he'd been alone the past two days. He'd stayed in his room for a while but the walls had begun to close in on him. He'd then roamed the house before coming back to his room. He'd scanned the TV channels but there was nothing that caught his attention for more than a few minutes at a time. He'd tried to read but kept drifting off to sleep. His mom had plenty of snacks on hand, but he was trying to stay in shape as much as possible until he could starting working out again. Maggie had been over a few times, but he'd gotten her to reluctantly agree to limit their time together, at least for now. He needed some space to sort through everything that had happened in the past couple of weeks.

But just the thought of Maggie made him smile. He still couldn't believe she'd quit her job. She'd showed him Connor's reply email after she'd submitted her registration. Riley liked this guy less and less and was glad Maggie wouldn't be working with him anymore. Quitting, Riley knew, had to have been hard for Maggie, but it hadn't seemed to phase her. She was happy and all smiles. He put his head back against the pillow and sighed happily.

When they'd said goodbye last night, he'd wanted to hold her forever. He recognized she'd walked out on him, but he also believed she truly regretted that decision. And now, she said she wanted to put that behind them and move forward together. He wanted that too—he always had. His thoughts were now turning back more often toward a proposal, but he still needed just a little more time to make sure she'd really decided what she wanted was a life with him and this just wasn't a reaction to his being injured.

Riley sighed and looked at his phone again. Still no change in Jeremy. But today was the day *after* Jeremy's twenty-fourth birthday. He'd made it. That blasted superstition be hanged.

Riley had just closed his eyes when his phone buzzed with a text from Cade:

Get to the hospital. NOW.

Riley sat up too quickly, grabbing for the side of the bed, feeling slightly dizzy. His heart was pounding as he waited for more from Cade and when there was nothing else, Riley texted:

Home alone. Can't drive. What's going on?

Cade replied:

On my way.

Riley texted back the thumbs up emoji but couldn't wait until Cade got there to know.

Tell me. Good news or . . . bad?

Riley watched his phone's screen for Cade's reply as he pulled a shirt over his head. "Come on, Cade." Riley grumbled just as the doorbell chimed.

Riley wasn't totally solid on his feet yet but steady enough to get to the front door quickly. He threw it open to see Cade with a huge, goofy smile plastered across his face.

"He's awake, Sully! He's still a bit out of it, but he's awake!" Cade said as Riley grabbed him in a loose hug before they slapped each other on the back. "I didn't want to give you the news in a text. This is just too big!"

Riley smiled but then staggered slightly.

"Hey, pard. You okay?" Cade asked, alarmed.

"Oh I'm fine, just excited and relieved. This is what we've been waiting, hoping, and praying for."

Looking over Cade's shoulder Riley saw Maggie coming up the walk, looking between the two of them, a hopeful look on her face.

"Do the looks on your two faces mean what I think they mean?"

"Jeremy's awake!" Cade blurted out before Riley could reply. "He's got aways to go, but the doc says it's looking good. I told Emily I'd come by the office and tell her as soon as there was news so, Maggie, can you get Riley to the hospital?" Cade said in a rush as he edged toward the walk.

Maggie laughed, trying to gage Riley's reaction to Cade's request. Riley's bright smile in her direction answered that question.

"I'll get a jacket. Hold on just a sec," Riley said, heading inside.

Maggie waved to Cade as he drove away and then turned as Riley came out and shut the door behind him.

"Word of warning," he said as he took the hand she offered to help him, and they started down the steps, "I get a bit lightheaded or dizzy once in a while so keep an eye on me if you wouldn't mind. Don't let me fall on my face."

"Oh Riley," Maggie said as he opened the passenger door. "Keeping an eye on you is one of my favorite things to do."

THE CROWD HAD ALREADY spilled into the hallway from the small ICU waiting area when Riley and Maggie walked in. The entire A Shift crew from Station Five was there, milling around. And for those who hadn't already seen Riley, they descended on him with slaps on the back and huge smiles. Maggie stood off to the side, keeping an eye on him, as she promised, but with a bemused and pleased look on her face.

Allie was beaming as she came over and gave Riley a hug.

"He's going to be okay," she said, wiping a tear before giving Riley another hug. "And I know *we're* going to be okay too. Thank you for telling me what that knucklehead was thinking. I can't believe he took all of that so seriously. Believe me, he'll be hearing from me about it. I'll forgive him—eventually." She smiled brightly up at Riley before moving to give Maggie a hug.

Cade and Emily made their way through the throng of people to Riley and Maggie.

"She insisted on coming," Cade said with a grin at Emily. "I'm glad."

"We're glad too," Riley said. He introduced Maggie.

"I hope we get the chance to visit more," Maggie said with a warm smile.

"That will definitely happen," Cade said, beaming at Emily.

Riley was happy for Cade. He and Emily made a great couple.

The doors to ICU swished open, and Mr. and Mrs. Ennis walked out, smiling from ear to ear. They were accompanied by Dr. Cary, whose eyes widened at the size of the group.

"Well, it looks like Mr. Ennis has quite the following," Dr. Cary joked as he looked around the room. "Mr. and Mrs. Ennis have asked me to share some about Jeremy's condition with you. Jeremy woke up approximately an hour and a half ago. He's alert, and we're confident he'll continue to progress quickly. We'll keep him in the ICU for a couple more days but after that, he'll be moved to a regular room. We'll monitor his progress from there, but his prognosis at this point is excellent."

Looking around the crowded waiting room once again, he said, "And I can see why with so much support. He's a very lucky young man."

"And we couldn't agree more," Mr. Ennis said, beaming a huge smile to the group. "Thank you, everyone, for being here before and for coming now. It means the world to Jeremy and all of his family."

Dr. Cary went on. "ICU has very limited visitation and is typically for family only but for today, Jeremy has asked to see Riley and Cade, but it has to be for just a few minutes."

Riley was jolted when he heard his name. He looked over at Cade and then to Maggie, who gave him a slight push as he joined Cade and walked over to Dr. Cary.

"Follow me please, gentlemen," he said as the ICU doors swished open. The atmosphere in ICU was solemn, a hushed silence interrupted only by intermittent beeping noises coming from different rooms and low voices of nurses and doctors talking in hushed tones. Dr. Cary led them past several glassed-in rooms with curtains drawn before entering another room that was lit by a florescent light directly behind the bed.

Jeremy watched as Riley and Cade entered, their eyes wide.

"Ten minutes, guys, and then you'll need to leave," Dr. Cary said before he stepped out of the room.

"Hey," Jeremy said weakly.

"Hey yourself," Riley said as he and Cade edged nervously closer to the bed. Jeremy was extremely pale with dark circles under his eyes. He had an IV in each arm, breathing tubes in his nose and various other tubes and lines attached with multiple monitors pulsing their readings.

"Well, look at you. How are you doing?" Cade asked softly.

"As they say, I've been better," Jeremy said with a grimace as he tried to move. "I hear there's quite a crowd in the waiting room. Are you guys charging admission? If not, you're missing an opportunity," Jeremy stopped, a bit breathless.

Riley and Cade looked at each other and then to Jeremy with concern.

"Don't look so worried, you two lunkheads. I'm sure I can't look *that* bad," Jeremy said.

"Well, actually, you do," Cade said, receiving a glare from Riley.

"Thanks, pard," Jeremy said, shaking his head slightly and attempting a grin.

"What? Just saying—you look like you've been through hell. And you have. Am I right?"

"Don't invite Cade for a visit if you want to be cheered up," Jeremy said with a roll of his eyes. Jeremy and Riley both looked at Cade, shaking their heads while Cade shook his own head in reply.

Turning serious, Jeremy turned to Riley. "What happened, Riley? I don't remember anything. I mean a few bits here and there. I remember there was a fire, and I heard you were in the hospital for a while. I've been trying to remember, but the pieces aren't coming together."

Turning somber as well, Riley glanced at Cade, unsure of how much to say. He didn't want to overtax Jeremy. Cade shrugged and gave a nod.

"Well, there was a fire at the The Lofts. A big fire."

Jeremy looked at him blankly, so Riley went on.

"We were on the second floor and had just gone into a vacant loft that the renovation crew must have been using for storage. There was a stockpile of cans stored there—paint, turpentine, paint thinner, you name it."

Jeremy's eyes widened. "I remember, I remember. Go on."

"Well, when you saw it, you turned and ordered everybody out, but before we could even move, the ceiling collapsed on top of the cans and they exploded. The force of the blast threw you onto a stack of crates."

Jeremy squeezed his eyes closed, remembering the concussion of the blast and being thrown in the air. The feeling of the impact came back to him, and he reflexively jerked, causing some of the monitors to beep loudly.

Riley and Cade looked at each other in alarm as two nurses rushed in and moved them aside.

"I'm okay, I'm okay," Jeremy said breathlessly as the nurses checked everything and studied him.

"Only a couple more minutes, guys. And please, don't excite him," one of the nurses said to Riley and Cade with a stern look.

"Jeremy, sorry man," Riley said, moving close to the bed once again.

"No, please. I need to know what happened. It's driving me crazy not being able to remember. I can remember the explosion now and landing on the crates. Go on."

Riley exchanged another look with Cade but continued. "You, me, and Grimes were the only three inside when the explosion happened, but you were the closest. Cap told me later that the crates you landed on were filled with decorative skylights. You caught most of the blast. So thanks to you, me and Grimes only had minor injuries. Grimes was dismissed a few hours after the incident, but I spent the night in the hospital with a concussion. I was released the next day. And so now, here we are."

Cade gave Riley a sideways look. "I didn't think you could remember much of what happened."

Riley shrugged. "Well, I actually don't remember much yet. Cap gave me the low down after the incident report was filed. Doc says the short-term memory will return eventually."

Jeremy listened closely as Riley recounted what had happened, trying to remember a more complete picture of what happened for himself but wasn't having much luck.

"But enough of that for now," Riley said, eager to change the subject. "How are you doing?"

"I can't really tell yet," Jeremy said weakly and tried to smile. "But they say I'm doing good."

"And you are," Cade piped in.

"Oh, and you, lunkhead? What's the deal with this?" Jeremy asked, holding up the rabbit's foot he still held in his hand. "I *do* remember giving this to you."

"Aw, Jeremy, you needed it more than I do," Cade replied, his cheeks flushing.

"Well, actually, neither of you really need it anymore," Riley said with a mischievous grin.

Riley moved closer to the bed as Cade moved closer on the other side. Riley gave Cade a conspiratorial grin before looking Jeremy closely in the eye. "Happy Birthday, Jeremy. You're officially twenty-four years old, yesterday as a matter of fact. And you're very much alive."

Jeremy's eyes widened, and he looked between Riley and Cade.

"Yesterday was my birthday?" he asked, a smile brightening his face. "I'm twenty-four?"

"Actually, twenty-four years and a day," Cade interjected.

The three laughed as Riley and Cade returned Jeremy's lopsided smile. Then Jeremy grimaced, and they all sobered.

"Time's up, gentlemen," the same nurse from before said from the doorway.

"Yes, ma'am," all three replied.

"We'll be back to see you tomorrow," Riley said as Cade nodded agreement. "I'm not sure what time. I can't drive yet so Maggie will need to bring me."

Jeremy's eyes lit up. "Maggie's here?"

"Yeah, our favorite lunkhead called her," Riley said, looking at Cade. "And I'm glad he did. Oh, and by the way," Riley added as he moved toward the door, "Allie has been here the whole time too. Just thought you'd like to know."

Jeremy's eyes widened and then he smiled. "I'm twenty-four and a day. I can't wait to see her."

"I think she's just as anxious to see you. Tomorrow," Riley said with a small wave.

"Take it easy, pard," Cade said as he and Riley walked out the door.

JEREMY SMILED TIREDLY AS he watched them leave. I'm twenty-four and a day, he thought. He sighed with relief. The Ennis curse had been broken. He closed his eyes and suddenly, he could see his whole life opening up in front of him again. He was ready to get out of the hospital and start living it. He thought of Allie, and smiled, drifting off to sleep.

JEREMY HAD JUST BEEN moved to a regular room after three days in the ICU, and the nurses were still fussing, making sure everything was set up according to the doctors' orders and making sure he was comfortable. Everyone in the ICU had been great, and Jeremy appreciated the care he'd gotten, but he welcomed the room change. Not just for the change of scenery but also because it meant he was getting better.

He could tell he was improving a little every day, but it still felt like he had a long way to go to get back to normal. For the time being, though, he was content to rest and follow doctors' orders. It wasn't like he really had a choice.

The nurses finished the adjustments they'd been making, gave him the call button control, and pulled the door closed behind them as they stepped out.

Jeremy looked around the room briefly but then soon drifted off to sleep. He wasn't sure how long he'd been asleep when he heard a soft knock and the sound of the door swishing open. He reluctantly opened his eyes but was quickly wide awake when he saw Allie approaching the side of his bed.

"Allie? Hey," Jeremy said, his voice raspy as he held out his hand to her.

Allie crossed the short distance quickly and took his hand in both of hers.

"Jeremy . . ." Allie said, her voice breaking.

"Hey, don't cry. Please, it's okay. I'm not good with tears, you know," Jeremy chided. He reached up with a slight grimace to brush a tear from her cheek.

"How are you?" she asked, her eyes on his before drifting to the monitors and the IV's before coming back to look closely into his eyes.

"I'm doing okay. Getting better."

Allie could feel Jeremy's hand trembling in hers.

"I've never been so scared in my life, Jeremy Ennis. I couldn't bear it if this had ended up—differently." Allie's voice broke slightly but she went on. "In fact, I should be furious, you know," she said with a sniffle, holding Jeremy's hand tightly. "And maybe I am."

"About what? There are so many things. Any one thing in particular?" Jeremy asked with a small, nervous smile.

"I'm serious, Jeremy. You break up with me for no good reason and then almost get yourself killed. You scared me, you really scared me," she added softly, looking at him intently as tears threatened again.

Jeremy laid his other hand over hers, the tubing from the IV in his hand trailing across the bed.

Straightening, she shook her head. "So, you see, I've got a lot to be upset with you about."

Jeremy looked closely into Allie's eyes as he gripped her hand. "You're right, Allie, and I'm truly sorry for what I did. I know I hurt you and upset you. But honestly, I didn't know how to tell you. Breaking up with you was the hardest thing I've ever done. I'd rather walk into a hundred burning buildings than do that again. I know this sounds trite, but it's really true—I broke it off for you. In my own stupid, clumsy way, I was trying to look out for you."

Jeremy smiled weakly. "But I've missed you, Allie. I've really missed you. Nothing's been right without you."

"I know that feeling all too well," Allie replied with a frown. "At first, I was just missing you, getting to be with you, talking to you, even texting. But after the fire? Not knowing you were going to be okay or even live? It was almost more than I could take. When we got word you were awake, I was so relieved that all I could do was cry. That's when Riley told me about the Ennis curse and why you broke things off."

Jeremy sighed and let Allie's hand go. He turned to look out the window, unable to bear seeing the pain on Allie's face.

"Allie, honey, I am truly sorry. It was hard to talk to anyone about it. I felt both foolish and afraid. My Grandpa Mars told me right before he died and it's been on my mind ever since. He was convinced of the curse and wanted me to know and be prepared. I know it sounds crazy," Jeremy added, seeing the uncertainty in Allie's eyes.

"I felt myself sliding further and further down that slippery slope," Jeremy went on. "The fatalities I'd see at work, Mr. Thornton's service the other day—all I could think of was that was going to be me and soon." He paused but rushed on before he lost the nerve to share his most personal fears.

"Allie, I thought a lot about what dying would feel like. What did the people who died while I was trying to save them see? What did they feel when that time came? I worried about leaving you, Riley, Cade, my family. I worried about not leaving anything behind." He looked up at her with a sad smirk. "I wondered how long it would take everyone to forget me. It was all just too hard to talk about with anyone."

Allie studied Jeremy intently. "You know, for some crazy reason, I felt bad that I hadn't been there for you to talk to about something that had you so bothered and worried. While the thought of you trying to look out for me is sweet, the next time, Jeremy Ennis, you think you're looking out for me, you'd better talk to me first," Allie said, her voice growing firm. "If we get back together, we're going to have to work on the bad case of hard headedness you seem to have developed."

Jeremy grasped Allie's hands tightly. "And are we? Can we get back together? I feel like I've been given a second chance and can look forward to living again, but I want you with me. I never wanted to break up in the first place, so please tell me I haven't blown things completely."

Allie could still feel Jeremy's hand trembling as she held it tightly. His face was pale, and he looked exhausted, but the earnestness in his eyes spoke directly to her heart. She leaned over, her face near his. "Oh, Jeremy." She placed one hand alongside his scruffy cheek, stroking it gently with her thumb. "You can't get rid of me that easily. I have a pretty bad case of hard headedness too, but one thing . . ."

Jeremy cocked an eyebrow, waiting, hopeful.

"You'd only walk into a hundred burning buildings rather than break up with me again?" Allie asked as she leaned closer.

"Well, maybe a hundred and one," Jeremy managed before Allie kissed him gently on the lips.

When she leaned back and saw his smile, her heart leapt. Jeremy pulled her down for another kiss only to be interrupted by a nurse clearing her throat as she entered the room.

"Well, Mr. Ennis, looks like you've come up with a lot better medicine than what we've got for you. I'd say it will probably speed your recovery along nicely."

Jeremy beamed, looking at Allie. "You have no idea."

RILEY HAD FINALLY BEEN cleared by his doctor at the hospital and was waiting on final approval from the fire department to start back at the station. Captain Jernigan had said it'd probably be within the next couple of shifts. Riley was ready.

Jeremy was improving daily. And after being moved to a private room, he never lacked visitors. He had so many visitors, in fact, the nurses had to make sure he had time to rest. The doctors hadn't said yet when Jeremy would be well enough to go home, but at the rate he was improving, it wouldn't be long. And with the holidays coming up, Riley was glad. After reaching his twenty-fourth birthday, it seemed Jeremy had regained the exuberance he'd been missing since his grandfather's passing. It looked like the curse was long forgotten.

Riley looked forward to his visits to see Jeremy at the hospital but he'd warned him he wouldn't be coming by today. Maggie had asked him to go with her to Dallas to clear out her office, and they'd decided to make a day of it. They'd go early and take their time on the way back. He checked his watch before throwing on a jacket. She should be pulling up any second. He'd moved back to his apartment and was just getting used to having his own space again. He smiled when he heard the knock at the door. Maggie was always right on time.

"Mags!" Riley said as he opened the door to see Maggie waiting, all smiles. His heart leapt seeing her standing there, her beautiful blond hair laying softly on her shoulders and her blue eyes sparkling. He wasn't sure with what. Happiness? Something more? He wasn't sure. But whatever it was, it seemed to light her up from the inside.

"Sully!" she replied with a grin. "You ready?"

"Ready."

She'd walked to the passenger door of the car and tossed Riley the keys. "Would you mind driving?"

A bit surprised, Riley said as he got in, "Of course I don't mind. Any particular reason?"

"No. Well . . ." Her smile faltered when he glanced at her.

"Maggie, what is it? You're not telling me something."

"Well, I don't want to make a big deal of it, but I am a bit nervous about going to the office and the possibility of seeing Connor."

Riley's eyes narrowed as he backed out and then headed toward the main street in front of his complex.

"Why are you nervous? Has this guy done something to scare you?"

"Well," she finally began, "he called after he'd got my resignation letter and after he'd emailed a reply. I guess he didn't want what he was going to say documented. He wasn't happy. He . . . well, he threatened to ruin my career if given the chance. He said since I was new, I'd need every reference possible. Thankfully, I already had this other job so I didn't take that part of what he said too seriously but . . ."

"But what?" Riley echoed, waiting, his fingers nervously tapping the steering wheel.

"Well, I think he may have had an interest outside of the office that I didn't share. It was strictly professional on my part, but I think it might have been different with him. That may be where his anger is coming from. He's the boss and considered by some of those in the office to be quite the catch, so he's not used to being rejected. Needless to say, he's not taking my resignation too well."

Riley's jaw clenched as he glared out the window.

"Riley?" Maggie asked softly. After a minute or so of no response, she asked again, "Riley?"

Riley startled, his mind on what he'd do to this Connor guy if given the chance. Maggie touched his arm, studying him with concern.

"Riley, it's okay. Really, it's probably just me overreacting. It won't take but a minute to grab my things, and then we'll have the rest of the day to ourselves. I'm looking forward to that, aren't you? We'll have to think about where we want to eat on the way back. I know I'm going to be starving by then!"

Maggie kept talking, trying to get Riley's mind off what she'd foolishly told him. She thought that she was probably just being paranoid and more than likely, they'd never even see Connor.

IT WAS A BEAUTIFUL drive. The colors of fall were starting to be seen in the trees and fields alongside the road. The hay fields had been mowed and the workers were starting to roll bundles to dry. Traffic was light and their conversation was interesting and nonstop.

Riley enjoyed the drive. But as they drew closer to Dallas, the urban sprawl began to take over. He began to feel the uncomfortable squeeze of losing the openness he was accustomed to, but he didn't mind making this drive with Maggie. The more time they spent together, the more he could sense a renewed purpose in Maggie, a content determination. He felt it about himself too. He felt the relationship healing and even deepening beyond what they'd had before. He was falling in love with Maggie all over again, and he was happy.

Maggie reveled being in Riley's company. She enjoyed the fall scenery, but she enjoyed being with Riley more. After so many months apart, she couldn't talk fast or long enough, sharing everything she'd been wanting to share with him all along. She pointed out a fall market in one small town they passed through, and they agreed to stop on the way back. She smiled as Riley reached over and took her hand and squeezed it. This was where she belonged—with Riley. At last, she was happy.

Three hours later, Riley pulled into a spot in the office's parking garage. Maggie took a nervous breath.

"There's no need to worry," Riley assured her. "I'll be with you every second. I don't like anyone hitting on my girl or thinking they can be mean to her."

Maggie's heart warmed at Riley calling her "his girl." Nothing could ruin this day now and hopefully they wouldn't even see Connor.

That hope was dashed when they stepped off the elevator and started toward the front door of the agency. Connor stood talking to Brenda, the receptionist. He'd looked up when the elevator dinged its arrival.

Riley felt Maggie stiffen beside him. "That's Connor," she whispered.

Riley put his hand to the small of Maggie's back and gave her a gentle pat as a reminder he was there. He pushed the door open, and Maggie stopped just inside, far enough for Riley to enter and close the door.

Connor's glare deepened as he looked from Maggie to Riley. The receptionist sat wide-eyed, looking between them.

Maggie nodded to Brenda with a nervous smile before turning to Connor. "Good morning, Connor. Riley, this is Connor Matthews. Connor, this is Riley Sullivan."

Neither man moved, and Maggie nervously cleared her throat.

"Connor, I've come to get the personal things out of my office, as promised. We won't be but a minute."

Maggie started to move to the hallway behind the receptionist, but Connor put a hand up, stopping her. "Employees only beyond this point," he said, looking at Riley.

Maggie started to object, but Connor went on. "But not to worry, Maggie. Your things were removed from your office and boxed up the day we received your resignation. Brenda, would you please retrieve Ms. Rawlings' things from the storeroom? I believe you'll find everything is there and in order," he said, looking back to Maggie, his eyes narrowing.

Brenda looked nervously between the three and quickly left. Nothing was said to break the uneasy silence as Connor and Riley continued to study each other. Brenda returned a few minutes later pushing a cart holding two boxes. She pushed it toward Riley and Maggie. They each picked up a box and took a step toward the door.

Connor lounged smugly against the counter. "It's been a real pleasure, Maggie. You know what I mean."

Riley stiffened and started to turn around, but Maggie put a hand on his arm. Under her breath but loud enough for Connor to hear, she said, "That would be nice, but really, he's not worth it."

They started toward the door again but stopped when Connor spoke again.

"So, I'm guessing this is the all-important fireman you rushed off to see."

Riley started to turn but Maggie stopped him by gently setting her box on top of the one he was carrying. She turned and walked slowly toward Connor, stopping within inches of him. In low, measured tones, she said, "Yes, Connor. Riley is a firefighter. He's one of those who runs into burning buildings when everyone else runs out. I left that day because he had been injured in a major fire, and I wanted, and needed, to be with him. Besides being a hero, Riley is also an overall great guy, and I'm crazy about him. I appreciate the opportunities I had here, but this is over and done. Please do not call, text, or email me again. I wish you well. Goodbye."

Seeing the shocked look on Connor's face, Riley bit his lip to hide a smirk. Connor evidently didn't know Maggie very well. Riley watched and listened with pride as Maggie pivoted and walked back to him. She picked her box up and looked up at him with a wry grin.

Riley returned her grin and opened the door into the waiting area for the elevators.

When they got onto the elevator, Maggie laughed nervously. Riley shook his head.

"That was absolutely incredible, Mags. I am so proud of you! But..."

Maggie looked up. "But what?"

"Hero? Really? That was a little over the top wouldn't you say?" Riley asked with a chuckle.

The grin slid from Maggie's face. "No. It wasn't over the top at all. I meant it. You *are* my hero, Riley. You always have been."

Riley wasn't sure what to say, but the look in Maggie's eyes made his heart skip a beat. As they walked up to her car, they set the boxes on the hood.

"Riley, I really appreciate you being here and ready to defend my honor." She put a hand on his arm. "And you really are my hero."

Riley couldn't resist. He pulled her to him and held her tightly. He didn't want to let her go but reluctantly did when a group of young guys in suits walked by, looking at them curiously.

As Riley opened the trunk and loaded the boxes inside, he said between gritted teeth, "If he'd ever hurt you, Maggie, in any way—career, personal, or otherwise—he would have me to deal with."

"I feel sorry for him then," Maggie countered with a wicked giggle as they slid into the car. "But you know what is much more important right now?"

"No, what?" Riley asked as he started to back the car out.

Maggie looked at him. "Where are we going to eat? I'm hungry!"

Riley laughed. "Well, alrighty then," he said, still chuckling. "Let's eat!"

RILEY AND MAGGIE HADN'T gotten back to Abernathy until late last night. They'd stopped for a nice lunch, enjoyed a leisurely tour through the fall market, and then an even more leisurely dinner, taking their time and stopping to see whatever struck their fancy along the way, enjoying the time together.

Cade had texted that he was on his way to the hospital the next morning, so Riley decided to join him, and they walked in at the same time. They walked past the nurses' station with its usual buzz of activity and sidestepped some gurneys and orderlies in the hallway. As they approached Jeremy's room, they could hear Jeremy's voice and laughter.

They stopped just inside the door watching and listening as Jeremy joked with one of the nurses. Looking at each other and rolling their eyes, they turned to hear Jeremy.

"Hey, guys," he said with a slight grimace as he tried to sit up.

Still smiling at whatever Jeremy had just said, the nurse pushed him gently back down into the bed.

"You're to lie still, Mr. Ennis," she said, re-adjusting the sheet around him.

"Mr. Ennis?" Cade said, plopping down unceremoniously in one of the guest chairs. "Who is that?"

"It would seem I get the respect I deserve around here. You two might want to take notes," Jeremy replied.

"Will you two please make sure Mr. Ennis lies still? That incision isn't going to heal if he keeps moving around. We try to keep him under control, but he keeps us busy," she said with a playful wink at Cade and Riley.

"We've known this guy for a long time, and we haven't had any luck yet keeping him under control," Riley said as he plopped down into the other guest chair. "But we'll do our best."

She left with a good-natured nod to Riley and Cade, but a stern look at Jeremy.

Jeremy grinned. "What are you two jokers doing here? Don't you have girlfriends to keep you out of my hair?"

"Well, Emily had to work a school event this morning," Cade said, taking a sip of the coffee he'd carried in with him.

"Maggie and I spent the day together yesterday. I went with her to pick up the stuff from her office. I'm glad I went, too," Riley said with a frown.

"Why? What happened?" Jeremy asked as he moved the nurse's call button from where the nurse had placed it.

"Her boss—or ex-boss now—is a real jerk. He said some things that if, well, if Maggie hadn't been there, I might not have been able to refrain myself from showing him exactly what I think of him."

Cade let out a low whistle as Jeremy nodded.

"Now that would have been something to see," Jeremy said. "I don't think I've ever seen you *that* mad. And believe me, we've seen you mad. I mean, I think *we've* even made you that mad before." Jeremy chuckled while Cade grinned.

"Yeah, you guys have made me that mad before. Kinda like right now," Riley said with a pretend glare.

"But enough about us," Riley went on. "How about you? How are you feeling?"

"Besides the incision, not too bad, actually. I'm getting waited on hand and foot. All I have to do is lie here and receive my loyal subjects."

Riley and Cade rolled their eyes.

Cade picked up the nurse call button and started playing with it as Jeremy watched, shaking his head.

Jeremy shifted uncomfortably in the bed then gasped. Riley looked at him sharply.

"You okay?"

"Yeah, yeah. I just keep forgetting. This incision is still really tender," Jeremy said through gritted teeth.

"Well, you'd do best to remember that you're still healing. The nurse said you were to lay still."

"Yes, Mother."

Riley grinned and shook his head.

Jeremy laughed and immediately grimaced again.

"Hey, sorry," Riley said, on his feet in an instant.

Jeremy waved him off. "I'm fine. All part of the healing process, or so I'm told. I'm just tired of being cooped up here."

"Well, I'm afraid you've got a little while yet to go so you might as well make the best of it," Riley said. He added with a wicked tease, "I hear they have outstanding jello."

Jeremy acted like he was looking for something to throw at Riley when someone tapped softly on the door.

Allie stepped inside looking between the three of them.

"So, looks like you might need rescuing, Mr. Ennis," Allie said walking past Riley to stand next to Jeremy's bed.

"So, I take it all is well again between you two?" Riley asked, looking at Allie, then Jeremy.

"Don't you have somewhere you need to be?" Allie asked with a quick smile at Jeremy then a pointed look at Riley.

"I think you just answered my question," Riley said, noting the happy looks on both Jeremy and Allie's faces.

"Actually, you know, now that you mention it, there is somewhere Cade and I both need to be," Riley said, getting to his feet. "Come on, Cade."

"What? Where do we need to be?" Cade asked, looking up from his phone.

"Tell Emily we all said hi while you're texting her back, but you and I are leaving. Come on."

Cade hit send on his text and stood. He and Riley started toward the door when his phone dinged with a reply. Reading the text, Cade chuckled. "Emily says hi back."

They all laughed.

"We'll be back later," Riley said over his shoulder as he and Cade stepped into the busy hallway.

Jeremy nodded and waved, but his eyes were on Allie.

A FTER LEAVING JEREMY, RILEY drove through a fast-food place and grabbed a burger and some fries. Cade was meeting Emily for lunch, and Maggie was having lunch with her mom, so Riley thought he'd work a few hours at Electronix Doc and make up some time. The workroom was quiet. All of the technicians were either out for lunch or on installations. Riley had just taken the first bite of his hamburger, when the back door opened with a tiny squeak and Winston entered.

"Riley!" he said and walked quickly across the room, his hand extended.

Riley swallowed his bite quickly and took Winston's hand, shaking it firmly.

"How are you, son?" Winston asked, studying him closely. "Sounds like you've really been through it the past week or so."

They both took seats on stools in front of the workbench.

"It's been something else, that's for sure," Riley said, pushing his food aside. "But thankfully everything is looking up. I'm sorry I've been away so long. I was hoping to help with some repairs this afternoon and get back on track."

"Well, there's no denying you've been missed, and we are a bit behind. But the more important thing is that you're okay. How's Jeremy? I heard he was hurt pretty badly."

"Yes, sir, he was. It was touch and go there for a while, but he's turned a corner and is improving quickly."

"I'm glad to hear it! Really glad. I know you boys have always been close."

Riley grinned. "We've been like brothers most of our lives. I couldn't begin to imagine what life would have even been like without him. Glad I don't have to find out. He's getting back to his old self quickly."

"Were you ever able to find out what was bothering him?"

Riley's chuckle was humorless. "Actually, he did tell me. Right before we got the call for the big fire."

Riley relayed what Jeremy had told him, and Winston let out a low whistle.

"I'm thankful Jeremy broke that streak, but I'm surprised at him getting so caught up in it, believing it was inevitable," Riley said as he pushed some of the smaller tools around absentmindedly on the work top.

Winston was silent for several minutes, then looked back to Riley.

"We never know what's going to strike a chord with any of us. Jeremy had gone his entire life without knowing about the supposed Ennis curse until a few months ago when his grandfather told him. Maybe it was connected to his grandfather's passing and the closeness they'd always shared. Or maybe it was a deep held fear Jeremy hadn't allowed to come to light. The mind is a complicated thing. We're never going to know the explanation or reasons behind a lot of what goes on up here," Winston said, tapping his head. "The main thing is that Jeremy is past it and is getting better by the hour."

Winston studied Riley.

"But how about you? Everything okay with you?"

Riley smiled. "Now that you ask, Maggie and I are back. Well, I guess you can say we're *working* on getting back together. Cade called and told her about the fire and she came. We're talking and spending time together, working on rebuilding what we had. For now, I'm happy with that."

"That's good news, Riley. I'm glad to hear it. But why aren't you with her right now instead of here working?"

"We spent the day together yesterday. Had a great time too. I really enjoy being with her, but honestly, I just needed some time to sort through some things. You'd heard about my friend, James Thornton, passing away, but I don't think you knew I was on that medical call and was the paramedic." Riley paused, unable to go on. "His service was the day before the fire so, you know, I've got some things to sort through."

"Yes, son, you do. But take your time, on everything. That's the best and safest course of action. It will all turn out the way it's supposed to in the long run."

Winston slapped his legs and stood. "But, in the meantime, there's work to be done. I'm glad to have you back. But more importantly, I'm glad that you're okay."

"Thanks, Winston. I appreciate it," Riley said, picking up the iPad for the next repair.

Winston chuckled and grinned. "It should be me thanking you. I'm certainly not going to be running into a burning building any time soon. Now, don't stay too long and don't overdo it."

"Yes, sir." Riley smiled, pulling his lunch back in front of him and taking a bite as he studied the iPad.

As Riley ate and began the phone repair, his mind wandered back to his day with Maggie yesterday. Connor was just a blip on the radar. The most important thing was what was growing between the two of them. He used to think he couldn't love her any more than he did, but he was finding out that he could and that he did. There was a new depth and a new richness to their relationship, which gave him a sense of peace. He and Maggie had always been close but since she'd come back and they'd spent more time together, that feeling had only deepened and intensified. He couldn't imagine living without her.

He looked up and paused. He was ready to propose. It had taken him awhile to be sure of Maggie but now, he was sure. He'd tucked the velvet ring box into a dresser drawer. It was time to pull it out and start thinking about how he wanted to propose. He knew he wanted to surprise her, and he also knew it had to be absolutely perfect. He smiled to himself. An idea was already beginning to form.

Cade sighed. It was his last day with the police department. He was excited—very excited—but there was still the unknown of a new job and if he had what it took to be effective. He knew he was making the right move, he just wanted all to go well.

His parents had thrown a celebratory good luck dinner the evening before. The whole family had been there, including his grandfather and both uncles who'd served as officers. It was a proud heritage, and he was happy to be continuing in the same line of service as his family. Riley and Jeremy said they were going to celebrate his new job when Jeremy got out of the hospital. They'd already decided they were going to use the occasion to celebrate everything they *all* had to celebrate. And there was a lot.

Cade stepped out of the locker-room to look for Crawford, but instead he was met by a hall full of officers waiting to shake his hand and wish him well. The support staff had brought coffee and donuts, of course, and each officer grabbed a cup and one or two donuts before Sergeant Dickson motioned for quiet.

"I speak for us all, Officer Marshall, when I say we wish you the best of luck in your new role at Abernathy High. You've worked hard and served the citizens of Abernathy with passion, dignity, and professionalism. I know you'll carry that forward and exceed at serving the faculty and students at the school with the same dedication. It's been an honor and a pleasure serving with you. You certainly live up to the fine tradition of service the Marshall family has given their community over the years." Sergeant Dickson shook Cade's hand and everyone applauded. Cade turned red with embarrassment at the praise and being the center of attention.

"Thanks, everyone," Cade said, uncomfortable as he looked around nervously. "I'm sure I'll be seeing you around. And don't hesitate to stop by campus. I think it would be a good thing for everyone to get acquainted. But anyway, thank you for all of this," he said gesturing with his hand. "It's been an honor and pleasure serving with each of you."

The gathered officers applauded again and made their way by Cade one by one to shake his hand and wish him well. The one officer missing, Cade noticed, was Crawford.

After the last officer had shaken his hand and Sergeant Dickson had given him a clap on the back, thrusting the box of remaining donuts in his hand, Cade turned to head toward the cruiser. He figured that Crawford was waiting for him, fuming.

Instead, as he started down the hall, he looked up to see Crawford waiting for him by the door.

"Officer Marshall," Crawford said brusquely before opening the door and walking out.

Cade sighed. It was going to be a long shift.

The morning, thankfully, passed quickly and Crawford had actually been friendly, talkative even. Most other days, conversation was scarce with edgy silence broken only by the radio or exchange of information while writing a report or completing information on a stop or call.

After talking about the weather and the forecast, they've moved on to talk about sports. Cade thanked Crawford again for coming to his youth team's tournament. To Cade's surprise, Crawford talked at length about the tournament game.

"Marshall, you've got a real talent for coaching. You're a leader, and you have the ability to inspire young men with the way you build them up through sports. I saw how those boys looked up to you. That's a gift. Don't ever squander the influence you have with those boys and what you will have with the students. They'll appreciate the lessons learned from you because you're *living* the lesson. They can see an actual example of how and what to be. The youth could use more mentors and coaches like you. This resource officer job is hard, and it will be demanding, but the results, the rewards, and the benefits are far reaching. Trust me."

Cade turned and looked at Crawford. "It sounds like you're speaking from experience."

"That's because I am," Crawford replied. But he didn't elaborate.

Curious, but not feeling the time was right to press, Cade just nodded. That was probably more words in one conversation with Crawford than they'd shared their entire time as partners. It had been an extremely pleasant morning. Not what he'd been expecting at all.

After making a quick traffic stop with a warning for a burned-out taillight, Crawford cleared his throat. "It's close to noon. Are you hungry?"

Cade looked at him in surprise. He'd never asked Cade if he was hungry the entire time they'd worked together. They'd operated on Crawford's schedule only.

"Well, sure," Cade said, stumbling over his reply.

"Good. Because we're eating here."

Cade looked up in surprise to see they'd pulled into the parking lot of one of the nicer steakhouses in Abernathy.

"I hope you like steak, Marshall. My treat," Crawford said, putting the car in park and opening the door.

Cade was stunned and sat unmoving for several seconds.

Crawford leaned over and looked back inside the car. "Thought you were hungry."

"Yes, sir. Coming." Cade hurriedly opened his door and followed Crawford inside.

It was evident the owner knew Crawford from his greeting at the door. They were shown to a nice table and given exceptional service. The food was outstanding and the conversation was even enjoyable.

Cade couldn't help but ask, "Bart, I don't want to pry, but you said you spoke from experience with youth sports. Have you coached before?"

Crawford wiped his mouth with the linen napkin and looked at Cade. "No, son. I was one of the boys on a football youth sports team."

Cade nodded and waited. Crawford seemed like he was gathering up something from inside before he felt comfortable continuing.

"My coach was much like you. I'm sure I looked like one of those boys you coach, all wide-eyed wonder. Coach Shaw saw something in me no one else ever saw or encouraged. He showed me how to believe in myself and grow confident in what I could do and be."

Crawford looked over at Cade who was studying him thoughtfully.

"He treated me like a son. My own dad never did and that hole was aching to be filled. Coach Shaw was a great man." Crawford cleared his throat and trailed off.

"Are you guys still in touch?"

Crawford shook his head, surprising Cade by becoming emotional. "He died. Sudden heart attack. He left practice and died in his sleep that night. I never got to tell him goodbye or how much he meant to me. In spite of the years, I've never forgotten him." Crawford stopped and cleared his throat.

Cade looked at Crawford with wonder. "What an inspiring thing to share with me," Cade said. "Thank you, Bart. I think that's the best going-away present I could ever receive."

Crawford looked over at him and actually smiled.

When they were about to get up from the table to leave, their waiter appeared with two large pieces of chocolate cake with ice cream. "Compliments of the house," he told them.

Cade's eyes rounded, as did Crawford's. "Officer," Crawford said to Cade, "I think you may have to drive this afternoon while I take a nap."

Cade chuckled as he took the first delicious bite. "I don't know . . . I vote for a shade tree and we *both* take a nap."

WHEN THEY PULLED UP at the station at the end of shift, Cade was almost reluctant for it to be over. He wished Crawford had shared this side of himself from the start. How different things could have been.

After changing out of their uniforms and walking out to the parking lot, Crawford stopped.

"Marshall," he said, turning to Cade. "I know I've been one sorry brute for the majority of the time we've been assigned together, and I'd like to apologize for that right now. I try to get my bluff in ahead of time and establish "my way or the highway mentality" with new partners. Sometimes I go a little over the top. I tried the same thing with you, but you either stood up to me when needed—respectfully, I might add—or you just let my uncalled-for comments pass when they didn't deserve a reply."

Crawford paused and studied Cade, taking a step closer. "Son, bottom line, and I've thought about this a lot. I believe I act the way I do—all the bluster and loud talk to keep everyone at arm's length. That coach I told you about? I've never gotten over losing him at a time in my life when I really needed a dad. I figure I'm forcing people away to avoid the risk of losing someone so close to me again."

"Bart, I'm not sure what to say except I'm so sorry for the loss you suffered. Life doesn't seem fair sometimes, does it?" Cade shuffled back and forth, unsure of what else he could say that would be helpful.

Crawford cleared his throat. "You've inspired me, Cade. I mean that. I'm going to work at being a kinder, gentler version of myself." He stepped back and smiled. "I wish you the best of luck. The school is definitely going to benefit from you being there. And if . . ." Bart trailed off, and Cade waited.

"Well, if . . . if you ever hear of a youth team needing a coach—football or basketball—I'd be interested."

Cade couldn't help the broad smile that spread across his face. "Absolutely, Bart. I know they're always looking for coaches when the seasons start. I'll let them know there's a great coach available. They'll be in touch. Thank you."

Crawford nodded curtly and stuck his hand out. "Marshall."

"Officer Crawford," Cade said. He shook Crawford's hand firmly. "Come by campus sometime. It'd be good to see you, and I'd like to show you around."

Crawford didn't say anything, but the pleased look on his face made Cade smile to himself.

Cade was still watching where Crawford's truck had pulled out of the parking lot, long after Crawford had left. Cade was actually going to miss that guy. What an interesting day this had been. Surprising himself, Cade realized he was already looking forward to Crawford's visit to campus.

RILEY WALKED IN THE back door of the station, duffel bag over his shoulder. He'd only been gone four shifts, but it felt like it had been much longer. It felt great to be back as he breathed in the familiar smell of brewing coffee. He also smelled breakfast cooking. Breakfast? It was his job as the rookie to start breakfast on the morning of shift. He double-checked his watch. He wasn't late. He quickly dropped his duffel bag in his room and hurried to the kitchen only to find the entire A Shift crew seated around the large square table waiting. Waiting for what? he wondered, as he careened to a halt.

The table was already loaded with every kind of breakfast food that would typically be served on a Sunday morning. Someone Riley didn't recognize was frying bacon and tossing strips onto a platter accompanied by what looked like a dozen fried eggs. Riley started toward the stove to start pitching in when Grimes exclaimed, "Sullivan!" with a wave from the far side of the table, bringing everyone's attention to Riley.

Riley stopped. Something was off. Grimes had just called him Sullivan—not Rookie.

"Why is everyone here so early?" Riley asked, continuing toward the stove before Brimly stepped to his side and steered him toward a chair at the table.

"Have a seat, *Sullivan*," Brimly said with emphasis as the others grinned and sipped their coffee.

The only person who had called him Sullivan at the station had been Jeremy. Something was up, and it looked like he was the only one not in the know.

He grinned, playing along, and joined them at the table.

"What's up, guys?" Riley asked, looking around the table. He looked up at Grimes with surprise as he accepted the mug of coffee he handed him.

"Well, there have been some changes around here while you've been gone," Brimly said, taking an open chair across the table.

The guy who had been frying bacon at the stove carried the platter to the table, adding it to the feast before turning back and starting another pot of coffee brewing. Poor guy, Riley thought, he looks nervous and a bit harried. He looks like a . . . rookie.

Before Riley could say anything or anyone could add anything else, Captain Jernigan's voice boomed from his office, "Sullivan! A word if you please."

Riley took a quick gulp of coffee and pushed his chair back. "Excuse me."

A few gave cursory nods as platters were passed and forks speared sausage, waffles, biscuits, and fingers grabbed piping hot pieces of bacon. Riley looked at it all longingly. He hoped there would be some left for him and the captain.

He hurried across the shiny linoleum and down the short hallway to the captain's office. Reaching the office, Jernigan motioned him to close the door and take one of the chairs. Being the start of shift, the office was fairly tidy. The shift roster was in front of the captain as he turned from the computer screen. Pulling his glasses off, Jernigan studied Riley closely.

"So, Sullivan, how are you feeling? Fit enough for duty? Doc's released you, but I want to hear from you firsthand."

"I'm ready, sir. I've been working out on my own, and I feel good. No side effects."

"That's good. Glad to hear it." Jernigan picked up his glasses and slipped them on. "We're making some personnel changes here at the station which involve you. They were already in the works, but with Ennis out for a while, we're moving forward, just implementing them in stages."

Riley nodded, wondering what could be coming. His curiosity was rising equally with his anxiety.

"First of all, you may have noticed a new face in the kitchen."

Riley nodded again, this time with a perplexed frown.

"That's Brett Reynolds, our new rookie."

Riley sat up straight.

"Rookie, sir?"

Captain Jernigan grinned, looking over the top of his glasses. "Yeah, sorry. I know that's probably upsetting."

"Yes, sir!" Riley agreed a little too quickly. "I mean, no sir," he amended with a dutiful shake of his head.

Captain Jernigan chuckled. "I'd worry if you were upset to lose such a worthy status." The captain sifted through a short stack of papers to his left, finally pulling one from the stack and studying it.

"Now, let's see. Your status on the engine was a temporary assignment. And since you're no longer the rookie and no longer riding the ambulance, what shall we do with you?" He looked over the edge of the paper, a teasing glint in his eye.

Riley shuffled his feet, silently begging the captain to get on with it. He hoped he knew what was coming but the suspense was killing him.

"Ah, yes," Jernigan said, running his finger down a list on the sheet of paper. "Here we go . . . new role assignments. It looks like Mr. Sullivan that you will now *officially* be riding the engine as a firefighter."

Riley wanted to spring from the chair and let out a whoop, but he managed a sedate nod and smile.

"Sounds good, sir. Thank you. I've been studying and working toward this, so I appreciate your confidence and the opportunity."

"Don't thank me, Sullivan, you've earned it. But speaking of studying," he pulled one of two binders on top of the filing cabinet at his side and plopped it on the desk in front of Riley. "This is for you. Study materials for the upcoming lieutenant's exam in March. I want you to take that exam, and I want you to pass it. Do I make myself clear?"

"Well yes, sir, of course. But—"

"No buts. I've got a lot riding on you passing this test. You've just moved up one rung from being a rookie. In Abernathy, you are typically not allowed to test for a lieutenant spot until you've completed at least two years of service. I've talked Battalion Chief Bentley into trying something new for the department—fast-tracking a candidate we feel qualifies and has the aptitude to be an officer. We both agree that you're one of those exceptions, so we're testing our theory on you. I need you to pass this test to prove me right."

"Wow, no pressure then, sir."

Captain Jernigan looked at Riley before going on. "This little fella," laying his hand on top of the remaining binder on the filing cabinet, "goes to Mr. Ennis. He, on the other hand, should have tested for lieutenant a long time ago. So, we're correcting that this go-round. I expect you both to take the exam and both pass. Besides, he needs something productive to occupy his time while he's recuperating. We need some additional officers around here since you successfully lost Lieutenant Cochran for us."

"I did what?"

"Cochran. You mentioned his name to Franklin Bradford, the drone company guy, about what a great fit he'd be to administer the new program for the department. Cochran is out of his mind with excitement, and I'm left with empty slots to fill."

"Sorry, sir. Cochran and I had talked about drones before that opportunity ever came up, and I could tell he had a passion for it. Mr. Bradford asked if I had anyone in mind if I wasn't interested, and I mentioned the lieutenant. I was excited for Cochran but didn't realize it would all happen so fast."

"Oh, we've got Cochran until Ennis gets back. But after that, he's off to admin and going to the birds as they say." The captain smiled and then stood and extended his hand.

"Congratulations, Firefighter Sullivan. I know you're going to do a great job on the engine and will make a great lieutenant. Now get your gear onto the engine. Your new assignment starts today. And oh yeah, enjoy some breakfast. The guys wanted to celebrate your return and break in a new rookie too. I just hope they left something for you."

Riley chuckled as he stood and shook Captain Jernigan's hand. "Thank you, sir. I'll work hard and make you proud."

"You already have, and I know you will. Go eat, Sullivan."

Riley stepped outside the captain's office and took a deep breath, a huge smile spreading across his face. He'd made it past being a rookie and to the engine permanently and was now a full-fledged firefighter. He realized he'd be on the ambulance now and then, but the engine was now his home. He couldn't wait to let Jeremy know.

Riley walked to the kitchen and watched the tableau of activity with the silly grin still plastered on his face. The station crew, his crew, were around the large square table that served as the center of the station's activities. He was thrilled to be here and a part of this group.

Walking to the table from the coffee pot, Brimly spotted Riley. "Well, well, well, look who's back. Got your gear on the engine yet, Sullivan?"

The others turned, some still chewing, and nodded in Riley's direction.

"Headed to do that right now," Riley said as he stepped up to the table and reached over Carrier to snag a piece of bacon. "And when I get back, I'm having breakfast. There'd better be some left, just saying."

"Eh, get outta here, Sullivan," Hayward said, turning back to his still heaping plate. "If you're fast enough, you might be lucky to get some leftovers."

Riley broke into a slight jog once he reached the bay. He retrieved his equipment from the locker area and proudly hung his bunker coat from the door behind the driver's seat and rolled his bunker pants down to the boots where he could quickly step into them. He then carefully laid his helmet, hood, and gloves on the seat and took a step back to take it in.

Riley stood with his hands on his hips, looking around the enormous bay—at the truck, the engine, and the ambulance. Their red paint and chrome sparkled and gleamed in the early morning rays slanting in through the bay door windows. The buzz of the florescent lights overhead was broken only by the occasional hum of cars passing by in front of the station. He loved it here and couldn't wait to start studying for the lieutenant's exam. He was going to justify the captain's faith in him.

He pulled out his phone and snapped a picture, texting it to Jeremy with the caption:

Permanently assigned to the engine. New rookie at the station. Hurry and get well.

A text immediately came back:

Congrats, Sully. On both counts. Working on it.

C HARLES ENNIS PULLED THE pickup to a stop in front of the wood shop. He killed the engine. He stole a look over at Jeremy, who he could tell was in some pain, but would never admit it. He'd asked him to pick him up from rehab today and drive him here. Jeremy hadn't said why, but Charles figured he'd be finding out soon enough.

"You okay?" Mr. Ennis couldn't help but ask.

"Yeah, Dad. I'm getting there." Jeremy opened the door and swiveled in his seat to put his feet on the ground but didn't make a move to get out.

Mr. Ennis didn't want Jeremy to have to ask, so he came around the truck and helped him to his feet, handing Jeremy a cane to steady himself and walked with him to the door. He pulled out his old set of keys and opened the door, then helped Jeremy through.

Neither spoke while Mr. Ennis flipped the light switch on, which set the neon lights blazing.

JEREMY TOOK IN THE familiar space, glad to see it again after so long. He hobbled carefully down the aisle, fingering each piece of equipment fondly. He finally made his way to the worktable in the center of the room. The last project he'd been working on sat in the middle, an elaborate carved end table, waiting for his return. He looked up at the skylights far overhead and over at the stack of lumber that had been delivered right before everything happened. It sat ready as he took in its fresh scent. The earthy but chemical scent of wood stain floated faintly in the air. He settled himself unsteadily onto one of the stools that sat alongside the worktable.

Jeremy was extremely pale and a light sheen of perspiration was on his forehead and upper lip. He felt a little shaky but was happy to see the workshop again.

His father eyed him with concern.

"I'm okay, Dad," Jeremy said, a bit out of breath. "It will just take a while for me to get back into shape. But I'm getting there."

"I know you are, son," his dad hurried to assure him. "I'm just thankful to have another chance to sit here with you like this. After those days in that waiting room not knowing? Well ..."

Jeremy put a hand up to stop him. "But, Dad, we're headed in the right direction, so we don't have to worry about that now." He held his arms out. "See, I'm here and mending well. All's good."

After looking around silently for a couple of minutes, Jeremy took a deep breath. "Dad, there is something I need to talk to you about though. That's why I wanted to come here."

Mr. Ennis leaned forward.

Jeremy took a deep breath and ran a finger across the smooth top of the worktable. "When we were here last time, you encouraged me to think about something to supplement my job with the fire department. At that time, I didn't think I was going to have any kind of a future past my twenty-fourth birthday."

Charles shook his head. "I could wring your grandfather's neck for putting all that nonsense into your head."

"Well, I did have it in my head, foolish or not. But thankfully, now we're past it, and I do have a future to look toward. I've been thinking about what I'd really like to do, and please don't laugh when I tell you."

Mr. Ennis held his hands up in mock surrender.

Jeremy surveyed the shop and reached up to finger the intricate leaves he'd carved into the legs of the end table on the workbench. "I love this space, Dad. I love working with wood, creating something solid that lasts but also something beautiful."

He looked intently at his dad. "You know how I've dabbled in woodworking for years and taken an occasional request or two, but never pursued anything seriously. I've been doing some research in my downtime between rehab appointments and placed a bare bones ad in the paper offering custom made wood pieces. I already have three actual orders and a lot more inquiries that I need to respond to. But Dad, I think this could be a real business. I can have as much work as I can handle. And who knows, I may need to hire a helper or two. What do you think?"

Mr. Ennis looked at his son. He saw the excitement and determination on his face and in his eyes. Thoughtfully stroking his chin, he stood and paced back and forth, shuffling sawdust that had accumulated on the floor. Jeremy waited anxiously, watching him closely.

He stopped and turned to face Jeremy. "You'll need a business platform to keep track of orders, payments, supply requests, and costs and ..."

Jeremy got to his feet as quickly as he could, moving to stand directly in front of his dad.

"You're saying you think it will work? You think it can be a viable business?" Jeremy asked, barely containing the excitement in his voice.

"Son, actually, I have absolutely no doubt. You said it best when you said you'll have as much work as you can handle. In fact," he went on with a mischievous smile, "I've been asked by several people if you sell what you make, and if so, they'd like to place orders for some pieces when you're ready."

Jeremy's face lit up even brighter. "Seriously? That's awesome!" He staggered a bit, getting off balance in his enthusiasm. His dad reached out to help as his face creased with worry.

Jeremy steadied himself, and with a rueful look said, "I've still got aways to go to get back to a hundred percent, but now I've got extra incentive to work hard to get there. Thanks, Dad!"

"No need to thank me. You're the one with the talent. But whatever your mother and I can do to help, all you need to do is ask. You know your mother used to have a small bookkeeping business. I bet she'd be glad to lend her services if you want. And all you need to do is tell me where and how you need my help."

Using the edge of the worktable to steady himself, Jeremy stepped across the narrow walkway and slowly over to the table holding the circular saw that had belonged to Grandpa Mars. Jeremy reached for the handle, wrapping his fingers around its smooth surface, relishing its feel in his hands.

He turned to face his dad, his face bright with excitement.

"Thanks, Dad. Rehab is slow, but I'm staying busy in my downtime, so I'll be ready to roll when I'm out. I can't wait to tell Allie. I ran this by her, and she thought it was a good idea too, but encouraged me to get your thoughts."

Mr. Ennis beamed his pleasure hearing that. He then asked, with a glint in his eye, "And speaking of Allie, needing any advice on that subject or anything you'd like to share?"

"Uh, no, Dad. I think I know what I'm doing there, at least I hope I do. But what you mentioned before? You know, about marriage? Well, that's ..." Jeremy looked at his dad and grinned widely.

"Yeah? Well, I'm glad to hear it and your mom will be too. She's been wanting me to ask," he said with a chuckle.

Jeremy wavered a bit and grimaced. Charles stood. "Time to get you off your feet."

"Yeah, I guess so, but I'm glad we had this visit," Jeremy said. He took another long look around the space and breathed in the familiar smell before picking up his cane and putting an arm around his dad's shoulder.

"Me too, son. Me too."

THANKSGIVING WAS HERE AND gone before Riley knew it. Between being on shift at the station, studying for the lieutenant's exam, working at Electronix Doc, and spending more and more time with Maggie, the days had flown by. They'd had some deep and heartfelt talks. He knew he couldn't live without her. And now, Maggie knew her true feelings and what she wanted as well. Riley had decided it was time to propose and was busily planning how.

Maggie's new job had turned hybrid, and she only had to make the drive to Dallas a couple of times a month and when she did, it was just for the day. She'd rented an apartment not too far from Riley's, which made it easier for them to spend time together.

Jeremy was dismissed from the hospital right before Thanksgiving but was having to stay at a rehab facility until he could get back fully on his feet. He expected to be discharged from there in another week or so. From there he'd move in with his folks for a couple of months, which meant he'd literally be home for Christmas. After that, he'd be back in full Jeremy mode.

Jeremy and Allie were definitely back to being "a thing," and it made Riley smile seeing how happy they were together. He still thought Jeremy would be a good brother-in-law but knew better now than to say as much. That couldn't stop him from hoping it would happen someday.

Cade's new high school resource officer job was the absolute perfect fit for him. The few times Riley had dropped by campus to see him, there were either students in his office hanging out or he was in the gym coaching some of the guys on physical fitness. Or he was in the cafeteria talking to a group or listening to them with rapt attention. You could tell he already had their respect.

And when visiting Emily in the office, she had stars in her eyes when she looked at Cade, and the same for him when he looked at her. Riley rolled his own eyes and wondered if he and Maggie had ever been that goofy-eyed. But he had to admit, they probably had been.

No plans had been made by any of the three families for the annual large Christmas gathering. It seemed that in light of everything that happened recently, everyone was content to spend time with their own family this year.

New Year promised to be a different matter entirely.

New Year's Eve was clear and frosty. Riley breathed the cold air deeply as he stepped out of his SUV. He stopped and looked up, sending a prayer heavenward for what was planned for the evening. The sky was velvety black and the stars shone brightly against the inky darkness. One star in particular caught Riley's eye as he gazed up. It twinkled even more brightly than the others, as if answering his prayer. Riley smiled as he headed toward Maggie's front door.

Maggie was staying at her parents' for the holidays and their door flew open just as he raised his hand to knock. She stood silhouetted in the warm light, wearing a midnight blue gown of velvet, pearls scattered across the bodice and down the elbow-length puffed sleeves. Against the soft skin of her throat, she wore the single diamond drop he'd given her for high school graduation. But the smile she wore was the most beautiful part about her.

"What are doing out here? Star gazing?" she asked with a small laugh.

"Maybe. But the brightest star I see is standing right in front of me," Riley said with a slight tease but looking solemnly into her eyes.

Stepping back, he gestured toward the SUV. "Your carriage awaits, my lady." He reached for the coat she had over one arm and helped her into it, pulling the door closed behind them. He caught Mr. and Mrs. Rawlings watching from one of the windows. He winked and gave them a thumbs up as he followed Maggie down the steps.

They talked of the weather, how happy the holidays had been, and how there was no better way to spend New Year's than together as they drove to the Country Club.

They pulled up, and the Club's familiar valet, Todd, stepped to Maggie's door and opened it for her, extending his hand to help her out. Riley stepped out of the driver's side as Todd came around.

"Good evening, Mr. Sullivan," Todd said with an easy grin.

Before Riley could reply, Todd went on with a knowing glint in his eye, "And yes sir, the usual. No dings, no dents, no—"

"Damage," they finished together with a laugh.

"You've got this down, my man," Riley said with a quick fist bump as Todd slid into the driver's seat.

Riley stepped across the drive and extended his arm to Maggie. She slipped her hand through, resting her hand lightly on top of his arm, looking up at him with a slight blush on her cheeks.

"You certainly are being very formal tonight, Mr. Sullivan."

"Well, it's not every day you get to escort a beautiful lady to dinner on New Year's Eve."

Maggie smiled happily, tightening her grasp on Riley's arm.

They entered the Club, but as they started toward the dining room, the maître d' intercepted them, his brows furrowed in worry and his hands shaking.

"Mr. Sullivan! I'm so glad I caught you. My sincerest apologies but a large party has booked the entire dining room for a New Year's Eve party. We will need to place you elsewhere this evening."

Stopping abruptly, Riley blanched and frowned.

"I beg your pardon? I booked these reservations weeks ago and nothing was mentioned," Riley said evenly, but with frustration in his tone.

"My sincerest apologies. The front desk was supposed to have notified all of those with previous reservations. Please, let me escort you to a different area and your table."

Riley looked at Maggie and grimaced but tried to shrug it off.

"I'm so sorry, Maggie."

"Riley, if I'm with you, anywhere is fine."

His heart beat faster as he looked into Maggie's eyes, and he gamely acted as if he were trying to smile.

Maggie patted his arm as they followed the maître d' across the lobby and toward the double doors that opened onto the patio overlooking the eighteenth hole of the golf course.

Riley looked straight ahead as Maggie looked between him and the maître d' questioningly. It was entirely too cold to sit on the patio.

The maître d' opened the door and preceded Riley and Maggie. With a grin and a flourish he said, "Your table, Mr. Sullivan."

Riley grinned as Maggie gasped.

Awash in candlelight, the patio was cleared of all but one table, which was illuminated by candles on either side of a bouquet of fresh pink roses, Maggie's favorite. The table was set for two with twinkling crystal goblets and sparkling china. Warmth from mobile heaters on the perimeter of the patio made the spot comfortable and cozy.

"Oh, Riley," Maggie managed to gasp as she looked up at him, her eyes shining. "This is . . . this is absolutely stunning."

Riley's grin broadened as he nodded to the maître d' and pulled Maggie's chair out for her, helping her off with her coat.

"So this was the plan all along," she said with a playful swat at his arm as he sat down and picked up the already opened bottle of wine on the table, pouring some into each of their glasses.

"To a great new year," Riley said, smiling and holding his glass aloft.

"To a great new year," Maggie echoed, clinking her glass to Riley's. Their eyes locked for several seconds over the rims of their glasses. Time stood still in that instant, and they both felt something shifting between them.

The waiter appeared quickly with their salads and disappeared just as quickly.

"What? No menu?" Maggie teased, setting her wine glass down and lifting her salad fork.

"Now, Mags, why waste time with a menu when we both know what we'd order anyway?" Riley asked, setting his glass on the table and taking a bite of salad.

"And you are so right," Maggie replied cheerfully, her eyes sparkling.

They ate in companionable silence until they'd finished their salads. The waiter appeared once again only this time, he placed a silver salver in front of Maggie. The waiter disappeared, having left nothing for Riley.

"We should call him back," she began. "He didn't bring your food."

"Maggie," Riley said softly. "I think you should lift the cover." He indicated the salver's silver cover with a nod.

With a puzzled look, Maggie lifted the cover. On the tray was a yellowed envelope. She looked at Riley with a questioning raise of her eyebrows.

"Read it," he said gently, looking from the envelope to her, his eyes glowing.

Maggie carefully lifted the envelope from the tray and gently removed a piece of paper as yellowed as the envelope. She unfolded it and read, "My Dearest Martha."

Maggie's eyes darted to Riley's, her lips parted in wonder. He'd told her about Mr. Thornton, about their talks, and about Mr. Thornton's "Martha." Riley had told Maggie Mr. Thornton was the reason for his continued efforts toward her, and she understood what she held in her hand was priceless.

Riley nodded and urged her to read it aloud. Maggie began in a hushed voice.

My Dearest Martha:

I should have told you a long time ago how I feel, but I don't know . . . things just felt so right between us, there really didn't seem to be the need. But now, I realize there certainly was.

I love you, Martha. I love you with all of my heart. I love you with everything I am and everything I ever hope to be. You are my world, my song, and the sunshine that brightens my days. I never want to be without your hand in mine, our sighs mingling, our joys shared, and our tears halved. You complete me, my sweet Martha, in every way. I've never felt this way before. And it rather scares me, but I'd rather live, scared as I am now, than to ever be without you.

Forgive my negligence for being so long in telling you my feelings. But know, my darling, my only desire has always been to share a life with you. To cherish you and be at your side. My love for you is never-ending and always true. Please be mine as I am yours.

Always and forever,
Jimmy

Maggie, her eyes swimming in tears, looked to Riley.

"There's something I need to ask you," he said.

Riley reached inside his jacket and pulled out a ring box. Opening the lid, he stood, and pushing his chair away, he knelt on one knee in front of Maggie.

"Maggie, I've known you most of my life. And for most of my life, I've known you were the one for me. The only one I want to spend the rest of my life with, the one I want to cherish and make happy, and the one I want to grow old with. I think you're an incredibly strong, beautiful, and amazing woman. Mr. Thornton said it so much more eloquently than I ever could, but the sentiments are the same. I love you, Maggie Rawlings. I love you with my whole heart and with everything I am. Would you do me the honor of marrying me?"

Maggie's hands trembled as she clutched the letter to her heart. Unshed tears of pure joy sparkled in the candlelight as she listened to Riley, on his knee in front of her and holding out the most beautiful ring she'd ever seen. The love in Riley's eyes, the words he was saying, the ring, the candlelight—it was all surreal. She never knew how truly happy she could be until this moment, and she wanted to remember it, just this way, for the rest of her life.

When Riley said that he loved her, her breath had hitched. It took everything she had to wait for Riley to actually ask her to marry him, but she waited. When he finally asked, she placed a hand on either side of his sweet, earnest face and looking him steadily in the eye said, "Yes, Riley Sullivan. Yes, I'll marry you! I love you too. I've *always* loved you."

Riley took her trembling hand in his own trembling one and placed the ring on her finger. It fit perfectly, just as he knew it would. They both looked at the ring, his hand holding hers, the ring's sparkle reflecting the candles' flames. Their faces inches apart, Riley's lips touched Maggie's lips with a tender kiss. When they parted, they shared huge smiles before Riley leaned in, pulling Maggie close. They kissed again, this time deeply with passion and overwhelming joy.

Gasping and then laughing, they moved apart, Riley reclaiming his chair and taking Maggie's hand. The waiter appeared with a huge smile and placed their entrees in front of them. They looked at their food, then each other, and laughed again.

"You have no idea how happy you've made me," Riley said, swimming in Maggie's blue eyes, large and bright with joy.

"Oh, yes, I do," Maggie said, placing her other hand on top of Riley's. "Because you have no idea how happy you've made me. What a beautiful proposal, Riley. And using Mr. Thornton's letter?" she paused. "What a perfectly lovely touch."

They leaned close and kissed again, slowly, lingering and relishing the moment.

After sharing a long look filled with love and promise, they began to slowly eat their entrees, their hands often taking hold of the others'. Maggie stopped several times and held out her left hand to admire the ring.

"Riley, the ring is absolutely stunning. It's exactly what I would have made if I were to design my own." She held her hand out and wiggled her fingers.

"You did design it," Riley said with a grin as he played with a bite of asparagus.

"I did?" Maggie asked, confused.

"You did. In junior high. You made a sketch in civics class when we were studying marriage laws. You slipped it in your notebook, but I slipped it out. I intended to put it back. But well, I've kept it all these years and now, here we are. And you know the ironic thing," Riley went on as he laid his fork down and looked at her, "I had it in my pocket the night you told me you were moving. Don't get me wrong, that was a hard night. But now? I'm the happiest guy in the world!"

"Oh, Riley," Maggie said, her face turning downcast. "I'm so sorry. I—"

"Oh no you don't. That's the past," he hurried to assure her. "We've got nothing but the best of times to look forward to, and I believe there's a wedding to plan!"

Maggie swallowed her regret. Riley was right. That *was* the past, and now, they were very happily in the present. The waiter brought a chilled bottle of champagne and two champagne flutes, a strawberry in the bottom of each.

"To us," Riley said with a clink to Maggie's glass after he'd poured the champagne.

"To us and our happily ever after," Maggie replied with a smile and sip of her champagne.

After finishing a dessert neither one would remember, Riley said, "You know, we've dallied so long, it's not too much longer until midnight." He placed his napkin on the table and rose. "I think we ought to crash that big party in the dining room."

"Oh Riley, no. We couldn't do that!" Maggie protested. "It's been a big night. I'd just like to be with you when we ring in the new year."

"Nope. They imposed on our plans. I think we should impose on theirs."

Riley grabbed Maggie's hand and her coat and started toward the doors. The waiter held the door open for them.

"Thanks, Joel. You did a great job tonight," Riley said with a nod.

Joel grinned and nodded knowingly in return as he walked hurriedly in front of them toward the dining room. The doors were closed but the low hum of a crowd could be heard beyond.

"Oh Riley, really. I don't want to crash someone else's party." Maggie began to pull back just about the time Joel threw the doors open.

Riley pulled the reluctant Maggie into the room and raising her left hand with the ring, he shouted, "She said yes!"

The room erupted. And it was then Maggie saw that the people filling the room were family and friends—her parents, Riley's parents, Jeremy and Allie, Cade and Emily, Winston, her brother, Lyle, the guys from the fire station and their wives, high school friends, and more.

Her eyes huge, Maggie couldn't help but laugh, looking up at Riley who was beaming at his success in pulling off yet another big surprise for the evening. How lucky could one girl be?

To the cheers of everyone, Maggie pulled Riley's face down to hers and kissed him soundly, fluttering the fingers of her left hand, the ring's diamonds sending flashes of light across the room. Riley picked Maggie up and swung her in a circle, hugging her tightly and laughing as their friends and families cheered.

T HEY WERE IMMEDIATELY SURROUNDED with well-wishers, receiving hugs, kisses on the cheek, and claps on the back. There were so many people there, Maggie wasn't sure how Riley had pulled this off successfully. She'd never had the slightest clue. Even her own parents were in on it. For her, it was an absolutely magical evening.

Riley never knew his face could get so tired from smiling, but he was learning. He didn't care. He was so happy and to have everyone here who meant so much to both him and Maggie. It was the best night of his life.

Riley snagged a couple of glasses of white wine from a passing waiter, handing one to Maggie while they smiled and talked with everyone. Waiters moved around the room, holding trays filled with glasses of wine and others passed canapes and hors d'oeuvres of all kinds. Riley had let his mom decide what to serve tonight, and she'd outdone herself.

The excitement dimmed and the hubbub had abated somewhat when Douglas and Lyle Swanson approached Riley and his dad.

Mr. Swanson pulled them aside. "May we have just a short minute of your time to discuss some business?"

Oh no, Riley thought. Surely they wouldn't bring the firm up tonight? Not when everyone was enjoying the special evening and he needed to be with his guests.

Ballard Sullivan frowned but nodded, as did Riley.

Lyle looked like a Cheshire cat while Douglas looked jubilant.

Steering them to a corner, away from the crowd, Douglas Swanson nervously cleared his throat.

"Riley, I don't believe I've thanked you appropriately for what you did a few months ago, saving my life after that allergic reaction I had. I'm now checking ingredients when it comes to all seafood, you can be sure. But I wanted to personally thank you."

Riley nodded, waiting for some indication of what was truly on Douglas' mind.

"Ballard, you and I have had an exceptional working relationship over the years," he began, turning to Riley's dad. "I think we can both say, without reservation, that our firm has a stellar reputation and an impressive track record. As you and I have discussed, at length, our dream has always been for our sons to follow in our footsteps and take over the firm one day. Our foolish wager on the golf course has put a strain on not just our working relationship but on our friendship as well. With Riley successfully joining the fire service, I know you were feeling added pressure to bring him back into the fold, so to speak, so you could retain controlling ownership. That hasn't happened and doesn't look like it will be happening."

Ballard started to speak, but Douglas held up a hand stopping him.

"When Lyle graduated and joined the firm several months ago, I thought the path ahead was clear for him to take over that management role. Turns out, I was wrong." Douglas reached over and put a hand on his son's shoulder. "Lyle has informed me he doesn't want to do litigation work and is really not interested in private practice at all."

Riley's mouth dropped open as he looked between Douglas and Lyle. He glanced at his dad, who also looked stunned.

"Lyle is going to be working with the City of Abernathy as legal counsel. The town is growing, and they're projecting continued growth at an even faster clip in the coming years. They're going to need some strong legal advice. The city approached Lyle a few weeks ago and things were just finalized. Turns out, it's something Lyle already had a keen interest in pursuing. I had no idea. But now, well, it looks like we're in the same boat, my friend," Douglas said, looking at Ballard with a rueful grin.

Ballard's eyes had grown round as he listened. Finally, he exhaled a relieved breath of air.

"This is good, Doug. I'm happy for both Riley and Lyle," Ballard said as he and Douglas shook hands while Riley and Lyle beamed relieved smiles.

"We'll figure things out as we go when it comes to the firm, but I think we can both agree that we have exceptional sons. We can be very proud."

Douglas Swanson nodded, looking proudly at Lyle as Ballard looked at Riley with love and his newfound respect. With another handshake and glance around the room, Ballard and Doug left the young men to join their wives.

Riley reached out and shook Lyle's hand. "Congratulations, Lyle. Looks like we're working for the same "company," Riley said, gesturing with air quotes.

Lyle grinned. "So it does. And I'll know who to call if somebody's life needs saving."

"And I'll know who to contact to get out of a parking ticket," Riley quipped back.

"Who got a parking ticket?" Cade asked, walking up with Emily at his side.

"Nobody," Riley laughed. "Besides, you're out of the traffic ticket business, remember?"

"Oh, that's right. I am," Cade said, looking at Emily and smiling.

"Cade's in what business, pray tell?" Jeremy asked, leaning on a cane, Allie holding his other hand.

Riley took a sip of wine and motioned toward Lyle with the glass. "Fixing parking tickets," Riley answered with a laugh. "Lyle is our go-to guy for that now."

Jeremy and Cade looked at Lyle in surprise.

"Meet the new city attorney," Lyle said, taking a mock bow.

"Is the city that hard up?" Jeremy asked with a smirk, giving Lyle a clap on the back.

"Yeah, whatever," Lyle laughed. "I'll remember that when you've double-parked somewhere."

"Don't worry, Lyle," Cade said, "these guys are amazingly law-abiding. It never ceases to surprise me. But then again, it's probably the good influence I've had on them."

"Oh, I am so sure that's what it is," Jeremy said with a roll of his eyes and shifting his stance.

"How are you doing, Jeremy?" Lyle asked, turning serious.

"Actually, pretty well. I'll probably be calling it a short night. But overall, I'm doing well."

"He has an excellent nurse, you know," Allie said, squeezing his hand.

"The best," Jeremy answered with a grin.

Riley rolled his eyes.

"Uh-uh," Jeremy said, brandishing his cane in Riley's direction. "Don't be rolling your eyes when you're the one who got engaged tonight."

Riley laughed. "I know, I know...In fact, I'd better find my fiancé. I don't want to start the new year in trouble, but I need to talk to someone first. I'll join you in a minute."

Riley caught Captain Jernigan's eye across the room and headed toward him. The band in the corner was playing softly and a few couples were dancing as Riley wove through them.

"Cap," Riley said, shaking the captain's hand with a nod to Mrs. Jernigan as he walked up. "I'm so glad you both could come tonight."

"It's our pleasure, Sullivan. I must say, you throw a great party. It was nice of you to invite the whole crew and their significant others." He looked around the room. "Looks like everyone is having a great time."

Riley followed his gaze and nodded, seeing members of the Station Five crew and their wife or significant other enjoying the celebration. He smiled. Having them here made the evening complete.

"I'm glad. I wouldn't want it any other way. Tonight is for close friends and family, and I consider the station crew family," Riley said earnestly.

Captain Jernigan studied Riley.

"Sullivan, you're going to be one hell of an officer. The sky's the limit for you, and as I told you when you were laid up in the hospital bed, you're going to go far. I've only come to believe that even more firmly."

"Thank you, sir. And I must say, I've got one hell of an officer as an example to follow."

Captain Jernigan smiled as they shook hands. "Now go on, Sullivan. You've got a beautiful fiancé to be celebrating with. I'll see you next shift if we don't talk again tonight."

"Yes, sir."

Riley found Maggie, who stood in deep conversation with his mom and hers.

"Riley!" his mother said, grabbing his arm. "What do you think about a fall wedding? We're thinking the service at the church and the reception here at the Club."

Caught by surprise, Riley just blinked. "Well, we haven't had time to talk about it . . ."

He could hear Jeremy and Cade snickering as they joined them.

Maggie laughed and took his hand. "We're just talking possibilities. We'll have to get busy though. There's so much to do!"

"What have I done?" Riley groaned, turning with a teasing look at the group.

They were interrupted by the sound of popping champagne corks, joined by cheers as waiters moved through the crowd, distributing flutes of champagne to toast the new year. Riley snagged two flutes, handing one to Maggie.

The sizzle and crackle of fireworks could be heard outside and the singing of "Auld Lang Syne" began, as the crowd drifted to the opened terrace doors to watch the show.

Jeremy pulled Allie close, giving her a smile and passionate New Year's kiss while Cade did the same with a blushing Emily.

"Happy New Year, Riley. And happily ever after," Maggie whispered with a smile into Riley's ear, taking his hand and lacing her fingers tightly with his.

"Happily ever after," Riley replied softly, his eyes full of love as they kissed on the first stroke of midnight and the start of a brand-new year.

RILEY GOT TO THE station early. Today was going to be a big day for his two best friends and neither of them knew what was coming.

Today was Jeremy's first day back on duty. He'd been missed at the station. Everyone was looking forward to his return and had made plans to celebrate. They'd gone all out, and Riley couldn't wait to see Jeremy's reaction. The first phase was not to acknowledge Jeremy's return or his being away. At least until the full plan was put into motion.

Emily had called Riley last week and said seniors at the high school were planning something to celebrate Cade. The student organizers had asked Emily to see if Riley and Jeremy could come, since Cade talked about them so often. Of course, Riley knew there was no way they'd miss it.

Riley had almost choked when the celebration for Cade ended up being the same day Jeremy returned to work, but with a little luck and careful timing, he figured it could all work. Riley didn't know what the students were planning; he was just glad they wanted to recognize Cade somehow. He knew Cade had given that job his all this past year.

With Cade's celebration, helping plan Jeremy's return party, and ongoing wedding plans, the two weeks since taking the lieutenant's exam had flown by in a blur. Riley was glad to have had so many distractions.

Riley thought he had done well on the test, but he also knew the competition was fierce. He had to be in the top four but just didn't know if he'd make it. He'd started strong but by the end of the second hour, he'd been second-guessing himself on his answers. Riley knew it was best to go with your first instinct, but he'd had to think hard about the answer to each and every question. He and Jeremy had been the last two to finish, after nearly three hours of testing.

They'd done their best, but they agreed they didn't want to let the captain down. He would not be happy if they didn't do well—really well—by being two of the top four. Captain Jernigan didn't know for sure when the test results would be announced, but it could be any day. Riley was anxious to find out. But then again, maybe not.

The rookie, Brett Reynolds, was in the kitchen with tea brewing in the microwave and a pot of coffee already made when Riley came in.

"Morning, Rookie," Riley said as he walked through the kitchen to his room to drop off his duffel bag. The crew drifted in and took their places around the kitchen table, smug looks on their faces. The planning had been completed last shift, and all were ready to welcome Jeremy back but not without giving him a hard time first.

Riley had just sat down at the table with a cup of coffee when Jeremy walked in. He paused and looked around the room as if waiting for something.

"Morning, everyone," Jeremy said cheerily, slightly bouncing on his toes in his excitement.

"Morning, Ennis," the group grumbled without turning around or looking at him.

Riley knew Jeremy would suspect something if he didn't say something. So, wiping the grin from his face, Riley turned to him. "Good morning, Jeremy. Have you met the new rookie?"

Jeremy frowned and looked a bit confused but recovered quickly.

"No, I haven't." He walked over to where Reynolds stood and stuck his hand out.

"Rookie, Jeremy Ennis."

"Brett Reynolds."

"Welcome to Station Five," Jeremy said with a glance toward the table.

"Thank you, sir. And welcome back," Reynolds said.

Heads jerked up from the table and glowers were sent Reynolds' way.

"Rookies," grumbled several.

Jeremy turned and frowned at the group before leaving to stow his gear in his room.

Riley had to stifle a snicker as did several others when Jeremy walked out.

When they all went to the bay to check their equipment and apparatus, Jernigan followed them. He clapped his hands to gather everyone's attention. "Alright, Ennis you're on the ambulance until further notice," he boomed.

Jeremy had been standing next to the engine, and his head jerked up at the announcement.

"Sir?" Jeremy asked with a stricken look.

"You heard. Ambulance until further notice. Carry on, everyone." Jernigan turned and walked back into the station.

Everyone was suddenly very busy when Jeremy turned to look, and Riley had to duck to the other side of the engine.

Thankfully, it was an unusually quiet day, with only one medical run, which Jeremy completed with the new rookie in tow. All was routine as usual until early afternoon when Riley and Jeremy left on "assignment," which was really going to the high school for Cade's surprise celebration.

"Apart from being assigned back to the ambulance, you'd have thought I never got injured or wasn't out and recuperating for months. What a fine welcome back," Jeremy groused on the way to the high school. "What's up with that anyway?"

When Riley didn't respond, Jeremy huffed and went on. "At least Cade has people who appreciate him."

Riley had to look out the driver's side window to keep from laughing. Jeremy was all huddled up in the passenger seat, his arms crossed in front of him with a fierce frown on his face. His bottom lip even stuck out in a little pout. He looked like the poster child for disappointment.

"I wonder what the kids have planned," Riley said to change the subject.

"I don't remember us ever doing anything like this for Officer Lane when we were in high school," Jeremy said, shifting in his seat.

"Maybe it's because Officer Lane wasn't as cool as Officer Marshall evidently is," Riley replied, pulling into the high school gym's parking lot and parking.

"Let's go blend in," Riley said, opening his door.

Jeremy looked down at his uniform and then at Riley. "Did you say blend in?"

Riley rolled his eyes.

They walked into the gym, whose floor was filled with teenagers milling around and talking excitedly. Emily saw Riley and Jeremy and steered them over to the side.

"You guys wait here. They'll let you know when to make your presence known. The kids have worked up a ruse to get him here. And then the fun begins," Emily said, her eyes shining with excitement. "This is going to be fun. He has absolutely no idea."

A few minutes later, an announcement was made to watch the big screen at the end of the gym.

The video showed a group of students hurrying Cade up to the entrance of the gym. You could hear them telling him about a disturbance where he was needed. Cade was all seriousness until the video showed him entering the gym and then he walked in the doors. When the students saw him, they started chanting, "Cade! Cade! Cade!"

Riley and Jeremy grinned seeing the stunned look on Cade's face when he stopped short in surprise. The students surrounded him and pulled him to the center of the gym floor.

Jake Turner, who Emily had mentioned was Senior Class President, motioned for silence. "Officer Marshall, we are here to celebrate you and the contributions you've been making to Abernathy High School. Everything this afternoon has been coordinated and planned by the senior class of Abernathy High. Officer Marshall, we are all here today to celebrate you!"

The students cheered until a video began playing of short clips of student after student telling what kind of impact Cade had had on them, how easy he was talk to, how he'd helped by hanging out with them, how he'd worked out with them in the gym or coached them where needed, and how he'd been a leader. They said it felt like Cade was one of them, that he'd made them feel important and made sure they knew they had a contribution to make.

Riley was impressed. Cade had really found his niche.

"Officer Marshall, we have some presentations we'd like to make to you," Jennifer Lewis, the Senior Class Vice President said when the video ended and waved a few students forward. They presented Cade with everything from tickets to a professional basketball game to gift cards, including one to his favorite fast-food place where they teasingly said he got the same drink every afternoon. He also received a personalized plate to mark his own reserved parking spot at the admin building.

"We know how much you love basketball, Officer Marshall, and since we couldn't get a video of everybody who wanted to say their thanks, we did this!" Jackson Brandt, Senior Class Treasurer said, gesturing to the group around them.

Students began tossing miniature basketballs to Cade one at a time. On the balls, the students had written messages in black marker, and Cade took his time to read each one, before dropping them into a mesh basket beside him. Riley saw Cade wipe at his eyes. This was getting to him, and Riley could clearly see why.

An errant ball bounced toward Riley and Jeremy, and Riley picked it up. He looked at the message.

Thank you, Officer Cade. I'm better today than I was yesterday and not as good as I'll be tomorrow.

Alicia K.

Riley showed the ball to Jeremy before handing it to the student who'd spied it sailing their direction. That had been Cade's mantra since middle school. He hadn't recited it lately, but Riley knew he kept it on a handwritten note in his wallet.

"Now, Officer Marshall," Jake began, "you've told us a lot of stories about two special friends you have and how much they mean to you. In fact, you've told us how the three of you played football for this school a few years ago and how strong your friendships still are. Since you've told us how important good friendships are to have in life, we knew you'd probably want those guys here today. So, Riley and Jeremy, come on up."

Jake looked to where Riley and Jeremy stood and waved to them to come to center court. Cade's head jerked toward where Jake was looking.

"I didn't sign up for this," Jeremy said through clenched teeth.

"I don't think we have a choice," Riley said, embarrassed. He didn't know this was going to be part of the afternoon. He shrugged. "Oh well, it's for Cade."

"For Cade," Jeremy agreed as they both started walking toward the center court, the students clapping and parting to clear the way.

"Guys, thanks for coming," Cade said when they reached him and awkwardly clapped each of them on the back, all three red-faced.

"We're proud of you, Cade," Riley said.

"Yeah, what he said," Jeremy added.

Jake moved to the middle of the group, speaking into the microphone. "On behalf of not just the senior class, Officer Cade, but the entire school, thank you for what you're doing and for always making us feel important."

Jake then started the chant. "Cade! Cade! Cade!" The crowd of students filed by, giving Cade a hug, a clap on the back, or quick fist bump.

As the celebration began to wind down, Sergeant Dickson appeared from the edge of the crowd to shake Cade's hand. "Officer Marshall, looks like you're doing an outstanding job and very impressively I must say. You should think about training other resource officers. I'll give you a call to discuss it. We need more like you."

"Yes, sir. I'd like that," Cade said, his face bright with excitement.

"We'll talk soon," Dickson said. And with a nod to Riley and Jeremy, he made his way out of the mingling students.

"For a lunkhead, you've done pretty good for yourself," Jeremy said, picking up one of the basketballs and reading what was written on it before putting it in the basket. "This was all quite impressive. Looks like that lucky rabbit's foot sure did its thing, doesn't it?"

Cade nodded seriously. "I think it did its thing for you too."

"Yeah, I guess," Jeremy mumbled, jamming his fists in his pockets and walking to the edge of the group.

"What's up with him?" Cade asked Riley, waving his thumb in Jeremy's direction.

"Oh, he's feeling a bit unloved at the moment," Riley said with a wink and a quick glance at his watch. "Which by the way, we gotta go. See you in just a bit," Riley said under his breath. "Oh, and congratulations. This was amazing and well-deserved. Way to go."

Cade grinned and nodded as Riley and Jeremy turned and started toward the door.

Emily walked up beside Cade with a big smile.

"You knew about this, didn't you?" Cade asked, pretending to be angry.

"Well. I may have helped, just a teeny, tiny bit," she said, smiling and holding up her thumb and index finger. "But it was all the seniors' idea. They came to Principal Whitman wanting to do something for you. They planned all of this themselves."

Cade looked around, shaking his head. "It's amazing, it really is. I just can't believe it."

"Well, believe it. You're having a huge impact on these kids, Cade. You truly are to be commended, and for *them* to see it and appreciate it? That's even more impressive."

Emily smiled up at him. "I can't wait until you read the notes on all the basketballs. Oh, and they made a copy of the video for you too."

Cade shook his head. "I really am overwhelmed."

"You showed them you cared, Cade. That means the world to teenagers. What you're doing is badly needed."

"You know, Sergeant Dickson said something about my creating some training for other resource officers. I'll have to think about that."

Emily punched him playfully in the arm. "Don't think about it, Cade. Do it! Wouldn't it be awesome to have students on other campuses feeling about their resource officer the way they do you?"

Cade studied Emily's earnest face for several seconds and nodded. "Yeah, that would be pretty cool. I like it."

IT WAS AROUND FOUR when Riley texted the captain, telling him they were on the way back. When Riley backed into the bay, they were met by Hayward, the engine's driver.

"Ennis, Cap asked me to tell you that he needs you to do a thorough inventory of the medical supplies and show the rookie your method."

"What?" Jeremy snapped irritably. "I've been gone four months—that is if anyone cared to notice—and you're telling me no one has shown the rookie how to do inventory? Seriously?" Jeremy continued to rant, so caught up in his frustration, he didn't notice the smirks on Hayward's and Riley's faces.

"Fine. I'll show the rookie." Jeremy stepped to the door into the station and bellowed, "Rookie. Bay. Now."

A few seconds later, Reynolds trotted out and shared a conspiratorial grin with Riley and Hayward before dutifully following Jeremy to the locked storage area.

Hayward and Riley hurried to the door into the station to help the others.

It took over an hour to train on inventory, thanks to the dozens of detailed questions from Reynolds about how to do it thoroughly and correctly. Jeremy had never seen anyone ask so many questions about the frivolous and simple details.

Finally, Reynolds ran out of questions, and Jeremy locked up while the rookie went into the station. Jeremy checked his watch. It should be dinner soon, and he was starved. Being ignored can make you hungry, he thought.

When Jeremy opened the door, it seemed unusually quiet for being close to dinner time. And no one was in the bay. Where was everybody? he thought. When he was almost to the kitchen, a blast of noise hit him that stopped him in his tracks, his eyes opening wide in surprise. The kitchen was full of cheering people—all of the Station Five crew, Chief Bentley, Lieutenant Cochran, and Cade, grinning his goofiest grin.

Jeremy's face grew red, and Riley stepped out and slapped him on the back.

"Do you seriously think we wouldn't celebrate you coming back?"

"Well, it sure seemed that way," Jeremy said, laughing as the crew surrounded him, giving him playful shoves or a slap on the back.

Captain Jernigan called for quiet. "I'd like to make a speech please," he began, as everyone groaned.

He ignored them and turned to Jeremy. "Ennis, son, let me say how thankful I am to have you back. Your injuries and sacrifices are a lesson to us all that we need to always be vigilant and that our lives, fragile as they are, are in each other's hands. We're glad to have you back, and as you can see, we're here to celebrate. Your favorite meal has been prepared—steak, I believe? But before we eat, we have something for you."

Brimly handed the captain a large box with a big red bow on top. "This is for you."

He set it on the table, and everyone gathered around as Jeremy opened it. When he lifted the lid, he saw his old bunker gear carefully folded laying in tissue paper. It was ripped and torn and covered in scorch marks, evidence of what had happened the night of the big fire.

Jeremy choked up, and everyone quieted.

"But, sir, I think I might need . . ."

Before he could finish, the captain broke in. "Oh, don't worry. This is just for you to keep. You've earned a brand-new set, which is hanging on the engine waiting and ready for the next call. We've been waiting on it to get here. That's why I put you on the ambulance the first part of shift."

Jeremy beamed, looking around the group of smiling faces. "Thank you, everyone. I really appreciate it. I've been so anxious to come back, and to not even get a 'how are you doing' this morning, well . . ."

"He was pouting all the way to the school and back," Riley interjected. "You'd never even know I'd been gone!" Riley mimicked as everyone laughed. Jeremy gave him a shove and laughed too.

"Well, let's eat," Jernigan said.

The steaks had just been pulled from the grill, and Jeremy was sent through the line first to get his pick along with a large baked potato, and homemade rolls, Captain Jernigan's wife had made. This was really something, Jeremy thought, unable to hide a smile. It sounded like everyone had contributed something. This had taken a lot of work and planning, and it meant the world to him.

When everyone finished with seconds and thirds, if desired, Jernigan announced it was time for dessert.

"Mr. Ennis, since we didn't have opportunity to celebrate your birthday with our normal memorable celebration, we will also celebrate that tonight. If you please," he said, turning to Brimly.

Jeremy smiled nervously as Brimly retrieved a huge cake from where it'd been left in Jernigan's office for safekeeping.

"Cap, really, this isn't necessary . . ."

Jeremy tried to stave off what he knew was coming.

"Oh, but we insist. Don't we, gentlemen?"

Everyone agreed, nodding emphatically as Grimes put two candles on the cake—a two and a four. Tanner Jones began in his country drawl, "Haaaaaaaapppppppppyyyyyyyyy—"

Everything broke loose, with everyone singing off key as badly and as loudly as possible.

"That was bad. I mean, really, really bad," Cade said, chuckling and drying his eyes with the back of his hand when the song was over.

Riley handed Jeremy a plate with a huge piece of cake and several scoops of ice cream. His eyes widened, but he picked up a fork and dove in.

"If you weren't already well, that'd put you back in the hospital," Cade said as Riley handed him a plate with another gigantic piece of cake. Everyone laughed and continued chuckling as they received their own heaping plate.

Riley had just sat down with his dessert plate when he noticed Battalion Chief Bentley pull Captain Jernigan aside and show him something on his phone. They both left, heading toward the captain's office.

A few minutes later while everyone was still talking and enjoying the cake and ice cream, the captain and the chief came back in, pleased looks on their faces.

Captain Jernigan motioned for quiet. He looked at members of the crew. "Everyone, sorry to interrupt dessert, but we've just received some information that will affect this station and this shift significantly. So while everyone is here, we wanted to share it with you. As you know, two of our number took the lieutenant's exam a few weeks ago. There were fifteen candidates testing for four open slots. It's a tough exam, and requires a significant amount of study and preparation. Typically, a firefighter must be with the department a minimum of two years before they're eligible to take the exam. But a new program has begun to fast-track candidates who may not have the prescribed number of years with the department but who are deemed qualified and who pass the exam."

Riley's heart jumped, and he felt his face burn as he looked at Jeremy, whose eyes had widened. Cade straightened from where he'd been leaning against the counter. All eyes were on Captain Jernigan in the quiet that had descended.

Everyone knew Riley and Jeremy were the two who had taken the test, so if this wasn't good news, it would be devastating for it to be announced in front of everyone. Riley held his breath.

Captain Jernigan looked around the room, enjoying the suspense he was creating. "I have here the names of the top six—those who scored the highest. The top four will be promoted to lieutenant in another month, and the next two will move up if any of the four can't be promoted for some reason. So, are you ready?"

Everyone groaned, and Jernigan grinned. "I take that as a yes. Alright, number six is Brock Caraway from Station One, B Shift. Number five is Glen Davis from Station Four, B Shift. Number four is Mike Taylor from Station Two, C Shift.

Jernigan looked up from his phone and grinned. "Number three is Riley Sullivan, Station Five, A Shift."

There was a quick cheer from the group, and Riley felt the breath of air he'd been holding whoosh out. There were only two more slots. Riley glanced at Jeremy, who gave him a quick nod and looked down.

Cap cleared his throat.

"Okay, just two more. Number two is Todd Barlow, Station One, C Shift."

Riley tried to breathe but his chest felt tight. Everyone seemed to lean toward the captain, waiting.

"And the number one slot is," the captain paused and looked around the room, his eyes landing on Jeremy. "Jeremy Ennis, Station Five, A Shift."

The room erupted. Jeremy's head flew up, a huge smile on his face.

Jeremy and Riley jumped up from their seats and after exchanging a loose hug, shook hands with each other, then with the crew and everyone there.

But Jeremy stopped and looked at Captain Jernigan, who stood watching with a proud but sad smile. Gradually the hubbub settled down, everyone coming to notice the captain's quiet reaction.

"Cap?" Jeremy asked, taking a step toward him. "What does this mean for us? For A Shift at Five?"

The rest of the room looked at Jernigan, with the same question on their faces.

"It means, gentlemen, that A Shift at this station will continue to need two officers. Lieutenant Cochran, as you know, has transferred to admin to coordinate the new drone program. The new Lieutenant Sullivan will take his place on the engine. As far as the officer for the truck? That will be the new Lieutenant Ennis."

The quiet in the room was deafening.

Jernigan cleared his throat nervously and went on. "As you guys know, I've been at this for almost thirty years. I've been thinking about this for a while, and now that I can see this shift and this station will be in good hands, I've decided to retire and enjoy some leisure time. You know, golfing, fishing, hunting. Taking it easy."

"But, Cap, you don't do any of those things," Brimly said.

Nervous laughter filtered around the room before Jernigan laughed himself. "That's why they call it leisure, Brimly. I'll be able to take my time and try a little bit of it all and see what I like best. And, I'll get to eat my wife's good cookin' and not suffer through a new rookie's cooking." Jeremy gave Riley a shove, and the crew laughed.

"Now come on. It's all good. We've got a lot to celebrate tonight. Where's my cake and ice cream?" Jernigan asked as Riley handed him and Chief Bentley full plates.

Battalion Chief Bentley clapped Captain Jernigan on the back and shook his hand while the rest of the crew came by one by one to shake the captain's hand and say a few words.

A few hours later, after the kitchen had been cleaned, Riley, Jeremy, and Cade wandered out to the back and sat on the patio table with either a glass of tea or soft drink in their hand. They sat silently and looked at the dark sky, stars dotting the blackness.

"Quite a day," Cade said with a satisfied sigh.

"Yeah, quite a day," Riley said. A few minutes later he added, "Did you notice how unusually quiet it's been? No runs at all this afternoon. It's hard to believe we were that lucky with so much going on."

"There's a reason for that," Jeremy said, taking a drink of his tea.

"Oh yeah? And what would that be? Besides maybe some good timing for the station?" Riley queried.

"I heard Bentley arranged it," Jeremy said. "Any calls for Station Five were diverted to other stations for a couple of hours. If it'd been anything major where multiple units were needed, the call would have come through, but otherwise, they were diverted. We're back online now. I heard him and Cap talking about it earlier."

"Wow," Riley and Cade said at the same time.

After several minutes, Cade said without looking at either one of them, "Proud of you guys."

"Proud of you too, Cade," Jeremy said, staring ahead. "That was pretty impressive today."

"You guys are the best friends anyone could ever hope for. You know that, right?" Riley asked, looking first at Jeremy and then at Cade.

"Yeah, we know," Cade said with a somber nod.

"You're right. We are awesome," Jeremy added.

Riley rolled his eyes. "Well, seeing how you're both also so modest, I have something to ask each of you."

Jeremy and Cade turned to look at Riley.

"Sure, pard," Jeremy said.

"You know we've got your back any time," Cade added.

"Well, you know I've got this wedding thing coming up," Riley began. "And I'm needing a best man. But seeing as how I have *two* best friends, I'd like to ask you both to be my best *men*."

Jeremy looked over at Cade and shrugged his shoulders. "I don't know that I've ever heard of two best men."

"Yeah, me neither," Cade said. "Which one would get to give the best man speech at the reception? Who'd get to carry the ring? And which one would get to plan the bachelor party?"

"Sully, hate to say it but you might just need to ask a neutral third party," Jeremy said unable to stop the chuckle that escaped.

"You guys! You actually had me worried there for a second," Riley said, laughing.

"No way we'd miss standing up with you, Sully," Cade said with a clap to Riley's back.

"Absolutely not," Jeremy added, clapping Riley's shoulder. "It will be our honor."

"We'll decide who carries the ring and who makes the reception speech," Cade said.

"And who plans the bachelor party," Jeremy added.

"There's just so much to do!" Cade exclaimed dramatically.

"Are you guys done?" Riley asked, shaking his head and grinning.

"Yeah, I think that's about it. What do you think, Jeremy?" Cade asked, leaning out and looking across Riley to Jeremy.

"Yeah, I think so . . . for now," Jeremy replied with a wink at Cade.

"Good, I'm glad," Riley said and sighed with a happy grin.

A comfortable silence settled around them until the tones suddenly sounded: "Truck Five, Engine Five, Med Five: traffic collision, multiple vehicles . . ."

"I F THIS IS SUPPOSED to be the happiest day of my life, why do I feel like I'm going to a hanging?" Riley groused as he pulled on the neck of the dress shirt he had on beneath his tuxedo jacket.

"It's this penguin suit," Cade chimed in.

"Could you not have talked Maggie into something less formal?" Jeremy added as the three surveyed themselves in front of a floor length mirror. They each tugged on a shirt collar or shirt sleeve or jacket sleeve.

They were in the groom's dressing room, as the room had been designated, to the front and off to the side of the auditorium. They'd been dressed and ready for thirty minutes and were just waiting for the signal that the ceremony was about to begin.

"Well, Sully, it's your big day. We've all been friends a long time," Jeremy said, looking at Riley. "And . . ."

"Geez, Jeremy. Are you going to get all mushy?" Cade asked, shuffling his feet back and forth.

Jeremy rolled his eyes. "As the best man, I'm supposed to say words of encouragement, you lunkhead."

"I thought we were *both* the best *men?*" Cade interjected again.

Riley laughed. "Guys, if you think you're helping my nerves, let me assure you, you are not."

"Let's make this simple," Cade said, stepping up to stand beside Jeremy. "We love ya, Riley. The three of us are like brothers, and we'll always be like brothers. Just because you're getting married, and when we tie the knot, that won't change. We're brothers—through thick and thin."

Cade ended with an emphatic nod and looked at Jeremy. "See? Was that so hard?"

"Okay, okay," Jeremy said. "What he said."

They all laughed and pulled together in a loose hug.

"I love you guys too," Riley said, his eyes suddenly welling with tears.

"Oh, gee, not you too?" Cade said and rolled his eyes dramatically, causing them all to laugh again.

The door opened and Ballard stuck his head in the door. "It's time. You guys ready?"

Riley, Jeremy, and Cade exchanged looks, clapping each other on the back one more time before turning to face the door.

"Ready," they chorused.

ACKNOWLEDGMENTS

SINCE WRITING MY FIRST book, *Brotherhood By Fire*, it has become even more evident to me it takes a community of friends, book professionals, and readers to contribute to a finished novel. *Brothers In Service—Through Thick & Thin* is certainly no exception. It's hard to know exactly where to start so let's just begin.

First and foremost, a huge thanks to my nephew, Zac Bell, who provided not only the premise for the novel but several of the story lines within it as well. It wasn't a conscious effort. Zac just talked about what was going on at the fire station while I took mental notes. Zac was very gracious in sharing his paramedic medical knowledge on particular scenes when asked. And I have to say, he REALLY knows his stuff!

A HUGE shout out to Sandy Saucier—alpha reader, cheerleader, reviewer, and friend. Thank you, Sandy, for your always cheerful willingness to brainstorm, inspire, and encourage me in my writing endeavors. Your creativity and "what if" ideas inspire me to reach for the next level.

Dayna Linton, absolutely cannot do this without you. Your professionalism, friendship, encouragement and support mean more than you'll ever know. Your dedication, long hours and hard work are greatly appreciated.

Sean Linton, editor extraordinaire—your thoughts, insights, and suggestions strengthened and expanded this book beyond its meager beginnings. Thank you for your attention to detail and for pushing me to dig deeper and make sure this book was the very best it could be.

Thank you to the Plano Fire Rescue personnel, A Shift Station 12 especially, for welcoming me into your station and onto the engine for the firsthand experience that means so much when writing. Your support and help in my research has been invaluable. First responders everywhere are due all of our thanks and utmost of appreciation. We never know what they see and deal with on a daily basis, but they do it with an humble servant's heart.

A very special thank you to my sweet Mom, for her continued love, support, confidence, and encouragement through the ups and downs, unknowns and adventures of being an author. Thank you to my family for their continued encouragement and interest in my writing projects and to see what crazy idea I've had next. Thank you to the many, many friends who have cheered me on, encouraged me, voted on titles, and support for everything in between. Even the tiniest word of encouragement carries me further than you can ever imagine, and you, my friends, have carried me a long, long way!

Most especially, thank you to the good Lord who has loaned me the skill, desire, imagination, and tenacity to follow my dream to write. Anything that resonates with you, as a reader, is a result of the gift the Lord has seen fit to share through me.

BROTHERS IN SERVICE DISCUSSION QUESTIONS

1. This book evolves around relationships—close friendships, romantic relationships, work relationships, and family. Which relationship resonated the most with you? Why?

2. Maggie takes a promotion and moves without talking to Riley about their relationship first. Given the circumstances, do you think Maggie handled the situation correctly? How would you have handled it differently?

3. While Riley and Jeremy go into the fire service, Cade goes into police work. Given their different and distinct personalities, why do you think the three have been able to remain so close?

4. Riley forms close friendships with two older men who serve as mentors, Winston Forbes and James Thornton. Do you have an older friend who serves as your mentor? What began that friendship and what is it that keeps it going?

5. Jeremy believes the prediction Grandpa Mars makes based on Ennis family history. Do you have a superstition that directly affects your life or have you ever had someone predict a life impacting event? Did you believe them? Why or why not?

6. Maggie faced potential sexual harassment at work. How do you think she handled the situation with Connor? How would you have handled it differently?

7. If you could pick one character with which to form a close friendship, which one would it be? Would you pick a character most like you or different? Why?

ABOUT THE AUTHOR

Lɪɴᴅʏ Bᴇʟʟ ɪs ᴀɴ avid reader and has been her entire life, enjoying a wide variety of genres. Lindy's love of reading is what led to her love of writing.

Brothers In Service—Through Thick & Thin is Lindy's second novel. Her first, **Brotherhood By Fire**, was met with widespread acclaim by both readers and firefighters. It has been recognized for the intensity of the emotions it elicits as well as for its powerfully accurate portrayal of the fire service. Her first book ***Jane Austen Celebrates, Holidays & Occasions Regency Style*** tracks each month's holidays and how they have evolved and been celebrated through the centuries.

Lindy's writing has also brought about opportunities to speak to a variety of groups as well as teach Adult Professional Education courses on Jane Austen and the Regency Era at Southern Methodist University (SMU). Lindy also presents live book reviews to book clubs across the Dallas/Fort Worth Metroplex and writes book reviews for the Novels Alive blog site. Lindy is a graduate of Abilene Christian University with a Bachelors degree in Business Administration.

When not writing, Lindy enjoys relaxing with an engaging novel, cross stitching and serving in a variety of ministries in her home congregation.

www.ingramcontent.com/pod-product-compliance
Lightning Source LLC
Chambersburg PA
CBHW061541190726
48289CB00004B/1119